PRETTY LITTLE SECRETS

Pretty Little Secrets

A PRETTY LITTLE LIARS COLLECTION

SARA SHEPARD

HARPER TEEN

An Imprint of HarperCollinsPublishers

alloy**entertainment**
Produced by Alloy Entertainment
151 West 26th Street, New York, NY 10001

Library of Congress Cataloging-in-Publication Data is available.

ISBN 978-0-06-212591-0

Design by Liz Dresner

11 12 13 14 15   CG/RRDH   10 9 8 7 6 5 4 3 2 1

First Edition

To K

He sees you when you're sleeping
He knows when you're awake
He knows if you've been bad or good
So be good for goodness' sake!

—"SANTA CLAUS IS COMING TO TOWN"

CHRISTMAS STALKING

Here's a pretty snow-globe scene for you:

It's December of Hanna, Emily, Aria, and Spencer's junior year. Snow is falling, blanketing Rosewood's perfectly manicured lawns and dusting the tops of luxury SUVs. Christmas lights brighten every window, and cherub-cheeked kids are busy making their lists for Santa. The whole town is at peace, especially the pretty little liars.

Now that Alison DiLaurentis's murderer is in jail and A is dead, they can finally relax. But little do they know that I'm going to pick up where A left off. I'm going to be the new A, and I've made a list of my own. Guess who's at the top of the naughty column? That's right: Hanna, Emily, Aria, and Spencer.

And these liars have been bad! Hanna got caught shoplifting and totaled her ex-boyfriend's car. Emily defied her parents so many times they sent her away to Iowa. Aria's after-school smooch sessions with her English teacher got him fired. And Spencer may have been the naughtiest of them all. Stealing her sister's fiancé wasn't enough—Spencer also took her economics paper and pushed her down the stairs when Melissa found out what she'd done. Tsk tsk. These liars deserve coal in their stockings—or worse. Luckily I'm here to make sure they get what's coming to them.

It's only a matter of time before the pretty little liars get their hands dirty again—especially now that they think A is gone. So what trouble will they get into next? Well, I'll just have to lie low . . . and watch. I'll watch and watch and come to understand exactly what kind of bitches I'm dealing with. I'll find out *everything*.

And once I do, I'll know how to take them down.

Let's start with . . . Hanna. This girl's undergone some major upheaval. Her mom ditched her for Singapore. Her estranged dad is moving in with his Stepford fiancée and her perfect daughter, Kate. At least Hanna has her loyal boyfriend, Lucas. Or does she?

Let the stalking begin!

—A

HANNA'S PRETTY LITTLE SECRET

1

HOME FOR THE HOLIDAYS

It was a blustery Wednesday in early December in Rosewood, Pennsylvania, a bucolic suburb twenty miles from Philadelphia. While many residents were cutting down Frasier firs at the local Christmas tree farm or adorning the outsides of their houses with pinecone wreaths, a moving van was pulling up to a Georgian house with the word MARIN stenciled on the mailbox. Three men disembarked and slid open the back door to reveal dozens of boxes. Tom Marin, his fiancée, Isabel Randall, and Isabel's daughter, Kate, stood in the yard as the movers shuttled their belongings through the front door. Hanna Marin, who had lived in the house since she was five, observed from inside the foyer, biting her fingernails.

"Be careful with that," Isabel screeched to the burly guy who was hefting a medium-sized box. "It contains my vintage doll collection."

"And that box goes upstairs," Kate called nervously to another mover. "Those are all my handbags."

Hanna snuck a peek at her soon-to-be stepsister, Kate, who had a slender body, long, lustrous chestnut-colored hair, and big blue eyes. She was carrying a Chloé bag Hanna had only seen on the pages of *Vogue*. When Hanna asked where Kate had gotten it, Kate had trilled that it was an early Christmas present, shooting a grateful smile at Hanna's father. *Ick.*

"Hanna?" Mr. Marin thrust a small box marked DELICATES at her. "Can you take this up to your mom's—er, *our*—bedroom?"

"Sure," Hanna mumbled, eager to get away from Isabel and Kate—one of them was wearing a perfume that kept making her sneeze.

She climbed the stairs, her miniature pinscher, Dot, following at her heels. Just a few weeks ago, before Thanksgiving, Hanna's mother, Ashley, had dropped the bomb that she was taking a job in Singapore—and Hanna couldn't come.

Hanna would have loved to start over somewhere else. She'd had a horrible year. She'd been taunted by an evil text-messager named A. Her old best friend, Alison DiLaurentis, who'd been missing for three years, had been found under a concrete slab behind her old house in September. It turned out Ian Thomas, Ali's secret boyfriend—who Hanna and her other best friends Spencer Hastings, Aria Montgomery, and Emily Fields had all crushed on when he was a senior and they were seventh graders—had murdered Ali the night of the girls' end-of-seventh-grade sleepover. The police had arrested him a few weeks ago. It had all come as a massive shock.

But instead she was stuck here, with her father moving in with his new family—his replacement wife, Isabel, the ex-ER nurse who wasn't nearly as pretty or interesting as Hanna's mom, and his perfect stepdaughter, Kate, who'd taken Hanna's place in her dad's heart and who hated Hanna's guts.

Hanna padded into the empty master bedroom. It smelled slightly of mothballs, and there were four heavy indentations on the carpet where her mother's sleek Danish-modern bed used to stand. When Hanna dropped the DELICATES box on the floor, one of the flaps popped open and a little blue gift box with a blank gift tag peeked out.

Looking over her shoulder to make sure no one was watching, she lifted the lid. Inside was a round white-gold locket with a cluster of pavé-cut diamonds in the center.

Hanna breathed in. It was the Cartier locket that had belonged to her grandmother, whom everyone, even nonrelatives, called Bubbe Marin. Bubbe had worn it religiously when she was alive, boasting that she didn't even take it off in the bathtub. She'd died when Hanna was going into seventh grade, shortly after Hanna's parents divorced; by that time, Hanna hadn't been on speaking terms with her dad. She hadn't known what had happened to the locket, or who it had been willed to.

But now she did. She touched the blank gift tag and felt an angry pang. Her dad was probably going to give it to Isabel or Kate for Christmas.

"Hanna?" a voice floated up from the first floor.

Hanna shoved the lid back on the box and stepped into the hall. Her father was standing at the base of the stairs. "Pizza's here!"

The tantalizing aroma of mozzarella cheese wafted into Hanna's nostrils. *Just half a slice*, she decided. Sure, her Citizens jeans didn't button so easily this morning, but she'd probably left them in the dryer for too long. She walked down the stairs just as Isabel was carrying a pizza box to the kitchen. Everyone sat down at the table—*Hanna's* table—and Mr. Marin passed out plates and silverware. It was weird how he knew exactly which cabinet and drawer to open. But Isabel wasn't supposed to be sitting in her mother's chair, using her mother's cloth napkins from Crate & Barrel. Kate wasn't supposed to be drinking from the pewter cup her mother had bought for Hanna on a trip to Montreal.

Hanna let out another sneeze, her nostrils tickling with someone's cloying perfume. Not one of them said *Bless you*.

"So when are your entrance exams for Rosewood Day again, Kate?" Mr. Marin said as he grabbed a pizza slice from the open box. Unfortunately, Kate would be attending the same school Hanna went to.

Kate took a dainty bite of crust. "In a couple of days. I've been going over geometry proofs and vocabulary words."

Isabel waved her hand dismissively. "It's not the SATs. I'm sure you'll ace the exams."

"They'll be thrilled to have you." Mr. Marin looked at Hanna. "Did you know Kate won the Renaissance Student prize last year? She excelled above her peers in every subject."

You've only told me that eight million times, Hanna wanted to say. She took a bite of pizza so she wouldn't have to speak.

"And her grades were outstanding at the Barnbury School," Isabel went on, referencing Kate's old school in Annapolis. "Barnbury has a better reputation than Rosewood Day. At least there, kids aren't stalking other kids and running them down with their cars."

She shot a pointed look at Hanna. Hanna reached unconsciously for a second slice of pizza and pushed it into her mouth. Nice how Isabel was basically blaming *her* for her ordeals with A, the stalker who'd almost ruined her life this fall, and for tarnishing Rosewood Day's sterling reputation.

Kate leaned forward and stared at Hanna with wide eyes. Hanna had a feeling she knew exactly what question was coming next. "You must be so devastated that your best friend turned out to be . . . *you* know," Kate said in a fake-concerned voice. "How are you holding up?" A tiny smile crossed her lips, and it was obvious what her *real* question was: *How are you dealing with the fact that your BFF wanted to kill you?*

Hanna looked desperately at her father, hoping he'd put a stop to this line of questioning, but he was also staring at her worriedly. "I'm holding up just fine," she mumbled gruffly.

Not that it was true. Hanna was so mixed up about Mona Vanderwaal, her best friend since eighth grade who'd turned out to be A, the person who'd taunted her with her secrets, publicly embarrassed her more times than she could count, and yes, tried to run Hanna over with her car. There were still days when Hanna woke up, grabbed her phone, and started to text Mona about what shoes she was wearing to school before she remembered. At Mona's funeral, Hanna had actually *cried*, eliciting gapes from her peers. Hanna knew she should despise Mona with all of her heart—and a big part of her did. But another part couldn't just forget all the time they'd spent together gossiping, plotting their rise to popularity, and throwing fabulous parties. Before everything with A happened, Mona had been a better friend to her than Ali ever was—they'd felt like equals. But now Hanna knew it was all a lie.

Hanna stared down at her empty plate. Two ravaged pizza crusts lay in a lake of grease, but she couldn't remember eating the rest. Her stomach let out an unattractive gurgle.

Mr. Marin wiped his mouth. "Well, we have a lot of unpacking to do." He touched Kate's arm. "You girls should take a break. Why don't you and Hanna go to that new mall that just opened. What's it called?"

"Devon Crest," Hanna piped up.

"Ooh, I heard that place is very nice," Isabel cooed.

"I've been, actually," Kate said.

Isabel looked surprised. "When?"

"Uh, yesterday." Kate fiddled with the bangle on her silver David Yurman bracelet, which she'd bragged was a gift from Isabel for winning an essay contest last year. "You guys were busy."

"You two could go together, get to know each other a little better." Mr. Marin looked back and forth between Hanna and Kate. "Go shopping. Buy something nice for yourselves. Leave the unpacking to us. What do you say?"

Kate took a long sip from her water bottle. "Thanks, Tom. That sounds really great."

Hanna snuck a peek at Kate. Surprisingly, she looked sincere. Was it possible Kate had changed since Hanna had seen her last at a dinner in Philly, when she'd ratted Hanna out for stealing Percocet from a clinic? Hanna was back in touch with her old best friends, Emily, Aria, and Spencer, but none of them were big fashion followers, and she was kind of dying for a new best friend to replace Mona. Especially since she and her old friends had started attending group grief therapy together. She needed a break from all the Ali and A stuff—stat.

"I suppose I have some free time today," Hanna said.

"Great. Run along, then." Mr. Marin rose from the table and cleared everyone's plates. "Izz? Which room do you want to unpack first?"

"*Uch*, let's start with the kitchen. I'm not drinking out of *this* for another second." She wrinkled her nose at one of Hanna's favorite mugs, a majolica goblet her parents had bought on a trip to Tuscany.

The two of them left the room, chattering about which box their wineglasses might be in. Hanna rose from her seat. "So, I'm ready to go when you are," she said to Kate. "Is their Nordstrom any good? Is it true there's a Uniqlo? That place has amazing cashmere sweaters for pennies."

Kate let out a snort. "*God*, Hanna," she said, her expression suddenly venomous. "I was just saying I'd go to the mall to get your dad and my mom off my back. Did you actually think I was going to go anywhere with you?"

She sauntered out of the room, her chestnut ponytail swinging. Hanna's mouth made an *O*. Kate had set a trap, and she was the dumb animal who'd walked right into its steel jaws.

Kate paused in the hall, pressed some buttons on her phone, and then held it to her ear. "Hey," she whispered to whoever had picked up. "It's me." She laughed flirtatiously. It figured. Kate had only been here for two days and she *already* had a boyfriend.

Hanna twisted her napkin so forcefully she was surprised it didn't rip. *Whatever*—she and Kate probably would've had a horrible time shopping together anyway. Then, she heard a faint snicker spiraling from somewhere close by. On instinct, she glanced out the windows, certain she'd see a blond flash slipping through the trees. That was crazy, though. A—Mona—was gone.

2

PUKE-A-TAN

A few days later, Hanna sat on the cushy microfiber couch at her boyfriend Lucas Beattie's house, in front of the soft glow of the family's tinsel-heavy Christmas tree. The TV was playing an infomercial for a new ab-crunching device—"Get your body ripped by New Year's!"—the overly loud sales guy kept screaming. On the floor in front of them was a gift tin filled with butter, cheese, and caramel popcorn.

"The Kate worship was even worse than usual at dinner yesterday," Hanna moaned as she pushed another handful of cheese popcorn into her mouth. "All my dad and Isabel talked about was this absolutely *wonderful* speech Kate gave during tenth-grade commencement last year. And Kate just sat there beaming, all *yeah, I know I'm awesome.*"

"I'm sorry, Han." Lucas took a sip from his can of Mountain Dew. "You really don't think you guys can become friends?"

"Absolutely not." Hanna had decided not to tell Lucas how Kate hadn't wanted to go to the mall with her. She couldn't believe she'd been so naïve as to fall for Kate's kiss-ass tricks. "I want nothing to do with her. And I think I'm allergic to her perfume—I've sneezed about five hundred times since she moved in. I bet I'm going to get hives."

She slumped dramatically back on the couch and stared blankly at the Disney-themed Advent calendar across the room. Hanna hadn't grown up with holiday decorations. She was Jewish, and after her dad left, she and her mom barely celebrated Hanukkah. But Lucas's mother was obsessed with Advent calendars—they had three different ones pinned up to the fridge, a cloth one with stuffed toys in each of its twenty-five pockets tied to the stair rail, and a small glittery one hanging up in the powder room. Lucas put his arm around her and began to stroke her hair. Hanna shut her eyes and sighed, feeling a teensy bit better.

When Hanna and Mona were BFFs—and ruling the school together—Lucas wasn't exactly the kind of guy on the top of Hanna's Boys I Want to Date list. He didn't hang out with the right clique, didn't play a cool sport like soccer or lacrosse, and he was more into after-school clubs and Eagle Scouting than wild weekend parties. In fact, in sixth grade, Ali had started a rumor that Lucas was a hermaphrodite, which had plunged him into dorkdom. More recently, Mona had made fun of Hanna's friendship with Lucas, even threatening that it would bring down their popularity quotient.

But Mona and Ali were gone, and Lucas was shaping up to be the best boyfriend ever. How many guys would listen to her whine for hours about how Mona had screwed her over or how sucky her new family situation was? How many guys would open the door this evening, gaze upon Hanna in her bloated jeans and oversized Philadelphia Eagles sweatshirt, and say she looked smoking hot?

"Can I hide out at your house for the foreseeable future?" Hanna begged. "I don't know if I can bear going back there."

"That would be awesome," Lucas said. "But—"

"It *would* be awesome," Hanna cut him off, sitting up. "We could do stuff after school, go to Rive Gauche every night, dress up and crash the holiday party at the Rosewood Country Club . . ."

Lucas bit his lip. "Hanna, I—"

"Maybe my dad would even let me stay overnight here!" Hanna added, getting more and more excited. "I could claim that my allergy to Kate's perfume is really, really serious. Do you think your parents would go for that? I could sleep in the guest room . . . but maybe you could sneak over in the middle of the night." She winked.

"Hanna." Lucas's pale blond hair fell into his face as he sat up. "Slow down. I'm actually going away. Tomorrow."

Hanna blinked. "Away?"

"My dad just sprung it on us. It's an early Christmas present—he's taking us on a fourteen-day trip to the Yucatán peninsula. We're going with my dad's best friend from college and his family."

The inside of Hanna's mouth suddenly tasted sour. "Fourteen days . . . as in two *weeks*?"

"Uh-huh." Lucas gave her a little smile. "I'm really psyched."

"But we're still in school," Hanna sounded out, reaching for another handful of popcorn. It was only December 7—Rosewood Day didn't let out for Christmas and New Year's until later in the month. "Why doesn't your dad wait until winter break?"

Lucas raised both shoulders. "They got an amazing deal on the flights and hotel rooms. And my brother's flying in from college for a few days, too. My dad worked it out with Rosewood Day—I'll take the makeup exams between Christmas and New Year's. And at least I'll be back for most of the break." Lucas gently took her hands in his and squeezed them. "You and I can spend every minute together then."

Hanna pulled her hands away from Lucas's, feeling a huge lump in her throat. "But I need you *now*."

Lucas threw up his arms helplessly. "I'm sorry, but I've wanted to go to the Yucatán for years. It has amazing hiking. Great beaches. And it's not like my folks could change their tickets now."

Before she could say anything, the doorbell rang to the tune of "Jingle Bells."

Lucas jumped up and parted the front curtains. A steel-blue Mercedes SUV had pulled into the driveway. "It's the Rumsons, the family we're traveling with. They're dropping off the itinerary. You'll love them. And I'll bet you have a lot in common with Brooke."

"Brooke?" Hanna asked warily, staying on the couch.

Mr. Beattie bounded in from the kitchen and pulled the door open, letting in a whoosh of cold air. "Wade! Patricia! It's been far too long!"

Mrs. Beattie emerged from the upstairs, grinning at her guests. "We are just *so* excited!" she squealed at the couple who had just stepped into the foyer. "And so is Lucas!" She pushed Lucas toward them. The husband, Wade, who wore a Burberry barn jacket and had blindingly white teeth, pumped Lucas's hand. The wife, Patricia, whose toothpick arms were apparent even under her snug-fitting cashmere peacoat, gave Lucas a kiss on the cheek.

"Oh. My. *God*," said a voice from the porch. The adults parted, and an overly tan, scarily skinny, gum-snapping teenage girl with long, teased black hair, wet-looking red lipstick, and jutting boobs marched right up to Lucas and clapped her long-fingernailed hands on his shoulders. "Lukey!" she screamed in a nasal voice. "You look *uh*-mazing!"

Lukey?

"Whoa. Brooke." Lucas smiled shakily. "You look . . . different."

The Rumsons nudged the Beatties. "You two have both grown up a bit since we last saw you, huh?" Mrs. Rumson said.

"Remember the kind of trouble they used to get into?" Lucas's mother clucked. "Remember all the secret clubs they formed?"

"They were inseparable. I always said those two would get married someday," Mrs. Rumson murmured before all the parents bustled off to the kitchen.

Hanna's head snapped up. *Married?*

Brooke poked Lucas's shoulder. "When you said I looked different, I hope you meant gorgeous!" She traced her finger over Lucas's T-shirt, then let her hand fall to the waistband of his jeans. "Has someone been working out? And where'd you get those sexy new clothes?"

"*Ahem.*" Hanna stood up and strode into the foyer. This flirtation had gone on long enough. *She* had been the one who'd encouraged Lucas to buy the True Religion jeans and streamlined polo from Armani Exchange he was wearing.

"Oh." Lucas glanced at Hanna. "Brooke, this is my girlfriend, Hanna."

"What's up?" Brooke took in Hanna's unwashed hair, schlumpy Eagles sweatshirt, and ratty old Sevens. A look crossed her face that said, *She's no threat.* She stepped closer to Lucas. "Aren't you *so* excited to go on this trip? I've heard the beachside parties there are amazing. And I can't wait to work on my tan."

Hanna pressed her lips together to keep from snickering. This girl was already so orange she looked like she'd been born in a tanning booth.

"It's going to rock," Lucas said. "I was just telling Hanna about it. There's amazing hiking, sightseeing, food . . ."

". . . *and* the nude beach," Brooke added, licking her lips.

"Uh, excuse me?" Hanna bleated.

Brooke slung her arm around Lucas's shoulder. "You're in for the treat of your life, Lukey—everyone sunbathes naked down there. And you and I are going to do Jell-O shots every night."

The cheese popcorn rose back up in Hanna's throat. She had to put a stop to this. "Um, I need to talk to you." She grabbed Lucas's arm and pulled him into the den, which was littered with video game boxes, old magazines, and three more Advent calendars, one of which looked like it was made entirely out of puff paint.

There was an innocent smile on Lucas's face. "Is everything okay?"

Was everything *okay*? Hanna took a few breaths to steady her nerves. "What do you think, *Lukey*?"

Lucas ran his hand over his hair. "Yeah, Brooke used to

call me that when she was little—she couldn't pronounce Lucas."

"It's horrible. It sounds like *pukey*." And they were going, Hanna thought, to the *Puke*-atán peninsula with Princess Puke-a-tan herself.

Lucas shrugged. "It's just a stupid nickname."

Hanna squeezed her eyes shut. "Are you seriously going on vacation with . . . *her*?"

"Are you jealous? Over *me*?" Lucas grinned like this was the most amusing thing he'd ever heard. "Hanna, you have nothing to worry about. Brooke's like a cousin."

Some people hook up with their cousins, especially when they see them sunbathing nude, Hanna thought bitterly.

She eyed Brooke in the other room. She was studying herself in the round mirror near the door, puckering her lips and slathering on more gloss. If Mona were here, they could nudge each other and make fun of Brooke's tacky press-on nails. If Ali were here, she'd freeze Brooke out and make her feel like the biggest dork in the universe.

A sour feeling streaked through Hanna's stomach. Dating a popular boy came with its pitfalls and insecurities, but she'd figured she would never, *ever* have to be concerned about other girls with a nerd like Lucas. Then again, because skanks didn't regularly throw themselves at Lucas, taking off their tops and tempting him with Jell-O shots, he had no immunity against this kind of thing. There were so many people who had dropped out of Hanna's life in the last few years—her dad, her ex-boyfriend Sean Ackard, Ali, Mona, her mom. All she wanted was someone stable who'd be around forever. But now even Lucas felt so precarious . . . and there was nothing she could do to stop him from going.

3

OLD HABITS DIE HARD

Hanna skirted around Brooke, marched out the door, and gunned her Prius as fast as it would go out of the Beatties' driveway. The last thing she wanted was to hear another word about Brooke's tanning goals, Jell-O shots, and thinly veiled double entendres of how Brooke was going to get Lucas into bed.

Her cell phone rang just as she turned at the end of Lucas's street. Lucas's name flashed on the screen. Hanna considered not answering, then sighed, picked up, and said hello.

"You have nothing to worry about," Lucas blurted. "I *promise.*"

Hanna didn't answer, instead squeezing the steering wheel so hard she was sure she was giving her palms blisters.

"My dad just told me that the hotel we're staying at has Wi-Fi. I'll Skype you every day and send tons of photos and tell you how much I adore you on Facebook every few hours."

"How about every hour on the hour?" If Lucas was constantly in touch with her, he couldn't get into *that* much trouble, could he? "And promise to get me a present—something good. And don't you *dare* look at any boobs on that nude beach."

When they hung up a few minutes later, she felt a little better. Hanna wound through the streets of Rosewood, the only sound in the car the whooshing noise of the heater. As she passed the busy shopping district, she noticed two headlights pull up behind her. They followed her as she drove by the school, the lit-up windows of Otto, the fancy Italian restaurant, and Fresh Fields grocery. With every turn, the car kept pace. She glanced at the dark figure behind the wheel in the rearview mirror, her heart starting to beat faster. Was she being followed? What if it was Ian—had he broken out of prison? She pulled over at an intersection and waited. The driver passed her by without slowing, and Hanna exhaled in relief.

Hanna looked at the street sign and realized where she'd stopped. This was Mona's old street—and Ali's.

Some of the houses on the block were already decorated for the holidays. The Hastingses' estate had twinkling lights that traced the perimeter of the roof. Jenna Cavanaugh's house had solemn candles in the windows. Ali's old house, which a new family lived in now, had a glowing wreath on the door. The Ali Shrine, which friends and strangers alike had set up shortly after Ali's body had been found, blazed at the curb. It was anyone's guess who kept those votive candles lit.

The Vanderwaals' property was dark. Hanna could just make out the long, five-car garage at the corner of the lot, the one she and Mona had climbed on top of and written HM + MV = BBBBBFF in big white letters on the roof. "Promise me we'll never be anything but besties," Mona had said after they'd finished and were washing the white paint off their hands with the garden hose. "I promise," Hanna had said. And she'd believed Mona with all her heart.

Now Hanna wanted to fire-bomb the garage. Or climb up there and leave a bouquet of flowers in Mona's memory. Her emotions veered so wildly from second to second it was hard to know *what* she felt.

And then, unbidden, the memory of the car that had roared toward Hanna in the parking lot two months ago flashed in her mind. Hanna had tried to run, but it had come at her too quickly. She remembered the sharp, binding terror she'd felt when she knew the car was going to hit her—that *Mona* was going to hit her.

"Don't think about it," Hanna whispered to herself.

Hanna drove slowly the rest of the way home, taking deep, cleansing breaths. After gunning the car up her family's driveway, she nearly crashed into a line of vehicles she didn't recognize. There had to be about fifteen sedans, SUVs, and crossovers parked in the circular drive. Then she noticed something blinking by the garage. Christmas lights. And was that a glow-in-the-dark Santa and an inflatable gingerbread man in the front yard?

She took tentative steps toward the house. Dot, wearing some kind of bizarre headpiece, yipped at her feet when she walked inside. Wait. Were those *reindeer antlers*? Hanna scooped him up and stared at the two plush stalks on his head. Each was tipped with a tiny jingle bell.

"Who did this to you?" Hanna whispered, ripping them off. Dot just licked her face.

She looked around the living room and gasped. Holly leaves snaked around the banister. A mechanical Mrs. Claus waved from the console table that had once held Hanna's mother's austere ceramic vases. A tall, tinsel-laden tree stood in the corner, and the fireplace, which Hanna couldn't remember the family ever using, was ablaze. "Rudolph the Red-Nosed Reindeer" played on the stereo at maximum volume, and the whole house smelled like honey-glazed ham.

"Hello?" Hanna called out.

Laughter floated out from the kitchen, first Isabel's goose-honk chortle, then her dad's booming guffaw. Hanna rounded the corner. The kitchen was packed with people holding champagne flutes and appetizer plates filled with mini quiches and wedges of Brie. Many of them wore Santa hats, including Hanna's dad. Isabel stood in the corner, wearing a red velvet dress tipped with Mrs. Claus white fur on the cuffs and hem, and Kate had on a tight-fitting red jersey sheath and black-and-white Kate Spade heels. Mistletoe hung from the chandelier, a carafe of mulled cider sat on the counter, and plates and plates of the most delicious-looking Christmas cookies and appetizers filled the island.

Isabel spied Hanna and glided over. "Hanna! *Feliz Navidad! O Tannenbaum!* Merry Christmas!"

Hanna sniffed. "Um, actually, I'm Jewish. And so is my father."

Isabel blinked dumbly, like she couldn't comprehend that anyone, let alone her own fiancé, could celebrate anything *other* than Christmas.

Mr. Marin appeared at Isabel's side. "Hey, sweetie," he said, ruffling Hanna's hair.

Hanna stared at him incredulously. "Since when do you celebrate *Christmas?*" She said the word like she might have said *Satan's birthday*.

Mr. Marin crossed his arms over his chest defensively. "I've been celebrating it with Isabel and Kate for the past few years. I told Kate to tell you."

"Well, she didn't," Hanna said flatly.

"We do the Twelve Days of Christmas every year. We always kick it off with a bash." Isabel took a sip of champagne. "It's a wonderful tradition. We started early this year with tonight—kind of a housewarming-meets-Christmas thing."

"And we'd like you to be a part of the tradition too, of course," Mr. Marin added.

Hanna stared at all of the red and green paraphernalia. Her family had never been *that* religious, but they lit

menorah candles every night of Hanukkah. On Christmas
Day, they ordered Chinese takeout, watched movie mara-
thons, and went on a long family bike ride if the weather
was decent. She liked *those* traditions.

The doorbell rang, and Isabel and Mr. Marin moved
toward the front door. Hanna wandered toward the drinks
table, wondering how much trouble she'd get into if she
poured herself a giant glass of Scotch. Then, a familiar,
red-sheathed figure swam into view.

"*That's* an interesting outfit for this party." Kate eyed
the oversized Eagles sweatshirt Hanna was wearing. "This
party is a big deal for Tom, you know. A lot of his new
work colleagues are here. You could have put in a little
more effort."

Hanna wanted to club Kate over the head with a
pepperoni stick from the food spread. "I didn't *know* there
would be a party."

"You didn't?" Kate raised a perfectly plucked eyebrow.
"I've known for a week. I guess I forgot to tell you."

She turned and flounced away. Hanna grabbed a petit
four and shoved it into her mouth without tasting it, staring at her dad across the room. He was schmoozing with
a gray-haired man in a tailored black suit and a slender
woman wearing enormous diamond earrings. When Kate
approached, Mr. Marin placed his hand on her shoulder
and made introductions, looking proud. He didn't turn
around and wave Hanna over so that he could introduce
her too, though.

She was just a big, unwanted lump in an Eagles sweat-shirt. A girl who wasn't invited to parties in her own house. She felt like Lady in *Lady and the Tramp*, one of Hanna's favorite movies as a kid. When Jim Dear and Darling had a new baby, they kicked Lady to the curb. Except Hanna didn't even have a scruffy bad-boy stray she could run off and share spaghetti noodles with because her supposed boyfriend was going to be hundreds of miles away soaking up the sunshine on a nude beach with a skank.

She plopped down on a chair in the far corner next to Edith, an old woman from down the street who wore giant glasses and perpetually looked as though she'd swallowed her false teeth. "Who's that?" Edith asked, leaning her ear toward Hanna's chair. She smelled faintly of violets.

"It's Hanna Marin," Hanna told her in a loud voice. "Remember me?"

"Oh, Hanna, yes, of course." Edith felt around for Hanna's hand and patted it. "Nice to see you, dear." She pushed a Saran-wrapped paper plate of chocolate-chip cookies across the table. "Have a cookie. I baked them myself. Tried to put them on the table with all the other food, but that new woman who lives here didn't seem to want them there." She wrinkled her nose as if she'd smelled something rancid.

"Thanks," Hanna mumbled, wanting to kiss Edith for not liking Isabel either. She placed a cookie on her tongue, swooning at the taste of sugar and butter and chocolate. "These are delicious."

"Glad you like them." Edith pushed another cookie toward her. "Have another. You're much too skinny."

Edith had said Hanna was too skinny even when Hanna was a chunky, ugly loser, but it still felt good to hear it. The sugar soothed her. A third cookie might even make her feel euphoric. *You shouldn't,* a voice said inside her head. *You had all that popcorn at Lucas's. You're wearing your fat jeans, and even* they *feel tight.*

But the cookies smelled so *good.* Hanna glanced up and saw Kate beaming at another one of her father's work colleagues, and something inside her broke open. *Don't,* she willed, but her hands seemed to move of their own volition, wrapping up six cookies in a napkin. Her legs had a mind of their own too, pressing up from the seat and weaving around the partygoers. Hanna got as far as the empty stairwell before she opened the napkin and started pushing the cookies in her mouth one by one. She chewed and swallowed with desperation. Crumbs fell on her chest. Chocolate was all over her fingers and mouth. It was like there was something inside her that told her she could only stop when she finished each and every one—only then would she be filled.

This was exactly what had happened the first time she'd met Kate and Isabel in Annapolis: She'd felt so nervous and awkward that the only thing that soothed her was eating copious amounts of food. Kate and Ali, who Hanna had brought along, had gaped at her like she wasn't human. And when Hanna had doubled over, her stomach aching, Mr. Marin had joked, *Did little piggy eat too much?*

It had been the first time Hanna had ever made herself throw up—and it wasn't the last. Over the years she'd worked hard to stop, but sometimes old habits were hard to break.

A high-pitched giggle pealed from the hall, and Hanna shot up straight. It sounded like *Ali*. When she looked out the front window, she swore she saw someone moving around in the bushes.

Hanna peered into the darkness. Then, she felt eyes on her back and turned. Her father and Kate were staring at her from the kitchen.

Their eyes flicked from Hanna's chocolate-smeared mouth to the crumbs on her chest to the cookies in her hands. Kate smirked. Mr. Marin's brow furrowed. Eventually, he lifted his hand to his face and made a sweeping motion at his lips. Hanna brushed off a chocolate chip stuck to her cheek. Kate turned away and covered her mouth, suppressing a giggle.

The remaining cookies tumbled from her hand onto the floor. Face burning, Hanna fled upstairs and slammed her bedroom door, giving the middle finger to the loud hoots of the partygoers and the booming Bing Crosby Christmas carol on the stereo. She'd had just about enough Christmas partying for a lifetime.

4

YOU'LL NEVER WORK
IN THIS MALL AGAIN

Tuesday after school, Hanna pushed through double doors that said WELCOME TO THE GRAND OPENING OF THE DEVON CREST MALL! on the glass. She entered a large atrium and breathed in. The air smelled like a mix of Auntie Anne's pretzels, Starbucks coffee, and a mélange of perfumes. A large fountain burbled, and well-dressed girls carrying shopping bags from Tiffany & Co., Tory Burch, and Cole Haan pranced past. It was similar to the King James Mall, Hanna's regular haunt, but just different enough so that it didn't evoke a single memory of her many shopping trips there with Mona.

Just being surrounded by retail made Hanna feel better. She should have visited the mall earlier, but she hadn't had the time. Yesterday, as part of the Twelve Days of Christmas extravaganza, she'd gone with her father, Isabel, and Kate to a performance of Handel's *Messiah* in Villanova—*snore*. The day before that, they'd attended an eggnog-tasting at the local Williams-Sonoma, and to Hanna's chagrin, she and Kate were only allowed to drink the nonalcoholic eggnog, which tasted like rancid non-dairy creamer. They had plans to go to a department store in Philly to see some kind of lameass light display tonight, but the department store had been closed because it was infested with bedbugs. *Huge* loss.

Now, Hanna passed a seating area with a small café that sold 208 different kinds of tea, and a gluten-free bakery. She pulled out her phone to check once more if Lucas had called or texted, but there wasn't a single email, voicemail, or tweet. He'd left two days ago and had already forgotten his promise to check in daily.

Whatever. She could trust Lucas. Right? Hanna thrust her chin into the air, trying to remain calm, and stopped to look at the mall directory. It had an Otter, her favorite boutique. She would drown her frustrations by buying the most amazing outfit ever.

"Hey, pretty girl."

Hanna turned her head to look for the passing college guy who'd surely made the comment, but there wasn't anyone there. Instead, she saw a Santa Land village replete with inflatable candy canes, a gingerbread house, and a bunch of bored-looking, college-aged elves in pointy shoes and hats. Santa Claus sat on a gilded throne, his hat askew.

"Nice smile, gorgeous," the voice said again, and Hanna realized it was *Santa.* He beckoned her over with his white glove. "Want to sit on my lap?"

"*Ew!*" Hanna whispered, skittering away. She could hear him *ho-ho-ho*ing all the way up the escalator.

Otter gleamed from down the corridor like a soothing fashion beacon. Hanna marched inside, bobbing to a loungey music mix. She lifted up a silk scarf and pressed it to her face. Then she inhaled the expensive scent of the buttery leather Kooba bags and ran her fingers over the denim jeggings and tie-waist Marc Jacobs chiffon dresses. Her heart rate slowed. She could practically feel her stress levels decreasing.

"Can I help you?" a voice chirruped. A petite blond salesgirl wearing a high-waist pencil skirt and the same polka-dotted silk blouse Hanna was ogling on the rack appeared next to her. "Are you looking for anything special?"

"I definitely need some new jeans." Hanna patted a pair of skinny J Brands on the table. "And maybe this dress, and this." She gestured to a cashmere sweater wrap by Alice + Olivia.

"Oh, that's *beautiful*," the salesgirl gushed. "You have great taste. Do you want me to pick some things out for you and start a room while you browse?"

"Sure," Hanna said.

"Great." The salesgirl looked Hanna up and down, then nodded. "Leave everything to me. I'm Lauren, by the way."

"Hanna." She grinned. This seemed like the start of a beautiful friendship. Maybe Lauren would put new stock aside for her to try on before other girls could get their grubby mitts on it, just like Sasha at the King James Otter did.

She did a lap of the store, selecting several more sweaters and dresses. Lauren chose other items she thought Hanna might like, including a stack of jeans, and whisked them to the back. When Hanna was ready to try things on, she noticed that Lauren had selected the biggest corner dressing room for her. Three other dressing rooms were occupied, but they were much smaller, as though those girls weren't nearly as important.

Hanna pulled the curtain closed, smoothed down her hair, and looked at the gorgeous wares swinging from their hangers on the post. It was time to do some credit-card damage. But suddenly, her gaze froze on a tag on one of the pairs of denim leggings Lauren had chosen for her sitting on the paisley-patterned upholstered chair.

Size *six*.

She frowned and inspected the next pair in Lauren's pile. This one was a six as well. She looked at the tags of the dresses Lauren had selected. *Also* sixes. There was nothing wrong with being a size six—for most girls—but Hanna hadn't been a six since before her makeover with Mona in eighth grade.

"Uh, Lauren?" Hanna stuck her head out of the dressing room. Lauren appeared at the end of the hall, and Hanna gave her an apologetic smile. "I think there's been a mistake. I'm a two."

An uncomfortable look washed over Lauren's face. "I

really think you should try the six. J Brand leggings run a little small."

Hanna bristled. "I have three pairs of J Brands already. I know exactly how their sizes run."

Lauren's lips pressed together. A long beat passed, and someone in one of the other dressing rooms sniffed. "Okay," Lauren said after a moment, shrugging. "I'll see if we have twos and fours in stock."

The curtain slid closed again. As Lauren padded down the hall, Hanna swore she heard a slight snicker. Was Lauren *laughing* at her? The other girls in the adjacent dressing rooms had become very silent, almost like they were listening—and judging.

Lauren was back in seconds with the new jeans. Hanna grabbed them from her hands and yanked the curtain closed again. How dare that idiot salesgirl snicker at her! And how had she looked Hanna up and down and just *assumed* she was a six? Weren't salesgirls supposed to have an accurate sense of what size a customer was? Didn't they go through some kind of training? Hanna had never been treated so inconsiderately at the *other* Otter. As soon as Hanna left here, she was going to call up Otter's corporate office to complain.

The denim of the size-two jeans felt soft around her bare ankles. Hanna stretched them over her calves, but when she pulled them up to her thighs, the cotton wouldn't give. Hanna stared at herself in the mirror. This pair was obviously defective.

She wriggled out of the size two and tried on the next size up. She could get these over her butt, but there was no way they were going to button. What the hell was going on?

As a last resort, she tried on the six Lauren had selected for her. She fastened the button and gazed at herself in the mirror. Her legs looked puffy. There was the tiniest bit of fat gaping over the waistband. The seams stretched taut as though they were going to burst any second. Hanna's heart started to pound. Could *all* of these jeans be defective?

Or had she gained weight?

Hanna thought about the cookies she'd eaten at the Christmas party. And the leftover party snacks she'd gorged on last night while watching TV in her room, hiding from her dad, Isabel, and Kate. And the pieces of fudge she'd grabbed from the open box on the island when she passed through the kitchen.

Her skin began to prickle. She felt one step away from backsliding into the chubby, ugly, dorky loser she'd been before Ali had befriended her in sixth grade. She peeked at her reflection in the mirror again, and for a split second, she saw a girl with poop-brown hair, pink rubber bands on her braces, and pimples on her forehead. It was the old Hanna, the girl she swore she would never, ever be again.

"No," Hanna said in a gurgling whisper, covering her eyes with her hands and sinking to the chair.

"Hanna?" Lauren's platform heels appeared under the door. "Is everything okay?"

Hanna eked out a *yes*, but everything was very, very far from okay. All of a sudden, it felt like everything in her life was spiraling out of control. And she had to do something about it—fast.

5

DOWN FROM MOUNT OLYMPUS

The next morning Hanna cycled around and around the elliptical trainer at Body Tonic, the upscale gym she'd been attending since the end of eighth grade. Each machine had a built-in TV with a zillion cable channels, a juice bar and spa stood next to the check-in desk, and the locker rooms boasted a eucalyptus steam room, a whirlpool bath, and Kiehl's products in all of the showers. All around her, fit men, women, and the occasional student from one of the many elite private schools in the area jogged on treadmills, pedaled on recumbent bikes, or did slightly vulgar-looking squats on exercise balls. A yoga class was taking place in the exercise room at the back, and at that very moment, the class was attempting the half-moon pose, their bodies making T shapes, their legs wobbling.

Sweat was in Hanna's eyes, her arms and legs burned, and she'd just seen an upsetting newscast on TV that mentioned Ian Thomas was proclaiming his innocence from behind bars. But she couldn't stop exercising now. There was no way she would remain a size six. She wouldn't let a salesgirl snicker at her ever again.

Her phone buzzed and she reached for it eagerly, checking once more to see if Lucas had called, texted, posted on Facebook, *anything*, but it was just Aria, asking to borrow Hanna's notes from English.

Hanna's chest felt tight. It made her feel unbelievably lame, but she *missed* Lucas—and it didn't seem like he missed her at all. She threw her phone back into the little plastic cup on the machine intended for water bottles, and cranked up the resistance another few levels. It didn't matter. She'd lose ten pounds, look fabulous again, and withhold all affection when Lucas returned.

Then again, she thought, what if Lucas didn't even care about her when he got home? What if he'd decided to ditch her for Princess Puke-a-tan?

"You're really going for it, huh?"

Hanna jumped, looked down, and saw a buff guy in a tight Body Tonic T-shirt, long mesh shorts, and gray New Balance sneakers standing next to her machine. He had the bluest eyes she'd ever seen, close-cropped dark hair, and gorgeous golden skin, and his muscles bulged without looking too bodybuilderish. Hanna recognized him instantly—when she and Mona used to come to Body Tonic together, they'd nicknamed him *Apollo*, for obvious reasons. He prowled around the exercise room, grinning at girls, occasionally lifting a weight or doing a stomach crunch, and training all of the super-rich Main Line female clientele. But the clincher was when they'd caught him sitting in his car in the parking lot, rocking out to "Stairway to Heaven," pretending the steering wheel was a drum kit. Apollo was a reformed dork, just like Hanna and Mona were.

Hanna glanced behind her to see if Apollo was speaking to someone else, but she was the only person on this row of elliptical trainers. "Uh, pardon?" she asked, trying to sound breezy. She wished she'd brought a hand towel to mop off her face.

Apollo grinned and gestured to the LCD readout on Hanna's machine. "You've been working out for eighty minutes. That's intense."

"Oh." Hanna kept pedaling. "I'm trying to get back into shape. I've been to a few too many holiday parties." She laughed self-consciously, then cursed herself for drawing attention to her Christmas-cookie bubble butt.

"The holidays can be tough." Apollo leaned on the machine next to hers. "I'm leading a fitness retreat that starts today designed specifically to get people through the holidays. It focuses on exercise, nutrition, and mental wellness."

"Sounds awesome," Hanna said. Kirsten Cullen, a girl she knew at Rosewood Day, had gone on a fitness retreat in St. Barts the summer between ninth and tenth grades and had returned twelve pounds lighter and with the most flawless skin ever. "A retreat to where?"

"Oh, to nowhere." Apollo shot her a sheepish smile. "We hold it here at the gym. But you'll *feel* transported—and amazing by the time it's done. Would you be interested in signing up?"

Hanna gazed at her sweaty reflection in the mirror in front of her. "I don't know." She wasn't really into group classes.

Apollo gave her a dazzling smile. "Are you sure? I think you'd find it really, really amazing. It's Hanna, right?"

Hanna's jaw dropped. "How did you know that?"

"I've seen you here before." This time when he smiled, he revealed two adorable dimples. "I'd love to have you in the class."

Her insides tingled. Was he flirting with her? For a split second, she couldn't wait to hop off the machine, call Mona, and tell her that Apollo from Body Tonic was practically begging her to be part of his fitness retreat—until she remembered, yet again. Every time she realized Mona had been A, and that she was dead now, it felt like someone had chucked a medicine ball at her chest.

"The pounds will melt off you," Apollo promised. "You'll be in the most amazing shape of your life. Please say you'll do it."

Since he put it that way, how could she say no? His sparkling blue eyes didn't hurt, either. "Okay, you've twisted my arm," she said, pausing the machine. "Count me in."

"Awesome." Apollo grinned again. Just being next

to him made her tingle all over. And he had *noticed* her. He *knew her name*. All thoughts of Lucas and Puke-a-tan Brooke flew out of her head. If Lucas could flirt, then so could she.

"My name's Vince," he added. "The class starts at five today, and we'll be meeting morning and night through the end of the year. I'm so thrilled you're going to do this, Hanna."

"I'm thrilled, too," Hanna answered, looking deeply into Apollo's—*Vince's*—eyes. And she absolutely, positively meant it.

6

THE BIGGEST LOSERS

That day after school, Hanna sat on the steps outside Body Tonic and cradled her cell phone between her shoulder and her ear. "Sorry, Dad. I swore I told you that I had plans tonight."

"But you're going to miss Santa's Village at Longwood Gardens." Mr. Marin sounded very disappointed. "It's going to be a blast."

Hanna resisted the urge to gag. In seventh grade, she, Ali, and the other girls had gone to Longwood Gardens, which was essentially just that—a big, boring garden. It was hot, crowded, and downright miserable inside, so they'd spent most of the time hanging out in the parking lot, gossiping about which boy at Rosewood Day they most wanted to kiss and which celebrities they'd invite to their fantasy birthday parties.

"I'm really sorry," Hanna repeated. "But I made these

plans before I knew about your Twelve Days of Christmas thing."

Mr. Marin sighed. "This isn't because you're uncomfortable with Isabel and Kate, is it? Kate says she wants to get to know you, but you keep yourself at a distance. She also mentioned you ditched out on going to the mall with her the day we moved in."

Hanna opened her mouth, then shut it again. Kate had some nerve. "This has nothing to do with them," she lied.

When she hung up, she rested the phone in her lap, wishing it would ring once more and she'd hear Lucas's voice on the other end. But it stayed silent. She stared at the cars swishing back and forth on the remote country road. Snow was falling lightly, making the pavement sparkle. Hanna heard a shuffling noise to the left and sat up straighter. It sounded like someone was lurking behind the corner.

Hanna shrugged it off—no one was stalking her anymore—and jumped to her feet. She headed inside the gym, an excited flurry in her stomach. She might have been resistant to the group fitness idea at first, but now she was pumped. Everyone would probably be pretty, young Main Line girls—maybe she'd even make a new friend or two. And Vince had said that the class incorporated fitness, nutrition, and well-being; perhaps that meant regular massages at the end of each session, by Vince, of course. On a strictly professional basis, so Lucas wouldn't get too jealous.

A printed sign that said HOLIDAY FITNESS RETREAT was pasted on the door of one of the regular exercise rooms. Hanna had expected that the class would be in a secret Body Tonic space—something for VIPs only—but whatever. She took a deep breath and pushed through the door, a huge smile on her face, half-expecting all the beautiful participants to spin around and welcome her with open arms, sort of like a group therapy session except way more glamorous.

But the lights, which were very bright, almost fluorescent, revealed an entirely different scene. Ten people sat on the floor with various mats, balls, bands, balancing apparati, and yoga blocks in front of them. All of them did indeed turn and stare at her, but they didn't spread out their arms to welcome her in a group hug. Not that she wanted to touch them. They were as far from glamorous fitness junkies as possible.

There was a woman with a triple chin. A man whose gut plunged over his waistband. Frumpy suburban mothers. Dumpy suburban dads. The kind of teenage girls who joined drama club or band or spent their lunch periods in the art room, not giving a shit about how their bodies looked. One girl had the biggest boobs she had ever seen. She was Hanna's age and sexily padded, with big hips and a large butt, like a fifties pinup girl. She had a punkish style—tall, lustrous black hair, copious eyeliner on her almond-shaped eyes, lots of red lipstick on her baby-doll lips, and a tattoo shaped like a swirly dagger on her shoulder. Normally Hanna wasn't into the look, but it kind of worked on her. Not that she would admit it out loud.

A glam fitness retreat this wasn't. It was more like a low-rent version of *The Biggest Loser*. Hanna hadn't seen a single one of them on the floor of Body Tonic, *ever*—it was like the gym had hidden these people away so as not to scare off the regulars. And every last person was wearing an oversized red T-shirt that said GET YOUR BUTT IN GEAR! in big white letters on the front and HOLIDAY FITNESS BOOT CAMP! on the back.

"Hanna!" Vince appeared from behind a set of stereo equipment in the corner and grinned at her broadly. He was also wearing a red GET YOUR BUTT IN GEAR! shirt—albeit a much tighter one. "Glad you could make it! Here, take a T-shirt!"

He tossed one to her, but Hanna didn't make any effort to catch it, letting it bounce off her chest and drop limply to the floor. Behind her, she heard a thin, high-pitched giggle and froze. A figure slipped around the corner, her long blond hair streaming. Had someone *seen* her? Would someone think she was part of . . . *this*?

"Let's start by introducing ourselves and saying why we're here," Vince began. He pointed to the pinup girl.

She jiggled her boobs at him and purred, "I'm Dinah Morrissey. I don't care about losing weight, but I do want to make a commitment to get healthier." She batted her lashes at Vince, who smiled broadly back at her.

"Nice to meet you, Dinah. Hanna, how about you go next?" Vince asked.

Hanna's mouth was sealed shut. She looked again at the lumpy misfits on the floor, let out a small squeaking noise, and spun around. She ran as fast as she could toward the main gym, back to where everyone was pretty and slender and normal.

"Hanna," Vince called out as she wound around the weight machines and treadmills. He cut her off in the hallway between the yoga studio and the macrobiotic snack bar. "What's the matter?"

Hanna shrugged awkwardly, noticing that Vince had followed after her with the red GET YOUR BUTT IN GEAR! T-shirt that Hanna had rejected. "I don't think that class is for me."

"The retreat? Why?"

Was he *high*? First of all, it was a *boot camp*, not a fitness retreat. Second, how could Vince think Hanna belonged in a class like that? Had he noticed her on the elliptical today and pegged her as someone out of shape, someone ordinary? Someone who salesgirls snickered at, fathers rejected, and best friends despised?

"Because it's a class full of fat people!" Hanna finally blurted.

Vince took a few steps back, his mouth forming a small *O*. "You're kidding, right?"

A techno version of a Rihanna song thumped in the background. When Hanna didn't answer, Vince shook his head. "The other members aren't fat. Okay, maybe some of them are a little over their healthiest weights, but don't you think it's great that they want to get back in shape? I feel like I can really help them."

You're like a muscled Mother Teresa, Hanna wanted to snap. "Well, I think I'll pass."

"You're going to pass on a fitness class that's going to kick your ass? Why, because everyone else doesn't look like they stepped out of *Vogue*?"

He was talking awfully loudly. Hanna looked around cautiously. The whip-thin girl at the check-in desk scanned two members' cards, the machine making two efficient little beeps. A college-age guy sprinted on the treadmill, his floppy blond hair bouncing. What if someone had been listening, someone from Rosewood Day? If anyone caught wind of this, she would be the school's biggest loser—in more ways than one.

Vince gave Hanna a knowing look. "I think I understand what's going on. You don't have it in you. It's not called boot camp because it's easy. You don't have the mental edge to go through such a rigorous program."

Hanna sniffed indignantly. "This has nothing to do with my mental edge."

"Nah, forget it." Vince waved his hand. "I should have seen the signs. Not everyone is cut out for this class—you have to really *want* wellness, really be ready to go for it. Don't worry about it, Hanna. I thought you were tough enough for it—but it's cool."

"I'm plenty tough," Hanna said so loudly that a twenty-something girl in a Hollis sweatshirt by the mats glanced up in alarm. "I'm sure I'm tougher than all of those other . . . *people* in there."

Vince squared his jaw. "Okay, then. Prove it to me. Show me you're serious."

His voice sounded gruff and stern, but his eyes were soft, almost yearning. Once again, Hanna felt a tiny inkling that he might be interested in her. And just knowing someone liked her eased the loneliness she felt whenever she thought about Lucas's MIAness. If she walked out of here, condemning the fitness retreat and its overweight participants, Vince would probably never speak to her again. And she hated that he thought she was a quitter. It was practically synonymous with *loser*—and there was no way she was going to be a loser ever again.

"All right," she groaned. "I guess I'll give it another shot. But I have one condition. I am *not* wearing one of those muumuus." She pointed to the T-shirt Vince was holding.

Vince shrugged and clapped his hand on Hanna's arm. "It's a deal."

7

MAZEL TOV!

Two hours later, Hanna slumped into the Prius, barely able to move. Vince was definitely right about one thing: The boot camp was anything but a relaxing spa experience. She had never squatted, kicked, jogged in place, bicep-curled, or sweat so much in her life. Vince jam-packed the session with so many activities, Hanna had barely noticed the other people in the class except when one of them collapsed in exhaustion or whined that they couldn't do one more bicycle crunch. The only person who stood out was Dinah. She kept pushing her boobs in Vince's face and asking if her poses were right. One time she even made him stand behind her while she was squatting, his hand on her back and dangerously close to her butt, just to be sure she was working the correct muscle group. Her shameless flirting reminded Hanna of Brooke, which made her feel nauseated about Lucas all over again.

She pulled into the driveway of her house, wanting

nothing more than to crawl into bed and watch hours and hours of bad TV. Strangely, her father's car was still in the driveway—not at Longwood Gardens. And the Christmas decorations that had festooned the front of the property were gone. When she opened the front door, it no longer smelled like fresh pine and cinnamon sticks but more like . . . potato pancakes?

"Hanna!" Mr. Marin appeared from the kitchen. "There you are! Come in, come in! We have a surprise for you!"

He whisked Hanna through the living room, but not before she noticed that the mechanical Mrs. Claus had vanished, the Christmas tree was unlit, and the stockings that had hung over the fireplace—there were monogrammed ones for Isabel, Kate, and Hanna's dad, and a blank one presumably for Hanna—had been taken down. The old silver menorah Bubbe Marin had given Hanna's parents sat on the mantel. Three candles blazed.

"What's going on?" Hanna asked suspiciously.

Mr. Marin turned Hanna toward the dining room. There was a huge spread of food on the table, and Kate and Isabel were sitting in high-backed chairs, tepid smiles on their faces. "Surprise!" Mr. Marin crowed. "Happy Hanna-kah!"

Hanna blinked at the items on the table. There were all the traditional Hanukkah foods her grandmother used to serve: latkes, jelly donuts called sufganiyot, kugel, chocolate coins, and a large brisket. Off to the side were the old dreidels she and her cousins had spun for hours, turning the game into a kind of truth or dare—if the dreidel fell on the *gimel* side, Tamar, her younger cousin, had to steal a dollar out of her mother's wallet, and so on. A blue foil banner with Star of David cutouts was draped across the windows, and candles glowed around the room. Small gifts wrapped in silver paper sat on everyone's plates.

"I thought you guys were going to Santa's Village," Hanna said slowly.

"Oh, we can do that any day," Mr. Marin said. "I thought you might be a little upset since we're doing so many Christmas activities, so we thought we'd celebrate *our* holiday tonight! Hanukkah—or Hanna-kah!" He gestured to the food on the table. "Kate and Isabel did some baking this evening, though some of this came from the kosher deli near Ferra's Cheesesteaks."

"Your dad says you know all of the Hanukkah stories, Hanna," Isabel said politely. "I'd love to hear them."

"This is all so nice." Hanna's heart expanded, just like the Grinch's. This was definitely the nicest thing her dad had done for her in a long, long time.

Her father passed around plates, and everyone began serving themselves latkes and pieces of brisket bathed in sauce. Hanna took a moderate amount of food, feeling virtuous from boot camp. Wine was poured—even Hanna and Kate got some—and everyone opened their gifts. Kate and Hanna got gift cards to Fermata Spa. Isabel got a small Christmas tree-shaped charm to add to her silver Pandora bracelet. Mr. Marin had given himself a new Swiss Army knife. He immediately unfolded the scissors and cut the tag off of Isabel's bauble.

Then, Mr. Marin launched into stories about Bubbe Marin, who used to make the best potato pancakes in the world. "We used to go over there every night of Hanukkah," he explained. "She'd always have huge gifts for Hanna."

"Isn't that sweet," Isabel trilled, looking surprised, as though she'd never imagined someone would shower Hanna with gifts.

"And she had this African gray parrot, Morty," Mr. Marin went on, spearing a latke. "He knew every swearword in the world."

"He was crazy!" Hanna giggled. "I think I learned some new ones from him!"

"And he loved to watch those tabloid shows—what were they called?" Mr. Marin's face was flushed.

"*E! News*," Hanna repeated. "He was obsessed with Giuliana Rancic. Remember? He said she was *such a pretty bitch* in that crazy bird voice!"

"Who's Giuliana Rancic?" Isabel asked, blinking quickly.

Hanna's father was too busy shaking with laughter to answer. Hanna laughed too, also not bothering to fill Isabel in. It felt nice to have an inside joke with her father again, something from their lives before Isabel and Kate.

They continued eating, sharing stories about Hanna's

grandmother's obsessions with yard sales, animal figurines, and her crush on Bob Barker from *The Price Is Right*. By the time the meal was over, Hanna and her dad kept bursting into laughter but not bothering to explain themselves. Isabel rose to clear the table, but Mr. Marin waved her to sit down. "I can clean up," he said.

"I'll clean up, too," Kate volunteered quickly.

Hanna set her jaw. "No, *I'll* clean up with you, Dad." The last thing she wanted was for Kate to usurp her father's love again.

Mr. Marin grinned. "Hey, if both of *you* are going to clean up, I guess you don't need me!" He stacked the plates and handed them to Hanna. "How about you wash, Kate dries?"

Hanna stared at the congealed latke on her plate, wondering if this was a trick on her father's part to get her and Kate to bond.

Kate was already filling the sink with soap by the time Hanna walked in with all the dishes. "So did you like your little celebration?" she said in an icy voice, handing Hanna a dishrag.

"It was very nice," Hanna answered just as frostily.

"My mom and I baked for *hours*." Kate wiped imaginary sweat off her brow. "You could have at least helped out. So where were you after school, anyway?"

Hanna plunged her hands into the scalding hot water. "Just . . . out and about. Doing some shopping. Going to the gym. I didn't know you were going to do this for me."

Kate raised an eyebrow. "For four hours? That's quite a marathon shopping session. *Or* a marathon workout."

She stared at Hanna for a long beat. Hanna held Kate's gaze, trying her hardest not to give anything away. There was no chance in hell she was going to tell Kate about the holiday boot camp. She'd never hear the end of it.

Kate leaned against the counter and narrowed her eyes. "I think someone's hiding something."

"No, I'm not," Hanna snapped a little too quickly. "Maybe *you're* hiding something."

Kate froze. "I . . ." She tossed the dish towel onto the island. "Neither am I," she said tightly, then whipped around and headed for the hall.

Hanna listened to her footfalls on the stairs, then the heavy slam of Kate's bedroom door. *Okaaay.* Kate's abrupt disappearance meant she'd have to clean up all on her own, but maybe that was all right. It felt like she'd just won an argument without even trying. And with Kate, that was nothing short of a miracle.

8

A SEXY STRETCH
DOES THE BODY GOOD

The following morning before school, Hanna gazed at herself in the Body Tonic full-length mirror and adjusted the straps of her black Lululemon tank top. Then she twisted around and checked out her butt in the matching black-and-pink short-shorts, pleased to see that her legs looked toned and sexy. She dabbed tinted moisturizer on her cheeks and nose, ran a tube of gloss across her lips, reshaped her shiny auburn hair into a ponytail, and spritzed a little bit of Aveda Chakra 4 on her pressure points. Every guy she'd met went crazy for the scent. Lucas had loved it—until he'd gone to a nude beach with Puke-a-tan and forgotten all about her. She still hadn't received a single text from him. She had flipped over all the pictures of him in her room so she wouldn't have to look at his cornflower-blue eyes and wonder if Brooke was staring into them right then.

Hanna was actually excited for class to start. At least

when Vince was barking out orders, she was too distracted to feel sad about Lucas. As she pushed open the door to the fitness room, she heard moans. "That feels so, *so* good," someone said.

Hanna paused, wondering if a couple had ducked into the room for an early morning make-out session—*ew*. But then she caught a flash of a familiar red T-shirt. One of the boot campers was lying on the floor, her legs up in the air. Vince was standing above her, pressing on her foot to stretch her hamstring.

"Is that releasing the muscle?" Vince murmured, grinning down at the girl.

"Oh, yeah," she answered dreamily. "It's amazing."

Hanna's hackles rose. It was Dinah Morrissey, the feel-my-ass girl.

"Want me to do the other leg?" Vince asked.

"Sure," Dinah purred in a gravelly voice, lifting a checkerboard Vans slip-on. Dinah couldn't even wear Nikes or Reeboks like a normal gym-goer.

Hanna leapt across the room as fast as her legs could carry her. Maybe she couldn't compete with Brooke from a thousand miles away, but she was right here in front of Vince, and the choice between her and Dinah was obvious.

"Um, Vince?" she simpered. "I was going to ask you to stretch me out, too. Yesterday's workout was a killer." She twirled a piece of hair around her finger. "Would you mind? I'm in *so* much pain."

Vince stood and looked from Dinah to Hanna. "Um,

sure, I guess I could," he said, releasing Dinah's leg. "We have a couple of minutes before everyone else is due to arrive."

Dinah sat up and crossed her arms over her ample chest. "What about me?"

"I'll stretch you after class," Vince promised.

Ha, Hanna thought triumphantly.

"Lie down," Vince instructed, and Hanna did as she was told. He told her to raise her left leg, knee bent, and cross her right leg over it. He leaned over her, his hands touching her legs lightly, and pressed. "How does this feel?"

"Really good," Hanna whispered, staring into Vince's eyes, which were a dazzling shade of turquoise. Once, when Hanna and Mona first joined the gym in eighth grade—back when they were just beginning their transformations into pretty, popular girls—Mona had stood behind Vince at the juice bar and dropped her change on the floor in an attempt to get his attention. When Vince turned those blue eyes on her, she'd felt hypnotized. "I couldn't say a word," she'd gushed. "He was just way too gorgeous."

Hanna hoped Mona was watching her now from whatever hell she was in, eating her heart out.

"You're really sore from yesterday, huh?" Vince murmured.

"Mmm-hmm," Hanna murmured. "But it's a *good* kind of sore, you know?"

"I'm sore, too," Dinah piped up, sitting cross-legged

next to them. She had the kind of cleavage guys could stuff dollar bills into. "And you'd be so proud of me, Vince. I had grilled chicken and veggies last night for dinner, just like on your meal plan."

"That's great." Vince sounded delighted. *Suck-up,* Hanna thought.

"So how long have you worked at the gym?" Hanna asked loudly, diverting the attention back to her.

Vince cupped his hands around Hanna's knee. "A while, I guess. Long enough to notice you. I've watched you run on the treadmill. You have great form." He laughed sheepishly. "Sorry. I hope that doesn't sound weird."

"Of course not," Hanna said quickly. "So have you always wanted to be a trainer?"

"Well, yes and no," Vince said. "I'd actually like to start my own spa. It would have personal training, but also a lot of body services as well."

"That sounds amazing," Hanna gushed. "I love spas."

Dinah giggled in that good-natured way that sounded friendly but Hanna knew was sarcastic. "*Everyone* loves spas," she said.

Hanna wished she could poke her out of the room with the ten-pound Body Bar propped up in the corner. Didn't she know it was rude to eavesdrop?

Vince was about to say something else, but then the door to the fitness room opened and the rest of the class trundled in, each of them wearing their GET YOUR BUTT IN

GEAR! T-shirts again. Hanna hoped they'd laundered them since yesterday.

"Okay," Vince said, releasing Hanna's leg and strutting to the front of the room. Everyone gathered around him. Hanna glanced over her shoulder, making sure no one was lurking in the hallway. She thought about Kate's suspicions yesterday after dinner. Kate hadn't followed her here, had she? The last thing Hanna needed was pictures of herself sweating and squatting with a bunch of losers getting on the Internet.

"So I wanted to talk to you guys today about nutrition and full-body wellness," Vince was saying, settling into a lotus position on the floor. "Being fit isn't just about exercising—it's about eating right, too. Making healthy choices. Feeling good in your skin. And I want everyone to make a pledge to be healthy and feel good in their skin during this retreat."

He passed out sheets of paper that said *Boot Camp Pledge* at the top. It was a long list, each item starting with *I vow to. I vow to eat only clean foods—no processed sugar, no high-fructose corn syrup, no artificial flavoring. I vow not to drink alcohol or smoke cigarettes.* At the bottom was a space for a signature.

"By the time this class is over, my goal is for *all* of you to feel good in your skin—no matter what your body shape is or how many pounds you've lost," Vince said. "And one thing that can help you feel good is this."

He held up a water bottle. Printed on the side was a

label that said AMINOSPA in minimalist letters. "This is the most amazing vitamin water I've ever tried. It gives you energy, it flushes toxins out—I even think it helps me concentrate better. I'm a licensed seller, but I'll give you guys a sample for free."

He pulled more bottles of AminoSpa from his gym bag and tossed one to everyone. "I think you'll like it," he urged. "If you want more, I can get you guys a case at a great rate."

"And you said you sell this, too?" Dinah asked, cocking her head and pursing her full lips.

Vince nodded. "It's a great part-time job—you can do it from home. If you guys are interested, I can give you the sales literature."

The business model reminded Hanna of the time in ninth grade when Chassey Bledsoe's mom had started selling Ginsu knife knockoffs from door to door, bragging about how she was working from home and was making *so* much money. She even convinced Chassey to bring samples with her to Rosewood Day to give demonstrations during lunch. As soon as the administration had found out Chassey had a suitcase full of knives on school property, they'd stopped it immediately.

But Vince looked so earnest about AminoSpa, like he actually believed it was making everyone healthier and happier. Hanna caught the bottle he threw at her, unscrewed the cap, and took a long swig. She fought the urge to spit it out. It tasted like watered-down margarita mix.

Vince clapped his hands. "Okay. Let's start sweating, shall we? The next couple weeks are going to be really intense—you're going to be pushed to your limits. A lot of our exercises are going to involve sparring, competing, and partner stretches, so I'm going to pair you guys up. The person I pair you with will be your partner for the rest of the class; you guys will be spending lots of time together. They'll be your check-in for your nutritional goals—and hopefully a lifelong friend."

At this, Vince shot Hanna a coy, fleeting look, and Hanna's insides swirled. It was definitely a signal: He was going to pair her with him. She could already picture it: the two of them shadowboxing, Vince rallying her on. The two of them running on the Marwyn trail, the other slowpokes far back in the distance. After each session, they'd drink lattes—or AminoSpas—together, blissfully spent. Then when Lucas got back, she would show him just how fine she was while he was gone.

"Tara, I want you with Josie." Vince pointed at two middle-aged women in the back. They smiled at each other pleasantly. "Ralph, you'll be partners with Jerome." Two barrel-chested, bandy-legged guys nodded. Vince continued around the room, matching one red-shirted member to another. His gaze kept sweeping past Hanna, skipping over her. Because he was leaving her for himself, of course.

Finally, Vince pointed to Hanna and grinned. "Hanna. You'll be with . . ."

Hanna expected him to thump his chest and triumphantly say *me*, so when he pointed at someone across the room, she didn't understand. She'd thought she was the only unpaired person left standing, but one other retreater remained. The girl's hands were on her full hips. She shifted in her checkerboard Vans. Her heavily outlined eyes were narrowed and her red lips were curled in a sneer.

It was Dinah.

9

FAKE BOYFRIENDS
ARE SO MUCH FUN

On Saturday afternoon, Hanna speed-walked into Momma's Sweet Shoppe, the brand-new-but-made-to-look-old ice cream fountain in the Devon Crest Mall. The floor was a black-and-white checkerboard pattern, there were old-fashioned chrome and leather stools at the counter, and a chalkboard listing types of floats, malts, and the various ice cream flavors of the day hung above the milk-shake machines. The waitstaff wore crisp white shirts, red-and-white-striped vests, and white paper hats, and fifties doo-wop blared over the stereo.

Her father, Isabel, and Kate followed, making *brr* noises at the bracing wind and subzero temperatures they'd had to endure in the parking lot. "Tell me again why we're getting ice cream right now?" Hanna said, her teeth still chattering.

Mr. Marin unwound his heavy red scarf from his neck. "Because this is what Kate and her mom did after every

Nutcracker performance Kate danced in. Right, ladies?"

"Right," Isabel said proudly, patting Kate's shoulder. "It was always a double scoop of mint chip for my little Clara."

Hanna suppressed a groan. It was the same saccharine phrase Isabel had been saying all day, from the trek into Philly to see a matinee of *The Nutcracker* at the Academy of Music to the curtain call at the end of the ballet to the long hunt for a parking space at the mall. Kate was her little Clara, the child lead in *The Nutcracker*, the role Kate had danced for four years with their local ballet troupe in Annapolis, and it had been Kate's favorite ballet ever since. Honestly, Hanna didn't get the ballet's allure—a rich girl's house is infested with mice; candy canes, snowflakes, and strange Russian men don't let her sleep; and then she and a Mouse King in a really ugly vest disappear into some giant beehive. It seemed like one long acid trip.

"I bet you're still an amazing ballerina." Isabel pushed a piece of hair out of Kate's eyes. "You should see her dance, Tom. She's just so graceful."

"Maybe you should take some classes again," Mr. Marin suggested. "You'd probably fall right back into it."

"You're too nice." Kate spun her silver David Yurman bracelet around her wrist. "But I'm way out of practice."

You just don't want to because you'd no longer be the best in the class, Hanna thought bitterly, remembering her one and only experience with ballet. She and Ali had taken a class at the YMCA, and when all of them did *grand jetés* across the room, Ali had collapsed into giggles, saying Hanna looked exactly like a hippo in a tutu.

Now, Hanna sighed. After her new family had thrown Hanna a Hanukkah bone a few nights ago, everything had gone back to normal shortly afterward. The Twelve Days of Christmas nonsense had resumed, though Hanna had been able to get out of a lot of it because of boot camp. She had to keep lying about where she was going, but so far her dad hadn't given her a hard time about it— probably because he didn't really want her there anyway. She'd tried to make a joke to her dad about Bubbe Marin and Morty the lewd African gray parrot during intermission today, but Kate had talked over her, telling Hanna's father about how Tchaikovsky had based *The Nutcracker* on an old children's tale. Her dad had nodded at Kate like it was the most interesting story in the world. Meanwhile, though Hanna had taken to obsessively checking Lucas's Facebook page, he hadn't uttered a peep. She was half-tempted to call his resort and ream him out for ignoring her.

As they waited in line for ice cream, Isabel launched into yet another Kate-was-such-a-beautiful-ballerina memory. Suddenly, listening to *Nutcracker* talk was just too much. "I have to use the bathroom," Hanna interrupted, stepping out of line. "Just get me a bottled water," she said, remembering the boot camp pledge she'd signed.

"We're going to browse around the mall with our cones," her father called after her. "Look for us in Brookstone, okay?"

"Uh-huh," Hanna answered absently, snaking around the little tables and enormous shopping bags from Saks, Build-A-Bear, and the Apple Store. Her chest felt tight, like she was about to cry. Her dad had bent over backward for her a few days ago, reliving old times, laughing and joking with her like they'd used to. But now that seemed like ancient history. Hadn't he noticed how much she'd appreciated it?

"Hanna," a voice called out, and Hanna swung around. Sitting at the little table in the corner, a small bowl of ice cream and a bottle of AminoSpa in front of him, was Vince from Body Tonic. For a moment, Hanna didn't quite recognize him. He was wearing jeans, a sweater, and heavy brown hiking boots.

"Hey," Hanna said, instinctively running her hand over her face to make sure there weren't tears running down her cheeks. "What are you doing here?"

"Shopping." Vince grinned.

"*And* eating ice cream." Hanna glanced at the nearly empty bowl, one eyebrow raised.

Vince lifted his hands in surrender. "You got me. Butter pecan is my Achilles' heel. This place is going to be the death of me." He motioned for her to take a seat.

"I never thought *you* would have a food weakness," Hanna said, settling into a seat opposite him. She gestured to the bunch of shopping bags sitting on the chair next to him. "Did you get everything on your list?"

Vince nodded. "The Toys 'R' Us bag has a gift for a kid in the homeless shelter. And the rest of it is for my family.

Is that your family over there?" He pointed to Isabel, Kate, and Hanna's father.

Hanna made a face. "That's my dad, my stepmom, and . . . Kate." She'd rather die than refer to Kate as her *family*.

She looked again at the Toys "R" Us bag on the chair. "It's nice of you to get a gift for someone at the homeless shelter. Is it the one in Yarmouth?" She remembered Spencer volunteering there in seventh grade, because it would look good on a college application. Only Spencer would be thinking about colleges in junior high.

Vince swigged from his bottle of AminoSpa. "It's something I do every year. A bunch of us from Body Tonic are going there on Monday to wrap the gifts everyone donated. It's a really rewarding experience."

"That's so sweet." Vince was sort of like Brad Pitt with his Hurricane Katrina crusade.

Mr. Marin finished paying, and he, Isabel, and Kate wandered outside. Just then a man in a Santa suit sauntered past. He peered into the ice cream shop and smiled lasciviously at Hanna.

Hanna grasped Vince's hand. "Quick. Pretend you're my boyfriend."

"Excuse me?" Vince's voice cracked.

"Just until Santa goes away." She nudged her head ever-so-slightly toward the window. Santa was still standing there. She wasn't sure where his eyes were looking because of the sunglasses, but she had a pretty good idea.

"He hit on me a couple of days ago, asking me to sit on his lap. I can't have him thinking I'm available."

Vince snickered and clutched Hanna's hand. Their palms fit together perfectly, and she felt suddenly calm and happy. "Okay, pretend I've just said something really funny," Vince suggested.

"Ha ha!" Hanna fake-laughed, throwing her head back. "You are too cute!" She reached out and touched the tip of his nose.

"No, *you're* cute," Vince said, touching Hanna's nose back. She wished he meant it and they weren't just pretending.

They fake-bantered for another few seconds until Santa shrugged and trundled away. "*Thank* you," Hanna breathed out.

"No problem," Vince answered. "You know, a friend of mine works at the Gap here, and she said something about Santa being a real letch, too. It's becoming a huge problem for the mall. I'm not surprised at all that he hit on you, though."

Warmth spread across Hanna's face. She bit her bottom lip and lowered her eyes, pretending to be fascinated with the mosaic pattern in the tabletop. Did that mean Vince thought she was cute?

The milk-shake maker whirred behind the counter. A little girl banged her spoon against her empty dish. Finally, Vince coughed awkwardly. "So I'm happy you decided to stick with boot camp. You're doing really well."

Hanna smiled. "I'm happy, too. Though I'm kind of surprised that you paired me up with Dinah."

Vince frowned. "I thought you two would be perfect together."

Hanna resisted the urge to snort. Yesterday morning, while Dinah had held Hanna's legs during sit-ups, she'd whispered, "Just so you know, I can see up your shorts." To which Hanna responded that Dinah's dark lipstick made her look like a corpse.

Then, during the partner stretch, Dinah had whined to Vince that Hanna was stretching her incorrectly, finagling it so that Vince would stretch her instead. And during the evening session, Vince had proposed a squat-off for the class, the winner getting a special prize. Determined to win, Hanna had squatted and squatted until her leg muscles felt like they'd oozed out through her knees. One by one, the other class members fell to the ground, groaning. The only other person who kept going, right next to Hanna, was Dinah. Down and up they went. In and out they breathed. "Amazing, girls!" Vince bellowed. "Keep it up!"

Finally, Hanna's vision had begun to tunnel. She'd dropped to the ground in a heap, and Dinah had let out a whoop. Dinah's prize had been a bottle of AminoSpa— *whoo hoo*. But she'd looked at Hanna, licked her finger, pressed it to her butt, and made a sizzling noise.

"You two are young and hungry," Vince explained now. "But more than that, I think you're a huge inspiration to Dinah. I'm not sure she's ever taken fitness seriously before, whereas you look like you've taken care of yourself for years. I think you can really help her achieve her goals."

Hanna perked up. *That* made sense. She'd never thought of herself as a fitness inspiration, but maybe she was. She could be just like Jillian Michaels or that long-haired, buff-bodied guy on her mom's yoga DVDs, giving Dinah tough love and lots of encouragement.

"Well, I'm glad I can help," she said, folding her arms on the table. "In fact, if you ever want to get together to talk about how I could be . . . *more* inspirational, I'd be happy to hear it."

Vince nodded contemplatively. "Sure. That would be great."

"I'd like to hear more about AminoSpa sometime, too," Hanna added, gesturing to his almost-empty bottle.

This made Vince's eyes light up. "Absolutely. I can give you the whole rundown."

Then Vince said he'd better get going. They both stood and said their good-byes, and Hanna pranced away from him, hoping he was getting a good look at her already-firmer butt. Her heart was racing, her cheeks felt flushed, and she felt beautiful, radiant, and desired.

But as she strode out of the shop, she caught sight of something outside the window. COMING SOON, a large placard said on a storefront across the walkway. RIVE GAUCHE.

She felt a twinge of guilt. Rive Gauche was the

restaurant at the King James Mall she and Mona used to hang out at religiously—and it was the place where Lucas worked. They'd re-met there, actually—Lucas had chased after Hanna when Mona had stuck her with a bill, and they'd developed a friendship that led to dating.

Maybe it was wrong to faux-hold hands with a guy when Hanna had a perfectly good *real* boyfriend vacationing across the continent. Just because Brooke was a skanky tanorexic didn't mean Lucas was going to fall for her tricks. Maybe there was even an excuse as to why he hadn't written to her yet. Maybe the Beattie family had been kidnapped by Mexican drug lords and they'd taken away his iPhone. She'd seen that once on *Locked Up Abroad.*

She pulled out her phone to check for news about the Yucatán, but before CNN even loaded, an alert popped onto her screen. *Lucas Beattie was tagged in a new photo*, it said. Hanna's heart lifted. So Lucas *was* alive!

She clicked on the link, and the browser called up her Facebook page. Lucas's photo was right at the top of the news feed; Brooke had posted it. There was no text, just a picture of him and Brooke sitting on a beautiful white beach, their arms around each other. Their bodies were pressed close together. Skin on skin. Lucas's smile took up practically the whole frame.

Hanna stared at the picture for what felt like hours. It felt worse than the most eye-numbing ice cream headache ever. Finally, she exited out of Facebook and checked her inbox for any texts or emails from him, but there were none. Nor had he tweeted or—God forbid—called. The message was loud and clear. Lucas had forgotten about her, trading in Hanna for Puke-a-tan.

Which meant just one thing. Hanna would trade Lucas in, too—for Vince.

10

THAT'S A WRAP

On Monday after school, Hanna pulled into a small parking lot in front of a squat building across from the Yarmouth SEPTA station. YARMOUTH HOMELESS SHELTER, said a sign in faded blue letters over the door. A pathetic plastic wreath hung in one of the windows, and someone had strung a few Christmas lights around the scrubby bushes up the front walk.

"Are you sure this is the place you volunteered at?" Hanna said into her phone. "It looks like it's going to fall down any second."

"I'm positive," Spencer Hastings answered on the other end. "And good for you, Han, for volunteering."

"Yeah, well, maybe the ordeal with A has turned me into a better person," Hanna murmured before pressing END. But really, it wasn't A that encouraged her to come to the shelter today. It was because she knew a certain gorgeous trainer was going to be here.

She was in full-on Make Vince Want Her mode. She hadn't let herself think about Lucas and Puke-a-tan since she saw that Facebook photo on Saturday. Granted, she'd also avoided Facebook since then, not wanting to see *more* posts of Lucas and Brooke canoodling on the beach. But if she was getting dumped, she was going back to school after winter vacation with a hot new body and an older boyfriend.

Rolling her shoulders back, she strode up the front walk and turned the knob of the door. The shelter smelled like old, slightly mildewed wood and sweat. An unoccupied desk was the first thing she saw, then a mini rotating Christmas tree on the floor. In the distance, she heard the sounds of crinkling paper, slicing scissors, and laughter.

"Hello?" Hanna called out.

A pie-faced woman in a reindeer-print sweater emerged from a door marked BATHROOM and grinned. "Well, hello! And you are . . . ?"

"Hanna." She gestured toward the crinkling-paper sounds. "I'm here for gift wrapping."

"Excellent. You came just in time—we got tons of gifts this year, so we need tons of help. I'm Bette."

The woman led Hanna down a long hall that was lit by ugly fluorescent panels and into a large room with a bunch of tables and a kitchen at the back. Gifts were piled high on the floor, and there were tubes of wrapping paper, bows, ribbons, and labels everywhere. "Rockin' Around the Christmas Tree" was playing on a portable radio, and a bunch of people were wrapping gifts and drinking what smelled like hot chocolate out of Styrofoam cups.

"Just grab a present and get wrapping," Bette said. Then she waddled back in the direction of the front desk.

Hanna gazed around at the mob of people. Most of them looked like Hollis students, wearing ripped jeans, Uggs, and Patagonia fleeces. She didn't see Vince anywhere. This *was* the place where he was volunteering, wasn't it? But then, a door off to the left opened, and she spotted his dark hair, broad shoulders, and bright smile. *Yes.*

Hanna raised her hand to wave, but Vince seemed distracted, smiling at something across the room. A girl sat on top of one of the tables, placing a shiny bow on a wrapped gift. Vince walked up to her, said a few words, and they both started to giggle. Then he walked away again, disappearing into one of the back rooms. Hanna's gaze remained on the girl. When she recognized the girl's beehive of black hair, she exhaled sharply.

It was *Dinah.*

Hanna stalked over and tapped her on the shoulder. "What are *you* doing here?"

Dinah swiveled around, her smile wavering. She crossed her arms over her chest. "Vince mentioned wrapping presents for the homeless shelter a few days ago. I thought it was a really cute idea, so I signed up, too."

Hanna narrowed her eyes. "Do you actually think he'd go for you?"

"I know he will." Dinah sniffed. Then she looked Hanna up and down in such a way that made Hanna feel self-conscious. She'd changed from her Rosewood Day uniform into a pair of skinny jeans from Madewell—a size four, thank you very much—and paired it with a loose-fitting silk top that tied at the neck and a pair of soft suede booties. Dinah, on the other hand, was wearing a checkered housedress that flared at the waist and showed off quite a bit of boob, and a pair of black Mary Janes. The only redeeming accessory was her small Chanel quilted bag, which sat next to her on the table. It looked exactly like the one all the starlets carried in *Us Weekly* and *InStyle*. Surely Dinah's was a fake, right?

Vince returned with a bunch of unwrapped presents in his hands. When he saw Hanna, his jaw dropped. "Hey!" he said, a smile spreading across his face. "It's so nice to see you here!"

Ha, Hanna thought. He probably hadn't said that to Dinah. "Just wanted to help out," she said, trying to sound humble.

"You girls are awesome." Vince passed Hanna a tube of wrapping paper and a pair of scissors. "I'm so glad you both decided to come. Doing this kind of thing is really good for the soul, you know?"

"Absolutely," Dinah trilled, lowering her long lashes. "I'm all for volunteering. My school encourages it."

"Volunteering is *mandatory* at my school," Hanna said. "What school do you go to, Dinah?" She fully expected

Dinah to say Rosewood Public, or maybe one of the alternative Quaker schools where everyone was forced to work on the campus farm.

"Larchmont Academy," Dinah answered primly. "It's in Haverford."

"I know where it is," Hanna spat, trying to hide her shock. Before she'd become friends with Ali in sixth grade, she'd begged her mom to switch her to Larchmont Academy. Not only had every famous person who'd grown up on the Main Line graduated from there, but the school offered classes like the History of Couture and let kids take internships as far away as New York or Washington, D.C., during their senior year.

If Dinah were anyone else, Hanna would have loved to pick her brain about Larchmont. There was always the option of going there for senior year if attending the same school as Kate was just too much. But she didn't want to give Dinah the satisfaction.

"Larchmont Academy sponsors us to volunteer in the most amazing locations," Dinah said to Vince, slicing a long sheet of wrapping paper. "Last year, I went on a trip to Somalia to work in a hospital. It was basically an open-air tent. The year before that, I rebuilt houses that were ruined in the Haiti earthquake."

"That's incredible," Vince gushed as he ripped a piece of tape from the dispenser.

Hanna opened her mouth, wanting to boast about some over-the-top volunteer work she'd done too, but she couldn't think of a single thing. She glanced at Vince, who was beaming at Dinah like she'd just invented penicillin.

Hanna turned to her gift, a large Lego space set, and taped wrapping paper around the sides, vowing to be the best gift-wrapper ever. The other volunteers stopped by every so often to grab tape or drop off a roll of colored ribbon, chatting briefly with Vince. Hanna recognized two girls from Body Tonic—one of them, Yolanda, was the Pilates instructor, and the other worked as a lifeguard. About a half hour later, Dinah slid off the table and excused herself to use the bathroom. This was Hanna's chance.

"So did you have to do a zillion bench presses to work off that scoop of butter pecan the other day?" Hanna teased, sidling closer to him.

Vince looked up. "*Shhhh.*" He glanced covertly at the Body Tonic trainers. "If they find out I'm an ice cream junkie, I'll never hear the end of it."

Hanna giggled. "What's in it for me if I don't tell?"

Vince raised an eyebrow flirtatiously. "Hmmm. Well, what would you want?"

Okay, *this* was more like it. Hanna cleared her throat and scooched up onto the table, her thigh pressing Vince's waist. "Let's get coffee sometime. Talk about . . . you know. Fitness. Pervy Santas."

Vince laughed. "That sounds awesome."

"Great. How about Wednesday?" Hanna asked.

The light faded from Vince's eyes. "Uh, I can't Wednesday," he said, avoiding eye contact.

Before Hanna could suggest another day, Bette called for Vince to come over and help her with a heavy donation. As Vince wandered off, Hanna's mind scrambled for answers. Had she done something wrong? Said something wrong? She heard a little snorting laugh emerge from the shadows. She whipped around, sure it had to be Dinah, but Dinah was nowhere to be seen.

"*Ahem.*" Hanna looked up and saw Yolanda, the Pilates instructor, gazing at her from the next table. "I didn't mean to eavesdrop, but I heard you guys talking," she said in a low voice. "Don't take it personally. Vince is always busy on Wednesday nights."

Hanna blinked at her. "Where does he go?" Unsavory options came to mind. A Sex Addicts Anonymous meeting. Getting together with a bunch of guys to play EverQuest. On a date with his mail-order girlfriend, a fifty-year-old cougar with silicone boobs.

Yolanda set down the present she was wrapping and walked closer. "He carols with his church every Wednesday evening. They go door-to-door in Hollis, singing religious songs and, like, being biblical and whatever. It's not really the kind of thing he likes talking about to girls."

"Oh," Hanna said quietly. Caroling with his church didn't sound *that* bad.

"He's just looking for a good Catholic girl to settle down with." Yolanda cast a motherly glance in Vince's direction. He was chatting with Bette and pointing to his bottle of AminoSpa.

Hanna nodded, her spirits lifting. *She* could be the good Catholic girl Vince was looking for—well, the good Jewish girl, but what was the difference? It was time to warm up her voice: On Wednesday, she was going caroling. And for once, Dinah wouldn't be there to ruin the mood.

11

I SAW SOMEONE KISSING SANTA CLAUS

On Wednesday afternoon after school, Hanna strutted through Devon Crest's double doors, walked right past Otter and the evil Lauren, and marched into the upper level of Saks. If caroling tonight was her one chance to make it or break it with Vince, she needed to find the perfect outfit to win him over. Something wholesome but pretty, like a nipped-at-the-waist Diane von Furstenberg wool coat. Or maybe one of those jackets with fur on the hood and at the cuffs. Something that said holy, not slutty.

"O little town of Bethlehem," Hanna sang quietly along with the Muzak over the speakers. Last night, she'd dug out Isabel's most religious Christmas CDs and learned the words, including all of the verses to "Joy to the World," the Latin version of "O Come, All Ye Faithful," and "O Christmas Tree"—what was the deal with Christmas carols starting with *O*?—in German. She'd also memorized the

Hail Mary and the act of contrition Catholic prayers for good measure, but had stopped herself before ordering a rosary from Amazon. At one point last night, Isabel had paused in front of Hanna's room, raising her eyebrows at the music emanating from Hanna's stereo. "Well!" she'd said, pressing a hand to her chest. "It's so nice that you're getting into the spirit, Hanna!"

A fresh blast of Chanel No. 5 wafted into her nostrils as Hanna walked into the department store. A saleswoman at the MAC counter greeted her, and after giving her a perfunctory wave and then doing a once-over of the new eye shadow shades, Hanna drifted toward the clothes department. Mannequins dressed in pencil skirts and cashmere sweaters were positioned beside tables of folded tees in the softest cotton imaginable. The air smelled like Gucci Envy, and when Hanna glanced at herself in the mirror, she couldn't help but notice that her butt looked smaller and her arms were definitely less puffy. The morning and evening trips to the fitness retreat were doing magic. Even Vince had commented on how great she looked this morning—then again, he'd also said that to Inez, who had linebacker shoulders, and Richard, whose stomach jiggled over the waistband of his shorts.

Her gaze clapped on an emerald-green Elizabeth and James wrap dress hanging on a rack. She breathed in, already picturing herself in it—it would make the perfect caroling outfit. The only one left on the rack was a size four, but she was sure she could fit into it. She moved toward it, but a figure stepped in front of her, grabbing it first.

"Hey!" Hanna cried. "I was going to take that!"

"Sorry," a familiar voice said. Then the figure turned. "*Hanna?*"

"Dinah," Hanna growled, taking in the dark-haired girl in the ugly fifties-style white wool coat, poodle skirt, and quilted mock-Chanel bag. It was like Dinah was her new A.

Hanna's gaze fell to the dress in Dinah's hands. "That isn't your size," she said, unable to hide the disdain in her voice. "It isn't really your style either."

Dinah clutched the dress to her chest. "How do you know what my style is? And I'm smaller than I look, Hanna. Not all of us have a flat ass and no boobs."

Not all of us have a flabby waist, either, Hanna wanted to snipe. She gestured to the dress. "Where were you planning to wear it?"

A sly smile washed over Dinah's face. "Somewhere," she said cryptically, and instantly Hanna's heart began to pound. Had she made a date with Vince? Were they doing another volunteer activity together?

"How do *you* know about Elizabeth and James, anyway?" Hanna demanded.

An exasperated snort emanated from Dinah's nostrils. "My aunt works at *Bazaar* in New York. I went to the Elizabeth and James runway show at Fashion Week last year."

"You *did*?" Hanna bleated before she could stop herself. She was dying to go to a 7th on Sixth show, even for one of the smaller designers—hell, even for one of the winners of *Project Runway*. And it must be amazing to have an aunt who worked for *Bazaar*.

Hanna wavered, considering letting Dinah have the dress, but then she pictured Vince grinning at her across the table in the ice cream shop. "I saw the dress first," she insisted.

"I touched it first." Dinah pressed the dress to her chest. "It'll look better on me, anyway."

"It absolutely won't look better on you." Hanna held out her hands. "Your boobs are too big."

"Yeah, well, your body is too straight-up-and-down." Dinah lifted the hanger over Hanna's head so she couldn't reach it.

Hanna grabbed for it. "You'll look pathetic in it."

"*You'll* get sick of it in a week." Dinah hid the dress behind her back. "I can tell you're a fickle bitch."

"I am not fickle!" Hanna shrieked. "*You're* whiny! And your tattoo is hideous! It'll clash!"

The girls glared at each other.

"Just give it to me!" Hanna lunged behind Dinah's back. "It isn't right for you, okay?"

Dinah stepped out of her way. Hanna let out a huff and dove for her again, yanking the dress out of her hands. "Ha!" she crowed, waving it over her head like a flag and running for the dressing rooms. A couple of shoppers looked up in surprise. A saleswoman paused at the counter, her mouth hanging open.

"Come back here!" Dinah screeched, right on Hanna's heels. Hanna wove around the racks of clothes, the entrance to the dressing rooms in full view. All of a sudden, she felt two heavy arms wrap around her waist and pull her down. Dinah fell on top of her, and for a moment Hanna was squished into the tattoo on her arm. She felt the dress being pried from her fingers.

"How dare you!" she muttered. "Get the hell *off* me!"

To Hanna's surprise, Dinah rolled off her, the dress still securely in Hanna's grip. Dinah wasn't even looking at her, instead staring at something in the dressing rooms. "*Shh!*" she whispered.

Hanna pricked up her ears, afraid she was going to hear the eerie high-pitched giggle that had been haunting her lately. But instead, she heard a loud smacking sound coming from inside one of the dressing rooms.

"What is that?" Hanna said, slowly rising to her feet. She crept closer to the dressing rooms, which were empty except for the noisy stall. Two pairs of shoes peeked under the door, one of them dark black boots, the other prissy black-and-white heels that looked vaguely familiar.

Hanna exchanged a knowing look with Dinah. With a slight nod of her head, Dinah encouraged her to move closer. Hanna tiptoed a few more steps toward the room. The shoes and boots under the dressing room shuffled. The slurping sounds increased in intensity.

Suddenly, the door flung open, and two people tum-bled into the corridor. Hanna pressed against the wall, pulling Dinah with her. There, reflected in the three-way mirror, was a guy in a red Santa suit, Santa hat, Santa beard, and shiny black boots. "You're so hot," Santa said in a skeevy voice.

He was sucking on some skinny girl's neck, and the girl was running her hand through his beard. Hanna stared at her. The girl's chestnut hair was swept into a messy French bun, her ass was nonexistent, and on her thin, ballerina-like wrist was a very familiar silver David Yurman bangle.

It was Kate.

Hanna grabbed her phone, which was conveniently in her bag's front pocket, and snapped a picture. Then she and Dinah sprinted out of the dressing room. Out of breath, they collapsed on a table of jeans and stared at each other for a pregnant pause. At the exact same moment, they both burst into peals of laughter.

12

SOUL MATES

A few hours later, Hanna sat on a ripped barstool at Snooker's, a college bar in Hollis. There were sports jerseys all over the walls and ugly green banker's lamps behind the counter, and the air smelled like fried mozzarella sticks and stale beer. An old Bruce Springsteen song played on the jukebox, and the room was packed with loud college kids.

"Okay, who would you rather hook up with," Hanna said, scanning the crowd, "Mr. I'm Taking Over Daddy's Company in Five Years, or Mr. The Only Interesting Thing About Me Is That I'm Irish?" She pointed at two college boys nursing beers in the corner. The first guy wore a preppy button-down and had a smug look on his face that only someone with a trust fund could pull off. The second guy had doughy features, red hair, was wearing a T-shirt that said DUBLIN on it, and was drinking–of course–a Guinness.

"Ugh, neither." Dinah popped the olive from her martini into her mouth. "Look at the girls they're with! Is that a *Burberry* bag she's carrying? That is *so* 2001!"

"Says the girl who wears poodle skirts," Hanna teased, poking Dinah on the arm.

Dinah pretended to be offended. "Poodle skirts are *retro*," she said haughtily.

"I forgive you," Hanna said. "After all, you've got an awesome bag." She pointed to Dinah's quilted Chanel on the stool. It turned out it *wasn't* a fake—Dinah's aunt who worked at *Bazaar* had put her at the top of the waiting list and scored her one from the New York flagship store.

The bartender set down another martini for Dinah and another vodka-cranberry for Hanna, and they clinked glasses. A warm sense of happiness washed over Hanna as she took the first sip. After she and Dinah had scampered away from Kate and Santa in the dressing room, they'd ditched the Elizabeth and James dress on a random table, called a truce, and decided to hit the college bars. Dinah had left her car at the mall, and on the drive over in Hanna's Prius, they'd chatted about fashion, beauty products, celebrities, and their favorite suburban boutiques, Hanna's four most favorite topics. The conversation had come naturally, as though they'd been friends for years.

But when they'd approached Snooker's, Hanna had been apprehensive. She didn't have a fake ID, and after getting caught shoplifting last fall, she didn't really want the cops after her again. Dinah had squeezed her hand and said, "Leave everything to me." She breezed up to the bouncer, who had a crew cut and wore a heavy gold chain around his neck, and said, "Hey, Jake! Remember me?"

The bouncer had smiled at Dinah appreciatively, but then asked to see the girls' IDs. Dinah had stuck her lip out in a pout. "C'mon, Jakie-poo. Don't be like that." She traced her fingers up and down his arm. Finally, the bouncer just shrugged and opened the door for them. Inside, Hanna gave Dinah a thumbs-up. It was just like something Ali might have done.

Dinah reached for a French fry from the plate they'd ordered. "We are so going against our boot camp pledges right now. I bet Vince is going to know and make us work out for five hours next session."

"Yep, I can feel the fat oozing back to my thighs," Hanna joked.

Dinah waved her hand. "As if you *ever* had fat in your thighs! Why did you join boot camp, anyway?"

Hanna rolled her eyes. "Uh, because I'm horribly out of shape and can't fit into any of my clothes?"

Dinah stared at her like she was crazy. "Are you one of those girls who looks in the mirror and sees a cow?"

"I'm not like that," Hanna assured her. Or *was* she? Every time she looked at her reflection, she found something wrong. Her hair looked oily. Her arms were puffy. Her face was too round. A lot of the time, she barely noticed all the hard work she'd put in with Mona in eighth grade. All she saw was the old Hanna, the loser she'd been back in middle school.

Hanna popped a fry into her mouth. "You know, I had this beautiful friend once. She was popular, gorgeous, the kind of girl *everyone* wanted to be. I was in her clique, but she always made it clear that I was hanging on by a thread. She made fun of the way I ate, how my jeans didn't fit, everything. After so many years of hearing that, it's kind of hard to shake."

Dinah leaned her elbows on the counter. "So what happened to this girl? You ditched her, right?"

Hanna kept her eyes fixed on the Absolut bottles behind the bar. "Actually . . . she's dead. Her name was Alison DiLaurentis. Maybe you've heard of her."

"*Maybe* I've heard of her?" Dinah's eyes popped wide. "That was only like the biggest story in all of Rosewood. They found her body not so long ago, right?"

Hanna nodded.

"Wow." Dinah knocked back the rest of her martini. "You know, I knew Alison."

"You did?" Hanna's head whipped up.

"Uh-huh." A faraway look clouded Dinah's face. "We met at a field hockey camp—I used to play in elementary school before I finally admitted to my parents how much I hated it. Alison was at the camp, too. She ruled a group of girls there, made them do everything she wanted. And for a while, *I* was their target. They called me Dinah Vagina. I didn't even *do* anything to them."

"That's terrible," Hanna said. "Ali used to call me Hanna Mon-TON-a. And a bunch of other names I don't even want to think about. Part of me wishes she could somehow see how much weight I've lost since then, how I've transformed."

Then Hanna sighed. "Actually, what am I saying? Ali would still probably find something about me to pick on if she was around now."

"Except now you wouldn't be *friends* with her, right?" Dinah said, linking her arm with Hanna's. "You're way too strong and independent to put up with that bitch."

"Totally," Hanna said shakily, although she wasn't really sure if that was true. Ali's jeering words still haunted her, especially when reincarnated through Mona as A. But she felt an even stronger kinship with Dinah now. Ali had touched them both, for better or for worse. They'd both been the girls Ali loved to tease.

A cheer rose up behind them, and Hanna turned around to see Mr. Irish chugging a bunch of beers on a back table. "Sexy," she murmured, nudging Dinah. "I just might have to go home with him tonight."

Dinah snickered. "I thought you were saving yourself for Vince."

"I thought *you* were," Hanna retorted. An awkward beat passed, then suddenly the girls burst into laughter.

Dinah sighed. "I don't know what that guy's deal is. I saw him outside of the gym a couple of days ago, and he went on and on about how he was so happy that you and

I were paired up together—he thought I could really *help you out* and *teach you something.*"

Hanna slammed the counter with her palm. "I don't believe it. He said the same thing to me—about you!"

One of Dinah's eyebrows rose. "Do you think he wants us to compete for his attention? That's probably been his grand plan all along."

"What a jerk," Hanna spat. "He acts all saintly, but he's really just trying to get us to throw ourselves at him." She hated to think that way about Vince, but maybe it was true.

"And what's with that vitamin water crap he keeps pushing?" Dinah rolled her eyes. "Every time I turn around he's swigging it."

"I bet it doesn't even have any vitamins in it," Hanna said. "And it's probably a zillion calories. He's been brainwashed."

"You know what?" Dinah got a determined look on her face. "He's a loser. We're better off without him."

"Agreed!" Hanna crowed drunkenly, feeling a surge of confidence. "And he really *is* a loser. Guess what he's doing tonight? He's going caroling with a group of people from his church. They sing super-religious songs and probably reenact the Nativity scene or something. It's a Wednesday tradition."

"Seriously?" Dinah made a face.

"Uh-huh. And I was going to crash it." Hanna paused to drink the rest of her vodka-cranberry. "Apparently,

Vince is looking for a good church girl to settle down with. But forget it. He's not worth the time."

"Good plan." Dinah nodded determinedly. "Let's grab some dinner instead. Vince will be singing, and *we'll* be having fun."

"Deal," Hanna said, giving her a high five. Then she giggled. "You know, Vince will probably make all of the carolers drink AminoSpa between songs."

Dinah almost spit out her drink from laughing. "He probably wrote a carol *about* AminoSpa!"

"He's probably going to try and sell it door to door while they sing it in German!" Hanna giggled, picturing it.

They doubled over in hysterics, eliciting a few strange looks from everyone around them. But Hanna didn't care. She didn't care that she'd just let Vince go, either. She'd made a new friend. Maybe that was what she'd wanted all along.

13

GOTCHA!

"Hanna? Hanna?"

Hanna opened one eye and saw her father standing in her doorway. She bolted upright. There was a dirty-sock taste in her mouth, and her head felt like it weighed a million pounds. She also had the sneaking suspicion she reeked of alcohol—she couldn't remember showering after she got back from Snooker's last night.

"Your alarm has been going off for a half hour." Mr. Marin pointed to Hanna's cell phone on the nightstand, which was blinking on and off. "Some of us are trying to get a little bit of extra sleep."

Hanna looked groggily at her phone, then pressed a button to stop the alarm noise. "Sorry," she mumbled. Her father grumbled something and shut her door.

She looked at the clock. It was 5:30 A.M., time to get up for the morning session of boot camp. Hanna groaned and rolled out of bed, regretting the tequila shot she'd done with Dinah last night in celebration that Vince was a loser. The shot had cut the night short—after downing it, Dinah's face had turned green, and she'd run to the bathroom. When she returned, she said she should head home. After that, the only thing Hanna remembered was stuffing enough money in the Hollis meter to leave the Prius parked there overnight, calling a cab, and stumbling blindly into the house. Luckily, Isabel, her father, and Kate had been out doing some kind of Twelve Days of Christmas activity, so no one had caught her.

She managed to pull on exercise gear, slide her feet into her sneakers, call a cab to retrieve her car in Hollis, and drive to the gym. As she walked toward Body Tonic's front entrance, she pulled out her phone and composed a text to Dinah. *Are you here today? Feeling as shitty as I am? If only I had some AminoSpa—ha, ha.*

She hit SEND, expecting Dinah to text her back immediately, but she got no reply. Maybe Dinah had ditched boot camp and was still asleep.

The inside of Body Tonic smelled like massage oil and fresh flowers, which made Hanna's stomach turn. The perky girl at the front desk gave her a wave, and Hanna trudged into the changing room without saying hello back. She checked her phone once more before throwing it in her locker, but Dinah still hadn't replied. Shrugging, she headed for the room where boot camp always met. When she pushed through the doors and saw Dinah standing against the mirror, her head thrown back in laughter, Hanna stopped short.

Dinah looked fresh and healthy, as though she hadn't drunk a drop of alcohol last night. She was standing next to Vince, an AminoSpa bottle in hand, grinning at him as though he was the Messiah. Vince was grinning at her, too.

"Your rendition of 'Away in a Manger' was amazing," Dinah cooed. "So heartfelt."

"Yeah, well, everyone was really into the way you put together that impromptu Nativity play on Mr. Larsen's lawn," Vince answered. "What made you think of doing something like that?"

"Oh, I don't know." Dinah lowered her lashes. "I've been caroling since my first Communion. I really know how to get people into the spirit."

She took Vince's hand. Vince wrapped his fingers around hers and squeezed. They looked into each other's eyes like they were soul mates, and then moved closer and kissed.

Hanna's mouth dropped open. She wanted to run out of the room, but the bottoms of her sneakers felt rubber-cemented to the floor. Dinah had gone . . . *caroling*? As in the caroling Hanna had told her about? Their conversation last night rushed through her mind. How *Dinah* had said Vince was a loser. How *Dinah* had said they were better off without him. How she'd skipped out shortly after Hanna had told her about Vince's secret caroling mission, claiming the tequila shot had made her sick.

Was it all a ruse?

A tortured-sounding squeak spilled from her lips, and Dinah and Vince turned. As soon as Dinah spotted Hanna, the corners of her bow-shaped lips curled into an evil smile. Vince gave Hanna a sheepish wave. Hanna grabbed Dinah's arm. "We need to talk."

She dragged Dinah into the hall, stopping next to a large stack of Pilates Magic Circles. "What the hell?"

Dinah rocked back and forth on her heels. "What the hell *what*?" Her voice sounded nothing like the awesome, friendly, conspiratorial girl who'd sat next to Hanna at Snooker's last night.

"I thought we called a truce! I thought we both decided he was a loser!"

Dinah started laughing. "I told you he'd go for me. All's fair in love and war."

Hanna's head swirled, knocking her off-balance. "I can't believe you," she whispered, feeling her throat get froggy and tears rush to her eyes. More images from last night flashed in her mind. How Dinah had said, off-handedly, that she'd love for Hanna to go to Larchmont Academy—she could use someone cool like Hanna there. How Dinah promised to introduce Hanna to her *Bazaar*-editor aunt when she visited for Christmas. How Dinah had given Hanna a big hug when they left, saying she'd see her tomorrow.

"I thought we were friends," Hanna sputtered.

"Oh please." Dinah rolled her eyes. "You're just pissed

because I tricked you. Like you wouldn't have done the same thing to me?"

"I *wouldn't* have. I *didn't*," Hanna squeaked, her voice sounding way more pathetic and vulnerable than she would have liked. And then, before the tears could spill down her cheeks, she whirled around and headed for the locker room. Her fingers shook as she worked the combination to her locker. She grabbed her bag and marched out of the gym without even putting on her coat.

As soon as she emerged into the chilly air, she let out a pent-up sob. The tears streamed hot and fast down her face. She staggered to her car and leaned on the hood, feeling like a huge water balloon inside of her had burst. She cried for Ali's death. The horror of Mona. The nightmare that was her new family. That she hadn't heard from Lucas at all. That she had pursued Vince at all, when who she really wanted was Lucas. Everything just felt so . . . *wrong*.

"Aw, is someone crushed?"

Hanna gazed across the parking lot through blurry tears. A figure stood on the other side of her car, a sneaky smile on her face. For a moment, Hanna was afraid it was *Ali*. But then her vision cleared. This girl had chestnut-colored hair, not blond. It was Kate standing there against the door of her Honda Civic, staring at Hanna at her worst.

14

MUTUALLY ASSURED DESTRUCTION

"W-what are you doing here?" Hanna stammered, straightening up.

Kate giggled. "Was boot camp just too much for you today, Hanna?" She stretched out something in her hands. It was an extra-large red T-shirt that said GET YOUR BUTT IN GEAR!

Hanna's stomach dropped. "I—I don't know what you're talking about."

"The program sounds really awesome." Kate waved the T-shirt tauntingly under Hanna's nose. "I'm sure everyone at Rosewood Day would love to know what you've been up to."

She pulled out her phone and showed Hanna a series of pictures. Hanna and the red-shirted boot campers running through a tire obstacle course behind Body Tonic, all of them fat and red-faced and ridiculous-looking. The boot campers gathered in a circle doing one of Vince's

AminoSpa chants. And the coup de grace: Dinah and Vince kissing, and Hanna standing in the doorway just now, looking devastated.

She'd seen *everything.*

"Give me that," Hanna said, grabbing for Kate's phone.

Kate held it over Hanna's head. "Not so fast!"

"Have you been following me?" Hanna shrieked. "Don't you have anything better to do?"

"What can I say? I love a good secret." Kate rocked back and forth in her fur-lined Uggs. "And someone gave me an amazing tip-off, so I followed you here."

A shiver snaked up Hanna's spine. Who could have done that? Immediately, A came to mind . . . but A was gone.

"Don't be ashamed of going to fat camp!" Kate went on. "At least you're making a positive change, you know?" She typed something into her phone. "I think this would make a lovely post on your Facebook wall. And maybe people would sympathize with you for losing the guy to that other girl!"

Hanna's heart pounded hard. "I'm not interested in Vince!"

Kate gave her a knowing look. "You keep telling yourself that, Hanna. But the photos don't lie. Now, what would be a good caption for Facebook? *Boot camp is so amazing, and look at my awesome new friends?* Or how about something simple, like *Getting my huge ass in gear?*"

Hanna let out a whimper. She was "friends" with all

kinds of people on Facebook. Naomi Zeigler and Riley Wolfe, two popular bitches who'd love nothing more than to hear about this. Senior girls who invited her to amazing parties. Mason Byers, James Freed, Noel Kahn, and her ex, Sean Ackard. That Mona had wanted to kill Hanna was bad enough—a post about boot camp would cement her status as a loser for good. She already saw herself sitting alone in the cafeteria at lunch. Spending every Saturday night in her room. Never being invited to a party again.

"Please don't post about this," Hanna cried. "I'm begging you. I'll do anything."

One of Kate's eyebrows rose. "What's in it for me?"

A stiff wind blew up, numbing Hanna's ears and the tip of her nose. She stared out at the empty road in front of Body Tonic and racked her brain. What did she have that Kate wanted? Hadn't she given up enough? Ever since Kate had set foot in Hanna's house, Hanna's life had gone from bad to worse. Kate had already usurped all of Hanna's father's attention. As soon as she started at Rosewood Day, she'd probably become the most popular girl in their grade, taking Hanna's place. How much more torture could she take?

What she wouldn't give for Mona right now—the Mona she knew before all the A stuff began. The two of them could laugh in Kate's face, tell her she wouldn't dare cross them, and then spin around and drive away in a cloud of exhaust. Having Ali here would be even better: She'd loop her elbow around Hanna's, lean in close, and whisper, "You've got something on her too, Han. That's what's so great about secrets—you can use them as currency."

Suddenly, Hanna's head shot up. It was as though Ali had spoken to her from beyond the grave. She *did* have something on Kate, something she'd almost forgotten.

She started to laugh.

"What?" Kate's eyebrows knitted together.

The giggles kept coming. Hanna rummaged around in her bag for her cell phone. "You're not posting anything on Facebook. Because if you do, I'm telling everyone about Santa."

Kate frowned. For a split second, a look of sheer terror crossed her face. "Huh?"

"*You* know," Hanna said mockingly, pulling up the photo she was looking for on her phone and thrusting it toward Kate. Santa caressing Kate's neck. Kate burying her hands in Santa's cottony beard. "A fitting caption would be *Someone's been naughty this year.* And haven't you heard that guy's a major pervert?" Hanna scolded. "He hits on twelve-year-old girls!"

Kate backed away from Hanna, her mouth opening and closing like a fish. "Please don't," was all she whispered.

"I think we have an agreement, then." Hanna pressed the UNLOCK button on her key chain. "If you post the boot camp pictures online, I'll post this. 'Kay?"

Kate didn't answer, but Hanna knew she'd gotten her. Head held high, she swung into the driver's seat, turned the ignition, and pulled swiftly and expertly out of her spot. "Bye-bye!" she trilled, waggling her fingers at her stepsister. Kate remained where she was, the red T-shirt limp at her side.

Hanna drove away without giving her stepsister a second glance. As she turned out of the parking lot, a phrase Ali often said and Hanna had adopted came to mind: *I'm Ali, and I'm fabulous.* Hanna felt pretty frickin' fabulous right now, too.

15

OPERATORS ARE STANDING BY!

Back at home, the kitchen was silent and unoccupied. Water in the shower ran upstairs, and Hanna could hear the muted sounds of the morning news from her father's room. Out the window, the six-year-old twins who lived next door whirled out into their driveway like dervishes, wearing matching Santa's elves hats.

Hanna downed a couple Advils and started to make coffee. For a few minutes, the only sound in the room was the water dripping into the carafe. She stared blankly at the front page of the *Philadelphia Sentinel*, willing her headache to go away. *Ian Thomas Maintains Innocence*, said a headline. She turned the paper over fast. It was the last thing she wanted to think about right now. Ian *had* to be guilty. Who else had a motive to kill Ali?

Hanna looked down at the paper again and flinched. In the lower left-hand corner was a giant ad for Body Tonic Gym and Spa. There, in black and white, was Vince's grinning face, telling potential exercisers that from now until New Year's, initiation fees would only be $50.

She couldn't believe Dinah—and she couldn't believe Vince had chosen a freak like her over Hanna. If she'd shown up caroling instead of Dinah, would Vince have gone for her instead? Why had he acted so into Hanna in the first place? Was something of what Dinah said true—was he just trying to get the two of them to compete for him?

After everything she'd been through with A, she should have known Dinah was going to stab her in the back. An image flashed into her mind. She saw Mona's car barreling toward her again. She felt the impact, her body flying into the air, the scream lodging in her throat. One person after another kept betraying her.

Hanna rubbed her temples and tried to take slow, even breaths. Was there anyone she could trust anymore? She glanced at her phone on the table, then scrolled through her contacts list, wondering if she should call Spencer. Or maybe Emily. Or Aria. She remembered a gift exchange they'd had in seventh grade, right before the holiday break. Aria had knitted all of them mohair bras, and they'd all tried them on over their clothes and danced around Ali's living room. Even Ali had been in a good mood that day, not making fun of how Hanna's bra stretched unflatteringly across her chest. Ali's brother, Jason, had walked into the room halfway through their dance party. He'd stared at them in their bizarre outfits, and they'd all collapsed into giggles.

There was a cough in the hall, and Hanna looked up just as her father strolled into the room in his bathrobe and slippers. "Hey," he said in a weary voice, ruffling her hair. "Mind if I have some of that coffee?"

"Be my guest," Hanna said.

Mr. Marin poured part of the carafe into the Doberman mug he'd used since Hanna was a kid. He sat down next to her, let out a long, tired sigh, and rubbed his eyes.

"Is everything okay?" Hanna asked.

His head bobbed up and down. "I'm just tired. These Twelve Days of Christmas activities are a little crazy this year. Isabel has me running all over the place."

"I'm sorry I haven't participated in all of them," Hanna said, feeling a little guilty.

Mr. Marin waved his hand. "Maybe you were smart to miss them." He gave her a covert glance. "Between you and me? I think I liked it better when we celebrated Hanukkah. At least that only went on for *eight* days. And it was much more low-key."

Hanna bit her bottom lip. "I liked it better when we celebrated it, too."

Mr. Marin opened his mouth like he was going to say something else, but then seemed to change his mind and just took another long swig of his coffee. A silence fell between them. The candy cane–shaped clock Isabel had hung up in the corner ticked loudly. A motor gunned outside.

Then, Mr. Marin patted Hanna's thigh. "Actually, that

reminds me. I have something for you." He rose, shuffled over to his briefcase by the door, and pulled out a small velvet box.

Hanna stared at it, recognizing it immediately. She lifted the lid and found the very same Cartier locket she'd discovered the day her father, Isabel, and Kate had moved in. She never thought she'd hold it again. "Is this . . . for *me*?"

"Of course it's for you. It was your grandmother's."

"I know," Hanna murmured, lifting the necklace out of the box. It glittered in the overhead light. "It's beautiful," she whispered. "I've always wanted this."

"I know," Mr. Marin said, hiding a smile. "Your grandma would've wanted you to have it. I want you to have it, too."

Hanna stood and gave her father a huge hug. "Thank you." She wanted to add, *for not giving it to Kate or Isabel*, but she was afraid it might ruin the moment. All of a sudden, everything felt a little bit better again. Maybe her dad hadn't forgotten her, after all. Maybe he still remembered, in some small way, that she was here, that she still mattered.

She turned around so that her father could clip it around her neck. The locket hung perfectly at her throat, and Hanna couldn't resist running her finger over its smooth oval shape. Mr. Marin finished his coffee, then pulled a bottle of water from his briefcase and took a long swig. "Well, I suppose I should get moving."

"Wait a sec." Hanna stared at the bottle in his hand. The label said AMINOSPA. "Where did you get that?"

Mr. Marin screwed the cap back on the bottle. "Some guy was selling it at the office. He said these drinks have a ton of vitamins in them and that I'd feel better once I start drinking a couple bottles a day. But I don't feel any different, to be honest with you. And it kind of tastes like rotten lime juice."

Hanna smiled sadly. "I think that stuff is a scam."

"Probably." Mr. Marin shrugged. "I think the whole point of selling this stuff is to recruit other people to sell it, too. The guy gave me this really long pitch about how I could be a part-time AminoSpa associate—I'd make tons of money and never have to change out of my pajamas." He chuckled good-naturedly. "The people who get recruited to sell this stuff are like cult members—they're totally brainwashed. And once they suck you in, there's no way to get out."

He placed the AminoSpa bottle on the counter and gave Hanna a kiss on top of her head. His slippers made soft slaps on the floor as he padded out of the room. Hanna sat motionless for a few moments, staring at the AminoSpa bottle on the counter. It was crazy to think she'd fallen for a guy who'd gotten caught up in a pyramid scheme. Dinah could totally have him.

Suddenly, an idea came to her. She stood, raced over to the bottle, and looked at the company information on the back. *To join our team, call now!* it said beneath a 1-800 number and a website.

Heart thumping, Hanna lifted her home phone off the receiver and dialed the number. "AminoSpa Industries!" a chipper voice answered almost immediately. "Are you interested in joining our team?"

"Uh, yes," Hanna said in her most professional voice. "My boyfriend sells AminoSpa, and I'd love to be part of it, too."

"That's wonderful!" the operator chirped. "What's your name?"

"Dinah Morrissey," Hanna said, grinning at her reflection in the window. She spelled it out, then gave the operator Dinah's address, which was on the boot camp call sheet Vince had given them the first day. "Please send me a hundred cases."

"One hundred?" The operator's voice rose. "Oh, honey, that's a lot for someone who's just starting out."

"I can handle it," Hanna urged, running her fingers over her new necklace.

"You realize there are no returns, right? You're responsible for every last bottle. And we'll bill you for those cases at the beginning of next month."

"I understand," Hanna said. "Like I said, I'm *very* eager to join the team!"

After giving the operator a few more details, Hanna hung up and grinned. Then she grabbed the half-drunk AminoSpa bottle her father had left behind, screwed the cap on tight, and dropped it in the recycling bin. Opening her phone, she composed a new text to Dinah. *I forgive you! I'm sure you guys will be very happy together in EVERY endeavor!* If Dinah wanted Vince, she could have him—but she had to take him, goofy pyramid scheme and all.

Her phone chirped less than a minute later, and at first she thought it was Dinah sending a reply. But to her surprise, Lucas's number flashed on the screen.

Got home early. Can you come over before school?

16

SUNGLASSES TANS ARE SO IN

After changing into her Rosewood Day uniform and gathering her books for school, Hanna pulled up to the curb at Lucas's house. His family's Ford Explorer was back in the driveway, the hatchback still open. The Mercedes SUV Hanna had seen the night the Rumsons had stopped over was here as well—meaning Brooke was here, too. Hanna wondered if Lucas had just invited her over to break up with her in person. Not that she would let him beat her to the punch. She would break up with him first.

Well, let's get it over with, she thought, grateful at least that she looked gorgeous after boot camp. Sighing dolefully, she slammed the door to the Prius and started up the front walk. As she was about to ring the bell, she caught sight of a faint flicker in the thick line of bushes that surrounded the Beattie property. It almost looked like someone was hiding there, but that was crazy. Who could be skulking around at 8 A.M. in fifteen-degree weather? When would Hanna stop thinking someone was following her?

Lucas answered the door almost immediately. His skin was golden, his blond hair was almost white, and he looked like he'd lost a couple of pounds. "Hey," he said, pulling her inside and giving her a huge hug. "I missed you *so* much."

Hanna recoiled. "It didn't seem like that when you were gone. I guess you were having too much fun to send me a text, huh?"

Lucas winced. "I'm so sorry. I thought we were going to have Wi-Fi, but the server was down. That's one of the reasons we're home early, actually—Mr. Rumson was freaking out because he couldn't check his BlackBerry. Brooke got onto Facebook for a moment, but none of us could get online."

"Yes, I *saw* that post." Hanna wasn't able to conceal her irritation. "You and Brooke looked very happy together."

Lucas searched her face. "You don't think we were . . ." He trailed off and pinched the skin between his eyes. "Oh, Hanna, I'm so sorry. It wasn't what it looked like."

"Uh-huh," Hanna said tepidly. She was sure he was just making excuses now that Brooke had to go home.

"I'm serious." Lucas guided Hanna over and sat her down on the couch. "After that first day, Brooke and I barely even saw each other. I went on these great hikes and on this amazing kayak trip, but all she wanted to do was tan." He moved closer, his voice to her ear. "She slathered baby oil on herself from morning to night. Which caused the *other* reason we had to come home."

At that, his gaze shifted to the hall. The two Rumson parents emerged from the kitchen, rolling their travel bags behind them. Brooke appeared next, wearing an ultra-short mini dress more suitable to warm climates and a pair of raffia wedges. Her face was peeling, she had a hideous sunglasses tan across her eyes, and she had some kind of white ointment slathered on both arms. The skin beneath the ointment looked like the blackened pieces of meat Hanna's father made whenever he attempted to use the grill. Hanna didn't know whether to laugh or cover her eyes.

"What happened to her?" she whispered.

"She got third-degree burns from the sun," Lucas answered in a low voice. "They were so bad we had to take her to the hospital. It was the scariest place I've ever been, Hanna—there were cockroaches in the waiting room, no one got a proper bed, and I swear none of the doctors had actual medical licenses. The guy that treated Brooke told her that if she went back into the sun for even one minute, her skin was going to fall off—*literally*. Her mom watched her like a hawk after that. Brooke moped around the house day and night, whining that she was really bored. I wanted to kill her by the time the trip was over. I think everyone else wanted to, too."

Hanna hugged a throw pillow to her chest. "So . . . you didn't sunbathe nude? You didn't do Jell-O shots?"

Lucas looked at her like she was crazy. "Have you ever done a Jell-O shot? Those things are nasty! Anyway, we couldn't make Jell-O if we'd wanted to—the water in Yucatán was undrinkable."

Just then, Brooke noticed Lucas and Hanna sitting on the couch and smiled weakly. "Hey, Lukey," she said in a nasal voice, walking over to him with the stiff gait of someone who was very, very sunburned. "I guess we're leaving now. But it was so awesome to see you. We have to do another vacay together soon. Maybe spring break?"

Brooke spread out her arms to give Lucas a hug. Hanna shot off the couch and blocked her way. "Lukey says bye," she said sharply. "Good luck getting over your burns."

Brooke stared at Hanna as though she'd never seen her before. Hanna held her ground. There was no way she was letting this bitch get close to Lucas ever again. It was a lesson she'd learned the hard way with Vince: If you wanted a guy, you had to fight hard for him.

After a moment, Brooke shrunk away, muttered goodbye, and skulked back to her parents. Everyone sounded weary as they patted one another on the back and said they'd see each other soon. When Lucas's parents shut the door, Mr. Beattie leaned against the jamb and pressed his face into his hands. "I hope to never see that girl again as long as I live."

Hanna couldn't agree more.

The engine roared in the driveway, and soon the Mercedes SUV rounded the bend out of the neighborhood. Lucas shifted closer to Hanna. "I'm so sorry we couldn't talk even once while I was away. I thought about you every day, though. And hey, now we can hang out all break! Whatever you want to do, I'm up for it—even going to that new mall."

"I'm going to hold you to that," Hanna said, warming to him a little. "But we don't have to go to that mall—it sucks."

Lucas started to rub Hanna's shoulders. "So did I miss anything while I was gone?"

Hanna pretended to pick an imaginary piece of lint off her Rosewood Day plaid skirt, thinking about boot camp, Vince, and Dinah. Was it wrong of her to have flirted with Vince? It wasn't like anything happened between them. And it hardly made sense to tell Lucas about boot camp— it wasn't like she was going anymore. Before coming over here, she'd tried on her skinniest jeans, and they'd fit just fine. It made her wonder if she'd really had that much weight to lose in the first place.

"Oh, not really," she finally answered breezily. "Except that you should never, ever take me to see *The Nutcracker*— it's still giving me nightmares."

Lucas snickered. "Got it."

Mrs. Beattie stuck her head into the living room and smiled at Hanna. "We don't have any cereal, so I'm going to whip up some French toast. Do you guys want some? There's plenty for all of us."

"Sure." Lucas looked at Hanna. "Wanna stay for breakfast?"

"Oh, that's okay." Hanna smiled politely at Lucas's mom. "I had coffee—I'm all set."

Lucas frowned and looked Hanna up and down. "You should have some French toast. You're really . . . *thin*."

Hanna placed her hands on her hips. "Isn't that a good thing?"

"Not exactly." Lucas circled a thumb and forefinger around Hanna's wrist. "I sort of liked you better the way you were before. Please have a couple pieces for me?"

The boot camp pledge flashed in Hanna's mind, along with all the sacrifices she'd made in the past few weeks. But then she thought of a stack of French toast, oozing with butter and syrup. It had been so long since she'd actually eaten a real meal.

"All right," Hanna conceded, standing up and pulling Lucas to her. "I guess I can have a piece or two."

"Excellent," Lucas said, leading her to the kitchen. Hanna followed behind him, absently touching the Cartier necklace at her throat. A calm feeling of well-being settled over her like a warm blanket. Everything in her life felt absolutely right again. And best of all, the only person who knew her secret about boot camp, Dinah, and Vince was Kate—and she wouldn't dare tell a soul.

UNHAPPY HANNA-KAH

For a so-called popular girl, Hanna could use some lessons on playing it cool. The chinks in her hot-girl armor are more obvious than Kate's lilac perfume. She's desperate for Daddy's attention, insecure about her love life, and in major need of a new bestie. (Ahem, she even tried to hang out with *Kate*.) But her biggest, baddest, most delicious fear: that she'll make one wrong move and become the chubby, ugly loser she was in middle school.

Maybe I'll just make her worst nightmare come true. Kate may have a reason to keep her Santa-kissing lips sealed, but I don't. And there's so much I could spill: her flirtation with Vince, losing to Dinah, fat camp, the cookie incident. And that's only the tip of the iceberg. If I reveal *everything*—the purging, the lies, the paranoid delusion that Mona is still out there, waiting to run her down again—all of Rosewood will see just how messed up Hanna is. And we all know where crazies belong: The Preserve at Addison-Stevens. Enjoy your size-two jeans while you still have them, Hannakins, because a straitjacket is one-size-fits-all . . .

One down, three to go. Now on to little miss Emily Fields, who is stuck in snowy Rosewood with her Christmas-loving family. And while Emily may be decking the halls and full of good cheer, her Christmas is about to get a lot less merry. Ho, ho, ho!

EMILY'S PRETTY LITTLE SECRET

1

ALL EMILY WANTS FOR CHRISTMAS

Late Friday afternoon, Emily Fields stood in her living room, pulling Christmas ornaments from the boxes her mother had brought up from the basement. Carols hummed from the stereo speakers, a fire blazed in the fireplace, and the piney scent of the Douglas fir they'd bought at the local tree farm filled the air. Emily's older brother, Jake, and sister Beth were home from college, and the whole family was gathered in the living room to help with the decorations.

"Oh, Emily, don't put Snoopy there." Mrs. Fields rushed to the tree and scooped up the Snoopy-embossed ball Emily had placed on a low branch. "He needs to be next to Garfield, see?" She pointed to a ceramic Garfield near the top.

Emily's sister Carolyn giggled, plucking a construction paper ornament covered in glitter and crayon squiggles from the decrepit box. "What *is* this?"

"That's the drum Jake made in preschool!" Mrs. Fields waved the ornament in Jake's face. "Remember this, honey?"

Jake stared at Mrs. Fields blankly from under his ARIZONA SWIMMING baseball cap and tugged on the ends of his chlorine-bleached red hair. "Uh, no."

Emily concealed a smile. Her mother was a Christmas-zilla, wanting everything to be as perfect as a greeting card. Every year they went to midnight Mass and waved around incense sticks. They always had a Christmas Day feast, which included a roasted turkey, stuffing, two kinds of cranberry sauce—a bowl of freshly made cranberry-orange relish as well as the store-bought cans—yams, mashed potatoes, and four different kinds of pies. Then they would sit down and watch every single Christmas special on TV, including *A Very Brady Christmas*, *To Grandmother's House We Go* with the Olsen twins, and a Justin Bieber concert in which he sang all of the holiday standards.

Mrs. Fields collapsed on the couch and admired the tree. "This is going to be the best Christmas ever!"

"Let's not go overboard." Mr. Fields laced his hands over his ample stomach. "My bonus was a little smaller than usual this year."

A tight expression washed across Mrs. Fields's face. "We'll make it work. We need a special holiday this year. We've all been through a lot."

She glanced at Emily, and Emily looked down at the worn beige Ugg slippers she'd gotten from her best friend

Alison DiLaurentis the Christmas before Ali disappeared. Her family *had* been through a lot this year—especially with her. The first family emergency was when Emily declared she was going to quit swimming, the sport all the Fields kids excelled in. While fighting over that—which ended with Emily not quitting swimming after all—Emily's parents also found out that she was dating Maya St. Germain, a new girl at Rosewood Day. Mr. and Mrs. Fields were the kind of people who raised eyebrows when someone from Rosewood Methodist dated someone who attended the Rosewood Abbey, so needless to say it hadn't gone over well.

After Emily had endured an ex-gay program, a purify-yourself-in-the-Bible-Belt stay with her extended family in Iowa, and a road trip where Emily's parents thought she was gone for good, they had finally accepted who she was.

"Hey, Em, we have something for you." Beth smiled reassuringly at Emily. She skipped into the kitchen and returned with a wrapped gift. "An early Christmas present. Jake, Carolyn, and I chipped in."

Emily slid her thumb under the tape and opened the package. Inside was a DVD box set of *The L Word*. Two women were kissing on the cover.

When she looked up, everyone was smiling at her eagerly, even her brother, who Emily was almost positive had never knowingly talked to anyone gay in his life. Emily had a feeling Mrs. Fields had told all of her children to put on a happy face about Emily's choices.

"A friend of mine at school watches the series." Beth

tucked a piece of reddish-blondish hair behind her ear. "She said it's really good. We'll watch it with you if you want."

"That's okay," Emily said quickly, an embarrassed flush rising to her cheeks. "But thank you."

"Speaking of which, there's a girl at church you should meet." Mrs. Fields paused from untangling two ornaments made out of Popsicle sticks. "She leads one of the youth groups. I've told her all about you. She has very short hair," Mrs. Fields added meaningfully.

It was amusing how, according to Emily's mother, girls with short hair *must* be gay. "She sounds really nice," Emily said, not wanting to sound ungrateful. But suddenly, all the we-accept-you-for-who-you-are attention was making her claustrophobic. "Um, I'll be back in a minute," she murmured, slipping out of the room.

She pulled on her coat and stepped onto the porch. The sun was at a low point in the sky, beaming straight into Emily's eyes. Emily let out a long sigh until her lungs felt absolutely drained of air. She knew she should be happy right now. A, the evil text-messager who'd been the one to expose Emily's relationship with Maya, was gone. Ali's killer, Ian Thomas, was behind bars. She was hanging out again with her old friends Spencer, Aria, and Hanna—after their last group therapy session, they all had gone bowling together. There was no more danger in Rosewood, no more trouble lurking around every corner, and her family was letting her be who she wanted to be.

So why did she feel so . . . *empty?* Maybe it was crazy, but even after Ali's body had been found in the concrete hole behind her old house, Emily found herself hoping against hope that her friend was still out there, alive and waiting for Emily to find her. She'd had so many dreams about Ali, and she'd even sworn she'd seen Ali the day of Ian's arraignment in the back of a Lincoln Town Car. Even now, it felt like a presence lingered somewhere close, ghostlike, as though someone she'd known forever was watching from the cornfield.

Emily glanced through the front window of the house. Her family was still decorating the tree, looking like a Norman Rockwell tableau. It was sweet how supportive they were being about her sexuality, but the last thing she could think about right now was a relationship.

With one final look inside her living room, Emily wheeled her bike out of the garage and took off down the street. Four minutes and thirty-nine seconds later—she'd timed it years ago—she was making the turn onto the road where Ali used to live.

The house loomed at the end of the cul-de-sac, its windows dark. Lit candles, wrinkled photos, ragged stuffed animals, Santa hats, and small wrapped gifts clustered at the curb, offerings for the Ali Shrine. At the back of the property was the concrete slab where Ali had been found. Yellow police tape hung limply around the perimeter, and there was an eerie, translucent haze over the opening in the ground. It was chilling to think that Ian, whom Emily and the other girls had talked to the night of the end-of-seventh-grade sleepover, had dumped Ali's lifeless body there just hours later.

Emily wheeled her bike up the lawn, stopped at a giant tree in the backyard, and gazed at the rickety remains of the old tree house in its tall branches. It was up there all those years ago that Ali had told Emily she had a secret boyfriend. Before Ali could reveal that it was Ian, Emily had leaned forward and kissed her.

Emily touched the tree bark with her fingers, finding the old spot where she'd carved her and Ali's initials. Despair flooded over her like warm rain. She'd loved Ali so much. Would she ever feel like that again?

A branch cracked to her left, and she froze. A figure emerged through the trees. "Hello?" Emily said shakily, thinking of Ian. His father had all kinds of connections and had a good shot at getting him out on bail—and Ian would probably want to punish the people who tipped off the police to his crime. What if he was here right now?

"Emily?"

Aria Montgomery appeared, looking just as surprised to see Emily as Emily was to see her. She was wearing a big coat with a furry hood, fitted jeans, and fur-lined brown boots that looked like Snuffleupaguses on her feet.

"Hey." Emily's heart began to slow down. "W-what are you doing here?"

Aria's blue eyes were wide. "I come here, sometimes. But I'm too afraid to go back *there*."

She pointed to the dug-up concrete slab. Emily nodded, knowing exactly what Aria meant. She hadn't looked inside the hole, either.

They stood in silence for a few beats. The sun sank lower into the trees, turning the sky an eerie purple. Christmas lights on automatic timers snapped on in the windows across the street.

Aria trudged over to a large boulder in Ali's yard and sat down. "It's weird, you know? That it's all . . . *over*. I feel like I'm waiting for the other shoe to drop."

"I know," Emily whispered.

"I mean, I'm *happy* it's over," Aria said quickly. "But it doesn't seem real. You know?"

Emily *did* know. Ali had been gone for years without any answers. And A—Mona Vanderwaal—had impersonated Ali so expertly, they'd all thought she was back until her body was uncovered.

"It is real, though," Emily said quietly, shifting her feet in the cold, spiny grass. She felt like crying as the words spilled from her mouth. As much as she wanted Ali back, there was nothing she could do to change the past. Ali was gone. End of story.

2

AWAY IN A MANGER

Forty-five minutes later, Emily parked her bike in the garage and walked back into her house. The beef stew Mrs. Fields had made for dinner was sitting on top of the stove, but there was no one in the kitchen to eat it.

Emily found her mother pacing around the den, her shoulder-length hair loosened from its ponytail and her green eyes wild. Emily's father was following behind her, rubbing her shoulders and saying, "It's okay. Calm down. *Please.*"

"What's going on?" Emily squeaked.

Mrs. Fields stopped in the middle of the round braided rug. "Something terrible has happened."

Emily's heart began to pound. Had Ian gotten out of prison after all? Was someone else dead? "Oh no," she whispered.

Mrs. Fields collapsed on the couch and placed her head in her hands. "My baby Jesus has been stolen! It was a precious antique!"

It took a few moments for the words to sink in. Emily recalled her mother hauling a ceramic baby Jesus out of the attic on Thanksgiving, nestling it into the backseat of the car, and proudly pointing it out in the Nativity scene on the church lawn every Sunday after that.

"I'm so upset," Mrs. Fields went on. "It was an heirloom from your grandmother!"

The phone rang, and Mrs. Fields pounced on it. "Judith?" she said into the receiver, springing to her feet and heading into the other room. Emily and her dad exchanged a look.

"That was Judith Meriwether at the church," Mrs. Fields said when she returned. "She and some of the other people on the church staff have a hunch about who stole the baby Jesus. They think it's a group of college girls home on winter break. They've been terrorizing neighborhoods, stealing decorations and messing up lawns. Apparently they call themselves the Merry Elves."

Before she could stop herself, Emily cracked a smile at the name, and Mrs. Fields shot her a look. "It's not funny. Judith says they call themselves that because they all work as elves at Santa Land at the Devon Crest Mall in West Rosewood. Judith works there as the assistant manager, and she's heard them say a few things that piqued her interest." Mrs. Fields scrunched up her face once more. "I can't believe they took the baby Jesus. They've probably smashed it to pieces!"

"Now, now." Mr. Fields rubbed his wife's back.

"I'm really sorry, Mom," Emily said, perching on the arm of the couch. "Is there anything I can do?"

Mrs. Fields dried her eyes with the embroidered handkerchief she always carried around. "We need to stop this blasphemy. But it'll take someone infiltrating the group and catching the girls in the act to get the proof we need." She placed her hand on Emily's arm. "The Santa Land at the Devon Crest Mall is looking for a new Santa—the old one was fired for hitting on girls." Mrs. Fields shuddered slightly. "Anyhow, I told Judith *you* could be the new Santa. It's a perfect way to spy on these girls."

"*Me?* A spy?" Emily blurted. There was no way she was taking a job as Santa Claus. She'd thought about getting a job over the holidays, especially after her father had mentioned that his Christmas bonus was going to be smaller this year, but she had been thinking of something more along the lines of a gift-wrapper at Macy's or a salesgirl at FrogLand, the swim specialty shop. Playing Santa sounded as challenging as being Mickey Mouse at Disney World. If you got it wrong, you'd ruin a kid's whole year. Not to mention that she didn't really fit the part.

"Please, honey?" Mrs. Fields's chin wobbled. "I really need you to do this."

"But I don't have any experience with kids," Emily protested. "And I don't think I'd be a good spy."

Mrs. Fields's eyebrows made a *V*. "You have plenty of experience with kids. You did lots of babysitting when you were younger. And what about when you were a Wilderness Guide at Rosewood Happyland Day Camp?"

Like *that* really counted. Emily and Ali had signed up to be Wilderness Guides the summer between sixth and seventh grades, mostly because Ali had a crush on the canoeing instructor. In the course of the first hour, a little girl peed on Emily's foot, a boy bit her, and a group of kids pushed her into a patch of poison ivy. After all that, Ali had discovered that Canoe Boy had a girlfriend. They'd quit after lunch and laughed about it all summer. Whenever Emily or Ali was in a bad mood, they'd say, *I'm having a Wilderness Guide kind of day.*

"And you would make an excellent spy," Mrs. Fields went on. "The elves are just a few years older than you are, and I know you can break into their clique and dig up some good information on them."

"Why can't Carolyn do it?"

Mrs. Fields's nostrils flared. "Because Carolyn already has a job over the break. She's working as a waitress at Applebee's."

Emily would gladly deliver sizzling fajita pans and margaritas to drunken patrons instead. "But Santa is usually a guy. Won't kids get confused when they hear my voice?" she asked as a last-ditch effort.

Emily's dad, who had settled on the couch, shrugged. "Just make your voice sound deeper. This really means a lot to your mom, Em."

Emily gritted her teeth. This was so classic: Mrs. Fields was always making decisions for Emily without actually asking her first. Like how she just assumed she'd be on the swim team year after year. Or how she bought Emily jeans from the Gap even though Gap jeans hadn't fit her properly for years. Or how she made reservations at a Broadway-themed restaurant for Emily's birthday even though Emily hadn't liked the restaurant since she was nine years old. Sometimes, Emily thought her mother *preferred* Emily when she was nine—obedient, sweet, no mind of her own.

But then Emily's gaze fell on the *L Word* DVD set on top of the media console. Below it was *Finding Nemo*, which Mrs. Fields had bought for Emily when she'd returned from Iowa, specifically choosing it because Ellen DeGeneres was the voice of one of the fishes. Her mom *had* finally come around about everything. What if she turned this down and her mom went back to freezing her out? Emily wasn't sure if she could take that.

"All right," Emily conceded. "I guess I can at least go in for an interview."

"Oh, nonsense." Mrs. Fields waved her hand. "You've already got the job. You're on the schedule for tomorrow. Saturday's one of the busiest days at Santa Land, so you'll be diving right in." She stood up and wrapped her arms around Emily. "Thank you so much, honey. I knew I could count on you."

Emily stiffly hugged her back, her mind starting to churn. She'd better get to work on her *ho ho ho*s—it looked like she was going to be Santa, ready or not.

3

YOU BETTER WATCH OUT, YOU BETTER NOT CRY . . .

The next day, it took Emily almost twenty minutes to find a parking space at the new Devon Crest Mall, a phoenix of marble, steel, elevators, and upscale department stores that had risen from the ashes of the West Rosewood flea market and fairgrounds. When she finally wedged her mother's behemoth Volvo wagon into a spot at the very back of a garage, it was almost noon, the time she was supposed to report for Santa duty.

She sprinted for the double doors, maneuvered around a group of women with strollers, nearly collided with a woman giving out free samples of some sort of anti-wrinkle skin product, and finally saw Santa Land at the end of the corridor, a vision of giant candy canes, fake snowdrifts, a gingerbread house, and an unoccupied golden throne with a mural of Santa, Mrs. Claus, and his eight tiny reindeer above it. There was already a line of kids waiting on a candy cane–striped carpet. Most of them were sobbing hysterically.

When Emily had read her horoscope in the *Philadelphia Sentinel* this morning, it had said, *Be prepared for an uncomfortable situation today.* No kidding.

Over the booming Christmas music, Emily heard the faintest, haunting giggle. She paused and whipped her head to the left, watching as the shoppers streamed past. Was someone watching?

"Emily?" A tall, graying woman in a red dress and a Santa hat rushed toward her. Even in the Mrs. Claus outfit, Emily recognized Judith Meriwether from church—she was always giving a reading or announcing a canned-goods drive.

"It *is* you!" Mrs. Meriwether breathed, taking Emily's hands. Her palms were ice-cold. "Thank *goodness* you're here. It's so nice of you to do this for your mother. For *all* of us."

Emily pressed her lips together to keep from saying that she hadn't really had a choice.

Mrs. Meriwether directed Emily to sit down in the little gingerbread house and fill out some tax forms. As Emily finished writing in her address, she glanced out the diamond-shaped window. Santa Land was wedged between an Aéropostale, a BCBG, and two kiosks. One sold glittery cell phone and iPad cases while the other hawked what looked like some sort of bottled water. DISCOVER THE AMAZING POWER OF AMINOSPA! said a banner draped over the booth. A buff, chiseled guy and a punky girl with jet-black hair stood in the thoroughfare, trying to get passersby to take free samples. The girl's red lips were drooped in a despondent frown, and she was practically tackling anyone who walked by.

"Here we are." Mrs. Meriwether bustled into the gingerbread house with a Santa suit in her arms. "It's fresh from the dry cleaner's. Our previous Santa wore it too, but he was much bigger than you are. We'll have to fill you out with some pillows." She held up the curly white beard to Emily's face. It felt like silky doll hair against her skin. "Perfect! No one will know you're a girl!"

Emily pulled the Santa suit over her clothes. When she looked at herself in the small mirror in the back of the gingerbread house, she looked, well, like Santa.

"Now, let me give you the rules," Mrs. Meriwether said after stuffing a bunch of pillows under Emily's jacket and down her pant legs. "Try to move the kids along as fast as you can, but always give them a few *ho ho ho*s and let them tell you a couple things they'd like for Christmas. Hold on to them tight for the picture—a lot of kids will want to squirm off your lap—and if someone pees on you, just laugh it off. Our previous Santa got angry, which upset a lot of parents." She made a face. "Our previous Santa *also* hit on thirteen-year-old girls. At least *you* won't be doing anything like that."

Emily clomped in her oversized black boots toward the gingerbread door, which had a wobbly knob in the shape of a gumdrop. "So where are these elves I'm supposed to be spying on?"

Mrs. Meriwether's eyes darted back and forth. "They're not here yet," she whispered. "Please keep your mission quiet, though. Sophie's father is the mall manager. He can't find out what we're doing until we have proof—I can't afford to be fired. But these girls need to be caught. Mrs. Ulster from the church swears they took the Santa sleigh from her front yard. And one of my neighbors woke up a few mornings ago to find her inflatable Frosty in a very . . . *compromising* position with the inflatable Ho-Ho-Homer Simpson." She winced.

"Well, I'll do my best," Emily assured her. Her phone beeped. She had one text message from Spencer: *Want to check out the new Ryan Gosling movie?*

I wish but I'm working, Emily wrote back. Then she opened the gingerbread door and stepped outside. All the kids' heads swiveled around at the sight of her. "It's Santa!" one of them screamed. "Santa, Santa!" the rest of the kids wailed, jumping up and down.

The girl at the front of the line barreled for Emily before she could sit down, latching herself onto Emily's leg. "Hi, Santa!" she bellowed. "I'm Fiona!"

"Hello, Fiona," Emily said, deepening her voice. She lowered herself onto the throne, and the girl climbed up onto her lap. She was about five years old, had her hair in two blond pigtails, and smelled like Lucky Charms. "What would you like for Christmas?" Emily asked.

"A *Little Mermaid* doll," the girl said promptly.

Emily couldn't help but smile. "*The Little Mermaid*

is one of my favorite movies, too." She'd kind of had a crush on Ariel.

Fiona's face brightened. "*Really?*" It was as though she'd just gotten a Santa exclusive.

"That's right," Emily said. "Ho ho ho!"

Mrs. Meriwether snapped a picture. Fiona gave her a huge hug, which filled Emily with a surprising sense of happiness. It *was* pretty cute. After the little girl skipped away, Emily assessed the line again. One child down. A zillion more to go.

The next kid, a boy of about seven, wanted a *Star Wars* Lego set. The girl after him wouldn't say a word, but Emily made her smile by pretending to pull a peppermint candy out of her ear. Fifteen or so kids later, a man in a police uniform and a badge that said O'NEAL plopped his daughter on Emily's lap. The girl, whose name was Tina, recited a very long list of Christmas wants, from several different American Girl dolls to a motorized car Emily had seen in an FAO Schwarz catalogue that cost $1,500. Her father nodded after each request, saying, "Santa will bring that for you, honey. And that, and that, and *that*." Emily wanted to scold him. On a cop's salary? Tina was definitely going to be disappointed Christmas morning.

There were some kids who cried, wiping their snot onto Emily's sleeve. There was one boy only a few years younger than Emily who was there with his little brothers, who wanted to sit on Emily's lap too, probably realizing she was a girl. Inevitably, a little girl peed on Emily's lap

out of excitement. Her mother whisked her off immediately, apologizing profusely. "It's okay," Emily said,
recalling Mrs. Meriwether's advice. She blotted the warm
wet spot on her knee and tried not to gag.

"You're much nicer than you were the other day,
Santa," the peeing offender said, showing off her missing front tooth. "You were mean to me then. You said I
was dirty."

"Oh, that was just a joke," Emily said quickly. "I think
you're great."

When there was a lull in the line, Mrs. Meriwether
emerged from the gingerbread house and marched over
to Emily. "You're doing a great job," she said. "Certainly
better than our old Santa, anyway."

"It's been fun," Emily answered. It was true. The job
was a whirlwind of activity, but it was fun to hear what the
kids wanted for Christmas. It was even better when they
squealed or hugged her, like she'd made their day.

Suddenly, Mrs. Meriwether gasped at something in the
distance. Emily turned to see four girls ambling toward
Santa Land. They were dressed in pointed hats, green
dresses, striped stockings, and shoes that turned up at the
toes. As they passed the Santa throne, Emily caught a
strong whiff of cigarettes and peppermint schnapps.

The elves. Though they definitely didn't look merry.

"Girls," Mrs. Meriwether called, waving. "Can you
come here for a minute?"

The tallest elf, who had bright blue hair, wore a lot of

makeup, and looked vaguely familiar, rolled her eyes and started over. The others followed. One had dreads and a nose ring, another was an Asian girl with hippie braids and a tough expression, while the final girl was tiny with short hair and a tattoo of a smiling jester on the inside of her wrist. Their eyes flickered cagily over Emily as if they didn't like what they saw.

"Girls, this is our new Santa. Her name is Emily Fields." Mrs. Meriwether put a hand on Emily's arm.

The blue-haired girl guffawed. "A *girl* Santa?"

"She's doing a very good job, Cassie." Mrs. Meriwether's voice rose in pitch. "Emily, this is Cassie Buckley. And Lola Alvarez"–that was Dreads–"Sophie Chen"–Hippie Braids–"and Heather Murtaugh"–Jester Tattoo. "They'll be helping you out with whatever you need."

The elves chuckled and nudged one another, as if to say *yeah right*. Emily's gaze returned again to Cassie, the blue-haired girl. All of a sudden, she realized why she looked so familiar: Cassie Buckley had been on the Rosewood Day JV field hockey team with Ali. But what had *happened* to her? She used to look like all the other field hockey girls: long, blond hair, bronzed skin, and an extensive wardrobe from J. Crew. Now, there were rings through her lip and eyebrow, and she was glaring at Emily with such animosity Emily immediately felt like she'd done something very, very wrong.

"What are you looking at?" Cassie snapped, noticing Emily's stare.

Emily whipped her head down. "Nothing."

"You'd *better* be looking at nothing," Lola threatened.

Emily glanced around for Mrs. Meriwether, but she had vanished. She might as well have left Emily alone with four rabid, unleashed dogs.

"And you better leave us the hell alone, Santa," Sophie rasped in a low smoker's voice.

"Yeah, we have a good thing going here," Heather growled. "So don't screw up our shit. Got it?"

"Got it," Emily whispered.

The elves laughed raucously, linked arms, and sashayed away in a booze-smelling cloud. Emily's heart sank to the soles of her black Santa boots. What had she gotten herself into? There was no way she could infiltrate the elves. It made breaking into Ali's clique in sixth grade look easy.

4

ELVES HAVE FEELINGS, TOO

The following day, Emily was on her Santa chair again, greeting kids with deep *ho ho ho*s. About a half hour into her shift, she heard the whispers.

"That one's *totally* going to puke on her. He ate a whole bucket of Chick-fil-A while waiting in line."

"I should tell that girl in the *Dora the Explorer* T-shirt to pull her beard."

"*I* should tell her that there's no such thing as Santa Claus."

"Girls?" Mrs. Meriwether's meek voice sounded from behind the camera. "Can someone please man the register?"

The four elves emerged from behind a large Frosty statue, pushed around a mother and two children in line without bothering to say *excuse me*, and slumped against the register. A man and two kids Emily had just visited with were waiting there. The man cowered a little when he saw the elves, drawing his children in closer.

"That'll be $19.95," Cassie said in monotone, looking at the man's photo order.

"Happy holidays," Heather said in a hissing voice she might use to deliver a ransom message.

"Actually, can I get their picture in *that* frame?" The man pointed to a silver frame mounted on the wall behind the register. It was the limited-edition Santa Land collector's item that cost $79.95. When Mrs. Meriwether worked checkout, she was always pushing people to buy it.

Sophie gazed at the frame and scrunched up her face. "*Uch*, that means we have to find it in a box in the back."

"It's really ugly up close," Cassie told the man. "And it's not real silver. It'll turn your fingers green as soon as you touch it."

"And it was probably made in China," Lola added righteously. "By a little girl in a sweatshop who gets paid a penny a day."

"Daddy?" The littler of the two boys gazed worriedly at him, looking like he was about to cry.

The man nervously tugged at his collar. "Okay. Just the regular photo frame, I guess."

The elves grumbled as if even this was too much effort. Cassie swiped his credit card, the bell on the end of her hat jingling.

Mrs. Meriwether stifled a sigh and scampered toward Emily. "Any luck?" she whispered.

Emily stared at her. It had only been twenty-four

hours, and the elves had barely *spoken* to her. Everything she did seemed to amuse them—and not in a good way. "I'm trying," she said.

After the elves rang up the man, practically shoving the frame at him and shooing him away, they all collapsed on the plushy reindeer sofa next to the gingerbread house as though they'd completed a twenty-four-hour shift in the emergency room.

"I think it's time for Starbucks," Cassie announced breathlessly. "I don't know about you guys, but my head's about to explode from all of this Christmas music."

"Agreed," Lola said.

The four girls grabbed their bags from behind a snowman-shaped podium and let themselves out through the white picket-fence gate.

"Guys, wait," Emily protested, hating how whiny her voice sounded. "We have more customers." She gestured to the huge line of kids waiting to talk to Santa.

Lola glanced blankly at the customers, as if she'd just noticed them. Heather and Sophie continued walking. "Oh well," Cassie said, linking elbows with the other girls and pulling them in the direction of Starbucks.

"Why don't *you* ring them up, Santa?" Heather called over her shoulder. "Mrs. Meriwether would *love* you for that."

"Santa and Mrs. Claus, sittin' in a tree!" Cassie trilled.

They burst into giggles and skipped away, taking a moment to knock over the giant inflatable bottle of

AminoSpa vitamin drink that stood in front of the kiosk in the middle of the promenade.

Emily pressed her fist into the Santa throne, hoping one of the giant foil stars that hung from the mall's ceiling would fall on the elves' heads. How was she going to befriend these girls? What would Ali do in this type of situation? Play by their rules? Make herself invaluable? Then again, Ali would never *get* in this situation.

Sighing deeply, she beckoned the line of kids to move forward. A little boy and girl climbed on Emily's lap and looked up at her with hopeful expressions. "And what would you like for Christmas?" Emily asked them, trying to sound chipper.

"I want to see the silver panther show in Atlantic City," the boy piped up. "It's supposed to be really, really awesome."

"And *I* want to go to Atlantic City to gamble," the girl added, pronouncing it as one word, *LantiCity*.

"I think you're a little too young to gamble," Emily said, eyeing the kids' mom, who was typing obliviously on her iPhone.

The little girl's mouth made an upside-down *U*. "I'm not too young! My mom said I could play the slots!"

The line slowly dwindled and the elves returned from Starbucks. Not that they did any work. Heather slipped a pair of Bose headphones over her ears and ate a couple of candy canes out of the wicker basket on the checkout counter. Sophie chatted with one of the Aéropostale

workers. Lola slipped around the corner of the gingerbread house to take a phone call. "So you're going to be
gone for four days?" she said to someone on the other
line. "No, it's fine, Mom. I said it's *fine*. It's just, like, I
think there's something wrong with the car, and . . ."
She trailed off. "No, I understand. Rocco needs you. I
got it."

She stabbed the phone to hang up, making a small
whimpering sound. When she turned around and saw
Emily staring, her eyes narrowed. Emily decided this
wasn't a good time to ask if Lola was okay.

The only girl who hadn't returned from Starbucks was
Cassie. Emily had watched the lead elf carefully, trying to
figure out how Cassie could have gone from such a freshly
scrubbed, super-popular Rosewood girl to someone who
looked like she'd just tumbled out of juvie. For once she
actually wished Cassie would recognize Emily from her
pictures in the papers after Ali had vanished or when Ian
had been arrested. If Cassie knew who she was, it might
bridge the gap between them.

As if sensing Emily's thoughts, Mrs. Meriwether
emerged from inside the gingerbread house and glared
around Santa Land. "Where's Cassie?"

Heather lifted a headphone from her ear. "On her
break."

Mrs. Meriwether's mouth became a small, tight line.
"She left for her break an *hour* ago."

"No, there she is." Emily pointed down the corridor. Cassie was sauntering unhurriedly back to Santa Land, a Starbucks cup in her hand.

Mrs. Meriwether darted over to her. "An hour break is *not* permitted."

One corner of Cassie's mouth rose in a smirk. "Sorry. I was busy."

"You were *busy*?" Mrs. Meriwether placed her hands on her hips, looking about ready to explode.

"Yeah, busy." Cassie hitched her purse higher on her shoulder, glaring at Mrs. Meriwether. They looked ready for a standoff of epic proportions.

"Wait a minute." Emily jumped off the Santa throne and waddled over to Mrs. Meriwether and Cassie, holding the pillow in her stomach so that it didn't slip into her crotch. "Uh, Mrs. Meriwether, I'm the reason Cassie took such a long break. I asked her to see if she could find me a new Santa hat. Mine is really, really itchy."

She scratched her scalp for effect, not daring to meet Cassie's gaze. Of course it was a lie, but Mrs. Meriwether needed to keep her job—and Emily needed to get on the elves' good side.

Mrs. Meriwether's brow creased. "Is this true, Cassie?"

"Uh, yeah," Cassie admitted. "I scoured the mall, looking. But sorry, Santa, I couldn't find a single hat."

"It's okay," Emily said quickly. "I'll live."

Mrs. Meriwether's eyes flickered from Emily to Cassie,

looking like she didn't believe either of them. "Just go back to work," she grumbled, turning around and trundling back to the gingerbread house.

Cassie gazed down her nose at Emily. "Thanks, Santa."

"You're welcome," Emily answered.

"You know . . ." Cassie ran her tongue over her teeth. "There's a party at my house tonight. Maybe you want to come."

Emily blinked hard. "Uh, sure. That would be great."

"What?" Heather slid the headphones from her ears and nudged Cassie hard. "Why are you—"

"Shut *up*." Cassie nudged her back, then turned to Emily again. "I live on Emerson Road in Old Hollis. You'll know the place because of all the cars."

"Great." Emily tried to sound nonchalant. "I'll see you there."

Cassie set off toward the back of Santa Land. The other elves followed behind her, whispering. Emily returned to her throne, feeling light-headed and giddy, but nervous, too. Was Cassie being sincere? What if this was some kind of setup? She stared at the swarming mall crowds. *If someone passes in the next minute with a Neiman Marcus bag, this is all going to end up okay*, she wagered.

Not five seconds later, a woman strutted past with not one Neiman Marcus bag, but *three*. If that wasn't a positive omen, Emily didn't know what was.

5

EVERY GOOD SPY NEEDS A PLAN

When Emily got home from Santa Land that evening, she flopped on the living-room couch with an old clothbound journal in her lap. Ali used to keep a journal, and because Emily had wanted to do everything just like her, she'd started one back in middle school. Emily had only recently found out that Mona Vanderwaal had pulled Ali's old journal from a pile of junk on the curb that Maya's family had thrown away from Ali's old bedroom. Mona had used the information in that journal—including Emily's and her old friends' darkest secrets—to become A.

In the twinkling light of the now fully decorated Christmas tree, Emily flipped through the old onionskin pages of her notebook. At first, her journal entries were mostly straightforward accounts of things she and her new friends had done together: trips to Ali's family's vacation house in the Poconos, manicures at the King James Mall, a sleepover where Ali dared Aria to prank-call Noel

Kahn, her crush. When Aria did, Ali had blurted, "She loves you!" before Aria hung up.

In April of that year, the tone of the entries had begun to change. The Jenna Thing happened, and they'd all become so scared and worried. Emily didn't refer to the incident directly on the pages—she was worried her mom might read it—but she'd put a sad face next to the day that it happened. Many entries after that were despairing and frantic, too.

The next school year, things began to spiral downhill even more. *Ali got a spot on the JV field hockey team, even though she's only in seventh grade*, Emily had written one day in late August. *She was talking about the team party she went to today and saying how cool the older girls were.* She hadn't drawn a sad face, but Emily remembered exactly what she was feeling: Ali would soon realize *she* wasn't cool anymore and drift away from her. Her time with Ali had always felt borrowed and precarious, and in the back of her mind, she was always waiting for the fantasy life to come crashing down.

A few journal entries later she mentioned that Ali and Emily had attended a field hockey party where Emily had met none other than Cassie Buckley. *Cassie bragged about how good vodka and Red Bulls were*, Emily had written. *When I asked if I could try one, Cassie ignored me, and Ali was like, "No, Em, I think vodka–Red Bulls are a little out of your league." She and Cassie laughed like it was the funniest thing in the world.*

Emily still remembered that party like it was yesterday. Cassie had answered the door with the front pieces of her long blond hair braided together and fastened at the back with a clip; only a few days later, Ali showed up to school with her hair done in the same way, and then all the other girls in their grade copied her. Once inside the house, Cassie had mixed drinks effortlessly, like she was an adult. She'd slung her arm around Ali's shoulder and invited her to a "secret" party upstairs, making it clear Emily couldn't come. Emily had wandered around the party for a little while longer, but no one spoke to her. She'd slipped out the door, holding in her tears until she was halfway down the block.

She closed the journal, pulled her laptop onto her lap, and typed Cassie Buckley's name into Facebook. A profile of the Technicolor-haired, pierced girl popped up. Emily scrolled through her pictures; Cassie wasn't smiling in a single one. Nor had she included any photos from her blond, preppy, field hockey days. Why had she undergone such a dramatic makeover? If Ali would have lived and remained friends with Cassie, would Ali have transformed, too?

"Who's that?"

Emily jumped. Carolyn stood in the doorway, a laundry basket in her arms. "Uh, no one," Emily said.

Carolyn dropped the laundry basket on the couch and studied the screen. "Is it a new girl you have your eye on?"

The words sounded forced coming out of Carolyn's

mouth. Emily wondered what Carolyn *really* thought about Emily's sexuality—she wasn't exactly the accepting type.

"Does Emily have a new girlfriend?" Beth asked, wandering into the room with a bowl of microwave popcorn.

"Maybe." Carolyn folded a Rosewood Day Swimming T-shirt and set it on the chair. "Show her, Em."

"Let me see, let me see!" Beth plopped down next to Emily and tilted the laptop in her direction. When she saw Cassie's picture, she frowned. "Whoa. She looks *tough*."

"She's just this girl who's working at Santa Land with me," Emily protested, figuring their mother had told her siblings about Emily's mission. "She's *definitely* not a girlfriend."

"What about *her*? *She's* cute." Beth clicked on another profile. It was tiny, gamine, short-haired Heather from Santa Land. In Heather's info section, it said she liked South Street Philadelphia, Ken Kesey and the Merry Pranksters, and *The Anarchist Cookbook*.

"What are you guys doing?" Jake grabbed a handful of popcorn from the bowl as he entered the room.

"Trying to find a new girlfriend for Emily." Beth clicked on the profile of a girl named Polly whom Emily didn't recognize.

"Are the girls hot?" Jake's eyes lit up. "I'll help."

"You *guys*!" Emily grabbed the laptop from Beth and slammed the lid shut. She suddenly felt like her siblings were turning this into a pet project. It reminded her of when she was little and they decided that she was half-girl, half-cat because she was so young, small, and nimble. *Felina,* they called her, as though she were a superhero mutant. They'd developed training sessions for Emily to make her even more catlike, squeezing her under fences, folding her up inside cupboards, and forcing her to walk across a balance beam that straddled the small pond down the street. Emily put up with it because she liked the attention—it was hard being the youngest and left out of everything. It was only when they started talking about letting Emily jump off the roof to see if she'd land on her feet that Mrs. Fields got wind of it and put a stop to things.

"I don't *want* a girlfriend," Emily said now.

"Sure, you do," Beth teased.

Emily groaned, stood up, and stormed into the kitchen, where her mother was standing at the stove minding a pot of pasta, a chicken-print oven mitt on one hand. When she saw Emily, she dropped the spoon into the pot and rushed over to the kitchen table.

"How did it go today?" she said in an excited whisper.

"Um, not too bad." Emily ran her hand through her hair. "They invited me to a party."

Mrs. Fields squealed giddily as though Emily had just announced she'd been awarded a full scholarship to Harvard. "That's *wonderful.* And you're going to go, right?"

So ironic. Usually, Emily had to beg her mom to let her go to parties. "You don't care that it's a Sunday night and I have school tomorrow?" she asked.

"You can go in late to school if you want," Mrs. Fields said.

Emily almost swallowed her gum. Who was this woman, and what had she done with her über-strict mother?

Mrs. Fields started listing off points on her fingers. "Now, be sure to tell me everything they say, including any pranks they might want to pull next. In fact, try to record it on your phone if you can. Or write it down so you don't forget. And don't drink." She wagged her finger at Emily.

"Got it," Emily said.

The kitchen timer sounded, and Mrs. Fields stood up again. "You'd better get upstairs and figure out what you're going to wear. I can have Beth set the table instead of you. Go on."

She nudged her out of the room. Emily scuttled up the stairs, walked into her bedroom, and opened her closet. Nearly identical Old Navy long-sleeved T-shirts, medium-wash jeans, and Banana Republic cable-knit sweaters hung in an unorganized jumble. What did one wear to a naughty elf party? She pulled out a pair of tight black jeans and an off-the-shoulder black top she'd bought on a whim with Maya.

Then, a flicker outside the window caught her eye. She ran to the window and squinted hard. Something was moving through the cornfield outside. It was definitely a person. And did she see *blond hair*?

Emily pressed her nose and mouth so close to the window that the glass immediately steamed up. But by the time she wiped it clean and looked again, the figure had vanished.

6

POOR LITTLE WALLFLOWER

A few hours later, Emily walked up the front steps of a huge white Victorian on Emerson Road in Old Hollis, the hip neighborhood next to Hollis College. It was the only house on the block with loud music pulsing from its seams, lights in every window, and cars parked on the grass, so Emily figured it was Cassie's. A couple of kids were making drunken angels in the light dusting of snow. Everyone seemed to know one another, and she already felt out of place. She'd asked Aria to come with her, but Aria had to help her dad get wreaths or logs or something ready for the Winter Solstice.

The front door was shut tight. Emily was deliberating over what to do—knock? Just go in?—when the door burst open and a girl wearing a very short dress and thigh-high snow boots and a guy in a Santa beard and a HOLLIS BEER CRAWL T-shirt tumbled out onto the porch, giggling. They held the door open for Emily, and she slipped inside.

The scent of stale beer instantly assaulted her. People crammed the rooms, talking loudly. A small Christmas tree decorated with white lights rotated slowly on a plastic pedestal. A high-tech-looking stereo pumped out music, and a flat-screen TV was tuned to Comedy Central, not that anyone was watching. A gray cat perched on the stairs, licking her paws. When a girl barreled down from the second floor, spilling her cup of beer as she went, the cat screeched and took off.

There was no one at the party Emily even remotely recognized. She passed through the living room into a dining room with a stately old table laden with booze, and then into the kitchen, which had a stainless-steel fridge and expensive-looking pots and pans hanging from a rack above the island. Pinned up to the fridge was a neon-yellow Post-it that said, *Cassie is a slutty beast!* There were black bananas in a hanging basket over the oven, and a ton of dishes were piled in the sink. Emily wondered if Cassie was holding down the fort while her parents were away on vacation.

When her gaze clapped on the view of the Hollis spire out the back window, a pathway connected in her brain. The field hockey party she and Ali had attended all those years ago was in this very same house. It had been in the dining room behind her that Cassie plied Ali with vodka and Red Bulls and ignored Emily completely.

"Oops," a voice said behind Emily. She turned just as a burly guy, wearing a T-shirt that had a drawing of a penis on it, spilled half his beer on her arm.

"Hey!" Emily cried, drawing back. Her sleeve was drenched.

"Sorry," the guy half-spoke, half-belched. He wandered away.

The hip-hop song rose in volume, making Emily's head ache. After toweling off her sleeve, she escaped back into the dining room, which was slightly less crowded. A guy stood behind the table, pouring vodka into a red plastic cup. He raised his eyes to Emily. "What are you having? Cassie's making me be bartender so no one hogs the booze."

"Oh, uh, I'll just have some orange juice." Emily pointed to the first nonalcoholic beverage she saw, thinking of her mother's advice not to drink.

A slow smirk rolled across the guy's face. "It's not like I'm going to card you."

"Really. Orange juice is fine," Emily insisted, feeling like the most prudish girl in the universe.

She took the red cup from the guy—at least now she had something to do with her hands—and wandered through the crowd, looking for Cassie and the elves. People stared past her apathetically as though she wasn't even there.

Then the crowd parted, and she spotted four figures lounging on plastic lawn chairs next to the radiator in the front room. It was Cassie, dressed in a leather skirt and a tie-dyed baby tee. She'd bleached her blue hair to white blond, though it was nothing like the blond hair from her field hockey days. Heather, Sophie, and Lola, each in similarly skimpy outfits, sat next to her, whispering and looking smug.

Emily pushed through the throng toward them. When only a few people stood between Emily and the elves, a tall boy leaned over Cassie, grinning mysteriously. "I heard you guys have been raising hell all over town. Is it true?"

Cassie gave him a cryptic smile. "That's what elves do, isn't it?"

"That's for us to know and you to wonder about," Heather added.

"You guys rock," the guy said, giving Lola a fist bump.

Then Cassie looked up and stared squarely at Emily. Emily felt a swoop in her stomach and waved, but Cassie just peered through her. Lola glanced in Emily's direction too, but she gave Emily the same blank, unwelcoming expression.

Emily shrank back. A high-pitched giggle lilted through the air. She knew the laugh was meant for her.

She drank the orange juice, pretending it was booze. So this *was* just a big joke. The elves wanted to make it clear how big of a loser she was. She ducked into the empty hall bathroom, feeling tears rush to her eyes. After fiddling with the old-timey glass knob so that the door actually shut, she plopped down on the side of the tub and placed her head in her hands. Talk about déjà vu—she'd locked herself in this very same bathroom at the party in seventh grade, shortly after Ali had headed upstairs with Cassie.

The pain she'd felt back then was still so palpable. It felt like Ali had been breaking up with her—and, in a way, she had been.

Emily stood up, padded over to the mirror, and stared hard at her reflection. "Get over it," she told the mirror. "You're not that seventh grader anymore. You're stronger than you used to be."

She splashed cold water on her face and walked into the front room again. The crowd was just as thick, but she used her elbows to maneuver between kids until she was face-to-face with the elves. Emily tapped Cassie on the shoulder. Cassie squinted at Emily, her mouth pinched into a sneer.

"Thanks for inviting me," Emily said sarcastically. "I've had a blast."

Cassie peered at her from under her white-blond bangs. "Who the hell are you?"

Emily wanted to groan. "You *know* who I am. Emily."

"Emily?" Cassie looked at Heather, Sophie, and Lola, who were now peering curiously at her, too. "Ring any bells, girls?"

"*I* didn't invite anyone named Emily," Lola said, slightly slurring her words.

"Me neither," Sophie and Heather piped up.

Cassie rolled her eyes. "Did my brother invite you? I told him we were way over capacity."

"*You* invited me!" Emily exclaimed. "It's Emily Fields! *Santa!*"

It was as if a light went on over Cassie's head. She smiled. "Santa? I didn't recognize you without your beard! Guys, it's *Santa*!"

"Santa!" Heather whooped. "Wassup?"

"Hey, Santa," Sophie said.

"You should have worn your hat." Lola looked annoyed. "How were we supposed to know it's you?"

"Hang on a sec." Cassie shot up and disappeared into a back room. Moments later, she appeared with another lawn chair and plunked it down next to her. "Here you go, Santa. Hang out with us. What can I get you to drink?"

Emily blinked at the empty chair, then stared at the two inches of orange juice left in her cup. "Um, how about a vodka and Red Bull?"

"Excellent choice." Cassie winked. "Those used to be my favorite."

I know, Emily wanted to say. She sat in the lawn chair, suddenly feeling kind of amazing. Just like that, the party had gotten much, much more interesting.

7

THE COOL CROWD

"More vodka, anyone?" Cassie raised a bottle of Absolut in the air and shook it. A bit of liquid sloshed in the bottom.

"Me, me!" Lola raised her hand. So did Heather and Sophie. Instead of topping them off, Cassie made a beeline for Emily, glugging a good three shots' worth into her cup. "I've barely seen you take a sip, Santa!"

It was about an hour later, and although the party was still raging inside Cassie's house, the elves and Emily had formed a little VIP section in Cassie's backyard, which had a big deck and a couple of heat lamps to fend off the cold. It was peaceful out there, though, with the stars in the dark sky making a chandelier over their heads and the heat lamps providing a soothing warmth on their skin.

The elves talked about the best college ragers they'd ever been to, how lame the Devon Crest Mall was, and tales about the previous Santa at Santa Land, whose name was Fletcher, and who'd apparently tried to make out with all four of the elves on the same day. "That dude was dying to get some," Cassie moaned, hand over her eyes. "He didn't even care who it was."

"Remember that prissy-looking brunette girl who actually fell for him?" Lola snickered. "I'm convinced those two snuck off somewhere."

"Yeah, right." Cassie sniffed. "She wouldn't have gone for him. Even she wasn't that stupid."

"Nasty, huh, Santa?" Lola giggled, tapping Emily with her foot. Emily nodded.

"Speaking of gross guys." Cassie propped her feet on the deck rail. "I can't believe what an asshole Colin's being tonight. He hasn't said one word to me, not even *thanks for inviting me to your party*. Do you think I should try and talk to him, or should I just let it go?"

"Forget him." Heather waved her hand as if to sweep him away.

"We're in the same boat." Lola slumped down in her chair. "I saw Brian disappear up the stairs with Chelsea. I guess that was his way of telling me it's over between us."

"At least he didn't break up with you in a Facebook post." Sophie lit a cigarette. "I'll never forgive James for doing that to me."

"That's a Yale boy for you." Cassie clucked her tongue. "And you should never go out with someone from your dorm."

Emily peered at Sophie. "You go to Yale?"

Sophie shrugged. "Yeah, but probably not for much longer."

Cassie snickered. "Oh, please. Sophie was valedictorian at Prichard. She probably still does her homework the night it's assigned. *And* the extra-credit."

"Nuh-uh." Sophie's braids bounced as she shook her head. "I've totally slipped."

"Okay, *Daddy* does your homework," Cassie corrected.

"Are you still going to be a doctor, just like Daddy wants?" Heather teased.

Sophie blew a smoke ring. "My grades this semester blew. I probably won't be able to get into the premed program if I keep this up. My parents are going to murder me when they find out." She said this toughly, but when she turned her head away there was a petrified look on her face.

Heather must have sensed her fear, because she snickered and said, "Poor little Sophie, under all that pressure. You were bound to crack sometime."

Sophie whirled back around and slapped the arm of her chair. "At least my parents *notice* when I'm a fuckup. Who's your dad spending all his time with these days? One of The Pussycat Dolls?"

Cassie let out a loud guffaw. Heather raked her fingers angrily through her pixie-short hair. "Ha frickin' ha," she said in a small voice, suddenly sounding sober.

"Your dad knows The Pussycat Dolls?" Emily asked, mostly to cut the tension.

The elves turned their attention to Emily, almost like

they'd forgotten she was there. "Actually, no," Heather snapped. "But he's a music producer and knows a lot of other artists."

"Knows them *intimately*," Lola said meaningfully. "He brought one of the runners-up on *American Idol* to Heather's graduation party and was all over her. You should have seen Heather's face!"

Heather kicked her chair. "Tell the whole world, why don't you? Like your life is so perfect? How's your brother? What rehab facility is he in these days?"

Lola's face paled. She didn't elaborate, but Emily remembered the name Rocco from the conversation Lola had had on her cell phone behind the gingerbread house earlier today.

A silence fell over the group. Sophie puffed on her Marlboro Light, staring into the middle distance. Heather tapped her foot against the porch rail. Emily shifted her butt in the uncomfortable lawn chair, wishing she could find the right words to say to make everything better. This reminded her of the dynamic between Ali, Emily, and her old friends at the end of seventh grade, especially when Ali hinted at a secret she knew about one of them but the others didn't. Maybe there was some deep-seated animosity within this group, too.

But in a strange way, hearing the elves' secrets was also kind of reassuring. Like Emily, the girls were human. Fallible. Vulnerable. They had secrets A might glom on to, if A were still around. It made her feel less alone.

Cassie stretched in her chair. "So what do you think, Santa? Do all guys suck?"

Emily pulled her hands inside her down coat. "Pretty much. That's why I'm into girls."

All four heads whipped up. There was a long tip of ash at the end of Sophie's cigarette, but she didn't flick it away. "Yeah, right," Cassie said.

"It's true." Emily tried to sound nonchalant. "I dated this girl named Maya in the fall." It felt weird saying it out loud—bragging about it, almost. But if there was a group she could tell this to without judgment, it was probably the elves.

Cassie's eyes were wide. "Are you *out*?"

"You could say that." Emily didn't bother adding that A had outed her against her wishes.

"What did your parents say?" Sophie gasped.

"They freaked," Emily admitted. "But they've come around, I guess."

"Whoa." Heather crossed her arms over her chest. "Maybe I should try saying *that* to my parents. That would probably get them in the same room at the same time."

Cassie leaned forward and blinked curiously at Emily. "What would you do in my situation with Colin? If Colin was a girl, and she wasn't speaking to you and acting all weird, would you confront her or would you just blow her off?"

Emily sat back, amazed Cassie was asking *her* for advice. "I would talk to him," she decided. "But I wouldn't be too clingy about it. Act like you don't really need him, like he needs you." If only she had done that with Ali when she'd had the chance.

Cassie nodded thoughtfully. "Yeah, that's what I was thinking, too." She cuffed Emily on the shoulder.

A loud screech of feedback suddenly sounded through two invisible speakers on the back porch. Then a song by Jay-Z blared out, and Lola got up and started twisting her hips. "Oh my God, I almost forgot," she said, pausing mid-twirl. "I brought something for us."

She disappeared into the house, returning a few seconds later with a crumpled paper bag that she upended on the ground. Cone-shaped fireworks spilled out. "We had these left over from the summer. I thought it would be fun to set them off tonight."

"Sweet." Cassie grabbed a rocket-shaped one from the bag without hesitation, placed it on the concrete, and lit the wick. Sparks flew off the long striped tube, and everyone stepped back. Emily's heart thudded hard. She would always associate fireworks with The Jenna Thing.

A high-pitched peal rang out in the air, and the firework shot into the sky and exploded just over the rooftops. "Yeah!" Lola and Heather bellowed, giving each other a high five. Emily looked around nervously. Wouldn't they get in trouble for this?

It wasn't something the elves were worried about, though. One by one, each of the girls sent a firework screeching into the air. Upstairs lights flipped on in the neighboring houses. Someone yelled "Shut the hell up!" from a window. Partiers stepped outside to see what was making so much commotion.

Cassie passed a bottle rocket and a book of matches to Emily. "Your turn, Santa."

Emily turned the firework over in her hands, wondering how her mother would handle the police calling her at 2 A.M. saying they'd taken Emily into custody. But she'd made so much progress with the elves. She couldn't turn back now. And she'd be lying if she said she wasn't having fun.

She placed the firework on the ground and struck the match. The wick lit immediately, burning down faster than she expected. She stepped back just as the rocket launched into the sky with a high-pitched wail. It crackled in the air, sending a shower of sparks toward the ground.

The elves cheered and slapped her hands. Emily's heart thumped with adrenaline. It *was* kind of amazing to send a sparkling, booming stick of dynamite careening into the sky. What was even better were the looks the elves were giving her, clapping her on the back and grinning broadly at her. It was like she belonged.

The back door swung open once more, and a frizzy-haired guy stuck his head out. "Your neighbor's on the phone, Cassie. He sounds pissed."

"*Shit*." Cassie looked at the other elves. "We'd better get inside. If it's Mr. Long, he's already called the cops."

The elves nodded and headed for the house. Everyone

at the party was staggering drunkenly for the door, the festivities winding down. Every counter, tabletop, and shelf was littered with red cups and empty bottles, and the house smelled like the bottom of a moldy keg. Emily told Cassie she should probably be going, and Cassie and the elves walked her to the front room.

"Thanks for inviting me tonight," Emily said when she reached the porch.

"No problem." Cassie twisted the doorknob. "It was fun."

"Maybe we can do it again sometime?" Emily asked eagerly. She'd relished their time in the backyard. It had been ages since she'd talked with a group of girls like that.

Cassie's face clouded. She exchanged an ambiguous look with the other elves. "Uh, we'll see about that, Santa."

8

MISSION IMPOSSIBLE

"Emily Fields?" crackled a voice over the Rosewood Day PA system on Monday afternoon. "Can you come to the office?"

Emily looked up from the English quiz on the themes of *A Farewell to Arms*. A couple of kids swiveled around and stared at her curiously.

"You can go after you're finished with your quiz," Mrs. Quentin, the English teacher, said. She was sitting at her desk reading a tattered copy of *To the Lighthouse*, her glasses perched low on her nose.

"Actually, I'm done." Emily rose from the desk and dropped the quiz in the wire box at the front of the room. She had no idea why she was being called to the office, and a nervous pit formed in her stomach. Had someone found out she'd set off fireworks at the party last night? Could she get in trouble at school for that?

Every footstep on the marble floor sounded like a

bomb exploding in Emily's head. Her vision was slightly blurry, as it often was when she hadn't gotten enough sleep. Perhaps that was because of how she'd tossed and turned until almost 5 A.M., trying to make sense of why Cassie and the elves had been so welcoming one moment and so cold the next. *We'll see about that?* What was that supposed to mean?

The Rosewood Day hall was empty of students. A bunch of posters for a holiday dance from three weeks ago still hung on the wall, and a cracked glass ornament lay on its side next to the door to the girls' bathroom. Through classroom door windows, Emily could see harried-looking teachers trying to keep their students on task. There was a jovial, let's-not-do-any-more-work mood in the air—the two-week break was only four days away.

She passed through the lobby, where a memorial to Ali's death still hung near the auditorium. It was a huge collage of photographs, old drawings, and memories from students, the words WE WILL MISS YOU in silver lettering around the perimeter. Emily was in quite a few of the pictures in the collage, her elbow linked with Ali's, her head resting on Ali's shoulder, the two of them laughing loudly in the auditorium.

She touched the display case with the tips of her fingers, her own ghostly reflection blinking back at her. Ali's school picture from fifth grade was in the middle of the montage; for a moment, it looked like she was making eye contact with Emily from inside the glass. Suddenly, a

second reflection behind her caught her eye. She whipped
around fast, sure she was going to discover someone standing in the lobby, watching her, but the lobby was empty.
The front door eased shut slowly, though, as if someone
had just run away.

The principal's office was on the other side of the
lobby. Emily slipped inside and stood there silently until
Mrs. Albert, the woman at the front desk, looked up.
"Oh, Emily." She shuffled a few papers. "Your mother's in
there." She pointed to a small office the guidance coun-
selors normally used.

Emily's heart started to hammer. Her *mom* was here?
Her mind scattered in all kinds of terrifying directions.
Something had happened to one of her siblings. Her
grandmother's melanoma had come back. Ian was on a
killing spree.

Emily burst into the room and found her mother sitting calmly at the round table, sorting through the clipped
coupons she always toted around in a little canvas pouch.
"What's going on?"

Mrs. Fields gave her a placid smile. "Hey, honey. I was
wondering if you wanted to skip eighth period and get a
manicure before your shift at Santa Land today–I received
a few coupons from the Welcome Wagon committee as a
Christmas gift. If you don't have anything too important
going on in eighth period, of course." Her gaze shifted
to the front desk and she smiled mischievously. "I told
Mrs. Albert that you had a doctor's appointment," she

said in a stage-whisper.

Emily gaped at her. Her mother pulling her out of school—something that *never* happened, not even the time Beth had been sent to the hospital for double pneumonia—was shocking enough, but girly spa days weren't something they did together. Emily had always *wanted* Mrs. Fields to be that kind of mom, but Mrs. Fields saw spas as frivolous indulgences. She'd even balked at her daughters getting their hair professionally done for school dances, insisting that they could do it themselves with enough bobby pins, flat irons, and hair spray.

"That would be nice," she blurted. "I have history eighth period, but we'll probably just watch a video." They'd been watching videos for the past week now as Mrs. Weir, the teacher, sat at the back and Christmas-shopped on her iPad.

"Great." Mrs. Fields stood and slipped the coupon pouch back into her Vera Bradley quilted bag. "Let's go, then."

Emily trotted behind her mom through the double doors in the lobby. A stiff wind kicked up, knocking the tree branches together and blowing a silver gum wrapper across the parking lot. She looked around, thinking about the figure she'd sworn she'd seen behind her in the lobby, but the parking lot was empty. It must have been a trick of her imagination.

"What's this on your arms?" The manicurist at Fermata Spa grabbed Emily's wrists and turned her forearms over.

Tiny red bumps speckled her skin.

Emily stared at them in alarm. Mrs. Fields looked over and clucked her tongue. "Oh dear. I washed your sheets in new detergent yesterday. I bet it's from that."

Emily groaned. Her mother was always buying different detergents based on whatever was on sale. Her sensitive skin couldn't keep up with all the changes. It looked like she had some sort of flesh-eating bacteria.

She sat back in the manicure chair and tried to relax. The foot-soaking baths bubbled peacefully. The air smelled soothing and fresh, like sandalwood mixed with fresh oranges. Aestheticians in black lab coats drifted past quietly, shooting Emily and her mother placid smiles. The only downer was that "Blue Christmas" was playing on the stereo, probably the most depressing holiday song ever written.

Emily's mother sat next to her, flinching as the manicurist clipped her cuticles. Emily suspected this was the first manicure she'd ever gotten—she'd puzzled for ages at the wall of Essie polishes before finally selecting an almost-clear pink. "So," Mrs. Fields murmured. "Tell me all about the party last night."

Emily had wondered when her mother was going to pump her for information about the elves.

"It was pretty good," she answered as the manicurist buffed her nails. "The elves opened up to me a little. One of the girls, Sophie, is flunking out of Yale. She kind of reminds me of Spencer—under way too much pressure.

Heather seems to be having family problems—I don't think her parents get along. Lola's going through some stuff as well—I think her brother is in rehab. I don't know much about Cassie yet, only that the party was at her house and her parents definitely weren't home. It seems like they all have to fend for themselves. Maybe they're pulling pranks to get attention."

"Yes, but what did you find out about the pranks themselves?" Mrs. Fields asked. "Are they planning anything big soon? Did they make any references to the baby Jesus?"

Emily chewed on her bottom lip. "They didn't mention any firm plans," she admitted. "And actually, when I pushed about hanging out again, they got sort of weird. I haven't even gotten real confirmation that they *are* the pranksters. It's not like they've talked about it."

Mrs. Fields pressed her lips together until the skin around them wrinkled. "Of course they're the pranksters—we know that. You've got to try harder. This is very important."

"I *know* it's important," Emily said petulantly. "But I can only go as fast as I can. I don't think they trust me yet."

"Well, earn their trust." Mrs. Fields wrenched her hands away from the manicurist, riffled in her purse, and plunked a small box on Emily's lap. "All of us at the church pulled together to get you this so you could catch them in the act."

Emily picked up the box. It was a brand-new iPhone.

"It has video capabilities," Mrs. Fields explained.

"You want me to videotape them?" Emily asked, stunned.

"How else do you expect to document what they're doing for the police?" Mrs. Fields spread out her fingers again, and the manicurist brushed them with polish. The chemical smell filled the air.

Jingle bells sounded as a group of women sauntered into the salon. Elvis continued to croon miserably about how his baby had left him for Christmas. Emily lowered her eyes to her lap. She thought about how Cassie had pulled up a lawn chair for her at the party. How they'd all cheered when she set off the firework.

"Look, I know you don't want to do this," Mrs. Fields murmured as if reading Emily's mind. "But I'll come clean with you. The baby Jesus they stole is worth a lot of money. I was thinking of selling it and using it for Christmas gifts since your dad's bonus wasn't what we expected." She sniffed. "I just want the holiday to be special this year."

"I understand," Emily said quietly. "But what if I can't get the baby Jesus back?"

"You *can*," Mrs. Fields urged. "You have to earn their trust. Win them over. Do whatever it takes."

She spread out her finished nails on the table. Emily shifted her feet, an uneasy pain growing in her stomach. But like the good girl she'd always been, she nodded and said she'd do as she was told. The problem was, Emily still had no idea how to infiltrate Cassie's clique. If she didn't come up with something fast, though, it would be a blue, blue Christmas for everyone.

9

ANTS IN HER PANTS

An hour later, her nails freshly painted a festive red, Emily rushed to Santa Land to begin her shift, passing a huge sale at Hermès, a mob of people at the diamond counter at Tiffany & Co., and a magician's performance outside a toy drive. There was already a long line of kids waiting on the candy cane–striped walkway at Santa Land, many of whom looked tired and cranky. Mrs. Meriwether greeted her at the gingerbread house.

"Have you seen the elves?" she asked, her voice an octave higher than its normal pitch.

"Uh, I just got here," Emily reminded her.

"They're *missing*." Mrs. Meriwether glanced around frantically. "They were supposed to come in an hour ago, and it's mayhem around here!"

Then she scuttled off, muttering to herself. Emily pulled on her Santa gear, wondering if the elves were bagging work because of Cassie's party last night.

In minutes, she was on the Santa throne. A familiar girl with brown pigtails strutted up first and plopped herself on Emily's lap. Her father, a broad man with a crew cut and wearing a police uniform, appeared beside her. Emily stared at his shiny badge. O'NEAL. This was the girl who asked for every gift in the world.

"Tina liked you so much that she wanted to pay another visit, Santa." Officer O'Neal gave Emily a wink. His badge gleamed under the hot photography lights.

"I wanted to add some things to my list," Tina boasted.

She started listing off items on her fingers. Her new requests included the Barbie Townhouse, the Barbie Vacation Jet, and the Barbie Limited Edition Snow Princess. Emily wasn't sure a girl Tina's age should even *know* the term *Limited Edition*. "Don't you think that's enough?" Emily said after Tina had named about twenty items. "Santa has to make space in his bag for toys for everyone *else* in the world, too."

Tina stuck out her bottom lip. "Daddy said Santa would bring me *everything*."

Emily cast a wary glance at Officer O'Neal, but he just shrugged sheepishly. "She's been a very good girl this year."

Kids continued to move through the line. One spilled a strawberry smoothie in Emily's lap and another burst into tears. Just as a girl presented Emily with a thick letter in an envelope that said *To Santa* in shaky writing on the front, Emily finally caught sight of Cassie, Lola, Heather, and Sophie trudging down the corridor. Their elf hats were askew. Their bodysuits sagged. Cassie and Sophie hadn't bothered to put on their pointy shoes, wearing sneakers instead. Even from far away, it looked like they were nursing massive hangovers. Emily wondered how late they'd stayed up partying after she'd been shut out.

The performing magician handed Cassie a balloon flower. "You girls look like you could use a pick-me-up," he said to the elves, pushing a balloon toward each of them.

"Fuck off," Cassie deadpanned. Lola knocked the magician's hat off his head. He slunk back to his stool.

Mrs. Meriwether hurried toward the elves. "Where have you girls been?" Her face was bright red, and her hands made tight fists. "You were supposed to be here an hour ago."

The elves just stared at her, seemingly too exhausted to retort.

Mrs. Meriwether raised a hand. "I want you four to clean up the inside of the gingerbread house." She pointed toward it. "A child just vomited in there. And the bathroom toilet is filthy."

The elves opened their mouths to protest, but Mrs. Meriwether stamped her foot. "*Do* it," she said through her teeth. Even Heather cowered back.

Grumbling, the elves stomped toward the gingerbread house. "What I wouldn't *give* to not be working today," Cassie growled under her breath.

"Let's hope an asteroid hits the mall," Lola agreed.

"Or at least Santa Land," Sophie said.

"Can you bring us that for Christmas, Santa?" Heather eyed Emily, acknowledging her for the first time all day.

Emily scratched absently at the red bumps on her arm, her head swirling. *Win them over*, she heard her mother's voice say. *Do whatever it takes.* She stared at the rash on her arm, a thought congealing in her mind.

Placing the SANTA'S GONE TO FEED THE REINDEER sign on the throne, she padded down the candy cane carpet and tapped Mrs. Meriwether, who was puzzling over receipts by the register, on the shoulder. She whipped around and gave Emily a withering stare. "Don't tell me *you're* going to give me trouble now, too."

"No trouble here," Emily said. "But I did want to tell you that I just found a bug in my beard."

Mrs. Meriwether's eyebrows furrowed. "Let's see."

Emily pretended to parse through the silky hair on her chin. "I guess it crawled away."

"What did it look like?"

Emily pretended to think, then described the ticklike creature she'd read about in the newspaper a few weeks ago. "It was kind of reddish-brown? Oval-shaped? It kind of looked like a beetle, but I'm pretty sure it wasn't."

The color drained from Mrs. Meriwether's face. "Good Lord. That sounds like a bedbug."

Bingo. Emily was glad she'd gotten the description right—a department store in Philly had to be fumigated for the creatures, and there was a huge news story about it.

She feigned surprise. "You *think*? Aren't they, like, impossible to get rid of?"

"Have you taken the Santa suit out of the mall?" Mrs. Meriwether looked furious. "Have you been anywhere that might contain bedbugs?"

"Of course not." Emily crossed her arms over her chest. "I leave the Santa suit here every night. But now that you mention it, I did notice these." She rolled up her sleeves to reveal the little red bumps on the insides of her arms. They looked exactly like the bedbug bites a department store worker had shown to a news reporter on TV.

A disgusted gurgle emerged from the back of Mrs. Meriwether's throat. "Oh good heavens." She gripped her head. "There are bedbugs at Santa Land! There are bedbugs in the mall!"

Heads perked up. Whispers started. The rumor spread like wildfire, and within minutes, all the families with kids waiting to sit on Emily's lap had fled the candy cane–striped walkway. Salespeople and shoppers wandered out of Aéropostale and J. Crew and spoke in tight clusters. Everyone started scratching their arms, necks, and scalps. Parents peered carefully at their children's skin.

A security guard pulled Mrs. Meriwether aside and started talking to her. Soon after, a bunch of men in business suits emerged from a back corridor and strutted over to Santa Land. "I'm Jeffrey Allen, head of operations," one of them said, sticking out his hand for Mrs. Meriwether to shake. "Did you say you found a bedbug?"

"That's right." Mrs. Meriwether pointed to the bumps on the inside of Emily's arms.

Mr. Allen inspected the bumps carefully, and then conferred with a few of the other executives. Emily caught the words *massive fumigation* and *huge profit loss* and *maybe there's some kind of mistake.*

"Bedbugs!" a passing mother screeched.

More parents gathered around the execs, wailing that they were going to have to burn all of their clothes and that they were going to sue if their children had bites tomorrow.

"Calm down, calm down," Mr. Allen said, making a *settle down* lowering motion with his hands. "I'm calling security right now. The mall will be shut down until tomorrow so we can clean out the problem."

Minutes later, the jolly Christmas music ceased, and an announcement blared over the loudspeaker that everyone needed to evacuate the mall immediately. Stampedes of shoppers headed toward the exit. As if on cue, the elves emerged from the gingerbread house. "Did I just hear that the mall was *closing*?" Cassie asked blearily, staring at the people rushing toward the double doors.

"That's right," Mrs. Meriwether said in a perfunctory voice. "Get your things. There's a bedbug investigation."

Cassie tucked a lock of white-blond hair behind her ear. "But we still get paid for today, right?"

"I suppose," Mrs. Meriwether said begrudgingly. "But leave your uniforms here—we're going to have them specially cleaned tonight. Emily found a bedbug in her Santa beard."

All four pairs of elf eyes swiveled to Emily, and Emily winked. Lola's mouth dropped open. Heather let out an incredulous giggle. When Mrs. Meriwether turned her back, Cassie sidled over. "A bedbug in your beard, huh?"

Emily glanced around cagily. "How unlucky, right?"

"Holy shit," Cassie whispered, grabbing onto Emily's arm and giving it a squeeze. "You're *awesome!*"

"You just saved our ass, Santa," Lola gushed. "I don't think I could've made it through today. I feel like death."

Emily removed her Santa hat. "I didn't really feel like working, either."

"We should do something to celebrate our unexpected time off," Cassie said, seemingly revived. She gave the other elves a secret look. After a series of unspoken hand gestures and nods, she turned back to Emily. "And you're coming with us, Santa."

"Really?" Emily squeaked, forgetting to play it cool.

"Really." Cassie linked her arm around Emily's elbow. "You look like you could use a little fun."

She pulled Emily toward the exit with the other scratching, panicked shoppers. A few people gave Emily wary sidelong glances, probably wondering why she was smiling so broadly in the face of a bug infestation. What they didn't know wouldn't hurt them one bit.

10

TAKE IT ALL OFF, BIG BOY

"Giant Pooh and Tigger on a sleigh to your right," Cassie called out a few hours later, jutting a fingerless mitt–clad hand out the slightly rolled-down driver's-side car window. "And, Jesus, is that Eeyore as the reindeer?"

"Poor guy." Sophie took a long drag on her cigarette. Emily leaned out the window to get a better look. Sure enough, there was a bluish inflatable donkey pulling the cartoon bear and tiger on a Santa sleigh in someone's front yard. Eeyore did indeed look miserable.

Emily sank back into the backseat of Cassie's car, where she was wedged between Lola and Heather. The interior reeked of a mix of cigarette smoke, cinnamon gum, and peppermint candy canes they'd grabbed from the Santa Land wicker basket. They were driving slowly around a neighborhood in West Rosewood, ogling the ostentatious decorations, listening to music, and passing around a flask of rum. Emily felt a nervous buzz in her chest, but it wasn't because of the alcohol, which she'd tried to avoid as much as possible. It was because of the iPhone nestled in the palm of her hand. Something was going to happen tonight, she could feel it. Before leaving the spa, she'd taught herself how to use the camera function, learning which buttons to press and how to zoom in and out. But part of her wanted to toss it out the window. Or, at the very least, tuck it back into her purse.

"This is where Colin lives." Cassie pulled to a curb and parked, peering out at a large Dutch Colonial–style house set back in the trees. Christmas lights traced the roofline, and a bunch of reindeer paraded up the long front walk. The windows were dark, and it looked like there was no one home.

"Has he spoken to you since the party?" Heather asked.

"Nope." Cassie set her jaw.

Lola leaned forward. "Do you want to . . . ?" She trailed off, glancing cagily at Emily.

Cassie rubbed her chin, the blinking Christmas lights flashing across her face. "Nah," she decided. "He's not worth it." Suddenly, she perked up at something in the opposite direction. "But what is *that*?"

All of the girls followed her gaze to a house across the street. Every window blazed. A ton of cars filled the driveway, and a deep, steady bass line vibrated from within the walls. Silhouettes moved in front of the big bay window, one figure standing out among the others. Someone was gyrating wildly, shaking her hips and butt exhibitionist-style.

"Whoa." Sophie chewed on the end of one of her braids.

Cassie thrust the door open. "*This* we have to see."

She shot across the front yard. Lola, Sophie, and Heather scrambled out of the car, too. "Come on, Santa." Heather gazed at Emily over her shoulder. "You're not going to wimp out on us, are you?"

Emily didn't know what else to do but to follow the other girls up the gently sloping front yard, iPhone in hand. They came to a stop behind a large holly bush and peered through the branches. A strobe light pulsed against the windowpane. A squeal went up as the gyrating person whipped off her shirt and tossed it into the crowd. Emily couldn't make out too many details, only that the person was wearing a red Santa hat on her head.

"Do you think it's a bachelor party?" Sophie whispered.

"Maybe it's just a Christmas party with strippers," Lola suggested.

"If Colin's in there, I'll kill him," Cassie growled.

Heather squatted in the snow. "I dare you to get a picture, Cass."

Cassie stood and extracted her phone from her bag. "That's hardly a dare." She marched toward the window, her shoulders squared. A twig snapped loudly in the woods, and she froze. "Was that one of you?"

Everyone shook their heads and looked around. The sidewalk was empty. There was no one lurking near the line of cars, either. Emily peered at the house next door, her heart thumping. She swore she'd just seen something move by the deck. What if it was the cops?

"Someone's on to us." Cassie marched back to the group. She shot Emily a sharp glare, as though it were Emily's fault.

Heather sniffed. "There's no one there. You're just scared."

"Fine. *You* do it," Cassie challenged, handing Heather her phone.

Heather turned the phone over in her hands, then cocked her head as if listening for something. No twigs snapped, but there was something fraught and dangerous in the air.

Sophie leveled her eyes at Emily. "How about if Santa does it?"

Emily's heart raced. "Um. Okay."

The elves turned and stared at her. "Good for you, Santa," Cassie said gruffly. "Go for it."

The volume of the music increased the closer she got to the window. Another cheer rang out inside the house, followed by someone bellowing, "Take it all off!"

She was only a few feet from the window now. She crouched down low. Prickles from the bush grazed her skin. The wet snow seeped through the knees of her jeans. When she glanced back, she half-expected to see Cassie's car peeling away, the elves laughing hysterically, but they were still hunched by the bushes, watching.

She slithered into the overgrown bush just beneath the bay window. A figure passed just a few feet above her and she froze, holding her breath. The music shifted from a fast techno song to something brassier with lots of horns. More cheers rose up, and Emily inched her nose up the siding until she could see into the room. A ton of women crowded a large space filled with floral-upholstered sofas, Tiffany-style leaded-glass lamps, and shelves laden with old-fashioned dolls in lacy petticoats. Everyone was holding a pink cocktail and staring at the stripper, who'd now climbed up onto the raised brick fireplace and was wiggling her butt.

Only, why would a bunch of *women* watch a girl stripper? It was doubtful there were *that* many lesbians in West Rosewood. Emily's gaze returned to the figure on the fireplace, and she bit down hard on her tongue to keep from laughing. It wasn't a woman stripper. It was a *man*.

He had shed almost all of his clothes, wearing only the red Santa hat and a red G-string. The women, who all looked like soccer moms, oohed and aahed, and every so often one of them would shove a bill into the waistband of his underwear.

With shaking hands, Emily raised her phone to the window and pressed the button to take a few shots. Suddenly, the front door creaked open, the music spilling out of the house. A woman stepped onto the porch and looked around. "Is someone there?"

Emily's heart leapt into her throat. She shoved the

phone back into her pocket and took off down the yard. "Hey!" the woman cried, but Emily kept going. The elves followed, and they all piled into Cassie's car, giggling hysterically.

"Drive!" Emily cried, glancing at the woman, who was now halfway down the walk.

Cassie screeched out of the neighborhood. Only when they were on Lancaster Avenue again did Emily's heart start to slow down. In a strange way, that had been exhilarating. She felt like a felon.

"Did you get any shots, Santa?" Heather asked.

Lola snorted. "I bet she didn't."

Emily passed the phone to Heather. Heather's eyebrows shot up as she clicked through the pictures. "The stripper was a *guy*?"

Sophie grabbed the phone. "Oh my God, that is the lamest thing I've ever seen."

"Does anyone know who he is?" Lola stared at the pictures, too. "I bet his wife doesn't know he's doing this."

Cassie pulled over so she could get a look at the pictures, then doubled over, laughing. "You rock, Santa. All this time we thought you were a narc. I guess we were wrong."

Sophie ran her tongue over her teeth. "Maybe we should even let her into . . . *you* know."

"I think that could be arranged." Cassie's eyes swept over the group. "Are we all in?"

"I am." Heather raised a hand.

"Me, too," Sophie said. Lola shrugged and said she supposed she was, too.

Cassie stuck her hand out for Emily to shake. "Congratulations, Santa. Welcome."

"Welcome to what, exactly?" Emily asked, even though she was afraid she knew exactly what the elves meant.

"You'll see," Cassie teased, pulling the car back into traffic and making a sharp left turn at a light. The other elves grinned at Emily like she'd just won the jackpot—and in some ways, she had.

But a part of her also felt grosser than the male stripper's Santa hat. *All this time we thought you were a narc.* She winced at the thought of Cassie and the others finding out how right they were about her.

Maybe she should just come clean. But if she did, the elves would never speak to her again. And suddenly, something became clear in Emily's mind: She *wanted* the elves to speak to her again. She wanted to be their friend—for real. For three long years, she'd longed for another clique to be part of, another group of friends to confide in. She had her old friends, sure, but it had never felt the same as it used to. And maybe the elves were wayward and a little bit crazy, but they were fun and loyal.

Emily dropped her phone in her purse. Forget saving her mom's baby Jesus. She was going to the dark side.

11

THE TRUE MEANING OF CHRISTMAS

"Hey, Santa!" Cassie's voice rang out just as Emily was changing out of her Santa suit the next day. She poked her head inside the gingerbread house. "Want to grab some food with me?"

"Uh, sure," Emily answered, kicking the ugly Santa boots off her feet. They had a slight chemical smell from the anti-bedbug treatments absolutely everything in the mall had been sprayed with. All kinds of signs hung around the mall, saying things like BEDBUG FREE! and TREATED WITH ENVIRONMENTALLY FRIENDLY CHEMICALS! Still, even though the mall had been cleansed of bedbugs—not that there had ever been any to begin with—the lines at Santa Land had been thin today. There had been only a smattering of people wandering the promenade as well, quite a few of them suspiciously scratching their heads and necks.

Emily emerged from the gingerbread house just as Mrs. Meriwether was locking up the big Frosty and Rudolph statues so no one would steal them. Cassie was waiting by the gate; she had changed into a pair of black jeans, a faded black AC/DC T-shirt, and red, thick-soled John Fluevogs. It all made her newly blond hair look even whiter.

"Where are the others?" Emily asked, looking around.

Cassie shrugged. "Is Bellissima okay?"

"That's fine," Emily answered, feeling pleasantly surprised that Cassie wanted to hang out with her alone.

As Emily let herself out of the gate, she glanced over her shoulder. Luckily Mrs. Meriwether was still occupied with Rudolph and didn't notice that Emily was hanging out with Cassie. Emily couldn't tell her and her mother that she was giving up spying. Hopefully, in a week or so, she'd just say she hadn't been invited along on any of their pranks. It would look like she'd tried and failed instead of deliberately giving up.

As for the baby Jesus paying for Christmas gifts, well, Emily had some thoughts about that, too. She'd received her first Santa Land paycheck yesterday and was astonished to see that Santa paid fifteen dollars an hour—way more than she would have made in another random holiday job. If her family was really hurting for cash this Christmas, she would hand over her earnings to her mom for gifts.

Bellissima, a little Italian bistro, was at the far end of the corridor. Crooning, romantic music—a nice change from Christmas carols—played over the speakers, and the inside of the restaurant featured lots of terra-cotta tile, roughly plastered, goldenrod-colored walls, and little tables covered with black-and-white checked cloths. Unlike the rest of the mall, Bellissima was filled with diners and patrons at the bar. Maybe people didn't think bedbugs could infiltrate restaurants.

A petite waitress with a high ponytail led the girls to a table in the corner and poured them glasses of sparkling water. "I'm probably just going to get a salad," Cassie said, opening the big laminated menu.

"Oh, me, too," Emily said, even though she wasn't the type of girl who ordered salads at restaurants.

They sat for a moment, studying the menu, and then Cassie tapped her lip. "Although the cannolis look really good, too."

"Ooh, let's get them instead," Emily squealed.

"*Whew.*" Cassie pressed a hand on her chest. "I was afraid you were one of those obsessive dieter types."

"Me?" Emily held back a laugh. "Um, definitely not."

The girls gave their orders, and the waitress swished away. Emily gazed around the restaurant, recognizing a few people she knew from school. Mason Byers and Lanie Iler sat in a corner booth, sipping Italian sodas. Kirsten Cullen and her family were eating bowls of pasta.

"So did you have fun last night?" Cassie swirled the ice around the water glass with her straw.

"Definitely," Emily admitted. "Those pictures of Stripper Santa were priceless."

"Totally." Cassie grinned.

"So how long have you known the other girls, anyway?" Emily asked. "Have you guys been friends for a long time?"

Cassie cast her eyes to the right, thinking. "We met last year—we were elves at the Santa Land at the White Birch Mall, which Sophie's dad used to manage, and decided to do it again this year. It's kind of a big joke between us. But we didn't go to the same high schools or anything. I went to Rosewood Day."

"I go there, too," Emily blurted.

A small smile appeared on Cassie's face. "I know you do. You were friends with Alison DiLaurentis, weren't you?"

Emily pressed her lips together. Just hearing Ali's name made her heart beat faster.

"I made the connection at my party," Cassie explained. "I remember you. I used to play field hockey with Ali on the JV team at Rosewood Day. She was really good."

"I remember you, too." Emily fiddled with the cloth napkin on her lap. "Ali thought you were awesome. She used to talk about you all the time."

Cassie pressed her tongue between her teeth, seeming a little embarrassed by this. "We had fun together. Ali was definitely mature beyond her years—all of us said so. We couldn't believe she was in seventh grade." She twisted a thick leather bracelet around her wrist. "I couldn't believe it when I found out about what Ian had done to her. He was a grade ahead of me. I only knew him by sight, but he always seemed so *nice* to everyone. Not the kind of guy who would . . . you know. But what kind of freak dates a seventh grader as a senior? That's just . . . wrong."

"I know." Emily's eyes inadvertently filled with tears. She wanted to claim it was the strong odor of Italian spices wafting in the air, tickling her nostrils, but she knew it wasn't true.

"She used to talk about you, you know," Cassie said.

Emily lifted her head. "Really?"

"Uh-huh. She said you were her favorite of all her friends. You guys had a special bond."

"We did," Emily said, her cheeks warming. "I miss her so much."

"I do, too." Cassie placed her hand over Emily's. "I've changed so much since Ali went missing."

A buzzer sounded from the kitchen. A group of women at a nearby table broke into a peal of laughter. Emily blotted her eyes with a napkin and peeked at Cassie's blond hair, heavily lined eyes, and the multiple piercings in her ears. Was it possible Ali's disappearance had made Cassie drop her perfect, preppy image and turn into a bad girl? It certainly had made Emily rethink a lot of things.

"I've never had another friend like Ali," Emily admitted. "Even though she could be mean, I would have done *anything* for her."

The waitress appeared with two cannolis, and Emily and Cassie dove into them at once. Cream oozed onto the plate as Emily cut into the pastry with her fork. "This is frickin' *delicious*," Cassie murmured.

"Much better than a salad," Emily said.

Then Cassie laid down her fork, leaned forward on her elbows, and gave Emily a serious look. "So listen. We've had a lot of fun with you, Santa. At first we weren't sure about you—it was so weird that Mrs. Meriwether brought in a girl to be Santa, and she kept whispering around you, and we were sure there was something weird going on. But you've proved us wrong. So we want to invite you somewhere very special tonight."

Emily almost choked on her bite of cannoli. Her heart began to hammer. A tiny voice inside of her pleaded, *Don't let it be a pranking mission. Anything but that.*

Cassie licked a bit of cream off her spoon. "Have you heard the stories about someone in Rosewood messing with people's Christmas decorations?"

Emily's heart sank. "I guess so."

"Well, that's us." Cassie thumbed her chest proudly. "Me, Lola, Sophie, and Heather. We call ourselves the Merry Elves. And tonight, we're going to pull our biggest prank yet." She scootched forward into her chair, her voice dropping to a whisper. "We're going to steal all the presents under the big tree at the Rosewood Country Club. All of the decorations, too. It's perfect timing, because tomorrow morning is the annual brunch where everyone opens their gifts. It's going to be just like *How the Grinch Stole Christmas!* Let's see if the snotty rich people gather around the tree when it's bare." She rolled her eyes. "Anyway, we'd like for you to help."

Emily kept her gaze trained on her half-eaten cannoli. "I don't know how I feel about stealing."

"Oh, we're not stealing the stuff." Cassie waved her fork in the air. "We're just moving it to the tennis courts. They can move it back the next day. It's just to mess with them. Screw with their perspective. It's like how, a couple of weeks ago, we stole this baby Jesus from the Nativity scene in front of a church. We wanted people to see the empty cradle in the manger and really *think* about things— what the holidays mean, what the symbols mean." She paused. "It was also really funny. Heather had to ride in the car with the Jesus on her lap. She kept screaming about how it was bad karma and that God was going to strike her down."

It took all of Emily's willpower not to tell Cassie that it was her mother's baby Jesus she was talking about. On the bright side, it didn't sound like Cassie and the others had smashed the baby Jesus to pieces. "So the pranks aren't about ruining people's holidays?" she asked timidly.

Cassie popped the last bite of cannoli into her mouth. "Not necessarily. It's more to draw attention to the commercialism of it. All good pranksters have a point to their actions. I mean, we're not complete thugs." She touched Emily's hand. "We'll have so much fun, I promise. Think of it as a Christmas crusade."

The bites of cannoli churned in Emily's stomach, and she stared out at the mall's promenade, with its massive Christmas tree and millions of shops. Maybe Cassie had a point. She thought about the line of kids at Santa Land, all of them asking for way too many things, and their parents nodding encouragingly. And there were all those stories on the news of shoppers tackling one another to get the last hot toy at Target or Walmart. All those commercials that made you feel terrible if you didn't buy your beloved a diamond ring or a Lexus or an It bag for Christmas. Even her mother's desperation to get the baby Jesus back: She was going to sell it in order to buy Christmas presents so she could turn this Christmas into, yet again, the best Christmas ever. Did it really matter when they had the most important thing: a healthy, happy family that was spending the holiday together?

Her fork dropped to her plate with a loud, clear clang. "Okay," she decided. "I'm in. Let's do it."

12

ALL THE WHOS DOWN IN WHOVILLE

"Should we have our usual turkey for Christmas dinner or try something else, like steak?" Mrs. Fields asked as she spooned squares of lasagna onto her children's plates that night for dinner. "Or how about if we went out for dinner this Christmas Eve? That would be special, wouldn't it?"

"I'm not sure we should be spending money on extravagant restaurants," Mr. Fields said as he filled the water glasses at the fridge.

"It's only once a year," Mrs. Fields interrupted, thrusting her chin into the air. "And anyway, I think we'll find a way to afford it."

She raised her eyebrows at Emily, but Emily kept her gaze trained on her empty plate. In one hour, she would be joining the elves on their pranking mission—but not as a narc.

Mrs. Fields launched into the regular family prayer, and everyone started to eat. "We'll have to decide about

Christmas Eve dinner soon," Mrs. Fields said as she spooned some green beans onto her plate, picking up on the topic again. "All of the restaurants probably book up fast."

"I vote for Ruth's Chris Steak House." Jake stabbed a piece of lasagna.

"*Uch*, that place is so boring." Beth bit off a piece of a roll. "Let's go somewhere nicer. Like somewhere in the city, maybe."

"I'm fine with Applebee's," Carolyn said meekly, always the sensible girl.

They argued about this for the rest of the dinner. Emily didn't dare contribute a word, feeling like a pent-up volcano ready to blow. Finally, fearing she was going to blurt out everything if she sat at the table for another minute, she rose from her seat. "Uh, I have to go to the library. I have a ton of homework."

"On a Tuesday night before the break?" Beth looked surprised. "Rosewood Day is working you hard."

"Uh, it's a last-minute test," Emily fumbled, carrying her plate to the sink.

Mrs. Fields rose too and caught her arm. "You hardly ate any of your dinner." Her eyes were wide and concerned. "Is everything okay?"

Emily kept her eyes locked on the chicken-printed trivet sitting next to the stove. "I'm fine," she mumbled, placing her plate on the counter. "See you later."

As she walked into the living room, she could feel her

mother's gaze on her back. *Don't turn around*, she silently willed. She made herself think about lyrics to Christmas songs instead, though the only one that rattled through her mind was "You're a Mean One, Mr. Grinch." Only when she reached the stairs did she glance over her shoulder again. When she did, her mother had turned away, like she didn't suspect a thing.

"Don't drive us into a ditch!" Heather cried as Cassie steered her car onto the side of a dark, secluded road that paralleled the Rosewood Country Club. The car pitched to the side, definitely off-balance, and Emily, Sophie, and Lola, who were riding in the back, squished together against the door.

"I know what I'm doing." Cassie jammed the gear into park and shut off the engine. When the headlights clicked off, darkness descended around them. A faint light glowed over the hills of the golf course, but otherwise, Emily couldn't see a foot in front of her face.

Cassie rummaged around the front seat, pulled out a flashlight, and snapped it on. Everyone squinted when the golden light beamed in their eyes. "Okay, bitches. We ready?"

"Totally," Lola whispered, pulling a black ski cap over her head. The other girls followed, Emily along with them. Then they climbed up the hill. Every nerve in Emily's body felt electrified. There was a sour taste in her mouth, and her stomach rumbled from the few bites of lasagna she'd eaten at dinner. She'd had to hide her hands under her butt the whole drive over so the elves wouldn't see how badly she was shaking.

Cassie's flashlight made golden crisscross stripes across the golf course. The girls darted over the green, circumnavigating the giant man-made pond and a couple of amoeba-shaped sand traps. Every few steps, Emily looked behind her, sure someone was following them. The rounded hills loomed in the distance, dark silhouettes against the purplish sky. She didn't see a soul.

The lights of the clubhouse glimmered on the horizon. Dread filled Emily as she took in the long windows and the stone façade. This had been the place where Mona Vanderwaal had held a party for Hanna after her car accident—the one that *Mona* had caused. And it was at this very party that Hanna realized that Mona was A—and that Mona wanted to kill them.

The girls looped around the country club until they found a back entrance to the kitchen. "*Voilà*," Lola whispered, pulling out a key on a Philadelphia Eagles ring, which she'd procured from a friend who worked in the kitchen earlier that day. The key twisted in the lock, and the door creaked open. Emily braced herself for alarms to sound, but none did.

They flipped on the kitchen lights, and Emily shaded her eyes. The pots and pans were neatly put away, the stainless-steel countertops gleamed, and a long spray nozzle dangled limply in the sink.

"Come on," Cassie hissed, tiptoeing toward a swinging door to the right. She pushed it open with her shoulder to reveal the dining room Emily had eaten in countless times with Ali's and Spencer's families. Thirty or so round tables with heavy wood chairs were scattered around the room. An Oriental rug stretched across the floor, and an oak bar took up the whole back wall. An enormous Christmas tree stood in the corner, its lights still blazing, tons of wrapped presents waiting underneath.

The elves got to work quickly, ripping off the glass orbs and strings of popcorn on the tree and placing everything into a bunch of cardboard boxes Cassie had dragged out from the kitchen. Emily helped Lola load the presents into a wheelbarrow Lola's kitchen friend had placed just outside the door for them, every once in a while examining the labels peeking out beneath the ribbons. She found a box for the Hastings family. There was another one for the Kahns and James Freed's parents. A fourth tag caught her eye, and she nearly gasped. THE DILAURENTIS FAMILY, the label said. Emily had heard rumors about Ali's family moving back here; they'd even been in the audience at Ian's arraignment. Had they already arrived?

Soon enough, Emily and Lola were wheeling a full load to the tennis courts up the hill. "Isn't this awesome, Santa?" Lola giggled.

"Definitely," Emily said, but it felt like a bomb was about to go off in her chest. The darkness was playing tricks on her. A bush seemed to scuttle to the left. The wind sounded like a high-pitched giggle.

They dumped the presents onto the ground next to the net and clumsily guided the wheelbarrow back to the clubhouse. Emily worked furiously with Cassie and Heather to pull the ornaments off the Christmas tree. They grabbed glass orb after glass orb, along with a mix of silver and gold stars. Emily tried to wrap them carefully in napkins, but the other girls threw them hastily into the wheelbarrow. Then the girls pulled down all the wreaths, garlands, and strings of mistletoe around the room, stuffing them into the wheelbarrow, too. Just before the last load went out, Cassie directed the girls to stand together in front of the stripped Christmas tree for a photo. "Say *Bah Humbug!*" Cassie squealed, setting the auto-timer feature on her digital camera and jumping into the picture, too. She took pictures with all the girls' phones, including Emily's.

Then they stood back and stared at their handiwork. "It's *awesome*," Cassie breathed.

Emily wasn't sure the effect was awesome, but it was definitely striking. The tree looked scrawny without any adornments. A bunch of needles had scattered all over the floor, and there were dusty spots from where the presents had been. Without the festive wreaths, candles, and tinsel garland decorations, the dining room seemed a bit shabby and sad, just like what the houses in Whoville looked like after the Grinch had stolen all of their decorations. What would the country club proprietors do when they found the place like this at brunch tomorrow morning? Sing peacefully around the tree, like the Whos did? *Right.* This was the Rosewood Country Club.

They hefted the door open once more and pushed the wheelbarrow out into the cold. The cart was especially full this time, and it took all five of them to push the thing up the hill. Every creak of the wheels, every elf giggle, made Emily tense. They were so close now. She didn't want someone hearing them.

They made it to the tennis courts, dumped the rest of the gifts, and ditched the wheelbarrow without incident. The elves started over the hilly golf course to the car. And that was when Emily realized: They had done it. They were running to *freedom.*

Emily's heart lifted as she ran after them. Never before had she felt so exhilarated in her life. She grabbed Cassie's hand and let out an excited whoop, and Cassie whooped back.

"Long live the Merry Elves!" Heather hollered.

When the floodlights snapped on, Emily thought it was just an automatic timer and kept running. But then a bullhorn sounded through the crisp winter night. "Down on the ground! We see you girls! The police are here! They've already surrounded your car! There's nowhere to go!"

Emily froze. All of a sudden, blue and red lights flashed over the bluffs. Her heart dropped to her feet. "No," she whispered.

"I said, down on the ground!" a second voice said.

Both voices were familiar. Emily turned toward them. Two figures in heavy winter coats stood by the tennis courts, staring squarely at Emily, Cassie, and the others. One of the figures was tall with graying hair. The other wore a felt jacket with a varsity letter *R* on the front. Even though Emily hadn't seen the back, she knew intuitively it would say ROSEWOOD SWIMMING in big blue letters. It had been Jake's old jacket when he swam varsity for Rosewood; now it served as the all-purpose coat for anyone in the Fields family when they were doing dirty work outside–shoveling snow, digging in mud, or climbing up and down the hills of a golf course, tracking down vandals.

Emily's mouth fell open. The first figure was Mrs. Meriwether. The second figure was her mom.

13

A MOLE AMONG US

"Down on the ground!" Mrs. Fields bellowed again through the bullhorn.

Slowly, the elves dropped to their knees and put their hands up. Emily did the same. Mrs. Meriwether and Emily's mother barreled up the ledge like FBI agents on a drug raid and surrounded them.

Mrs. Fields grabbed Cassie's arm and pulled her to her feet again. "You think you're so clever," she hissed in a gruff voice Emily had never heard from her before. "Your pranking days are over."

"We've got the whole thing recorded." Mrs. Meriwether held up a digital camera. "A good half hour of footage of you ravaging that Christmas tree and taking away all of the presents. Don't you know some of those gifts go to children? You should be ashamed of yourselves!"

"We didn't get *rid* of the presents," Cassie spat, squirming. "They're on the tennis courts! Don't you see?

The country club owners can just put everything back tomorrow!"

"It's vandalism of private property." Mrs. Fields held fast on to Cassie's arm. "It's a very sad thing that you girls don't understand how wrong that is."

A police officer in a West Rosewood PD uniform bounded over the hill from the opposite direction, his flashlight shining and walkie-talkie squeaking. Emily stared at him. It was Officer O'Neal, the same guy who'd brought his daughter to Santa Land a couple of times, promising her every gift imaginable.

"These are the girls who've been causing so much trouble?" O'Neal jogged to Mrs. Fields, took Cassie from her, and pinned Cassie's arms behind her back. Cassie let out a whimper and went still.

"That's right," Mrs. Meriwether piped up. "They broke into the country club. These are also the girls who vandalized all the other properties. The Sign of the Dove Church. All the front lawns. They've been causing mayhem for weeks."

The cop looked the elves up and down and shook his head. "Come on, ladies," O'Neal said, corralling the girls toward the SUVs. The elves trudged off with their heads down, not saying a word. Emily began to follow them, not daring to look at her mother.

Mrs. Fields grabbed her sleeve. "What are you doing, Emily? You can come home with us."

Emily winced. The elves whipped around and stared

at Emily and her mother. "Wait. How do you know her name?" Heather asked.

"Why does she get to go home?" Sophie piped up.

"She stole the stuff right along with us," Lola spat.

Mrs. Meriwether shifted her weight. Emily's mother smiled smugly. Emily saw the realization slowly strike each girl.

"Holy shit," Sophie whispered.

"I told you!" Lola screamed. She jammed a finger at Emily. "I told you guys she was a narc! I could just tell the day she showed up as Santa! But you didn't listen!"

Heather spat in Emily's direction, which got her a cuff on the arm from one of the cops. Cassie glared at Emily with blazing eyes. "Is it true?" she said in a low, disappointed voice. "Did you set us up?"

Emily shook her head desperately. "I didn't say a word about this prank to anyone. Honest." She turned to her mother, who was now leaning against the Volvo wagon with her arms crossed. "How did you know we were going to be here?"

"We tracked your iPhone." Mrs. Fields looked proud of herself. "Officer O'Neal suggested it. I suspected something was up tonight, so I called Judith and Officer O'Neal and we followed you."

Emily thought of the iPhone still nestled in her bag. "You were spying on me . . . spying on them?" she sounded out.

"You were carrying that around to spy on us?" Cassie shrieked.

"It wasn't like that!" Emily pleaded. "I mean, yeah, they gave me an iPhone, but I never used it on you guys! I swear! You know me, Cassie! Why would I do something like that?"

Cassie made an incredulous face. "Actually, Santa, I'm not sure I know you at all."

"Cassie . . ." Tears rolled down Emily's cheeks. "I'm sorry."

"Oh, Emily, what do you care what these brats think of you?" Mrs. Fields yanked the car door open. "They deserve a strict punishment, and you helped us catch them in the act. Maybe we'll even get my baby Jesus back."

Suddenly, Emily thought she might explode. "Do you even care about your baby Jesus?" she bellowed at her mother. "You're just going to sell it to buy stupid Christmas presents for everyone, gifts we probably won't even remember next year! Why do you care so much about making the holiday picture-perfect? Why isn't what we have right now enough?"

The words had flowed out of her mouth before she'd taken the time to think them through. Mrs. Fields stiffened and a hurt look crossed her face. Without saying a word, she marched around the car to the driver's side, climbed in, and slammed the door shut.

The policeman pushed the elves into his squad car one by one. Just before O'Neal guided Cassie into the vehicle, Cassie swiveled around once more and gave Emily a seething stare. "Ali would hate you for this, you know."

A tiny whimper escaped from Emily's mouth. O'Neal slammed the cruiser door shut. The engine growled, and the car pulled away, sirens blaring. Emily didn't move from her spot on the golf course until she could no longer see the lights or hear the sirens. It was only then that it hit her for real: She was alone again. She had no one.

14

SANTA TO THE RESCUE

Later that night, Emily slipped out the front door, locked up, and pushed the Volvo down the driveway so her parents wouldn't hear the engine start. She wasn't supposed to be out this late, but she couldn't lie in her bed for a second longer, listening to Carolyn snore and seeing Cassie's wounded face in her mind again and again.

A light snow had begun to fall, dusting the streets, the rooftops, and the tree branches. She passed Rosewood Day, which was all lit up with lights around its stone perimeter, and then the turnoff to Ali's street. But she didn't feel like stopping by Ali's house tonight. She felt too ashamed about what she'd done. It was almost like she was accountable to Ali, like Ali was watching her from beyond the grave.

Emily couldn't get Cassie's words out of her mind. *Ali would hate you for this.* It was absolutely true: Ali might have teased the four of them, she might have been growing apart from them at the end of seventh grade, but she never deliberately sold them out. The five of them had always had a pact, covering for one another when they got in trouble. It was why Emily, Aria, Spencer, and Hanna had told Ali's parents all kinds of stories about where Ali might have been the morning after she'd vanished. They'd figured Ali would have wanted them to. Never in their wildest dreams had they thought she was dead.

Emily merged onto the bypass and followed the signs for West Rosewood. So what kind of person had she become now? Had she known, deep down, that her mom and Mrs. Meriwether were tracking her? Had she willingly led them right to the girls? She should have told Cassie and the others exactly what her mom was making her do. Even if it meant she wouldn't have come along on the prank, even if it meant they wouldn't have welcomed her into their clique, she would have extricated herself from the situation. But as it was, she just looked like a conspirator. A traitor. A narc.

The green sign for the exit for West Rosewood glowed in the distance. Emily hit the blinker and turned onto the off-ramp. Soon enough, she was pulling up to the West Rosewood police station, which she'd Google-mapped before she left home. It was in an old farmhouse. A bunch of squad cars sat in the parking lot, and a single light glowed in one of the ground-floor windows.

The elves were being held in the jail inside. If only there was something Emily could do, some way she could get them out. But how? Claim that she was the master-mind of the operation? Volunteer that she'd broken into the country club and stolen all that stuff herself? Her mother and Mrs. Meriwether had captured all of it on camera. The elves definitely looked guilty.

She pulled out her phone and looked at the picture of herself and the elves gathered around the barren Christmas tree inside the country club. Cassie had her arm slung around Emily's like they were best friends. She clicked through the other photos she'd taken of the elves that week. Lola and Emily staging a sword fight with two long candy canes at Santa Land that afternoon. Cassie and Emily lounging in the gingerbread house on a break. There was a shot of the girls in the car after they'd spied on Stripper Santa. And then the photos of Stripper Santa himself, waving a T-shirt in the air, the housewives stuffing bills into his G-string.

All this time we thought you were a narc, Cassie had said that night. *I guess we were wrong.*

The door to the precinct opened, and Emily slid down in the driver's seat. A uniformed cop strolled out of the station, lit a cigarette, and leaned against the brick wall. As he moved into profile, Emily realized it was Officer O'Neal. He shut his eyes as he took long drag after long drag, looking completely content, maybe even proud. It was probably a big win to capture the Merry Elves. Maybe he'd even get a bonus for this—maybe *that* was how he was going to pay for his daughter's ever-growing Christmas list. How else was he going to buy all those toys on a cop's salary?

A light flickered on in her head. She studied the smoking figure for a minute longer. There was something familiar about him, the shape of his broad shoulders, the jutting contours of his chin. Underneath his uniform, Emily was almost positive he had washboard abs and a broad, well-defined chest.

She fumbled for her phone again and called up the Stripper Santa photos. She looked at O'Neal once more, squinting hard. She looked from photo to cop until she was absolutely sure. "Oh my God," she whispered, lowering the phone to her lap and starting to giggle.

Stripper Santa was . . . *Officer O'Neal.*

15

A CHRISTMAS MIRACLE

Emily leapt out of the car and bounced toward Officer O'Neal. "I need to talk to you!"

O'Neal squinted at her. "Who's there?"

Emily stopped next to him on the slate path. Snow spiraled around them. An ashtray filled with cigarette butts stood to their left, the burning ember from O'Neal's cigarette right on top. "I'm Emily Fields," she answered. "I was at the country club."

"Oh, right!" O'Neal grinned. "You're the girl who led us to them. Good job—they didn't know what hit them."

"Actually, I didn't help bust them. In fact, I think you should let the elves go."

O'Neal stared at her blankly. "Excuse me?"

"You heard me. Let them walk. They've learned their lesson."

He drew up to his full height and barked out a laugh. "That's a good one, Miss Fields. But I've already started their paperwork. They're of age, you know. They might be facing jail time. Or at least some pretty strict community service."

"They weren't doing anything wrong," Emily said. "Well, okay. They shouldn't have broken into the country club and messed with private property. But they were just trying to send a message. They weren't looking to hurt anyone."

O'Neal crossed his arms over his chest and studied her. A few flakes of snow fell on the tip of his nose, but he didn't wipe them away. "I don't know why *you* care. They stole your family's property, too. They confessed to everything."

Then he turned on his heel and headed back into the station. "Wait!" Emily cried, pulling out her phone. "There's something you need to see."

She pressed the phone into his hands. When he looked down at the picture, the color drained from his face. "Where the hell did you get this?"

"Does it matter?" Emily snatched the phone away from him before he could delete the image. "But I don't think you want this getting around."

O'Neal's eyes grew very wide. He seemed to shrink back a little. "You wouldn't."

"Believe me, I don't want to." Emily stepped a little closer. By the frightened look in O'Neal's eyes, she knew she had him.

"What do you want me to do?" O'Neal asked in a defeated voice.

"Strike the elves' confession from the record," Emily said, thinking quickly. "Give them a slap on the wrist for breaking into the country club, make them go back there and return everything to where it belongs, but say you have no evidence about the other pranks and can't charge them. Let them go free."

O'Neal's nostrils flared. "So you want me to lie?"

"No . . . just selectively forget. Make the elves take back everything they stole—that should placate the victims, right? Just make it go away. Oh, and you don't need to tell my mom about my coming here, either. Or else . . ." She rocked the phone back and forth in the air, the photo of O'Neal in his Stripper Santa outfit still on the screen.

O'Neal stared off into the parking lot, chewing on the inside of his cheek. Emily's heart thudded against her ribs, wondering what she'd gotten into—she was basically blackmailing a cop. She glanced around the parking lot, suddenly certain someone was watching. A shadow fluttered behind one of the parked cruisers. The tiniest sigh sounded from next to a row of dumpsters.

"Fine." O'Neal threw up his hands. "I suppose I can make that happen." He shook a finger in Emily's face. "But if anything else goes missing in Rosewood—even something as small as a lightbulb from an outdoor lighting arrangement—I'm coming to you for answers, got it? *And* I'm telling your mother everything."

"Understood," Emily said.

She held out her hand, and O'Neal shook it. Just

before he went back inside, she called out, "One more thing. Don't tell the elves I negotiated their release."

O'Neal raised an eyebrow. "Don't you want them to thank you? They're rich girls. They could probably buy you an amazing present."

Emily stared off at the dusting of snow that now covered the parking lot. An amazing present wasn't the same as being part of the elves' clique . . . and she would never be welcome in their group again. In their eyes, she would always be a traitor, a girl they didn't want to know. This could just be her anonymous Christmas gift to them—her way to make up for what she did. She shook her head.

O'Neal slipped back inside. Emily stood by the window and watched him traverse the lobby, pull a couple of papers from his desk, tear them up, and shoot them through the large shredder in the corner of the room. After he was finished, he ambled over to a holding cell and tapped on the bars. Four figures appeared. Cassie, Lola, Heather, and Sophie were still wearing the thick down coats they'd had on at the country club. Their hair was matted, and their eyes and noses were red as though they'd been crying.

The snow was making a fine layer on Emily's eyelashes, but she didn't blink, not wanting to miss a moment. O'Neal said a few words to the girls, then fished in his pocket for a set of keys. He opened the jail cell and stood aside so the girls could file out. They stared at him skeptically, and then smiles bloomed on their faces. But for once, the smiles weren't wry or self-assured or mischie-vous. They were smiles of gratitude. Relief.

Emily backed away from the window, feeling like everything was right with the world again. She slid silently into her car, started the engine, and reversed out of the parking space. By the time O'Neal escorted the elves to a cruiser in the parking lot, Emily was long gone—they would never know it was her who set them free. But their grateful smiles were reward enough.

16

THE WHOLE WORLD WAS AT PEACE

The following afternoon, Emily was in the kitchen, rolling out a long log of flour to make Christmas sugar cookies. It was her favorite Christmas tradition, mostly because she loved licking the sugary frosting off the beaters. This was the first available time she had to do it—playing Santa had taken up a lot of her time. Mrs. Meriwether had called this morning, though, and said that Emily no longer had to report to Santa Land for duty—she had found a suitable Santa replacement and was letting Emily off as a thank-you.

Emily was surprised to realize she was disappointed to not be going back. She'd ended up really enjoying being Santa.

Someone coughed behind her. Emily's mother loomed in the doorway, her hands clasped at her waist. She glanced at the empty trays of cookie sheets Emily had ready next to the oven.

"Want to help?" Emily asked, avoiding eye contact. She and her mom hadn't really spoken since Emily had lashed out at her in front of everyone at the sting last night. Emily knew she should apologize, but she didn't really know what to say. She'd meant every word. Why should she take it back?

Mrs. Fields didn't answer, settling stiffly into a kitchen chair and making a big deal out of examining a loose thread on one of the place mats, which was printed with a chicken wearing a holly wreath on its head. Emily rolled out the dough, feeling more and more uncomfortable.

Finally, her mother let out a sigh. "You were right, you know."

Emily's head whipped up. "Pardon?"

"What you said last night about the baby Jesus." Her mother chewed on a thumbnail. "Maybe I *have* lost sight of things. Maybe it was crazy to want the baby Jesus back just so I could sell it to buy gifts. It's just . . . I wanted Christmas to be extra-special this year. Because of everything we've all been through. Because of you and that A girl. Because of Alison."

When she looked up, her eyes were wet, which made Emily tear up, too. "I know how much she meant to you," Mrs. Fields said in a choked voice. "I know how hard it's been to accept she was . . ." She trailed off, not daring to say the word *murdered*. "And the thought that it was someone we knew, someone so close to all you girls . . . I couldn't bear the idea that it could have been you instead.

Your dad and I are just so grateful that you're here. I just wanted to make sure you knew that."

Emily moved from the counter to the seat next to her mother and placed her hand lightly on her wrist. "I don't need a ton of gifts to understand that," she said gently. "All you have to do is *say* it."

"I know." Mrs. Fields rested her head on Emily's shoulder. Emily shut her eyes and thought about how Ali's murder must have affected every parent in Rosewood. It had probably been terrifying for them. But in other ways, maybe Ali's death could bring parents and kids closer. Maybe it could help those who were still alive.

"I'm sorry I got you into that Santa mess," Mrs. Fields murmured. "I shouldn't have put you in that position."

"Actually I'm glad you did," Emily muttered, suddenly feeling drained. "It was kind of fun. And even though you won't believe this, they *were* nice girls."

She wondered what the elves were doing right now—Mrs. Meriwether had mentioned that she had also found all new elves for Santa Land, too. Were they lounging at home right now? Trying to connect with their distant and disjointed families? Suddenly, Emily felt a little sorry for them. Their problems were larger than life. Sophie was flunking out of Yale. Lola's brother was an addict. They still had to find a way to deal with all of those things.

Her mother blotted her tears with a napkin, stood, and shuffled out of the room with her head down, just like she always did when she'd shown a little too much emotion.

Emily returned to her Christmas cookies, feeling a lot better. When the doorbell rang a few minutes later, she wiped her hands on a dish towel and padded through the living room to answer it. Four shadowy heads shifted back and forth through the sidelight. Emily drew in a breath—the elves.

Swallowing hard, she pulled open the door, making the jingle bells on the knob rattle. The four girls on the porch eyed her. None of them were smiling. Emily's heart began to thud in her chest.

"We know what you did," Cassie said in a wooden voice.

Emily's throat felt dry. "I *know* you know," she said. "But it wasn't like that. I really wasn't part of the sting. I swear."

The four girls continued to glare. Emily was sure they could hear her galloping heart. She was about to apologize again, but then Cassie burst out laughing, lunged forward, and wrapped Emily in a huge hug. Heather circled her arms around Emily, and then Lola and Sophie joined in, too. Emily remained stiff for a few moments, and then tentatively squeezed back.

"We know it was you who got us free," Cassie said. "We saw you through the window talking to O'Neal. But how did you do it?"

Emily pulled away and blinked hard. So much for remaining anonymous. "He was the stripper we saw in the window that night," she said shakily. "I had pictures."

The elves exchanged a glance, and then all of them gave her high fives. "You're a badass, Santa," Heather said. "O'Neal let us out without even a fine. The only thing we had to do was clean up the country club this morning and put the gifts back under the tree."

"I'm really sorry about what happened." Emily leaned against the siding of her house. "I swear I didn't know my mother was following us. I had no idea she'd tracked us through my phone. I did initially get the Santa job to spy on you guys—you were right. But I gave that up soon after I met you. I'm not cut out to be a narc."

"We know, Santa." Cassie touched Emily lightly on the wrist. "You're cool."

"And actually, we have something for you." Lola disappeared into the bushes and unveiled something wrapped in a large blue quilt. She set it down on the stoop and pulled the blankets away; nestled inside was her mother's baby Jesus. It didn't have a scratch on it. The little ceramic baby was sleeping peacefully, same as always.

"We thought your mom might want this back," Cassie said with a wink. "She was getting pretty worked up about it last night."

Emily touched the baby Jesus's head with the tip of her finger. "Thanks, you guys. This will mean a lot to her."

"No worries." Sophie looked at her watch. "We'd better go, guys. We have that . . . *thing.*"

The elves nodded mysteriously. Emily felt a hurt twinge, wishing they'd tell her where they were going, but maybe that was asking for too much.

Cassie stepped off the stoop and waggled her finger. "Don't tell anyone about this, okay, Santa?"

"Of course not," Emily said. "Don't tell my mom on me, either."

"We promise."

"Maybe we'll meet up next year at Santa Land." Lola suppressed a giggle. "I kind of like being an elf, to tell you the truth."

"It's a deal," Emily said.

The elves sauntered back to Cassie's car. Emily hugged her arms to her chest for warmth, watching as they drove away. A twig cracked in the distance, and she glanced toward the cornfields, feeling that old, familiar sense of unease. This was too much of a coincidence: *Someone* was back there. Someone was watching her. "Hello?" she called, stepping off the porch.

But no one answered. Whatever—or whoever—it was had vanished.

BAD SANTA

I might have disappeared into the cornfield, Em, but I'm not going anywhere.

I have to admit—I'm kind of impressed with how our little Emily has grown. Bribing an officer of the court? Who knew she had that in her? Then again, she always did have a soft spot for her friends. If I've learned anything, it's that the key to Emily's heart is the best friend she loved and lost. If Emily thought there was any chance that her dear Ali was back, she'd go to the ends of the earth to find her.

It is a weakness full of possibilities. I could make Emily break laws for me. I could make her accuse people of all kinds of things, all in the name of Alison. And when I make my move, it will be so easy to lure Emily into my trap. All it will take is a few simple words . . . and one simple kiss. I can only hope that the others will be as easy to manipulate . . .

Next up: Aria. She, Byron, and Mike are geared up for some kooky Yuletide fun, but I have the sneaking suspicion that the surprise waiting for them at the Bear Claw Lodge is *not* the new knitting wool Aria wanted for Christmas. And that's not all that's going to unravel in Aria's life this holiday season.

Mwah!

ARIA'S PRETTY LITTLE SECRET

1

THE MORE THE MERRIER
AT SOLSTICE TIME

"Don't you just love didgeridoo music?" Byron Montgomery steered with his knees as he shoved a CD into the slot in the Subaru's stereo console. Australian pipe music began to play, and he bopped his head back and forth. "It's so . . . spiritual. The perfect soundtrack for the Winter Solstice."

"Uh-huh," Aria Montgomery said absently, examining the gray wool scarf she was knitting. The car went over a bump, and she almost stabbed herself with a wooden knitting needle.

"I think didgeridoos are lame." Aria's brother, Mike, kicked the back of her seat. "They sound like a combination of a buzzing wasp hive and an old man farting."

Byron frowned and ran his hand through his scraggly hair. "You kids need to get into the spirit. I'd better not be the only one chanting during the Solstice celebration."

Aria resisted the urge to roll her eyes. It was December 24, and the family was on their way to the Bear Claw Lodge in the Pocono Mountains, where Byron would ski, Mike would snowboard, and Aria would knit and journal. Every other car on the Northeast Extension was packed full of prettily wrapped gifts, cases of wine, and maybe a frozen ham or a fruitcake. The Montgomery vehicle, on the other hand, contained three yoga mats, incense burners, a jug of homemade mead Byron had brewed in the basement, and a large, splintery Yule log. Aria's family celebrated the Winter Solstice instead of Christmas, Hanukkah, or Kwanzaa. Even though both her parents had been raised Episcopalian, they'd never done Santa or church or caroling. While everyone else received gifts sometime in December, all Aria got, year after year, was a head wreath made out of ivy.

Aria had never really minded the Solstice celebrations before—she'd accepted long ago that her family was kind of . . . *different*—but this year, after her old friend Ali's death, the evil text-messager A, and finding out that Ali's murderer was Rosewood's golden boy Ian Thomas, she longed for the comforting Christmas traditions her family had eschewed. Gathering around a decorated tree. Exchanging gifts. Staying indoors and watching cheesy holiday movies instead of schlepping through the wilderness, beating their chests like apes, and being one with nature.

As she gazed out the window at the passing cars, she felt envious of the excited kids' faces peering out from the backseats. When a sign for a Christmas tree farm swept past, she considered asking Byron if they could chop one down. She knew exactly what he'd say, though: *That tree has a soul! It would hate for us to defile it in such a tacky way!*

"I wonder what Ella's doing right now," Aria said as the Subaru barreled past a VW Jetta with tinted windows.

Byron poked his finger through a hole near the cuff of his sweater, an awkward look rolling across his face. "I'm sure your mom's somewhere over the Atlantic Ocean as we speak."

Aria turned and stared out the window at a billboard for the newly opened DEVON CREST MALL. WE HAVE THE TRISTATE AREA'S BIGGEST SANTA LAND! it said at the bottom. Ella was on her way to Sweden right now for some meatballs, Volvo-ogling, and sightseeing. Aria had hoped Ella would take her with her—the Montgomerys had lived in Reykjavík, Iceland, for three years, and Aria had cried the whole plane ride back to Rosewood this fall. Getting away to Europe would have been the perfect way to decompress after all the drama of first semester, but Ella had told her she needed to make the trip alone.

Aria understood her need to get away. Her marriage to Byron had crumbled this year when she found out he was having an affair with Meredith Stevens, his old student. A—aka Mona Vanderwaal—had been the one to reveal the tryst, also adding that Aria had known Byron's secret. Ella had been so angry at Aria that she'd banished her from the house, but they'd since made up. Byron was still living with Meredith in a dumpy apartment in Old Hollis, but luckily she was spending the holidays with her parents in Connecticut. Not so long ago, Meredith had dropped the bomb of all bombs: She was ten weeks pregnant . . . and planning on keeping the baby. She had also announced that she and Byron were going to get married as soon as his divorce went through.

Byron reached over the seat divider and placed a hand on Aria's knee. "I know it's sad that your mom's not here. But this is our chance to hang out together. I promise we'll have a good time."

"I know," Aria said softly, patting her dad's hand. As much as she wanted to despise Byron for splintering the family, she couldn't—he was still the absentminded, caring, goofy father she loved. It *would* be nice to spend some time together, especially since Meredith wouldn't be there. While Aria had stayed with Byron and Meredith when she and Ella weren't speaking, she hadn't warmed up to Meredith at all.

One didgeridoo song ended, and a second one—which sounded exactly like the first—began. Aria picked up her knitting needles and looked at the scarf. It was almost six feet long. She'd intended to give it to Ezra Fitz, the guy she'd met at a college bar the day she'd returned home from Iceland *and*—as she'd only discovered after they'd kissed—her English teacher at Rosewood Day. Just after they'd professed their affection for one another, A had exposed their relationship. Ezra had resigned from his teaching position immediately and taken off to Rhode Island.

Since he'd been gone, Aria felt like she had PTED—Post-Traumatic *Ezra* Disorder. She couldn't stop thinking about him. She'd written him tons of emails, but Ezra hadn't responded. Had he moved on to someone else? What about all those things he'd said about how amazing she was and how he'd never met anyone like her? What if she *never* got over him? What if she never kissed another guy *again*? She'd had other boyfriends before—her first was a guy named Hallbjorn Gunterson in Iceland and she even dated Sean Ackard, a Typical Rosewood Boy, last semester. But she'd never felt about anyone the way she felt about Ezra.

After a quick pit stop where Byron picked up some snacks and made a phone call, they pulled into a turnoff with a big sign that said BEAR CLAW. Byron gunned the engine up the long driveway, and the lodge came into view. It wasn't a lodge at all, but a behemoth stone mansion. The grounds were covered in glittering, pristine snow. A gondola carried skiers to the top of the mountain. There were more wooden signs pointing to a spa, indoor tennis courts, a gym, the ski rental shop, an ice-skating rink, and dog-sledding tours.

Aria's mouth dropped open. Mike's did, too. "I am *so* going snowboarding this afternoon," he said.

"Why didn't you tell us how nice this place was?" Aria gushed. She'd been positive the Bear Claw Lodge was going to have outdoor plumbing, raccoons living in the rafters, and a creepy caretaker à la *The Shining*.

"I thought we should go somewhere special for the Solstice this year. You kids deserve it." Byron swung the car into the round driveway. Several valets approached, pretending not to notice the Subaru's cracked taillight, the duct tape that held the passenger-side mirror in place, or the many stickers Aria and Mike had affixed to the back bumper. They didn't say anything about the Yule log, either, cheerfully loading it onto the luggage cart with the rest of the family's bags.

Aria stepped out of the car and stretched her shoulders, suddenly filled with optimism. The air smelled so fresh, and all of the guests were ruddy-cheeked and smiling. A big, beautiful Christmas tree stood in the front window. She could pretend it was all her own. Maybe she'd even learn how to ski.

A footstep sounded behind her, and she twisted around. A figure slipped behind the building, as though whoever it was didn't want to be seen. Aria's thoughts instantly darted to A, who had stalked her for months. But she was just being paranoid. A—Mona—was gone.

"I have another surprise for you." Byron pointed toward the lodge entrance. "Want to see what it is?"

Aria and Mike followed him through the double doors into a cozy, wood-paneled lobby. People wearing Fair Isle sweaters rested by the fire. A kind, grandmotherly woman waved at Aria from behind the front desk. "Maybe the surprise is something awesome like tobogganing," Aria whispered to her brother. "Or a helicopter ride over the mountains."

"Or maybe it's actual *presents* this year," Mike said back, his eyes glittering. "I'm dying for an iPad. Or one of those sick four-wheelers like Noel Kahn has."

Byron stopped halfway into the lobby and pointed. "Look!"

Aria followed his gaze to the bar. A man and a woman sat with their backs to them, drinking Bloody Marys. Two college-age boys wearing ski goggles like headbands finished the last of their Heinekens. A thin college-age girl in tight jeans and an oversized black sweater slumped on a stool in the corner, drinking a ginger ale. When she turned and revealed her slightly swollen belly, Aria's heart dropped to her feet. *No.* This couldn't be happening.

"Hey!" Meredith's eyes lit up, and she slid off the stool. "I'm so happy to see you!" She ran up to the family, bypassed Aria and Mike completely, and gave Byron a long kiss.

A Yule log–sized lump formed in Aria's throat. So much for quality time with just her dad and Mike.

2

SNUG AS FOUR BUGS IN A RUG

As the sun sank lower in the sky and an ethereal violet mist gathered over the mountains, Aria, Mike, Byron, and Meredith sat around a large square table in the lodge dining room. A harpist in a ball gown played soothing Christmas carols. Families to their left and right glugged red wine and eggnog, exchanged presents, and joked about Christmas memories of the past. And what were the Montgomerys talking about?

Puking.

"I can't believe how fast the vomit urge comes on," Meredith was saying, taking a tiny sip of ginger ale. There was a beautiful vegetable entrée of eggplant, mushrooms, broccoli, and quinoa before her, but she hadn't dared take a single bite. "It's like, one second, I'm totally fine, and the next—*bam*! I'm hugging the toilet or pulling over to the side of the road to throw up. I've even puked into a paper cup at the mall."

"Sweet." Mike leaned forward on his elbows. "Is it, like, projectile?"

"Sometimes," Meredith said, clutching her head wearily.

Um, we're eating? Aria wanted to say, staring down at the ravioli the waiter had served her. It sort of looked like puke now, too.

"You poor thing." Byron pushed a lock of hair off of Meredith's forehead. "There are some amazing Solstice healing rituals that might help, though. I brought a lot of calming herbs with me, too."

Meredith cupped her hands around her glass. "I can't wait to celebrate the Solstice. It just sounds so magical and spiritual."

"We're so thrilled to have you here, too. Aren't we, Aria?" Byron peered pointedly at her.

Aria picked at an imaginary string on her skirt. It was obvious Byron wanted her to welcome Meredith with open arms—even Mike was being a good sport about it, probably because Byron had promised him an unlimited snowboarding pass. But Aria felt far too wounded.

After Meredith had appeared, Byron had explained that her plans in Connecticut had fallen through at the last minute—her parents had decided to visit her brother in Maine instead. So he'd gone ahead and just invited Meredith to the lodge instead of letting Aria and Mike be part of the decision.

"I know we'd planned for it to just be us three, but I hated the idea of her being home alone," Byron had said in such a caring, concerned voice that Aria almost sympathized with Meredith, too. But then she'd looked at Meredith again. There was a crafty smile on her face, like she'd somehow orchestrated this whole scheme just to make Aria miserable.

The concierge had profusely apologized that their rooms wouldn't be ready until after dinner, and so the four of them had toured the grounds for a few hours, looking at the dogsled track, the toboggan runs, and the skeet-shooting fields. Meredith had behaved like an old lady on the walkways around the resort, terrified she was going to slip on a nonexistent patch of ice. She'd made Byron spend forty-five minutes in the gift shop, picking out a perfect gender-neutral baby onesie. And she'd asked him to walk her to the women's room the *eleven times* she'd had to pee. While they'd waited in the hall during Pee Break #4, Byron had given Aria's shoulders a quick squeeze. "Are you doing okay?"

"Never better," Aria had answered, her voice icy, resisting the urge to pull out her own hair.

Now, Byron picked up his glass of wine and held it in the air. "To the Solstice." Meredith touched his glass with hers, and Aria and Mike reluctantly followed with their glasses of Sprite.

"Let's go over the schedule of events for the next few days," Byron went on after taking a hearty swig. "Tomorrow I thought we'd go on a nature walk and do the Circle of Trust." He turned to Meredith. "That's where we join hands in the woods and breathe together as one, welcoming the change of seasons."

"Of *course*," Meredith said, as though she'd celebrated the Solstice for years.

"We'll definitely burn the Yule log that night." Byron cut a piece of tofu lasagna and popped it in his mouth. He wasn't a vegetarian except during Solstice time. "According to Scandinavian lore, burning it makes the sun shine brighter. And then the next morning, we'll do the naked run."

"A naked run?" Meredith's brow furrowed. "You mean outdoors?"

Mike snickered lasciviously, then looked around the dining room. "I should recruit *her* for that." He pointed to a pretty blonde eating dinner with her parents.

Byron dabbed his mouth with his napkin. "The naked run is very invigorating. We usually do it quite early in the morning so no one disturbs us. And we usually keep our underwear on," he said with a smile. "Americans aren't the most open-minded about these rituals."

"I'm not sure it's a good idea for me to run." Meredith patted her stomach. "The cold might hurt the baby. Or what if I trip and fall on my belly?"

Aria leaned forward. "Ella always loved the naked run. She told me once that she even did it when she was six months pregnant with Mike." She peeked at Meredith's face. She looked crestfallen. Good.

Byron's mouth twitched. "Well, that's true, but maybe Meredith's right."

Meredith lowered her glass defiantly. "Never mind. I'm in." She shot Aria a brief, sharp look that seemed to say, *You can't get rid of me that easily.*

Aria turned away, her gaze landing on the Christmas tree in the corner of the room. It was decorated with tiny glass birds, strung kernels of popcorn, and white grosgrain bows. Presents were stacked underneath, and a model train circled the perimeter. A young couple and their two children, a boy and a girl of about four and six, stood in front of the tree holding hands. The father lifted the boy so he could get a better look at one of the bird ornaments. Aria couldn't hear their conversation, but she definitely heard the mother say the word *Santa.*

Tears filled her eyes. That family was making amazing memories. Not long ago, *her* family had been making similar memories—okay, *Solstice* memories, which were kind of kooky, but at least they were all together. They'd been so happy in Iceland. It seemed like her parents had fallen back in love while they were there, but it had all come apart when they returned to Rosewood.

They finished their entrées and ordered a bunch of desserts to split, including tapioca pudding and crème brûlée, both of which Aria hated. When they arrived, Meredith breathed in, turned green, and pushed back her chair.

"I just have to . . . ," she blurted, her cheeks bulging. She ran toward the bathroom and clamored through the door. Her retching noises could be heard throughout the dining room. The diners gazed in the direction of the bathroom in alarm.

"*Nasty*," Mike said.

A porter in a red suit appeared at Byron's side. "Sir, your guest quarters are ready. We've already taken your luggage there."

"Excellent." Byron pressed his hand to his forehead, suddenly looking exhausted. "I think we could all use some downtime right now."

The porter handed him a key and told him to go to the fourth floor. Once Byron paid the check, they picked up Meredith from the bathroom. She leaned on Byron's arm on the walk to the elevator, making huffing and puffing noises as though she were already in labor.

"I call the TV remote," Mike said to Aria in the elevator. "There's a sweet ultimate fighting match on tonight."

"Whatever," Aria said wearily. At this point, she'd watch any of Mike's stupid shows—getting away from Byron and Meredith in their own room was reward enough. "I get first pick of the minibar."

"Byron, hurry!" Meredith urged from farther up the hall as Byron fumbled through his pockets. She turned around and clutched her belly, her face sheet-white. "I think I'm going to puke again."

"Okay, okay." Byron shoved a key into a room and opened the door. Meredith darted inside, slammed the bathroom door, and more disgusting noises commenced.

Byron strode into the little hallway for the room

and put his hands on his hips. "Well, this looks lovely."

"What about our room?" Aria asked.

Byron cocked his head. "*This* is your room."

Aria stared at it. Slowly, the realization swept over her. "We're all staying in a room *together*?" She'd assumed that since Meredith was along, Byron would have changed the reservation.

Byron blinked. "Honey, this place is really expensive. And anyway, the resort was fully booked." He flicked on the lights, revealing two big rooms, a kitchenette, and the closed door to the bathroom. Meredith let out a weak cough from inside. "This is a suite—you guys can have your own space if you sleep on the pullout couch in the living area."

A cramp squeezed Aria's stomach. A pullout couch wasn't good enough. She'd still be able to *hear* Byron and pregnant Meredith through the door.

She felt like a geyser about to blow. This was *her* time with her dad. Her time to bond. Didn't Byron understand that? Didn't he know how hard the past few months had been? He could have told Meredith not to come. He could have decided, just this once, that Aria and Mike came first.

"I have to go," she blurted. She grabbed her canvas bag from the luggage cart and started out the door.

"Go where?" Byron called after her. But Aria didn't turn back. She stormed down the hall, pushed through the stairwell, and clomped down to the oak-paneled lobby. A woman was playing "Jingle Bells" on the baby grand piano in the corner. People were drinking free cider from a carafe by the front desk. Kids were making angels in the freshly fallen snow. It was a beautiful place, and Aria wanted nothing more than to stay, but she knew that she absolutely, positively couldn't.

She was getting the hell out of there.

3

ANOTHER SURPRISE

Aria's cell phone said 9:57 P.M. when the bus pulled into the Rosewood Greyhound station parking lot. Feeling groggy and grimy, she staggered down the stairs, grabbed her luggage from the undercarriage compartment, and darted around the snowdrifts toward her old friend, Emily Fields, whom she'd called and asked to pick her up. She took out her cell phone again.

Back in Rosewood, safe and sound, she wrote to Byron. *Have fun tomorrow.*

After Aria had marched out of the shared room at the lodge, Byron had followed her to the lobby and tried to cajole her into staying. But Aria had stood her ground. With a heavy heart, Byron had driven her to catch the next bus to Rosewood. Before she'd boarded, he'd placed his hand on her shoulder and given her a meaningful look. Aria had thought he was going to tell her something profound. Or apologize.

"Don't forget to slather butter on the front door of Mom's house," he'd said instead. "Otherwise, you won't be protected from spirits for the rest of the year."

Snow began to fall as Aria slid into Emily's waiting car. "Thanks for coming to get me," Aria said.

"Of course." Emily eased her car out of the station and started down Lancaster Avenue. "But are you sure you don't want to stay at my house? Won't you be lonely spending the holiday by yourself?"

"I don't want to intrude," Aria answered. Emily was dropping her at Ella's—there was no way she was going to stay at her dad and Meredith's creaky apartment in Old Hollis. "And honestly, after everything that's happened, maybe I just need a little time to myself."

There was barely any traffic, and every stoplight in Rosewood was green. Emily sped past Rosewood's main drag, the Hollis campus, and the turnoff for Alison DiLaurentis's old street, reaching Aria's mom's house in record time. Hers was the only property on the block that wasn't aglow with Christmas decorations. It looked like a missing tooth in a mouth of pearly whites.

After saying bye to Emily, Aria unlocked the front door and dropped her bags in the foyer. The only noises in the house were the soft hum of the refrigerator and the hiss of air through the radiator pipes. When she looked out the window, the snow had already left a dusting on the front lawn. According to weather reports, they were supposed to get a foot by tomorrow morning.

"I'm dreaming of a white Christmas," Aria sang softly. Her voice echoed in the empty room, filling her with regret. What was she going to do with herself for the next few days, knocking around this big house all by herself? What was she going to make for Christmas dinner—frozen organic macaroni and cheese? Maybe she should have brought Mike with her—but he hadn't seemed that bummed out to be with Byron and Meredith. He'd probably spend the next few days skiing, snowboarding, ice fishing, and skeet shooting.

She trudged upstairs and flopped down on her bed, knocking a book to the floor. It was her well-loved sketch journal. She grabbed it, feeling a discomfited prickle. She was almost positive she'd left the sketchbook on the desk, not the bed. Had Ella moved it before she went to Sweden? Had someone else been in here?

The spine cracked as Aria opened to the first page. She'd had this journal since the beginning of sixth grade; one of the first sketches she'd drawn was of Ali the day she'd marched out of Rosewood Day and announced that her brother had told her where a piece of the Time Capsule flag had been hidden. It was eerie how accurately Aria's younger self had captured the curves of Ali's heart-shaped face, the wry twist of her smile, the sparkle in her eyes. It was like Ali was staring back at her from the paper.

She turned past sketches of Ali, Spencer, Emily, and Hanna—she'd drawn them hundreds of times after they'd become friends. Then came pictures of Iceland—the cute row houses, a sleeping old man at a coffee shop, a quick sketch of Aria's parents sitting together on the stone wall outside their house, looking totally in love, and a drawing of Hallbjorn, Aria's first boyfriend in Iceland.

Aria flipped ahead, the journal opening naturally to a particular page. She drew in a sharp breath. It was a side profile of Ezra Fitz standing at the board in English class. Aria stared longingly at his small, slightly sticky-outy ears. That amazing broad chest she'd loved to run her fingers over. Those full lips she'd kissed countless times.

She flopped back on the pillow. Where was Ezra right now? Celebrating the holidays with his family? Taking a moonlit Christmas Eve walk with a new girlfriend? Tears welled in Aria's eyes. Part of her wanted to check her email again to see if Ezra had written a Happy Holidays note, but why bother? There wouldn't be one. Aria didn't matter to him anymore.

The house let out a creak, followed by a loud thud. Aria sat up straighter and looked around. That didn't sound like the wind.

Another thud came, and she shot to her feet. She crept out into the hall and peered out the large square window that overlooked the front yard. There were no cars parked at the curb, no figures poised on the street.

Then something started to rattle.

Aria leaned over the stairs and gasped. The doorknob at the front door was wiggling back and forth, like someone was trying to force their way in. "Hello?" she called in an eggshell-thin voice, grabbing a lacrosse stick from Mike's room. Should she call the police? What if it was *Ian*, sprung from jail? At his arraignment, he'd whirled around and stared at Aria and her old friends, a look of sheer hatred in his eyes.

"Hello?" Aria cried out again, wielding the lacrosse stick in front of her like a sword as she tiptoed down the stairs. "Who's there?"

From the foyer, she glanced at the side panel to the left of the front door, her heart in her throat. A shadow shifted on the porch. It was definitely a person.

Knock knock knock.

Aria grabbed the cordless phone in the hall. "I'm calling the police! You'd better get the hell out of here!"

The figure didn't move. Aria pressed the TALK button on the phone. "I'm dialing!" She shakily hit the digits for 911. The ring tones bleated in her ear.

"Aria?" a muffled voice called from the porch.

Aria lowered the lacrosse stick an inch. The shape shifted in the window. "Nine-one-one, what's your emergency?" a dispatcher's voice asked on the other end of the phone line.

"Aria?" whoever was outside called again. Aria frowned. It was a familiar guy's voice. And was that an Icelandic accent?

"Hello?" the 911 operator said, a little more impatiently now. "Is anyone there?"

Aria walked toward the window. Standing on the

porch was a tall blond guy with broad shoulders and a square jaw, wearing a navy-blue anorak that said ICE-LANDIC SKI TEAM on a patch on the chest. She let out an incredulous laugh.

" . . . Hallbjorn?"

"Yes!" the voice said. "Can you let me in? It's freezing out here!"

Aria opened the door. A tall figure was standing on her porch, snow all over his head, shoulders, and face. She pressed the red OFF button on the phone. "Hallbjorn," she whispered again. He was here . . . in Rosewood. At her house.

Aria wouldn't have been more surprised if it had been Santa Claus.

4

ICELANDIC BOYS ARE HOT

Hallbjorn stomped into the Montgomerys' foyer and kicked his snowy boots. "I didn't know it got this cold in Pennsylvania," he said in the crisp, jaunty accent Aria had missed since she'd left Iceland. "This feels just like home!"

"W-what are you doing here?" Aria stammered, not having left her post by the door.

Hallbjorn pulled his bottom lip into his mouth playfully. "I missed you. I wanted to see how you were doing."

"At ten o'clock at night on Christmas Eve?"

"My plane was rerouted here because of weather–I'm trying to get to New York, but there was a bad storm. Flights have already been canceled for tomorrow, too. I tried calling your house from the airport, but there was no answer, and I didn't know your cell phone number. I thought I'd take a risk and just come." He looked around. "I'm not interrupting anything, am I? Did I wake your family?"

Aria leaned against the wall, feeling dizzy. "They're all out of town. It's just me."

There were a million questions she wanted to ask him, but her mouth couldn't form the words. She hadn't seen Hallbjorn in two years, but he looked even better than she remembered: His tall, reedy body now had a bit more muscle on its frame. His white-blond hair had grown to his chin. He still had the same handsome, angular face, but his eyes seemed even more piercingly blue than ever. And when he smiled, he had perfectly straight, white teeth, the kind that deserved their own Aquafresh commercial. Just looking at him made her heart flutter.

He'd had braces when he and Aria had met. A week after her family had moved to Reykjavík, Aria had taken a bike ride around the town, feeling lonely and displaced and mixed up. It was only a few months after Ali had disappeared, and that still weighed heavily on her mind. She had hoped that getting away from Rosewood would help her recover from everything that had happened, but it still felt so fresh and raw.

She'd heard music playing in a local coffee shop and had wandered in. A band had been playing on a small stage at the back, and a bunch of people were gathered around. During a break in songs, a blond guy had turned to Aria and asked her something in Icelandic. Aria had blushed and said the only two Icelandic words she'd learned so far: *English, please.* The boy had smiled. "Are you American?" he'd asked in perfect English. When Aria said yes, he'd welcomed her to Iceland and said his name was Hallbjorn.

After a few minutes of exchanging musical tastes and getting Aria's general impressions of Reykjavík, Hallbjorn had insisted on showing her around the country. The next day, he'd arrived at Aria's curb in the biggest SUV Aria had ever seen—everyone in Iceland drove massive-tired vehicles that could propel them over lava fields, glaciers, and snow. He'd taken her to see important Icelandic landmarks—the beautiful, clear waterfalls that looked like something out of the Lord of the Rings movies, the giant craters, the burbling volcanoes, and the Akureyri Puffin Island, where puffin colonies spent part of the year before they migrated to Greece. They'd talked during the whole tour, never running out of things to say. Aria had found out that Hallbjorn was two years older than she was and wanted to study architecture, that he'd learned to drive a snowmobile at five years old, that he was a DJ in his spare time, and that he was addicted to American reality shows like *Big Brother*. In turn, Aria had told him about the boring little suburb she'd come from, how her father was doing a research study here about the Icelandic beliefs in *huldufólk*—elves—and how, this past summer, her best friend had mysteriously disappeared.

At the end of the day, Aria had suggested going to Blue Lagoon, the all-natural salt hot springs the travel magazines couldn't stop raving about, but Hallbjorn had scoffed and said that was for tourists. He'd taken her to a secret hot spring instead. As they'd soaked in the warm, sulfuric-smelling water—Hallbjorn told her she'd get used to the smell—he'd leaned in close, took her hand, and kissed her. It had been Aria's first kiss.

They'd dated for four months, going to concerts, art openings, and Icelandic pony shows. Hallbjorn taught Aria how to drive a snowmobile, and she taught him how to knit and use her prized video camera. The whole thing felt like a dream. Aria might have been in Ali's cool clique in Rosewood, but boys still hadn't paid attention to her—they only wanted Ali. In Reykjavík, however, there was no Ali to make her feel like second best. More than that, there was no Ali telling her that she was being too kooky, too unapproachable, and too . . . *Aria*. Aria hadn't changed a thing about herself in Iceland, even leaving the pink streaks in her hair and the fake ring in her nose, and Hallbjorn had liked her anyway. In fact, he seemed to like her *more* for her uniqueness.

In February of that year, something horrible happened: Hallbjorn got a scholarship to a special boarding school in Norway for kids who wanted to study architecture. He'd left on Valentine's Day, and Aria had cried herself to sleep for months. They'd written back and forth at first, but after a while, Hallbjorn's letters had stopped coming. Aria had dated other Icelandic boys after him, but none of those relationships had been quite as special.

"How did you know my address?" Aria asked now.

When her family had left Iceland, Hallbjorn had still been in Norway.

Hallbjorn peeled off his mittens. "When I got back from boarding school this fall, I stopped by to see you, but the new people who were living in your house said you'd moved back to the States. They gave me your address."

"Who are you visiting in New York?"

Hallbjorn gave Aria a blank look, almost like he hadn't expected this question. "Uh, some relatives," he said distractedly, vigorously rubbing his reddened nose. "But like I said, the plane was rerouted because of weather." He smiled at her sheepishly. "Do you mind if I stay here for two nights? The next plane to New York isn't until the twenty-sixth. I can pay you."

"You don't need to pay me," Aria scoffed. "I'm happy for the company."

She led him down the hall and told him to sit on the family-room couch while she made tea for both of them. As she waited for the water to boil, she called out, "So how is Iceland these days? I miss it so much."

"It's okay." Hallbjorn sounded dismissive. "Not too exciting."

Aria grabbed two mugs from a high shelf. "Do your parents mind that you're away for Christmas?"

"Uh, I'm not really sure."

"Is everything okay with them?" Hallbjorn's parents were two sturdy, athletic Icelanders who dressed alike and ran ultramarathons together. Aria briefly entertained the notion that Hallbjorn's parents might be going through the same stuff Ella and Byron were, but she just couldn't imagine it.

"No, no, everything's fine. I just planned this trip at the last minute." A bell tinkled from the other room. "Hey!" Hallbjorn exclaimed. "You've still got the wind chimes from that shop on Laugavegur!"

Aria carried the mugs of steaming tea into the family room. Hallbjorn was now stretched out on the couch, his long legs propped up on the ottoman. A tingly rush went through her as she settled next to him on the couch.

"So how's *your* family?" Hallbjorn asked.

"A little messed up right now," Aria admitted. She explained that her parents weren't together anymore. "My dad and brother are celebrating the Winter Solstice upstate. Remember how we used to do that?"

Hallbjorn's eyes lit up. "You hugged all those trees in the Hallormsstadarskogur! And you did that naked swim in Mr. Stefansson's pond!"

Aria groaned—she'd blocked out that unfortunate incident. "Yeah, and my dad didn't *ask* Mr. Stefansson beforehand. Thank goodness you showed up and explained everything to him." Hallbjorn's family lived only a mile away, and when Mr. Stefansson had appeared with a rifle, threatening to shoot the Montgomerys as they cavorted, Solstice-style, in the pond, Aria had quickly called Hallbjorn for help.

Hallbjorn removed the tea bag from his mug.

"Remember how your dad tried to get Mr. Stefansson to participate in the Solstice ritual with him?"

"Oh God, *yes*." Aria smacked her forehead. "Mr. Stefansson looked at him like he was crazy. My dad was like, 'but Mr. Stefansson, you believe in *huldufólk*! Why can't you believe in the Solstice, too?'"

"He's very serious about his *huldufólk* beliefs," Hallbjorn said. "Remember that shrine he built to them in the rocks?"

Aria giggled. Mr. Stefansson was convinced Icelandic elves lived at the back of his property. "He used to yell at us if we got too close to it." She smiled at Hallbjorn.

Their eyes met for a long beat, the steam from their untouched mugs of tea swarming around their faces. Then Aria looked down at her lap. "I cried so hard when you went to Norway."

"You could have visited me at school." Hallbjorn touched Aria's hand.

"I didn't know if you wanted me to." In fact, she *had* visited Norway with Ella a few months after Hallbjorn had left for boarding school, even passing through the little village where the school was. Ella had urged Aria to inquire about Hallbjorn at the school's front desk, but Aria had been too shy and scared. What if Hallbjorn showed up to meet her with a girlfriend in tow? What if he laughed in her face?

"Of course I would have wanted you to." Hallbjorn scooted a little closer to her. "I thought about you a lot when I was away."

When she looked up again, Hallbjorn was staring at her intently. It felt so natural for them to pick up where they'd left off.

Aria smiled to herself. She'd thought what she needed was a quiet break to herself to get over Ezra and all the A drama, but maybe what she really needed was a new romance.

5

SEXY STRADDLE

On Christmas morning, while everyone else was opening presents—or, in Byron, Meredith, and Mike's case, frolicking with deer—Hallbjorn cooked Aria organic pancakes and tofu sausage for a Christmas breakfast. Then he decorated the cactus in the family room with various red items from the house—a mitten, a plastic spoon, a long ribbon he'd found in a drawer. "How did you know I wanted a Christmas tree?" Aria gasped.

Hallbjorn just grinned. "I just had a hunch."

After that Aria had texted Merry Christmas to Emily and Spencer—Hanna was Jewish—and she and Hallbjorn made their way to South Street in Philadelphia. Once there, they skirted around giant snowdrifts that were already yellow with dog pee. The air was biting and crisp, and there was hardly anyone out except for a couple of hard-core joggers and a bunch of tourists with expensive cameras around their necks. The only establishments that were open were a few sex shops and a Walgreens pharmacy, which was already advertising 50 percent off Rudolph and Santa decorations.

"Look, this place sells hemp outerwear!" Aria pointed at a shuttered boutique with a giant marijuana leaf decal in the window. "That's eco, right?"

"As long as it's not made in a sweatshop." Hallbjorn twisted his mouth. "You have to be very careful about organic and hemp fabrics."

Aria nodded sagely, as if she'd known this all along. They'd spent the whole morning playing the green version of "I spy," pointing out the vegetarian restaurants on South Street, the city's many recycling bins, and the fact that some of the buses ran on natural gas. Hallbjorn had told her that he'd recently dedicated himself to saving the environment. He looked so sexy and earnest while talking about carbon emissions, and Aria found herself wanting to prove just how green she was, too.

"So what made you become so environmentally conscious, anyway?" Aria asked as they passed a vintage store she loved. "I don't remember your being so committed when I was in Iceland."

"I started becoming aware while I was in Norway, but I really got into it when I started university this year," Hallbjorn admitted. "I joined an activist group that was trying to stop a big corporation from dumping their waste into the river near the school. A girl named Anja ran it. She set up some amazing protests."

There was a wistful look on his face. "Was Anja . . . a girlfriend?" Aria asked, trying not to sound jealous or prying.

Hallbjorn stepped around a large blue parking meter that had a plastic Christmas wreath hanging from it. "Yes. But a month ago she joined a Greenpeace boat that attacks whalers off the coast of Japan. I wanted to go too, but she told me she needed to be alone."

"I'm sorry about Anja," Aria said as a passing car honked its horn to "Santa Claus Is Coming to Town." "I recently had my heart broken, too."

"Really?" Hallbjorn raised an eyebrow. "What happened?"

Aria told him some of the details about Ezra, leaving out that he'd been her teacher. "It really hurt when he left. I thought I'd never get over him. But he's probably with a new girl by now."

"Yes, that's how I feel about Anja," Hallbjorn said miserably. "She changed my life. Pushed me to do things I wouldn't have dreamed of. And now . . . *poof*." He cupped his palm under his chin and blew, miming a dandelion seed scattering in the wind. "Now she's with a guy who, when not saving whales, chains himself to trees in the rainforest that are about to be bulldozed."

Aria snickered. "He's probably not that great. I bet he wets his sleeping bag every night."

"Or perhaps he secretly eats endangered rainforest monkeys," Hallbjorn said, playing along.

"Or he doesn't *recycle*!"

"What can your ex-boyfriend's new girlfriend's flaw be?" Hallbjorn tapped his chin. "That she's actually a man?"

Aria burst out laughing. "Maybe she doesn't know how to read. Or maybe she's incredibly hairy, even her butt!"

"Seriously, though," Hallbjorn said, staring deep into her eyes. "We never had any of those problems. Everything with us was just so . . . easy."

"I know," Aria said, suddenly feeling shy. "We were such a good fit."

Suddenly Hallbjorn froze on the sidewalk. His already pale skin turned even whiter, and he darted around a corner and dove into a small alleyway.

"Hallbjorn?" Aria followed him into the alcove. It smelled like rotting garbage and cigarette butts. A bunch of bicycle tires were propped up against the building. "What's the matter?"

"*Shh.*" Hallbjorn pressed a hand over Aria's mouth. His eyes shifted back and forth from the street corner to the traffic lights. A police car slowly rolled across the intersection. A woman walking a Great Dane passed by on the other side of the street.

Finally, Hallbjorn tiptoed out of the alley and looked around. The color had come back to his face, and he was breathing easier now.

"What was that all about?" Aria asked as she followed him.

"I thought I saw someone I knew."

"Someone . . . Icelandic? Or one of your family members from New York?"

"It doesn't matter." Hallbjorn took a few more steps down South Street, but then froze again. Aria gazed around to find what could possibly be spooking him. The two old people out for a stroll? The squirrel lurking by the pathetic little tree at the curb?

He ducked into an open door. Aria followed. It was dark and chilly inside the building, and the scent of essential oils made Aria dizzy. A waterfall burbled, and wind chimes clanged together in the window. DOUBLE MOON YOGA STUDIO, said a sign on the far wall. There were posters of lithe people in various poses all over the walls. Several pairs of shoes rested in square cubbies off to the left, and a few people calmly waited for a class to begin in a large, airy room to the right.

A girl wearing a Santa hat beamed at them from behind the front desk. "*Namaste*," she said in a Zen-like voice. "Happy holidays. Are you here for the couples class?"

"Uh, yes," Hallbjorn said. He glanced at Aria. "Is that okay?"

Aria stared at him crazily. They hadn't discussed doing yoga. She pivoted and peered out the window again. What did he think he saw outside?

Then she realized Santa Hat had said *couples class*. Meaning sexy stretching . . . with Hallbjorn. "It's totally okay," she answered, plunging her hand into her wallet and plunking twenty dollars on the counter.

After changing into some clean sweats from the studio's clothes exchange bin, Aria and Hallbjorn emerged from their respective dressing rooms. Hallbjorn looked much calmer, but Aria touched his arm anyway. "Are you okay? You were acting strange back there."

"I'm fine," Hallbjorn answered. "I was just a little stressed. Yoga always makes me feel better."

They grabbed mats and walked into the practice room. The Santa hat–wearing girl who'd manned the front desk stood against the mirror in the front. A tall guy with a Jesus beard, droopy eyes, and wearing spandex leggings without a shirt joined her and turned to face Aria, Hallbjorn, and the two other couples in the room. "I'm glad you could all be with us today. This is a very special couples class, being that it's on Christmas Day," he said. "Lie down on the floor. Breathe in and out in the same rhythm. Feel as one."

Hallbjorn dropped to his mat. Aria lay in corpse pose too, trying to ignore the fact that the mat kind of smelled like feet. She peeked at Hallbjorn next to her. His chest was rising up and down in an even cadence.

"This practice is all about being bound together in acceptance, unity, and love," Santa Hat explained after they'd breathed for a few more minutes. "It will lead to being more open and productive as a couple. First, we're going to do something called the double tree."

She told the three couples in the room to stand hip-to-hip and wrap their arms around each other's waists. Aria did so, shooting Hallbjorn a nervous smile. His arm felt strong and secure around her back.

"Now raise your opposite legs into tree pose," Jesus Beard said, demonstrating with Santa Hat. "Touch the palm of your free hand to your partner's. See? It binds you together."

Aria felt Hallbjorn's balance shift as he bent his knee and placed his foot on the inside of his thigh. She did the same, pressing her hand into Hallbjorn's. Instead of leaving his hand limp against her palm, as the instructors and the other couples in the room were doing, he laced his fingers with hers and squeezed.

"*Thaaaat's right.*" Jesus Beard's eyes were closed. "Feel the energy. Feel your equality. You are two trees in nature, holding one another up."

"This is a lot like your Solstice rituals, no?" Hallbjorn asked.

Aria giggled. "Next they're going to ask us to run naked up South Street."

Hallbjorn raised his eyebrows. "I'd do it if you would."

It took everything in Aria's power not to blush.

"Now we're going to move into the double straddle." Santa Hat lowered her bent knee to the ground. "This really helps you and your partner get over all sensitivities and insecurities with one another. Sit on your mats. Open your legs in a *V*, face each other, and hold hands. Just like this."

The instructors moved into the pose. Both of them were extremely limber; their legs jackknifed into two nearly perfect splits. They inched forward toward one another until their groins were practically touching.

Aria giggled nervously. Hallbjorn was already stretching his legs into a straddle. Aria did the same, then grabbed Hallbjorn's hands. Slowly, they pulled each other closer together, leaning forward so that their faces almost touched. Aria caught Hallbjorn's eye and didn't look away. Hallbjorn didn't either.

She flattened her spine, inched forward, and touched her lips to his. His mouth was warm and firm and tasted like honey. And for the first time in months, she didn't think about Ezra or Ali or A at all.

6

SOUND THE ALARMS

"Remember this picture?" Aria held up her laptop and pointed to a photo she'd uploaded of her and Hallbjorn standing at the edge of Laugardal, one of Reykjavík's biggest public pools. Snow was flurrying all around them, sticking to their bare skin. In Iceland, outdoor public pools remained open all year round because they were geothermally heated. "That place had the scariest waterslide ever!"

"You were such a wimp." Hallbjorn poked her. "All those kids were waiting behind you in the freezing cold, begging you to take your turn."

"I know, I know." Aria winced at the memory. She'd been too scared to slide down the enormous waterslide, turning around and walking down the wooden staircase instead.

It was Christmas evening, and they were snuggled under the covers of Aria's bed. This had definitely turned into Aria's best Christmas ever. Hallbjorn was an even better kisser than she remembered, and for the last twenty minutes, he'd been rubbing the kinks out of her neck, which made her shudder with glee and never want to leave this room for the rest of her life.

Aria flipped to the next picture and burst out laughing. "The ponies!" It was a photo of Hallbjorn's Icelandic horses, Fylkir and Fyra. Aria was on Fylkir, the shorter, fatter, and more docile of the two, but there was still a terrified look on her face. Hallbjorn was next to her on Fyra, who was the color of cinnamon and had giant nostrils.

"You made me go along that steep cliff on our first ride," Aria scolded Hallbjorn. "I could have killed you. I was so sure we were going to fall over the edge."

"Icelandic ponies are sure-footed," Hallbjorn protested.

"Well, I didn't believe you at the time." Aria looked at her younger self in the picture. "It's no wonder my brother was afraid of them. They look so small and untrustworthy."

Hallbjorn burst out laughing. "Mike was *afraid* of Icelandic horses?"

Aria slid lower under the covers. Oops. That was one of Mike's biggest secrets. "Uh, forget I said that."

"Who's this guy?" Hallbjorn scrolled to another picture on the laptop. Aria's photos were in no particular order, and the next shot was of Noel Kahn at one of Ali's seventh-grade parties. Aria had covertly taken the photo, peeking around the corner and pressing the shutter when she knew Noel wasn't looking. Ali had teased her merci-lessly when she'd found out Aria had camera-stalked him.

"Oh, that's someone I used to like before I moved to Iceland," Aria said nonchalantly.

"I think you told me about him." Hallbjorn stared hard at Noel's image. "Alison stole him from you, right?"

"He was never mine to steal." Aria peered at Noel's image. He was wearing his lucky University of Pennsylvania Nike lacrosse shirt—typical. "Besides, every guy was into Alison. I thought it was mean of her to go out with him, though. She knew I liked him." Worse, Ali had gone out with Noel for only one date before dumping him. It felt to Aria like she'd done it just to prove she could get any guy she wanted—or any guy Aria wanted.

He propped himself up on one elbow. "He was an idiot to pass up the chance to date you. You're so amaz-ing. I cared a lot about Anja, but I never forgot about you. You were my first love."

"Love?" Aria squeaked, the word almost palpable in the air around them.

Two pink splotches appeared on Hallbjorn's cheeks. "Yes, *love*."

Suddenly, a twig snapped outside the window, fol-lowed by a peal of laughter. Aria slid off the bed and parted the curtains. The night sky was hazy. There was a thin, glossy sheet of ice over the snow. Around the perim-eter of the property was a set of crisp, fresh boot tracks leading straight to the back door.

"Oh my God." Aria stepped away from the window. "I think there's someone out there!"

She ran down the stairs, Hallbjorn right behind her. As they reached the foyer, there was a crash out back, like someone had knocked over one of the metal garbage cans. Aria grabbed Hallbjorn's arm and squeezed.

"It's okay." Hallbjorn pulled her close. "It's probably just an animal."

"It's *not* an animal." Aria's heart was beating so quickly she felt woozy. "Someone is following me. Trying to get in."

"Why would you say that?"

"I've had a stalker for months, remember?" She'd filled him in on the A drama that afternoon.

"Yes, but didn't you say your stalker was dead?" Hallbjorn tiptoed toward the patio. "It's an animal. I'll scare it away."

"Don't go out there! I'll call the police," Aria said, picking up the hallway phone.

All the blood drained from Hallbjorn's face and he lunged for the phone, banging it back on the receiver. "No! Don't call the police!"

Aria stepped back in shock. "Whoa. What is going on with you?"

For a second, Hallbjorn looked like he was going to protest that nothing was wrong, but then his shoulders sagged, and he crumpled in on himself. "I'm so sorry. I didn't want to tell you . . . I'm wanted by the police in

Iceland. I'm afraid the police here might know, too. It's why I've been hiding and avoiding cop cars. They could be after me. So please don't call them. I'll go check out the noise and then I'll explain everything." Hallbjorn made his way to the back door.

A sick feeling spread through Aria's stomach and she retreated into the living room, where she sank down on the couch. She wondered if she should call the cops anyway. But this was Hallbjorn. There had to be a good reason he was wanted.

"It was just a raccoon," Hallbjorn announced as he came back into the front hallway. "I saw it running away."

Aria looked up at him. "Why are the police looking for you?"

"I led a protest against the destruction of a local puffin sanctuary outside of Reykjavík. I took you there once."

"I remember," Aria said slowly. "It was the place where the baby puffins hatched." She'd fallen in love with the baby puffins as soon as she'd seen them, desperate to steal one and take it home as her pet.

Hallbjorn raised his head and gave her a plaintive look. "They were going to tear it down and build a mall. Displace all those puffins. Bulldoze their habitats. I couldn't let that happen. So I protested, and I was arrested. But I put up a fuss, and then I escaped custody. The police were after me for days. I hid out at a friend's, but then I realized I had to get out of the country. I took a boat to Norway and caught a plane out of there. My passport wasn't flagged in Norway since no one was look-ing for me internationally yet."

Aria blinked at him, trying to take this all in. "So . . . you weren't coming to the States to see family after all?"

Hallbjorn shook his blond head. "I have some friends in New York who said I could stay with them. But when they diverted us to Philadelphia, I thought of you." He took her hands. "I'm sorry I didn't tell you right away—I was afraid of what you might think of me. I was desperate. I couldn't turn around and go back to Iceland. They'd throw me in jail. Can you forgive me?"

Aria pulled her hands away and curled them on her lap. She didn't like that Hallbjorn had lied to her—so many people had deceived her in the past few months. But then, would she have let him in if she'd known he was wanted by the cops? She'd had enough police interaction lately to last her whole life.

She looked up. "You were thrown in jail just because you protected some puffins?" In this country, he'd prob-ably get a slap on the wrist and probation. Eco groups like PETA and Greenpeace would make him their poster boy.

"Iceland is very strict," Hallbjorn insisted. "Protesting and running from the police are practically as bad as com-mitting murder." A contrite look washed across his face, and he put his face in his hands. "I don't know what I'm going to do."

Aria moved closer and wrapped her arms around his shoulders. "You were just trying to save the puffins—I would have protested against them tearing down the sanctuary, too. Maybe you could stay in the States for a while. Get a student visa and go to university here."

As soon as the words spilled from her mouth, she began to play it out in her head. Maybe Hallbjorn could go to Hollis or Moore College of Art in Philly; Aria could visit him every weekend. The two of them could drive to New York so she could show him the sights, just like he'd shown her around Reykjavík. It would be wonderful to have someone to talk to, a date on the weekends, a connection to Iceland again.

But Hallbjorn shook his head. "I *can't* stay here. My travel visa only lasts for another week. The only way I stay here is if I hide, and I'm not sure I want to do that, either."

"There's got to be another way." Aria leaned back against the couch and thought for a moment. Her gaze bounced around the room, noting the pile of laundry on the floor, the diamond-shaped God's eye hanging from the mirror, and the empty picture frame on the side table. Not so long ago, the frame had held a picture of Byron and Ella on their wedding day, lovingly embracing under a canopy of trees. When Aria was little, she used to gaze at that photo for hours, thinking that her parents were the most romantic people on the planet.

It was like a lightning bolt suddenly struck her brain. She sat up straighter. "Hallbjorn, what if we got married?"

Hallbjorn barked out a laugh. "Pardon?"

"I'm serious. If we got married, your visa would be

extended indefinitely. You could go to school here. Get a job. And eventually, when enough time has passed and we hire you a good lawyer, maybe we could work it out with the Icelandic police, and you could go back there and visit your family."

Hallbjorn ran his tongue over his teeth. "Is it even legal for us to get married here?"

"I think the legal age is sixteen? Seventeen?" Aria shrugged. "Even if we have to get a parent's consent, I could forge my mom's signature. I'm sure no one really checks as long as we pay the fees." She grasped Hallbjorn's hands, her heart suddenly pumping hard. "It's the best idea. It solves all your problems. And wouldn't it be fun to be husband and wife? We could go to Atlantic City! Make a weekend of it and get married in one of those little chapels in the casinos! I have some money saved up—we could stay in an amazing hotel. Order room service. Drink champagne. Play blackjack. Live it up."

Hallbjorn didn't look convinced. "We're talking about marriage. It's a serious commitment. Are you sure that's something you want to do?"

Aria tucked her feet under her butt. It was true that she sometimes threw herself headfirst into situations without thinking them through—her romance with Ezra was one example. But this was different. Hallbjorn was practically her age. They had so much fun together, had so much in common, and they could talk for hours. What more was needed in a marriage besides that? Look at Byron and

Meredith: What on earth did *they* have to talk about? Aria's marriage to Hallbjorn would probably outlast theirs.

And it wasn't just Hallbjorn the marriage would benefit: Aria had a feeling it would do wonders for her life, too. Marrying Hallbjorn would mean he'd never leave her, as so many other people had. He would be her life buoy in a rocky sea. She could make her marriage work, doing the opposite of everything her parents had done.

"It's definitely something I would want to do," she decided. "But what about you? Are you saying you wouldn't want to marry me?"

Hallbjorn's face softened. He leaned forward and pushed a hair out of Aria's face. "I *do* love you. But this is a huge sacrifice you're making, all so I don't have to go back to Iceland."

"It's not a sacrifice." With every word, Aria's conviction felt stronger and stronger. "This is something I believe in with all my heart. I promise."

She stared into Hallbjorn's eyes, trying to convey everything that she felt and wanted. Hallbjorn stared back, his icy-blue eyes wide. Finally, a tender smile spread across his face. "Let's do it." He sank to his knees. "Aria Montgomery, will you marry me?"

"Yes!" Aria exclaimed, falling into Hallbjorn's arms. "Atlantic City, here we come!"

7

PARTY LIKE A ROCK STAR

"Welcome," a porter told Aria and Hallbjorn the following afternoon as they walked through the revolving doors at the Borgata Hotel Casino & Spa in Atlantic City. "Enjoy your stay!"

"Thank you," Aria chirped, pulling her wheelie bag behind her. She and Hallbjorn had just endured a very long journey to get to Atlantic City—he'd insisted that they wait six hours in the cold bus station for the only Greyhound that ran on natural gas.

But none of that mattered now. Aria looked around the lobby, her heart skipping a beat. It was a sprawling space of marble and glass that smelled like a mix of expensive perfume and seared steak from a restaurant down the hall. Through an archway, slot machines stretched as far as the eye could see. All of them hummed, sounding like a massive swarm of bees. A couple of old ladies were sitting at the machines, robotically pulling the levers. A cheer went up from a blackjack table, and a croupier gave a roulette wheel a spin. It all felt very glamorous, and suddenly what they were about to do hit her again. They were getting *married*!

"Reservation for Montgomery," Aria said to a woman at the front desk who wore her dark hair in a French twist and had a pin on her jacket that said MAUREEN, RESERVATION ASSOCIATE.

"Of course." Maureen clacked her long nails across the keyboard. "Aha. Here you are, in room 908. The suite overlooks the ocean. Also included in your stay is a complimentary dinner at Wolfgang Puck's restaurant and two tickets to tonight's floor show."

Aria paid for the room in cash, using money from the small nest egg she'd amassed from a couple of paid essays she'd written recently about her experience with Monaas-A. She'd felt a little squeamish exploiting the situation, but she was happy she had the cash now, especially since most of it would be needed for the marriage license and the application fees for Hallbjorn's permanent visa.

Another porter who looked like the human equivalent of Humpty Dumpty loaded their luggage onto a cart and gestured for them to follow him to the elevators. When the doors shut behind them, Aria shot Humpty a smile. "Excuse me, do you know of any wedding chapels in the area?"

Humpty raised his eyebrows. "I do. If you'd like, I can have our concierge make all the arrangements."

Aria and Hallbjorn exchanged grins. "That would be great," Hallbjorn said. "Maybe for tomorrow evening?"

"Certainly." Humpty grinned and tugged at his collar, which looked like it was buttoned too tightly. "We can even have a limo pick you up and take you there."

"Not a limo," Hallbjorn said quickly. "A bicycle built for two."

Aria balked—biking in the snow? But Humpty didn't bat an eye. "Not a problem. I can just tell by looking at you two lovebirds that you'll be very, very happy together."

Aria took Hallbjorn's hand and squeezed it lightly.

The elevator doors swung open with a *ding*. Humpty carried their luggage down the hall and unlocked the door to room 908, which was tucked into a back corner. Inside was an enormous bedroom with sweeping floor-to-ceiling windows that offered an uninterrupted view of the Atlantic Ocean. A chilled bottle of champagne sat on the glass table in the corner, as well as a basket of small bags of chips and candy. A giant flat-screen TV was mounted on the wall. The king-sized bed was huge and had about a zillion pillows, and the claw-foot tub in the bathroom was bigger than the hot tub at Spencer's house.

"This is *amazing*," Aria breathed.

"I'm glad you're satisfied. Just let us know if we can get you anything else." Humpty placed their luggage on a little stand at the foot of the bed. Aria handed him a ten-dollar bill, and he bowed and backed out of the room.

Then she faced Hallbjorn and bounced excitedly on her toes. "We're getting married tomorrow!" she squealed.

"Yes, we are." Hallbjorn walked toward her and took her hands. "You'll be Mrs. Gunterson."

"Mrs. *Montgomery*-Gunterson," Aria corrected him. Then she widened her eyes. "I have to find a dress!" In her hasty packing, she hadn't brought one. "And flowers! And what should we do about a wedding cake?"

"We could order a whole cake from one of the restaurants," Hallbjorn suggested. "Have it delivered here through room service."

"I bet room service is kind of expensive." Aria glanced out the window. "I think I saw a Wawa on the way in. They probably have Tastykakes."

"I'm always up for gluten-free organic cookies, if we could find some of those," Hallbjorn said.

Aria pressed her lips together. Gluten-free organic cookies as a substitute for full-fat, full-butter, full-gluten wedding cake made her kind of sad. Not that she'd imagined her wedding very often, but she'd always thought she'd have a three-tiered confection with two figurines on the top. Except instead of a bride and a groom, they'd be a horse and a pig. Or two Lego space people. Or a knife and a fork.

She sat down on the edge of the bed and flipped through the binder that had come with the room, searching to see if this place had a spa. It would be nice to get her hair done for the wedding, not that she had money for that, either.

Hallbjorn pulled her backwards onto the bed, which was as plush and comfortable as Aria had imagined. They kissed for a few long beats, the sounds of the pounding surf in the background.

"I'm going to take a lot of pictures," Aria murmured as Hallbjorn flipped her onto her back. "I'm going to hang them up all over my room so I'll remember this weekend for the rest of my life."

Hallbjorn let out a chuckle. "*Your* bedroom? Won't it be both of ours, once we get married? Or do you expect me to live somewhere else?"

Aria frowned. She hadn't really thought about the logistics of what would happen *after* they got married. Would she have to tell her parents? Would she get in trouble? Then again, what could they really say? Byron and Ella had eloped their last year of college; their parents had come around eventually. But what would Mike think? And what if people from school found out? They would never understand. Not that Aria cared what people thought about her, of course, but gossipy whispers behind her back were getting kind of old.

"Let's worry about where we're going to live later," Aria said shakily. "We'll have plenty of time to figure it out."

"Whatever you say." Hallbjorn leaned forward and kissed her forehead. Aria tilted her chin so that their lips met next. They kissed for a long time, disappearing into the mound of pillows, and just like that, all of her concerns dissipated. This was about *them*, not their families or people at Rosewood Day.

Hallbjorn slid Aria's T-shirt over her head, and she did the same to him, letting out a pleased groan as their bare skin touched. She rolled over, accidentally squashing the remote. The TV clicked on at maximum volume.

Aria looked up. The hotel's in-house channel, which advertised the resort's various restaurants, casinos, and pay-per-view options, was on the screen. Then, two silvery panthers appeared. "Now at the Borgata, Biedermeister and Bitschi will blow your mind," an overenthusiastic voice said. Then came a snarling eighties guitar lick, and two magicians marched onto a stage. They waved their capes like bullfighters. The panthers roared, and the crowd looked dazzled.

Aria snickered. "Do you think our floor show tickets are for *that*?"

"I hope not," Hallbjorn said, pausing from kissing her to glance at the screen.

Suddenly, a faint giggle sounded outside the door. Aria hit MUTE on the TV. "Did you hear that?"

"What?" Hallbjorn raised his head.

Another giggle floated through the vent. "*That.*" The hair on the back of her neck rose.

"It's just someone laughing." Hallbjorn massaged Aria's shoulders. "You're being paranoid."

"It's *not* just someone laughing." Aria stood and crept

past the bathroom as the giggle intensified. It sounded like the person was standing at their door, wanting to get in. She pulled on a robe, took a deep breath, and whipped the door open.

The hall was empty. All of the doors were shut; an empty room-service tray with two drained glasses of red wine waited on the carpet outside room 910.

Aria slumped against the jamb and rubbed her temples, wondering if Hallbjorn was right. Maybe she *was* just being paranoid. Maybe she was hearing things that didn't really exist.

8

PANTHER PORN

"Another glass of champagne?" a cocktail waitress in a slinky beaded gown and a feathered cap asked Aria as she and Hallbjorn sat in the lobby lounge later that evening.

"Don't mind if I do." Aria extended her flute. The waitress dropped a few strawberries into the liquid, and it fizzed dramatically.

Aria took a sip and shut her eyes, suddenly feeling deeply relaxed. The day had been absolutely lovely. They'd lounged around in bed for hours, then had a delicious, romantic, and free dinner at the Wolfgang Puck restaurant. When they'd finished, Aria had poked into a little vintage shop down the block that was still open. She'd found an adorable red polka-dotted frock, which she was wearing tonight, and a gorgeous white tea-length dress with lacy accents at the neck and tiny pearl-shaped buttons running down the back for the wedding tomorrow. It had a tiny rip at the neckline, but it wasn't anything a needle and thread couldn't fix. With any luck, she could also dye it lime-green and wear it to the prom.

And now, she and Hallbjorn were waiting in front of the theater to see the Biedermeister and Bitschi silver panther show—it was, indeed, the free show comped with their stay. A swarm of other guests, many of them elderly, waited in front of the theater as well. Suddenly, the doors to the theater burst open, and the ticketholders rushed inside.

Aria stood, careful not to spill her champagne. "Shall we?"

Hallbjorn glanced at the poster for the show, which stood on an easel just outside the double doors. The magicians, whose stretched, catlike faces looked like they'd undergone tons of plastic surgery, had twin mullet hairdos and stared intensely into the camera lens. The silver panthers sat next to them like obedient dogs—except that they were baring their enormous, pointy teeth.

"This doesn't seem like my kind of thing," Hallbjorn murmured uneasily. "Those guys look like assholes. And did I ever tell you that I was traumatized by a magician when I was younger? It was a clown who'd come to my friend Krisjan's eighth birthday party. He had the most terrifying laugh."

"Of course you were scared of him—he was a *clown*." Aria hit him playfully. "Magic shows aren't my thing, either, but hey—it's free. We should take advantage of all the perks, don't you think?" She grabbed his hand.

"Besides, we'll have a funny story about what we did the day before our wedding to tell people ten years from now."

Hallbjorn shrugged and drained the rest of his champagne. Together they entered the theater, which had psychedelic-print carpet, velour seats that were almost filled to capacity, and portraits of other stars who'd visited—a lot of country music names Aria only vaguely recognized, comedians like Jerry Seinfeld, and about a dozen different Cirque du Soleils—over the stage. The lights lowered just as they plopped down in two seats next to the aisle.

"That Sven Biedermeister is just so handsome!" a blond, pudgy woman who looked a lot like the Rosewood Day school librarian crowed from the row in front of them.

"I'm a Josef Bitschi girl myself," her companion, a gray-haired woman with lipstick on her teeth, swooned. "I just want to tackle him and smother him with kisses!"

Aria and Hallbjorn nudged each other and tried not to laugh. A beat later, the silvery curtain parted. A line of showgirls in feathered headdresses, tiny tanks, and high, glittering heels marched across the stage with enormous smiles on their faces. They did a kicky dance to the same sort of snarling eighties music that had been on the commercial that afternoon, and everyone cheered. Aria looked at Hallbjorn, shrugged, and started clapping, too.

Mist began to swirl. A kettledrum rumbled. Then two

silver panthers strutted onto the stage. Biedermeister and Bitschi sat atop them, waving their arms like cowboys. They'd even put little saddles on the panthers, as though they were ponies.

The audience went wild. The ladies in front of Aria and Hallbjorn looked like they were about to faint. The magicians dismounted their panthers and took a bow. "Hallo!" the dark-haired magician boomed in an Arnold Schwarzenegger accent. "Are you ready to be wowed?"

"Yes!" the audience answered.

Aria tried to exchange looks with Hallbjorn, but his eyes were fixed on the magicians.

The showgirls started kicking again, and then the show began. Biedermeister and Bitschi swirled their capes and made the panthers disappear. With a wave of their hands, one of the showgirls began to levitate. They stuck their heads in the panthers' mouths and coaxed the panthers to let out a few deep roars. After that, the lights went up and the magicians plopped down on stools and whistled for the cats. Two handlers walked them out on long metal leashes. The cats dutifully sat down next to the magicians as though they were sweet kittens from the ASPCA.

"We rescued Arabelle and Thor from poachers in Africa," Biedermeister—or was it Bitschi? Aria couldn't tell them apart—said in a now-it's-story-time voice. "It was a dramatic mission, but we knew it was right to save them from their brutal fate."

A screen lowered behind the magicians and showed a picture of a helicopter landing on the Serengeti. The next photo in the slideshow depicted a bunch of people running commando-style through the jungle, presumably to capture the cats. There were more pictures of the silver panthers in the wild, the dens where they lived, and a silver panther pelt hanging in an African market. The crowd booed.

"They were just babies when we rescued them," the other magician said, patting one of the panthers on its alabaster muzzle. "We nursed them to health. Raised them as our own." More photos showed the little panthers in Biedermeister's and Bitschi's arms, frolicking in a backyard, meeting a golden retriever, and playing with an oblivious-looking child.

"*Awww*," the audience cried. The women in front of Aria dabbed at their eyes.

The magicians went on about how much they loved the panthers for a little while longer, and then it was back to the show. They trapped a showgirl in a box, stuck fake knives through an audience participant, and encouraged one of the silver panthers to disappear through a flaming hoop. It reappeared in a glass cage on the runway that extended into the audience. A young girl reached up to give the creature a hug, but one of the animal handlers leapt forward and intervened.

When one of the magicians coaxed a panther to

balance on its hind legs and dance with him, Aria began to applaud—it *was* kind of cute. Hallbjorn kicked her. When she looked over, he was staring at her in horror.

"What?" she whispered.

Hallbjorn just stared. Aria slumped down in her seat. What was *he* so grumpy about?

After another half hour of bad eighties guitar riffs and more crowd swoons, Biedermeister and Bitschi disappeared into a puff of smoke. Everyone went wild. Hallbjorn grabbed Aria's hand and yanked her up even before the magicians could return to the stage for their curtain call. He walked so quickly out of the theater that she could barely keep up. In the lobby, Hallbjorn glared at the poster of the magicians, then kicked it off its easel.

"What was that for?" Aria cried.

"How can you even ask that?" Hallbjorn's eyes were wild. "Wasn't that the most disgusting thing you've ever seen? Those guys need to be arrested for animal cruelty!"

Aria glanced at the closed theater door. The crowd was still cheering. "You thought they treated the panthers badly?" she said slowly. "But what about that story they told about rescuing them from Africa? Poachers were going to turn them into carpets! Biedermeister and Bitschi fed them bottles and let them sleep in their beds!"

Hallbjorn snorted. "They didn't rescue those panthers—they stole them from their natural habitat. And for what? To be chained up twenty-two hours of the day? To be forced to walk on their hind legs? They rode them onto the stage like horses! Where's the dignity?"

"How are you so sure the panthers are chained up for twenty-two hours a day?"

"I just have a hunch," Hallbjorn spat. "I gave this show a chance—I thought they would be kind and compassionate to the animals. But it was disgusting. I'll bet you any amount of money these panthers live in tiny cages, sleep in their own feces, and have no chance to roam free. People shouldn't be clapping for those magicians. They should be shooting them."

Aria recoiled. But before she could protest, the doors to the theater opened, and the crowd began to spill out. Aria steered Hallbjorn away from the stream of people, afraid he was going to tell someone who'd had a perfectly good time that the magicians were no better than Michael Vick. "I didn't realize they were being treated so badly," she said quietly. "If it's true, I'm sorry I dragged you to that. That really sucks."

"It *does* really suck." Hallbjorn placed a curled fist into his palm. "There must be something we can do. I can't stand by and just let this happen."

Aria gave him a wary look. "I can't stand by either, but let's just relax tonight, okay? Have some fun." She leaned forward and pressed her lips against his. She felt him softening. "Didn't you tell me you're a master at roulette? I bet I can win more money than you can."

Hallbjorn paused. He glared at the people leaving the theater, then at the Biedermeister and Bitschi poster, but then he took a deep breath, grabbed Aria's hand, and smiled. "You're on," he said, and led them to the casino.

9

BIG WINNER!

A few hours later, Aria and Hallbjorn were standing over the roulette wheel, watching as it spun around and around. The air was hazy with cigarette smoke, and Aria's brain was starting to go to mush with the maddening sounds of a zillion slot machines all chirping at once.

"I'm telling you, I think number seventeen is jinxed," she whispered when the little ball fell into the double zero slot and the croupier raked everyone's chips away. "We haven't won once. Maybe we should bet on another number."

"But seventeen is lucky," Hallbjorn argued. "My birthday is August seventeenth. My family lives at Seventeen Bergstadastraeti. And the café where you and I met? It was at Two Hundred Seventeen Laugavegur. I think it's a sign." He shuffled the remaining chips in his pile. "Just one more bet on seventeen? Please?"

Aria pressed her lips together, staring at the fuzzy

green felt on the table. Since there were no windows in this place, she had no concept of what time it was, but she and Hallbjorn had made the rounds of the blackjack, poker, and craps tables, sometimes winning a little, but mostly losing. It had been a lot of fun—Aria had worried about Hallbjorn being opposed to gambling, saying it was wasteful or that the chips were made out of non-biodegradable materials, but he'd seemed just as into it as she was, using his own savings to play the tables. But they were down a hundred dollars—money they couldn't afford to lose.

"Really, we should be done. We need money for our marriage license and your visa." Aria looked again for a clock on the wall before she remembered there wasn't one. "Besides, I bet it's getting late."

"But I have a really good feeling about this." Hallbjorn gathered the remaining chips in his palms. "One more on number seventeen. And if I don't win, I'll figure out how to get the money back. I'll work washing dishes."

He plunked down all of the chips they had left—two hundred dollars' worth—onto number seventeen yet again. Aria shut her eyes, not able to watch the spinning wheel.

"All bets, all bets," the croupier called. Suddenly, Aria's skin began to prickle. She looked over her shoulder, feeling someone's eyes on her back. But everyone was entranced in their own games. Even the obsequious cocktail waitresses were preoccupied.

The wheel made *clack* sounds as it spun. It began to slow, and Aria heard the ball plunk into a slot. Hallbjorn grabbed her hand. "See! I *told* you!"

Aria looked down and gasped. The little ball had landed on seventeen.

Everyone at the table began to applaud. "Big winner!" the croupier said. An old lady in a mink stole winked at Hallbjorn from across the roulette table.

The croupier pushed a pile of chips toward Hallbjorn, and then another. Some of the chips were black, one-hundred-dollar denominations, but nine were blue, the likes of which Aria hadn't seen before. She turned one of them over and gasped. *One thousand dollars*, it said around the perimeter. Hallbjorn had won $9,800 in just one spin.

She scooped up Hallbjorn's winnings and raked them into the little plastic bucket that had BORGATA emblazoned on the side. "We are done gambling for tonight," she murmured to Hallbjorn. "There's no way we're losing this amount of money."

"How are you going to spend it, honey?" the old lady in the mink stole cooed. "A swanky vacation with your girl? A new motorcycle?"

Aria wondered what they would do with the money, too—since they were getting married, technically it would be *theirs*. It would certainly pay for quite a few months' rent on an apartment. Maybe it would even solve his legal problems in Iceland.

Hallbjorn grinned at the old lady. "I know exactly what I'm going to spend it on. It's going to a good cause."

He grabbed the bucket from Aria and strode toward the neon-lit cashier's booth in the corner. Aria trudged behind, all of her excitement suddenly drained. He was giving it to a *good cause*?

She caught up with him just as Hallbjorn was passing the bucket to a dishwater-blond cashier. "So, um, you're donating the money to Save the Whales or World Wildlife Fund, huh?" she asked, trying to keep her tone even.

Hallbjorn leaned against the counter as the cashier tallied up the chips. "Not *that* kind of good cause. I'm buying you an engagement ring."

"*What?*" Aria stepped back. It felt like she'd just gotten an electric shock. "Why would you do *that*?"

He smiled. "Because you deserve it. And I'm not taking no for an answer."

Hallbjorn signed the paperwork at the cashier's stand, pocketed the cash, and dragged Aria across the casino floor, zigzagging around a couple of showgirls, dumpy tourists with fanny packs, and a group of skanky-looking girls at the bar until they came to an archway that said SHOPS in glittering gold letters. The lights in all of the stores blazed brightly, and the shop doors were open wide. After passing a Godiva chocolatier, a place that sold tuxedos and upscale gowns, and a vintage wine boutique that was holding a tasting by the register, Hallbjorn turned into a jewelry store called Hawthorne & Sons that had a lozenge-sized diamond in the window.

"You don't have to get me a ring," Aria insisted.

"Of course I do," Hallbjorn called over his shoulder. "We're getting married. The man has to buy the woman a ring."

"I'm not that traditional," Aria said, but suddenly, a little thrill went through her. It *would* be nice to have an engagement ring, something to spin around her finger in class. It would make the wedding seem so much more official.

The salesgirl, who barely looked older than Aria, glided over to them. "Looking for something special?"

"We need an engagement ring." Hallbjorn gestured to Aria.

"Certainly," the salesgirl said brightly, and brought out a tray of diamond solitaires. Each was sparklier than the last. Aria was kind of afraid to touch them.

"This one is a good value." The salesgirl pointed to a huge round diamond on a thick white-gold band. "You get maximum bling for minimum price. All girls like bling," she added to Hallbjorn with a tight smile.

Aria held out her finger, and the girl slid on the ring. It had some heft to it. She spread out her fingers and turned her hand this way and that, watching as the diamond threw prisms all over the room. The ring wasn't that much different than the sparkler Jessica DiLaurentis wore. Spencer's mom had a ring that looked just like this, too. But did she really want to look like someone's *mom*?

Hallbjorn cleared his throat uncomfortably and made a face, like he smelled something bad. "Aria, I don't think we should be supporting the diamond trade."

"Agreed." She wriggled the ring past her knuckle and handed it back to the salesgirl. Then she slid off the stool and peered around the shop, her eyes sweeping over the cultured pearls, sapphire pendants, and pink diamond tennis bracelets. There had to be something in this place that didn't scream *I'm Rich, I'm Suburban, and I'm Totally Boring.*

And then she saw it.

Sitting in a display case in the corner was a thick white-gold ring carved to look like a coiled snake eating its tail. Sapphires formed its two beady eyes, and bands of onyx made up its striped scales. Aria darted across the room and pressed her face to the glass.

"Can I see this one?" she asked, pointing.

The salesgirl scrunched up her face. "That's not an engagement ring."

"Who cares?" Hallbjorn strolled over to Aria and peered at it, too. "That thing is awesome. And look! The gems were mined according to fair-trade laws!"

It felt like fate. The ring slid on Aria's finger as easily as the glass slipper fit Cinderella's foot. The snake head peered at her, its sapphire eyes glittering both menacingly and protectively. It seemed like a talisman, a good luck charm. As long as Aria wore this ring, nothing bad would happen to her. This snake would make sure her marriage to Hallbjorn was happy. It would ward off bad luck and evil spirits.

It would make sure A never, ever came back.

10

I DO

"You have the most amazing skin," a makeup artist named Patricia, who had a bunch of tattoos and smelled overwhelmingly of Head & Shoulders shampoo, said to Aria as she dusted some powder on her cheeks. "I hardly have to use anything on you at all."

"Be sure to make my eyes smoky and dramatic, though," Aria reminded her. "I want to look awesome for photos."

"You got it." Patricia rummaged around in her case. "So you're getting married, huh?"

"That's right," Aria answered, puckering her lips for some gloss.

"Are you excited?"

"Definitely." She shook her shoulders, feeling a little shiver.

It was the following afternoon, and Hallbjorn had surprised Aria yet again by booking her an in-room massage—with eco-friendly oils, of course—a visit from Patricia the makeup artist, and a professional blowout by Lars, who wore the tightest pants Aria had ever seen. The hotel room had been transformed into a salon, with Adele playing in the background, cucumber sandwiches and a pitcher of mimosas on the tray in the corner, tons of gossip magazines stacked on the bed, and the smell of massage oils lingering in the air. Hallbjorn had disappeared as soon as Patricia and Lars had come through the door, saying he'd wait to see Aria's transformation when it was finished. Aria had taken a shot of him with her digital camera just as he left the room. She was trying to document everything today, from Patricia's messy makeup bag to the seven earrings snaking up Lars's ears, not wanting to forget a single detail.

"You're going to be such a cute bride," Patricia murmured now. "What are you, twenty-one? Twenty-two?"

Aria nodded noncommittally, not wanting to say she was only seventeen. Her age was kind of an issue—when the porter had delivered the marriage license paperwork this morning, Aria indeed needed a parent's signature to allow the state of New Jersey to marry them. She'd forged Ella's name and included her own cell phone number, figuring she'd pretend she was Ella if anyone from the courthouse called to check.

She glanced at her cell phone on the bureau, feeling a guilty twinge. Should she call Ella and tell her what she was about to do? Or maybe she should call one of her old friends. It felt weird going through with this without anyone knowing. But this was between her and Hallbjorn, and the last thing she needed was someone trying to talk her out of it.

Soon enough, Patricia had completed Aria's makeup and Lars had blown out Aria's locks to perfection. She shut herself in the bathroom, slid the dress she'd found yesterday over her head, and stared in the mirror at the results. She'd fixed the rip at the neckline, and the dress fit perfectly at her waist and hips. With her straight hair and smoky eyes, she looked like a movie-star version of herself.

When she glided out of the bathroom and spread out her arms in a *Ta-da!* pose, Patricia whooped. "You look amazing."

"Stunning," Lars seconded, leaning coquettishly against the bureau. "You have your old, new, borrowed, and blue stuff, right?"

Aria looked at them blankly. Patricia and Lars both put their hands to their mouths. "Something old, something new, something borrowed, something blue?" Lars repeated. "You've never heard that? A bride wears each on her wedding day! It's good luck!"

Aria had heard it, but she'd just forgotten. She peered down at her dress. "Well, this is old," she volunteered. "But it's also new . . . to me."

"Here's something borrowed." Lars slid a leather bracelet off his wrist. It had spikes on it and said BADASS, but it was just the right rock-star touch.

"And wait a minute . . ." Patricia darted into the hall and returned with a bunch of violets.

"Where'd you get those?" Lars placed his hand saucily onto one hip.

"The vase by the elevator." Patricia put her finger to her lips. Then she tucked a sprig behind Aria's ear. "Perfect."

It was time to go, and they rushed her down to the lobby. Someone in a tuxedo waited by the revolving doors, his back to them. Aria didn't realize it was Hallbjorn until he turned around and smiled at her. "Wow," she gasped.

"I was just about to say the same about you," Hallbjorn answered, taking her hand.

They were silent for a moment, and then burst into giggles. *This is really happening*, Aria thought. *I'm really getting married.*

Aria threw on her coat, and Humpty, the porter from the day before, ushered them outside and showed them the bicycle built for two he'd rented. It had banana seats, streamers hanging from the handlebars, and no gear shifts in sight. "I could only find you a beach cruiser," he said sheepishly. "I hope that's okay."

"It's better than okay." The seat was covered in sand and the gears were a little rusty, but she couldn't imagine a better wedding transport.

The temperature was much warmer than the day before, and all of the snow had been plowed off the streets. Hallbjorn climbed onto the front part of the tandem bike and set off, giving the bell a little ring. It wasn't easy for Aria to pedal in heels, so she let her feet dangle for much of the ride. A few people waved as they passed, and a couple of horns honked. Aria thought she caught sight of someone lurking behind them, but when she looked over her shoulder, whoever it was had ducked around a corner . . . or maybe hadn't been there at all. She shook off her worries. Nothing was going to ruin her wedding day.

They reached the chapel, a small white building wedged between a pawnshop and a tattoo parlor. It said CHAPEL OF LUV in red lettering over the door, and there were heart-printed curtains in the windows. Hallbjorn helped Aria off the bike, then gave her a long, meaningful look.

"You are so beautiful, Aria Montgomery," he said.

"So are you, Hallbjorn Gunterson," Aria said, her voice trembling a little.

He leaned in and kissed her.

They walked up the stairs together. The inside of the chapel was swathed in red draperies, tall white columns, and vases overflowing with red and white roses. A glittering chandelier hung from the ceiling, and a few rows of seats were positioned on either side of a red-carpeted aisle. The room smelled like a mix of perfume and flowers, and soft music played through the speakers. A door opened at the end of the chapel, and someone in an Elvis costume, complete with the spangled jacket and bell-bottom pants, the bouffant hair, and the aviator sunglasses, strutted out and smiled at them. "Hey there, lovebirds," he crooned in a perfect Elvis voice. "I'll be marrying you today."

Aria laughed. It was too perfect.

Elvis asked for the license paperwork, and Aria handed it over. He tucked it into his pocket without even looking at it. "Now, do you kids have witnesses?"

Aria looked at Hallbjorn. "Uh, no . . ."

"We'll be their witnesses," a voice came from the left. A tall, slender showgirl wearing a plume atop her head was sitting next to the spitting image of Cher.

Elvis returned to the front of the chapel and instructed Hallbjorn to join him. Cher jumped from her seat and ushered Aria into a little anteroom just off the aisle, which contained a couple of chairs and a full-length mirror. Aria stared at herself, taking in her vintage dress and the flowers tucked in her hair. Cher stood behind her, fixing her hair from the back.

"Thanks for being our witnesses," Aria whispered.

"Oh, I just love weddings, honey," Cher answered in a deep voice. Aria caught sight of her enormous hands in the mirror and smiled wryly. Of *course* Cher would be a dude in drag.

Canon in D played through the speakers. After a few beats, Cher offered Aria her arm. Aria took it as though it were perfectly normal for a drag queen to be walking her down the aisle instead of Byron, her gaze anchored on Hallbjorn at the front of the chapel the whole time. There was a giddy smile on his face. His hands were clutched at his waist, and one of his feet tapped the ground.

She came to a stop next to Hallbjorn just as the music ended. Cher kissed her on the cheek, whispered, "Good luck," and then sat down next to the showgirl. Elvis faced the two of them, opened a large leather book with gilt-edged pages, and cleared his throat.

"We are gathered here today to unite Aria Marie Montgomery and Hallbjorn Fyodor Gunterson." He stumbled a little over Hallbjorn's name, and Aria nervously giggled.

Elvis continued with all of the typical marriage lines Aria had heard in countless movies and read in hundreds of books. He made them repeat how they would take each other for better or worse, through sickness and in health, in good times and in bad, as long as they both shall live. Aria's hands shook as Hallbjorn slid the snake ring on her finger. She reached for the plain gold band they'd bought for Hallbjorn at the same jewelry store and pushed it past his knuckle.

"I now pronounce you man and wife," she heard Elvis say, and then suddenly Hallbjorn was kissing her, and Cher and the showgirl were cheering. Aria's heart thrummed fast, all of this feeling like a dream. When she opened her eyes, confetti was falling from the ceiling. A band appeared from the back, quickly plugged their instruments into amps, and Elvis grabbed the microphone he'd spoken into to marry them and began belting out "All Shook Up."

The chapel turned into a dance party. Hallbjorn swung

Aria's hands back and forth. Cher grabbed Aria and gave her a little twirl. The showgirl shook her boobs and did some high kicks. A few elderly tourists in heavy wool coats wandered in, and Elvis invited them to join the celebration as well. Aria paused for a moment, drinking the whole thing in. It was all so . . . *her*, down to the stolen flowers behind her ear and the fact that Hallbjorn had forgotten to rent shoes with his tux and was still wearing his Icelandic climbing boots. A rush of happiness washed over her, and she broke into a wide, euphoric grin. She couldn't have imagined a more perfect wedding.

11

THE COUPLE WHO BREAKS
THE LAW TOGETHER . . .

When Aria and Hallbjorn emerged from the Chapel of Luv an hour and a half later, their voices croaky from singing along to Elvis songs and their feet aching from dancing with Cher, their tandem bicycle now had a flag affixed to the back that said JUST MARRIED in pink letters. A bunch of empty cans had been tied to the back, too.

"That was the best wedding *ever*," Aria said, climbing aboard the bike. "Now I can't wait to get you back to our hotel room, *husband*."

"I agree, *wife*." Hallbjorn turned his new wedding ring around on his finger. "But I want to show you something first."

"Is it another surprise?" Aria asked, her mind whirling. Maybe Hallbjorn had arranged some kind of amazing dinner. Or booked them tickets on a mini-honeymoon.

"You'll see when we get there." Hallbjorn threw his leg over the seat and began to pedal.

They took off down the street, the cans clanging. Instead of turning into the Borgata's main entrance, Hallbjorn bypassed it and banked left into a back driveway. They snaked through a bunch of parking lots and loading zones until they stopped at a large metal garage door. Hallbjorn dismounted from the bike and dusted off his tuxedo, which had gotten sprayed from some salt on the road.

Aria looked around. Not a soul was in sight, and they were hemmed in by huge, dirty snowdrifts. A bunch of semitrucks stood waiting, their cabs unoccupied. She thought she heard a cough and froze, but as she waited, no more sounds came.

"Why are we here?" she asked shakily.

"I'll show you." Hallbjorn walked to the garage door and began to pull on the small handle at the bottom. Before Aria could stop him, he'd hefted up the door to reveal a small, dark room. The smell of cat pee hit Aria's nostrils immediately, and she suppressed a gag. When Aria's vision adjusted, she saw two black cages on opposite ends of the room. Large shapes huddled behind the bars. Then she heard a loud, menacing roar.

She turned to Hallbjorn, momentarily dumbstruck. "Are these the panthers from the show?"

"Yes." Hallbjorn flipped on a light, which just made the beasts growl louder. They looked even bigger up close, their bodies solid muscle, their eyes glowing yellow. They were shut into two tiny cages barely big enough for them to properly turn around or lie down in. Their food and water bowls were empty. There was poop all over the floor, and the room seemed way too cold for an animal to be comfortable.

"How did you find them?" Aria gasped.

"I did some poking around while you were getting your makeup done," Hallbjorn explained. "It was easier to find them than I thought. No one looks after them for most of the day. They're only important when they have to perform." He gestured to one of the panthers. It was now huddled in a ball, shivering.

Tears came to Aria's eyes. "The poor things."

Hallbjorn turned to her, his face suddenly full of excitement. "But we can help them. I want us to set them free. Give them the life they deserve."

Aria squinted at the panthers' cages. There were several huge locks on the doors. "How are we supposed to do that?"

"I think I've figured it out. Between seven and eight A.M., their handler unlocks the cages so that they can get some exercise—which is just them getting led around on short leashes. Tomorrow morning, I could distract the handler and you could sneak in there, open the doors, and set the panthers free."

"*I* have to set them free?" One of the cats yawned, and Aria pointed to its enormous canine teeth. "And risk them tearing me limb from limb?"

"Then I'll unlock their cages. You distract the handler."

Hallbjorn looked exasperated. "The point is that we'll be letting them out. Freeing them from their oppressors."

"So they can wander around Atlantic City?" Aria took a small step away from him. "Hallbjorn, this isn't exactly their natural habitat. Where are they going to live? Under the boardwalk? What are they going to do if it snows? What will they do for food?"

"It's better than the situation they have here." Hallbjorn swept his arm toward the cages. The panthers both let out mighty roars as if in response.

"But a loose panther could hurt someone!" Aria cried. "Think about those old people at the chapel just now. Do you seriously think they could outrun a panther?"

Hallbjorn put his hands on his hips. "I'm sure they're very gentle. And they won't try to hurt anyone—they just want to be free. They'll probably head straight for the marshland out of town."

Aria stared at him, waiting for the moment Hallbjorn would start snickering and say that he was just kidding—he was just going to call the ASPCA and have them take care of the situation. But the laugh didn't come. He stared at her fixedly, his face utterly serious.

"I want to share everything with you now that we're married," Hallbjorn said. "And I also want our marriage to be about something bigger than just us. We should conquer the world together."

Aria took another step out of the garage, her heel landing in a pile of slush. "But not like this. We could really get in trouble. I thought you came here to *escape* trouble."

Hallbjorn's face fell. "Well, *I* thought you'd be into the idea. I thought you *cared*."

"I *do* care. I love how committed you are to causes like this, and I want to share in your passion. But not by breaking the law."

Aria glanced over her shoulder. They could get in trouble just by being here. Biedermeister and Bitschi could sue them for trespassing. And this place was so grim. All of the snowdrifts had turned black from truck exhaust. The smell of cat poop was making her eyes water. She looked down at the snake ring on her finger. Suddenly, the jocularity of their wedding ceremony seemed long ago and far away.

"Maybe we should think about this a little bit more," Aria said, winding her arm around Hallbjorn's waist. "If you really want to help the panthers, we should call some sort of authority—someone who can take them to a safe place. Besides, this is our wedding night. Wouldn't you rather be doing wedding-night things instead of planning how to set panthers free?"

Hallbjorn's mouth twisted. Aria could tell he was cracking.

She traced a pattern on his back. "Just think. Tomorrow morning we could wake up together as man and wife, watch the sunrise, have breakfast in bed . . ."

She walked her fingers up his back and pushed a lock

of hair out of his eyes. Hallbjorn glanced again at the panthers in their cages. Aria tilted his gaze away and lightly kissed his neck. "Please?"

Finally, Hallbjorn sighed. "How can I say no to you?"

"You can't. I'm your wife. You have to do everything I say."

Chuckling, Hallbjorn shut the garage door and mounted the tandem bike once more. Aria climbed on the back, and they rode to the hotel's main entrance. As they rounded the corner, Aria heard another tormented roar. Hallbjorn's back muscles tensed. But he kept pedaling, and eventually, the sad, lonely growl faded away.

12

MASS PANIC

Aria opened her eyes. She was standing on a lawn outside a courthouse. A whole town spread out before her over the hillside. It was Rosewood. From her vantage point, she could see Rosewood Day and the Hollis spire. She could even see the top of the Hastings house with its antique rooster weather vane.

But how did she get here? Did it have something to do with her marriage to Hallbjorn? Was she in trouble for forging Ella's signature? She peered again at the ground and wrinkled her nose. The snow was gone. In fact, the grass looked kind of . . . *green*. How could a foot and a half have melted so quickly?

The doors to the courthouse flung open, and a flurry of people and reporters with cameras and microphones burst onto the steps. "Mr. Thomas, Mr. Thomas!" Ian Thomas rushed down the stairs with his lawyer and ducked into a waiting car at the curb.

Aria's head began to pound. She'd witnessed this scene before. This was Ian's arraignment. Last month.

"Hey."

Aria swiveled around. When she saw the blond figure with the heart-shaped face standing before her, a scream froze in her throat. "*Ali?*" she whispered.

"In the flesh," the girl said, curtseying. "Did you miss me?"

Aria stared at her. It was Ali . . . but it *wasn't*. She was taller now. Older. Her boobs were bigger and her face thinner, but her voice was eerily just the same. So were those haunting blue eyes, the ones that always gleamed with mischief whenever she proposed a new dare, the ones that always narrowed whenever Aria or the others said something she deemed uncool.

Aria gripped the side of her head as though to keep her brain from exploding out of her skull. She glanced back at the crowd in front of the courthouse. The reporters were surrounding Ian's car, banging on the windows. But they should be talking to Ali, not Ian. Why didn't they see her?

"Don't bother getting their attention." Ali coolly reached into her jacket pocket and pulled out a cigarette. "Only you can see me."

Aria widened her eyes. "What do you mean?"

"I'm here just for you." The words on their own could have been a compliment, but Ali's tone twisted them to make them sound menacing and scary. "I'm keeping tabs on you, Aria. I'm watching your every move."

"Why?" Aria blinked hard.

Ali lit the cigarette and blew a smoke ring. "You know why." She offered Aria a drag of the cigarette, but Aria shook her head.

"He doesn't really love you, you know."

It felt like Ali had dumped a bucket of cold water over Aria's head. "Excuse me?" she sputtered.

Ali stubbed out the cigarette with her high-heeled bootie. "No one could ever love a kook like you. Noel didn't want you. Ezra couldn't get away from you fast enough. Hallbjorn is just using you." She sauntered toward a waiting Town Car that had pulled up from out of nowhere and slid into the backseat. "I was your only real friend, and you let me die. You don't deserve to be loved."

"Ali?" Aria cried, taking a few steps toward the car. "Wait! Where are you going?"

Ali didn't answer. The Town Car pulled away from the curb with a sputter of noxious exhaust. Aria got a big mouthful and staggered backwards. It felt like there were shards of glass in her lungs. A high-pitched giggle spiraled over the trees.

Aria shot up in bed, breathing hard. Her heart pounded in her ears. Her feet kicked under the sweaty covers. She looked around. She was in the room at the Borgata. Sun streamed through the windows. The clock on the side table said 9:03 A.M.

She rubbed her eyes for a long time. The images had

been so vivid. Ali's telltale laugh. Ali's haunting blue eyes. But it was all a figment of Aria's psyche, right?

The details of last night slowly came back to her, thanks to some clues around the room. The remains of the room service dinner she and Hallbjorn had eaten were still on a tray by the window. A drained bottle of champagne was tipped over on the floor. Hallbjorn's tuxedo lay in a crumpled pile on the chair along with Aria's vintage dress. The JUST MARRIED sign, which they'd propped up against the mirror, had fallen over. After they'd eaten, they'd collapsed into bed, swigging flutes of champagne. The alcohol had hit them both quickly, and they'd passed out before they could make the marriage, er, official.

The TV flickered, again tuned to the resort's in-house channel. The commercial for the silver panther show appeared, the magicians parading around the stage in their ridiculous shoulder-padded costumes. Aria hit MUTE, not wanting Hallbjorn to be reminded of those poor panthers again.

Only, where *was* Hallbjorn? His side of the bed was empty. He wasn't at the little dining table. There were no noises coming from the bathroom, either, and his hiking boots, which he'd kicked off by the minibar fridge, were gone.

Aria reached for her iPhone before she remembered— there was no way to reach Hallbjorn, as he'd ditched his phone before leaving Iceland, worried the police might be able to track it. She called down to the concierge instead, asking if they'd seen a very blond boy wandering through the lobby. Maybe he'd woken up early and gone to breakfast.

"I haven't seen anyone by that description," the perky woman who answered at the front desk said. "But I could page him for you. What was his last name again?"

"Gunterson." Aria spelled it out. "Yes, please page him. Tell him his wife is looking for him." It felt weird to say *wife*.

"I'll have him call you if he comes to the desk," the concierge said, then hung up with a click.

Aria paced around the hotel room, occasionally pulling back the curtains and staring at the empty beach out the window. After a few minutes, she couldn't stand being in the room for another second and grabbed her keys. The hallway was eerily empty. A door quickly shut, as if someone didn't want to be seen. The elevator cables creaked and moaned, sounding like screams. The dream throbbed in Aria's mind. *He's just using you*, Ali had said.

She rode the elevator to the ground floor and checked the fitness room, but only a couple of chubby women were walking on the treadmills, drinking something called AminoSpa. She popped her head into the little restaurant that served the buffet breakfast, but Hallbjorn wasn't there, either. She pushed through the revolving doors that led to the valet parking area. What if the Icelandic police had tracked Hallbjorn here and took him away while Aria was sleeping?

Suddenly, Aria wanted nothing more than to see Hallbjorn's blond head appear over the dunes. She craned her neck, hoping. When someone appeared, her heart lifted, but it was a middle-aged woman in a down coat instead. She was running at top speed.

"Take cover!" the woman screamed, shooting past Aria and through the revolving door into the hotel. A man sprinted up from the dunes next, glancing nervously over his shoulder. More people followed, terrified looks on their faces. All of them kept checking behind them, as though they were trying to outrun a tsunami.

A guy Mike's age grabbed Aria's arm. "Get back inside!" he shouted. "It's dangerous out here!"

"Why?" Aria squinted at him.

"Didn't you hear?" The guy looked at Aria like a tree branch had just sprouted out of her head. He pulled Aria inside and pointed to a TV screen tuned to CNN in the corner of the lobby. The Atlantic City skyline was on the screen. An anchor stared excitedly into the camera.

"Apparently, the incident happened just a few minutes ago, and we're getting the very first footage of the rampage in Atlantic City," the reporter said.

Rampage? Atlantic City? Aria moved closer to the TV. Was a serial killer targeting the city? She glanced out the window again, fearing for Hallbjorn's life. What on earth had she done, dragging him here? What if he was hurt?

Then she turned back to the TV screen. A banner had appeared at the bottom. *Deadly Cats Loose in Atlantic City, NJ.*

Aria opened her mouth to scream, but no sounds came out.

A picture of the two silver panthers appeared, along with a shot of Biedermeister and Bitschi in their magician's capes. "Panthers are very dangerous," the CNN correspondent said. "They've been known to maul humans, so please, everyone in Atlantic City, stay inside."

Aria sank into a chair, feeling dizzy. The next shot on the screen was of the tiny cages where the panthers had been held that Aria had seen the night before. Both doors were wide open, the locks broken. Words had been spray-painted on the cement floor in front of the cages. *Panthers have rights, too. Animal cruelty is wrong.*

"I can't believe someone could do such a thing," a woman who had come to a stop next to Aria murmured. "Do you think it's al-Qaeda?"

Bile rose in Aria's throat. She inched away from the woman as though she were culpable, too. She knew exactly who had done it. Without a shadow of a doubt.

Hallbjorn.

13

MISTAKES WERE MADE

In a matter of minutes, every guest of the Borgata was cowering in the lobby, too afraid to go outside and face the loose panthers. Rumors of panther sightings swirled. People had seen them on the beach, near the local diner that was famous for its blueberry pancakes, and roaring outside the Trump Taj Mahal. Apparently one of the panthers had trapped a child under the boardwalk; a couple of people had thrown hamburger meat on the sand, distracting the cat and allowing the kid to escape. The other panther had found its way into a strip club. Every stripper and patron was forced to evacuate, the girls standing in the parking lot in next to nothing.

Broadcasts of the panthers' rampage played on every television screen in the Borgata's lobby, bars, and restaurants. News vans from everywhere in the tristate area screeched into the Borgata parking lot, and the lobby quickly transformed into a makeshift studio. Biedermeister and Bitschi were being interviewed over by the Starbucks kiosk, looking haggard and distraught. "I don't know who would do this to us," Biedermeister said, shaking his head. "We have no enemies."

Aria rode back up to the room and flopped down on the bed, still not believing this was happening. She couldn't believe Hallbjorn had gone through with it. Was he planning on returning to Aria and telling her what he'd done? Did he expect her to be proud of him?

She looked again at his crumpled tuxedo on the floor and felt an unexpected pang of longing. Their wedding ceremony had been so perfect, a memory she thought she'd treasure forever. Now, it felt tainted and tarnished. She picked up the tuxedo jacket from the floor and hung it neatly on a hanger. The rose corsage the showgirl had poked in Hallbjorn's lapel was still there. When Aria pressed the jacket to her nose, it smelled like Hallbjorn, a mix of chocolate and mint and the brisk winter air.

Underneath the jacket was the shirt, cummerbund, and socks, but the tuxedo pants, which had a satin stripe running up the side, were nowhere to be seen. Aria peered around the room for Hallbjorn's suitcase, thinking he'd stuffed the pants in there. She could have sworn he'd left his bag in the closet, but it was also nowhere to be seen. Nor was it in the bathroom, on the armchair near the window, or in one of the bureau drawers.

She froze in the middle of the room, suddenly knowing. Hallbjorn had taken his bag with him. He'd never planned on coming back here. Apparently, Aria's refusal to help free the panthers was grounds for abandonment.

So that was *it*? Had he seriously ditched her for some panthers? She thought about how he'd said he loved her. How excited he'd been to get married yesterday. It was all a ruse?

Tears rolled down her cheeks. She ripped the snake ring off her finger and set it on the desk, then changed her mind and winged it across the room. The ring clanged against the heater and fell onto the floor atop a few sheets of paper.

It was their marriage license. Aria crouched down and stared at the red seal from the state of New Jersey. It looked so official. Binding. But then she stared at Ella's signature, all loops and swirls, nothing like Ella's real signature. Aria had signed it with a glittery purple pen. The license made a crinkling sound when she stuffed it in her bag. She shoved her feet into her shoes, grabbed her room key and the ring, and rushed out of the door, suddenly fueled with purpose. There was something she needed to do.

There wasn't a single soul on the streets, and when Aria walked up the steps of the Atlantic City courthouse, the guards waiting at the metal detectors gave her startled looks. "You went outside with the panthers on the loose?" one of them blurted. Aria plunked her bag on the conveyor belt without answering.

A woman at the info desk directed her to a small office on the second floor that was packed full of papers and smelled like stale cigarettes. Aria approached a clerk behind a bulletproof-glass-protected window who was glued to a report about the silver panthers on a mini TV. "The last spotting of the panthers was in an alleyway behind Caesars," a reporter's voice said. A bunch of guys in jumpsuits that said ANIMAL CONTROL were on the screen. They pointed enormous blow-dart stun guns at a green BFI dumpster.

"Excuse me." Aria passed the marriage documents through the little slot in the window. "I need to come clean about something. These documents are not valid."

The woman wrenched her gaze from the TV and stared at the papers. "Why is that?"

"I'm seventeen." Aria held up her driver's license. "And I forged my mom's signature. She has no idea I got married. I doubt she'd allow it."

The woman pushed her glasses lower on her nose and gave Aria a long, disgruntled stare. "You know that it's illegal to forge someone's name, right?"

"I know." Aria hung her head. "I wasn't thinking." She wondered, suddenly, if she would get in trouble. What was the penalty for forgery? A fine? *Jail*?

The woman just shrugged and lifted a stamp over the license. "I'm going to have to make this null and void." Then she clucked her tongue. "Who wants to get married at seventeen years old, anyway? Why be weighed down by a husband? They're nothing but trouble. A modern woman should be free and unencumbered."

Aria almost laughed. That sounded like Hallbjorn's argument for freeing the panthers.

The clerk shook her head. "Does the guy you married know you forged your mom's signature?"

The TV screen behind the clerk caught Aria's eye. The Animal Control guys were still stalking the dumpster. Suddenly, one of the silver panthers appeared. They tried to shoot it with a tranquilizer, but it pounced toward them and they all scattered. The cameraman started to run, too. He got a parting shot of the panther as he fled. It looked anxious and scared. Not happy, like Hallbjorn predicted. Not free.

For a split second, she considered telling the clerk that Hallbjorn had set the panthers loose. All of Atlantic City was looking for him, after all. They needed to bring him to justice for what he did.

But she couldn't quite form the words. Hallbjorn might have been a lunatic, but he was *still* her husband—at least for a few more seconds, anyway. And deep down, she knew his heart was in the right place.

"I don't think our marriage is at the forefront of his mind right now," Aria answered glumly.

The noise of the VOID stamp hitting the paper was deafening. The woman asked Aria if she'd like to keep the license as a souvenir, and Aria reluctantly grabbed the paper through the slot and turned toward the door.

"Hey," she called, and Aria glanced over her shoulder. The clerk's grumpy expression had lifted and softened. "You'll get married when the time is right," she said. "I work as a part-time psychic. I know these things."

"Thanks," Aria said. And for some crazy reason, it made her feel better.

She pulled her coat closely around her as she exited the courthouse. The air was turning bitter, and clouds were rolling in. It would probably be best if she got out of Atlantic City before it started to snow again. She looked up and down the boulevard. The casinos gleamed in the distance. The ocean roared beyond, filling the air with a salty scent. A few streets away, sirens wailed.

Aria reached into her purse and pulled out the defunct marriage license. *Aria Marie Montgomery is married to Hallbjorn Fyodor Gunterson.* Slowly, methodically, she tore it into lengthwise shreds until it was tiny pieces of confetti, not that different from the confetti that had rained down on her and Hallbjorn's heads at the Chapel of Luv. She opened her palms and let the breeze pick up the shreds and blow them away. The bits drifted under cars, swirled into treetops, and whisked around corners, never to be seen again.

"Good-bye, Hallbjorn," Aria muttered, knowing she'd never see him again, either.

14

BLOWIN' IN THE WIND

Aria had just paid the cabdriver and let herself into the garage at Ella's house when she heard a rattling sound behind her. The Subaru was pulling up the driveway, Byron at the wheel. Meredith sat in the front passenger seat, and Mike climbed out of the back. When he saw Aria, he waved.

It took Aria a moment to wave back. The days had gotten away from her. She'd forgotten that Byron and Mike were returning from the Solstice trip this afternoon.

Byron spotted Aria in the garage, turned off the car, and climbed out. "Where have you been? I've been trying to call you for hours."

"Uh, I was on a bike ride," Aria answered, saying the first thing that came to mind.

Byron glanced at Aria's bike, which was tucked behind some old tires and black plastic bags full of clothes meant for Goodwill. It was an obvious lie, but Aria was too tired to explain herself.

"Byron?" Meredith opened the car door. "Would it be weird if I used the bathroom here? If I don't pee I'm going to burst."

Byron looked at Aria for permission, and she shrugged and gestured toward the door that led to the house—the last thing she wanted to see was Meredith *bursting*. Meredith elbowed past, taking butt-clenching steps and practically diving headfirst into the powder room.

The rest of them headed inside, too. Byron remained in the laundry room, seeming a bit hesitant to enter his old house. Mike, on the other hand, barreled into the kitchen and opened the fridge. "There's no food," he whined. "What did you eat this whole week, Aria? And why is it so frickin' *cold* in here?"

"It *is* cold in here." Byron walked across the kitchen and peered at the thermostat. "The power didn't go out, did it?"

Aria hung up her coat on a hook by the washer so she didn't have to look her dad in the eye. "I just turned down the heat for a few days. I was trying to save electricity."

"That's a very noble cause, especially during Solstice time." A regretful look fell over Byron's features. "It's really too bad you missed our celebration, Aria. We did the most amazing nature walks. And burning the Yule log was truly magical. A lot of the other guests joined in the festivities, and we all really bonded."

Mike, who was drinking orange juice out of the carton, let out a cross between a choke and a cough. Aria caught his eye, and he made a pained face.

"Of course, I wish Mike would've spent more time outdoors with us instead of watching television." Byron glanced at his son and shook his head.

"But then I would have missed the biggest news story ever!" Mike set the OJ container on the island, switched on the little TV in the corner, and turned the channel to CNN. "Did you hear about this, Aria? The panthers?"

Aria ran her tongue over her teeth. "Uh, no," hoping she sounded convincing.

"Check it out." Mike pointed at the screen. It was a shot of the Borgata lobby. Police cars were parked under the covered drive. Biedermeister and Bitschi hovered nervously near the bar, talking on their cell phones. *Panthers Still on the Loose*, the banner said at the bottom.

"Panthers got loose in Atlantic City," Mike explained. "It's caused this mass panic."

"Oh crazy," Aria said evenly, as if this was the first she was hearing of it.

Meredith appeared in the kitchen doorway and glanced at the screen. "Uch, Mike, turn that off. It's terrible."

"Are you kidding?" Mike moved even closer to the TV. "This is the craziest thing I've seen in a long time! Apparently one found its way into a strip club." He smiled lustily. "I could have saved those strippers."

A breaking news starburst popped up on the screen. The camera cut away from the reporter and focused on a blond guy in handcuffs. When the cameraman zoomed in on his face, Aria almost screamed. It was Hallbjorn. His eyes were wild, he was thrashing back and forth, and he was bellowing something over the sounds of the police sirens and the reporters. "Those panthers deserve to be free! They were being tormented in those cages! Support panther rights!"

Meredith crept closer to the television. "Is that the guy who did it?"

"He looks like a psycho," Mike said.

Byron squinted at the screen. "Is it me, or does he look familiar?"

Aria pressed her lips together, afraid she was going to throw up. The cops pushed Hallbjorn into a police car. The reporter's voice cut in. "The police apprehended the self-proclaimed eco-terrorist today, after he tried to flee on a bike," she explained. "I'm getting word that he thought the panthers were 'oppressed' and 'not able to live out a pantherly existence.'"

"*Pantherly existence.*" Mike snickered.

"I swear I've seen him somewhere." Byron squinted at the screen. Hallbjorn's head was hanging out the car window. "Panthers have souls, too!" he bellowed, waving his arms around. His name scrolled across the bottom of the picture. *Hallbjorn Gunterson, Eco-Terrorist*, it said in big yellow letters.

Byron rubbed his chin. "That's an Icelandic name."

The reporter appeared on the camera. "We're just getting details about Mr. Gunterson. He only arrived in this country a few days ago, fleeing from police custody in

Iceland. He's wanted there because he tried to blow up an office at the demolition company that was hired to tear down an Icelandic puffin sanctuary."

"*What?*" Aria exclaimed out loud. Everyone turned to look at her, and she shrugged sheepishly to cover her reaction. Hallbjorn had certainly glossed over *those* details. Suddenly, all of her regret and nostalgia disappeared. Hallbjorn truly was a lunatic.

Mike placed a hand to his chin. "Actually, didn't you date someone in Iceland named Hallbjorn, Aria?"

"Uh, yeah." Aria wound a piece of hair around her finger. "But it's a pretty common name."

"It *is?*" Mike looked skeptical.

"Of course it is." Aria tossed her hair over her shoulder and sauntered out of the room. There was no way she could watch another minute of the newscast without giving her secret away. And that, she had decided, was absolutely out of the question. It was like the question of the tree falling in the forest: If no one knew Aria got married, if no one *saw*, then it had never happened. She'd gotten the marriage annulled before it was logged into any permanent records. No one would be able to trace Hallbjorn to her.

The only real proof Aria had left that a marriage had taken place was the snake ring. She felt for it in her pocket as she climbed the stairs. Some pawnshop would buy it. She'd steal into Philly next week, go to a neighborhood where she definitely wouldn't be recognized, and get rid of it once and for all. And as for the money she'd get, maybe she'd give it to the poor kid who'd gotten trapped by one of the panthers under the boardwalk. Or to the strippers who'd had to run out of the club half-naked because a panther had gotten loose inside. Or maybe she'd use it to take a *real* vacation over spring break.

But no matter what, this was something she never had to think about again. No one knew, after all—and she was planning to keep it that way forever.

A VERY MARRIED CHRISTMAS

Lions and tigers and silver panthers, oh my! Biedermeister and Bitschi's pet cats weren't the only dangerous things running around Atlantic City. Aria thinks the sole witnesses to her marriage and annulment were some celebrity look-alikes and a grumpy court official, but I had front row seats for the whole affair. And unlike the state of New Jersey, I'm not going to pretend it never happened— especially when I learned sooooo much from the *un*happy couple.

Like . . . while Hallbjorn may know how to detonate an explosive, Aria's the one with the self-destruct button. She ruins everything she touches: Ezra's career. Her parents' marriage. Her own relationships. Yet for someone so easily burned, Aria keeps playing with fire—she falls in and out of love faster than you can say "I do." I can only imagine who her next relationship will be with—another artist, another Typical Rosewood Boy?—and how it will end. Unless, of course, I end it for her.

This is the problem with artsy girls. They treat life like a blank canvas, painting over their missteps and never learning from their mistakes. Every new guy, every new town is simply an opportunity to try on a new persona. But moving to Iceland doesn't fix a broken family, dyeing a vintage wedding dress lime-green doesn't make it fabulous new prom-wear, and nothing, absolutely nothing, gets Aria and her friends off the hook for what they did.

The honeymoon's over, Aria. And reality is going to bite.

That's something Spencer has to find out, too. She still hopes that she can start fresh with her damaged family. But don't worry, my pretties. Spencer is about to learn that not everyone deserves—or gets—a happy New Year . . .

—A

SPENCER'S PRETTY LITTLE SECRET

1

DEEP FREEZE IN THE
WARM FLORIDA SUN

The day after Christmas, Spencer Hastings sat squished
in a narrow leather seat of a private plane as it touched
down at the airport in Longboat Key, Florida. Through
the window, she watched the heat rise up from the tarmac,
making the palm trees look like they were swaying and
shimmering. The sun beat down ruthlessly on the traffic
controllers, who strutted about in T-shirts, shorts, and
sunglasses. It was a huge change from the seventeen-
degree weather and two-foot snowdrifts in Rosewood.
Spencer couldn't think of a better time to take a vacation
to Nana Hastings's Florida beach house—although given
that her family was, as usual, barely speaking to her, she
could think of many better groups to travel with.

Spencer's mother, who sat farther up the aisle and
was dressed in her requisite flying uniform of a cashmere
hoodie and yoga pants, lifted the satin sleep mask from
her eyes. "Peter, did you remember to rent a car?"

Spencer's father paused from typing on his Android phone and let out an exasperated puff of air. "Of *course* I did. I rented a Mercedes SUV."

"The G-class?"

"No." He stood and grabbed everyone's bags from the overhead compartment. "The ML350."

Spencer's mother made a face. "But the G550 has more legroom."

"Veronica, everything is walkable in Longboat Key— we don't even really *need* a car." He dropped Spencer's mother's travel-sized Louis Vuitton bag on the empty seat next to her.

The captain interrupted, telling the family that they'd landed—*duh*—and that Gina, the flight attendant, would open the door so they could disembark. Spencer eased out of the aisle behind her parents. Her sister, Melissa, fell in line behind her, keeping her head down and her iPod earbuds securely in each ear. She hadn't said a word the whole flight, which was odd—normally, she didn't shut up about the town house she was renovating, how well she was doing at the University of Pennsylvania Wharton School of business, or how generally fabulous she was.

Spencer knew the reason for Melissa's silence. A month and a half ago, Melissa's boyfriend, Ian Thomas, had been arrested for murdering Spencer's old best friend Alison DiLaurentis. Apparently, Ian and Ali had been secret lovers; Ali had pushed Ian to expose their relationship, and Ian had killed her in a frustrated rage. As Melissa's boyfriends were usually blue bloods groomed to make partner at daddy's law firm or become the next state senator, Ian's circumstances represented a bit of a step down. Melissa didn't believe Ian had really done it, but that didn't matter. The rest of Rosewood sure did.

The situation was made even more complicated by the fact that Spencer had been the one who'd turned Ian in—she had recalled seeing him the night Ali went missing. In the month since Ian was thrown in jail, Melissa had been extra-frosty with Spencer—an impressive feat, considering the sisters didn't have a good relationship to begin with. Over the past few months, things had gone from bad to worse: They'd fought viciously over a boy, aired their dirty sisterhood laundry in front of a therapist, and had gotten into a colossal argument that ended with Spencer accidentally pushing Melissa down the stairs. Not to mention that Spencer had stolen Melissa's AP Econ paper and claimed it as her own, winning a prestigious Golden Orchid essay contest as a result.

Gina opened the hatch, and the family climbed down the rickety staircase onto the runway. The Florida heat and humidity enveloped Spencer immediately, and she shucked her North Face jacket. The Hastings family walked stiffly and silently into the terminal, their synchronized footsteps the only indication they even knew each other at all.

Inside, a uniformed man held up a small sign that read HASTINGS. He led them to their waiting SUV, on loan from the local car rental place. Spencer's father signed some papers, loaded their luggage into the back, and everyone climbed in, slamming their doors loudly behind them. Spencer's father stepped on the gas, hard enough that Spencer's body lurched back against the plush leather seats.

"Ugh, it stinks like cigarettes in here." Her mother fanned the air in front of her face, breaking the silence. "Couldn't you have had them clean it out, Peter?"

Her father sighed audibly. "I don't smell anything."

"I don't smell anything, either," Spencer put in, wanting to stand up for her dad. Her mom had been ragging on him for days now.

But this just earned her a chilly look from them *both*. Spencer knew why. Against their wishes, she had declined the Golden Orchid award last month, admitting to the judging committee that she'd plagiarized her sister's paper. Her parents had wanted her to keep quiet about it and just accept the award, but dealing with Ali's death, discovering the identity of her killer, getting stalked by Mona Vanderwaal–as–A, and having Mona nearly push her off a cliff had put everything in perspective.

Spencer sank down in the backseat and stared out the window as her father turned onto the main boulevard. She'd been to Nana's house so many times she could walk this street blindfolded—first came the marina, with its enormous private yachts, then the yacht club, which had a tasteful sign out front that said LUAU DECEMBER 28, 9 P.M., then the bridge that was raised whenever a particularly tall boat passed through, followed by the many overpriced shops and fancy restaurants. And everywhere, women in sprawling sun hats and oversized sunglasses peppered the sidewalks and outdoor patios, while men, looking fresh in their golf clothes, parked their convertibles and flashed their whitened teeth.

Mr. Hastings rolled up to the gated community where Nana Hastings lived. A guard with tanned, leathery skin and wearing a polyester uniform checked them off on a clipboard and waved them through. After passing a brilliant green golf course, a multitiered pool in which Spencer had spent many hours swimming, a private shopping area, and a world-class spa, they turned on Sand Dune Drive and approached the huge white compound that looked like a mix between the White House and Cinderella's castle at Disney World. Doric columns flanked the front façade. Terraces lined the sides and the back. A tall turret jutted into the sky. The yard was elegantly landscaped; not a single flower was anything less than wedding-arrangement perfect. As Spencer's father opened the car door, she could hear the roar of the ocean. It butted up to the back of the house; a private deck looked out onto the beach.

"Now, *this* is more like it." Mr. Hastings put his hands on his hips, arched his back a little, and stared into the brilliant blue sky.

They unlocked the front door and pulled their bags into the foyer, creating a fort of name-brand luggage. The house smelled like expensive floor wax, a smattering of sand, and lavender laundry detergent. It was utterly silent inside, and Spencer was about to ask where Nana was before she remembered she'd left for Gstaad, Switzerland, with her new boyfriend, Lawrence, yesterday morning. Nana Hastings wasn't really into interacting with her family—she was rarely around when they visited. She in particular had never taken to Spencer. It must be genetic.

Spencer carried her bags up the sweeping, Southern plantation-style staircase to the bedroom she always stayed in, which was flooded with sunlight, had cheery yellow-and-white-striped wallpaper, a fluffy white rug, and an old brass bed. The room had a closed-up smell to it, as though no one had stayed in here for a long time.

She hoisted up her bag, pulled at the zipper, and began neatly unpacking her Florida wardrobe—bright sundresses, high-waisted sailor pants, and form-fitting polo shirts, which she refolded and placed into empty drawers. She unearthed her felt-lined travel jewelry case as she stood in front of the gleaming white bureau, ready to line up her necklaces and rings in the antique wooden jewelry box her grandmother had long ago cast off. She opened it, noticing a pair of chandelier-style earrings glistening from the top shelf. She gasped as she lifted them up, recognizing them instantly. She'd left them here the last time she'd visited, which had been over Memorial Day weekend in seventh grade. But the earrings weren't hers—they were Ali's.

Ali's family also had a place down here, just across the man-made lake, and she and Spencer had divided their time between the two houses, lying out on the sand, swapping clothes, sneaking slugs from Spencer's parents' Dewar's bottle, and flirting with boys downtown.

Ali had lent Spencer the earrings the night they had been invited to a house party a few streets over from Nana Hastings's. Spencer had struck up a conversation with a guy named Chad who'd dated Melissa one holiday break; after a while, she'd felt Ali's eyes on her. "You're acting really slutty," Ali had whispered nastily when Chad turned away. "Isn't it bad enough you already hooked up with *one* of your sister's boyfriends?"

Ali was referring to how Spencer had kissed Ian Thomas behind Melissa's back a few weeks earlier. But Spencer *hadn't* wanted to hook up with Chad—she was just talking to him. She and Ali had gotten into a huge, blowout fight; they didn't speak for the rest of the vacation. Ali hung out with some older girls from town, always laughing exaggeratedly when Spencer passed by. And Spencer wandered around alone, too proud to apologize.

Now she sank down on the bed and cradled the earrings in her hands. She *should* have apologized. If only she'd known that Ali had been seeing Ian—that that was why she was being so weird about Spencer kissing him. Maybe she could have somehow steered Ali away from Ian. Maybe she could have prevented Ali's murder.

Placing the earrings on her nightstand, Spencer stood

back up, changed into a pair of shorts, a soft American Apparel top, and a pair of Havaianas flip-flops, and walked downstairs. A warm, sweet-smelling scent wafted from the white-tiled kitchen.

"Hello?" Spencer called out, looking around. Her voice echoed throughout the empty first floor.

She heard loud voices on the patio and peeked out the sliding-glass door. Her family was sitting at the teak table that overlooked the pool and the ocean; there were bowls of chips and nuts, a marble slab containing several cheeses, and an open bottle of white wine on the table. Spencer's mouth watered.

The ocean roared loudly as she opened the patio door, right in the middle of a wild gesture her mother was making. Melissa looked like she'd eaten a sour plum, but Melissa always looked like she'd eaten a sour plum. Spencer glanced at her father, who was tapping on the iPad they'd given him for Christmas, probably playing Angry Birds. He'd only had it for a day and already he was obsessed.

She dragged another chair to the table just as Melissa popped a slice of aged cheddar in her mouth.

"Mom, do you want some cheese? It's really good," Melissa asked.

"What I *want*, Melissa, is for your father to put down his little toy and actually talk to us for once," her mother snapped.

Spencer froze. Melissa looked like she'd been slapped. Their mother usually reserved that tone for Spencer. Their father only sighed and continued tapping on his screen.

"Hey, how about we rent a movie tonight?" Spencer suggested, trying to ease the tension.

"A movie might be nice," Melissa offered. "Good idea, Spencer."

Spencer stared at Melissa with wide eyes, unsure how to respond. When had Melissa ever used the word *good* in any kind of relation to Spencer?

But then their mother snorted, as if the notion of a family movie night was outlandish, and that Spencer was an idiot for having suggested it. The family lapsed back into silence, and her parents, armed behind their invisible fortresses, stewed in their own private anger.

Spencer stifled a sigh. After everything that had happened this fall—Ali, Ian, even A—Spencer had hoped to spend the next few days sunning, getting spa treatments, and winning over her family. And then when she returned to Rosewood for second semester, she'd feel restored and rejuvenated.

But with World War III brewing in Nana Hastings's beach house, she'd be lucky to get any peace at all.

2

CUTE BOYS MAKE
EVERYTHING BETTER

The following morning, Spencer emerged from the ocean, staggered to her towel, and squeezed out her wet hair. She lay back and closed her eyes, letting the sun warm her shoulders, wondering what she should do next. She supposed she could get a head start on *The Sun Also Rises*, which she would have to write a paper on in English. Or she could go for a run—jogging on the beach always gave her calves great definition.

A shadow passed over her, and she opened her eyes.

"Hey." Melissa stood next to Spencer, her hand shading her eyes to the sun.

"Hey," Spencer said warily. Sure they'd shared a look at the table last night, but Spencer couldn't remember the last time Melissa had voluntarily spoken to her.

"So Mom and Dad are kind of out of control, huh?" Melissa said, plopping down next to Spencer. She scooped up a handful of sand and poured it over her toes.

"Aren't they always?" Spencer asked, taking a sip of water from her Nalgene bottle. It was only 10 A.M., and it was already eighty degrees and humid.

"Well, they don't usually snap at *me*," Melissa pointed out.

Spencer rolled her eyes, but she had to admit it was true. Her parents thought Melissa was perfect in every way.

"I was thinking," Melissa said, toying with a pearly pink conch shell, "that if we're going to have any fun on this vacation, it will have to be with each other."

Spencer sat up straight, stunned. "You want to hang out?" she asked skeptically. "With me?"

"Don't look so shocked. Who else am I going to hang out with here?" Melissa asked.

A wave crashed so far up on the shore that the water rushed up to the edge of Spencer's towel. She pushed her sunglasses up on her forehead and studied her sister. "I thought you hated me for turning Ian in?"

"Look, I don't think you're right . . ." She opened her mouth like she was about to say more, then changed her mind. "Whatever. The point is, I need a distraction from thinking about it, and you're all I've got."

"Gee, thanks," Spencer said wryly.

Melissa elbowed her in the side. "Don't be so sensitive. You know you're bored, too," she said, getting to her feet and dusting the sand off her legs. "Want to walk up to the club with me? We could do a spa day."

Spencer hesitated. A man with a yellow Lab jogged

by, and down the shore two grade-school girls were hard at work on a sand castle. Melissa was right. Spencer was lonely. And if Melissa was ready to bury the hatchet—for a few hours at least—maybe Spencer should give her a chance.

"Um, okay." Spencer threw on her cover-up and stuffed her towel in her canvas tote. Together they started up the sand, deciding to walk along the main route to the club.

There were a bunch of people out and about, and all the store doors were flung open, air-conditioning on full blast. Each shop was a trip down memory lane: There was Samantha's, the boutique where Spencer had bought a dress for her fifth-grade birthday party. Melissa pointed out the fudge shop where the sisters had had a fudge-eating contest when Spencer was eight—Melissa had won, of course. There was the store in which Spencer's dad had bought a long board and tried to teach himself how to surf. He'd spent the week paddling fruitlessly in the waves, too afraid to catch any.

She was looking at the Quiksilver T-shirts and Billabong hats through the window of a surf shop, when suddenly a shape shifted behind her. When she turned, someone ducked around a corner. Her stomach flipped.

"You okay?" Melissa asked, a concerned look on her face.

"Yeah," Spencer said, forcing her voice to remain steady. It was hard to shake the feeling that someone was following her. Taking a few deep fire-breaths, she reminded herself that Mona was dead. A was gone.

After accepting a sample from Ye Olde Saltwater Taffy Emporium and buying iced lattes at the Blue Dog Pancake House, Spencer and Melissa strolled to the Longboat Key clubhouse, a gorgeous white building at the edge of the bay. Twenty golf carts were parked in the front spots. Guys in polo shirts and khaki shorts shouldered golf bags, and women in visors gossiped in clumps.

The sisters followed the loud *thwock*s of balls hitting rackets on the tennis courts. Posters announcing an upcoming tournament on New Year's Day were tacked to the fences, and two guys were involved in a heated game. Both were dressed in white shirts and shorts—the club was as strict as Wimbledon, shunning colorful tennis gear—and looked to be in their early twenties. A dark-haired guy with an angular face, taut limbs, and a tight, squeezable butt was clearly the more talented of the two, making impressive drop shots and cross-court volleys. A crowd of girls had gathered on the perimeter of the court, their heads swiveling back and forth in time with the fluorescent-yellow ball.

"Did you know Colin's ranked ninety-second in the world?" a girl wearing a terry-cloth Lacoste dress and grosgrain-ribbon flip-flops whispered to her friend, who had on an equally short sundress and sky-high wedge heels. "He told me."

"He told *me* he's playing in the New Year's tournament," Wedge Heels said back.

Lacoste Dress rolled her eyes. "Of course he's playing in the tournament! He's totally going to kick ass!"

Spencer settled against the chain-link fence next to Melissa, resisting the urge to roll her eyes. Groupies were so lame.

But Colin, the guy with the cute butt, *was* fun to watch, especially as he decimated his opponent. His serve was blisteringly fast, whipping past the other player's face before he even had a chance to react. Every time he scored a point, he twirled his tennis racket and pretended not to be pleased with himself, but Spencer totally caught him smiling into his chest.

"I'm going to head inside and check out the spa menu," Melissa said, fanning herself. "You want in on a mani-pedi?"

"Sure," Spencer said absentmindedly, keeping her eyes on the match. "I'll meet you at the spa in a few."

When the game was finished—a complete rout—Colin and his buddy shook hands, walked to the sidelines, gulped down two bottles of something called AminoSpa vitamin water, and stripped off their shirts. Spencer coolly picked at her cuticles, not wanting to stare too pointedly at Colin's absolutely perfect abs. He was definitely hot—maybe even hotter than Wren, the boy Spencer had stolen from Melissa earlier this fall. If he weren't so mobbed with fans, he might just make the perfect winter-vacation fling. It had been ages since Spencer had gotten excited over a guy.

"Hey, Colin," Lacoste Dress cooed, winding a piece

of blond hair around her finger. "That was some amazing tennis."

"You're *sooo* good," another girl drawled. "Do you practice every minute of the day?"

"Pretty much." Colin wiped sweat off his face and opened another bottle of AminoSpa. "My trainer's down here for the winter—sometimes we play with the pros. The other day I saw Andy Roddick on the courts."

The girls nudged each other. "That is amazing," one of them said. "Nike should so sponsor you."

Colin just grinned. He finished loading his gear into a big lime-green Adidas bag and started in the direction of the clubhouse. Suddenly, he stopped and stared straight at Spencer. She could feel his eyes boring into the top of her head as she pretended to smooth a wrinkle on her cover-up. "Hello."

All of the girls' heads swiveled toward Spencer, too. "Hey," she answered, looking up and trying to remain poised and confident.

Colin took a few steps toward her. "Are you a new member of my cheering section?"

Spencer cocked her head. "I don't really *do* cheering sections—unless I'm the athlete being cheered on. But maybe I could make an exception."

The groupies began nudging each other. "Who *is* that?" one of them whispered.

"I bet she isn't even a club member." Wedge Heels didn't even bother to lower her voice.

Spencer glared at them, and every groupie looked away en masse. Suddenly, they reminded her of her parents. Excluding her. Acting like she didn't belong. Acting like she wasn't good enough to be here.

She turned to Colin again. "Like I said, I'm more into *doing* than *cheering*. What I'd rather do is volley with you sometime. If you ever need a partner, that is."

Colin raised an eyebrow. "Do you play?"

Spencer flicked her hair over her shoulder. "Of course I play." Her parents had made her take lessons since she was four.

Colin leaned back and eyed her carefully. After five long beats, he looked down and pulled out a BlackBerry from his bag. "You're on, then. What's your name?"

Spencer told him, and the girls started whispering again. "Let's play tonight," Colin decided, tapping something into his phone. He didn't bother to give Spencer *his* name. He probably assumed she already knew it. He was right—and she liked his confidence.

Spencer pretended to mentally check her schedule. "I think I could arrange that."

"Good." Colin tossed the empty AminoSpa bottle in a perfect arc into the trash can. "See you tonight at five-thirty. Same court. Winner buys drinks."

Spencer suppressed a smile and slipped her sunglasses back over her eyes. Had they just made a *date*? And he had assumed she was old enough to drink. *Score.*

Colin shot her a wink and sauntered away. Spencer

was dying to watch him climb the stairs and glide toward the locker room, but she restrained herself, not wanting to seem too eager. When she turned toward the gate, she came face-to-face with Colin's groupies, who were still staring at her.

She looked them straight in the eye. "Is there a problem?"

The girls flinched. Their mouths dropped open into matching round *O*s.

"I didn't think so," Spencer said breezily. She pulled her tote higher on her shoulder and strode off the court to meet Melissa in the spa. She could feel their gazes on her back the whole way down the sidewalk. The sun felt brighter, the air more fragrant, and when she glanced up at the blue sky, she saw a floating cloud that formed a near-perfect heart. She had a tennis date with a hot guy, and she already knew what the score would be: love–love.

3

SOME GIRLS GET ALL THE BREAKS

Smack.

Spencer couldn't help but watch in awe as her serve arced through the cool evening air, forming a perfect path over the net like a shooting star.

When Colin raised his racket in preparation to meet the ball, though, she turned her attention to more important things—namely, the way a strip of tanned, taut skin peeked out from over the waistband of his shorts as he swung to meet her serve. She let out a deep breath when his swing, which had looked so powerful and targeted from her side of the court, instead met the ball at a wrong angle, weakly, causing his volley back to dribble out of bounds. She hid a smile. Colin was so clearly letting her win.

"Good job, Spencer," Colin huffed, zipping up his racket into its case and flashing her a grin. She could feel him looking her up and down as she approached the net, ready to shake his hand, and was glad she'd put on her shortest tennis skirt and most fitted tank.

"You too," she cooed, reaching out her hand. Their

palms met, and Colin held on to her hand just a smidge too long. It had to be intentional.

"You weren't kidding—you are good," he added, still breathing heavily.

She ducked her head and grinned. "My parents insisted on lessons when I was a kid. My sister and I started playing in tournaments when we were still in grade school!" She pulled out the rubber band from her hair and hoped the light would catch its sheen as it spilled over her shoulders. "What about you? How did you get the bug?"

"Whoa," he laughed. Up close, she realized just how chiseled his cheekbones were, and he had a tiny dimple in his left cheek when he smiled. "That's a conversation way too involved to have on a tennis court. Are you hungry?"

"Starved," she admitted.

"Well, then, it's lucky I brought us a little picnic." His eyes twinkled as he led her to a grassy knoll on the south side of the courts and spread out a towel.

Spencer inhaled deeply, taking in the faintest trace of Colin's spicy cologne. It mingled with the salt air and the smell of grilled fish and steak that lingered from the restaurant just across the patio. Colin reached into his bag and pulled out two ready-made fruit salads, a wrapped cheese plate, and two bottles of AminoSpa. He placed a toothpick directly in the center of each cheese square, then arranged the AminoSpas side by side, labels out.

Spencer laughed. "You're as OCD as I am," she said, pointing to the meticulous platter.

"Guilty. I even hang my tennis polos by color," Colin said with a sheepish grin. "I suppose it's an athlete thing. Like how Nadal has that whole routine before he serves or how Sharapova can't step on the lines of the court when the ball's not in play."

"A small way to have control in a tense situation, I suppose," Spencer said, thinking of how organizing always made her feel calm in times of stress. She unscrewed the cap of the AminoSpa drink, took a long sip, and gagged. "What *is* this stuff?" It tasted like rotting grapefruit.

"It's full of vitamins." Colin pointed at the nutritional information on the back. "I swear it's made me a stronger player. Some guy was trying to get me to sell the stuff myself—he said I could easily turn my tennis buddies and trainer on to it, but I told him I'm too busy to take on any endorsement deals."

"So it's true what your groupies said? You're really training to go pro?"

Colin nodded modestly. "Well, my coach thinks I have a good shot of getting a wild-card draw at the US Open this year. I've got that tournament coming up later this week, and I've enrolled in a lot more, too—I've gotta get my ranking up. I want to get into the top fifty."

Spencer was impressed. "So do you live here in Longboat Key? Or are you just here for training?"

Colin popped a grape in his mouth and grinned mischievously. "If we keep talking about me, how will I ever learn more about you? Where did the mysterious girl with serious tennis skills come from?"

Spencer pushed a piece of hair behind her ear with her newly manicured nails—she and Melissa had spent a fun but slightly awkward afternoon together at the spa—thrilled that he was as curious about her as she was about him. "Well, I'm certainly not a pro tennis player or anything nearly as exciting as that. I live outside Philadelphia. I'm staying at the big white house at the end of Sand Dune Drive."

Colin's eyes widened. "You're in Edith Hastings's house?"

"Yep. She's my grandmother."

He chuckled. "I've heard she's a feisty one!"

Spencer made a face. "Nana? Feisty?" Whenever she thought of her grandmother, all she pictured was a frowning woman who yelled at her for getting the floor wet when she came in from the pool.

Colin shrugged. "I've been to the country club once or twice since I got here, and she's big into the ballroom dancing lessons they hold every week. Always comes with a new boyfriend, too. Guys can't get enough of her."

They can't get enough of her money, Spencer thought wryly. "So Nana's a player, huh? I guess she *does* look pretty good for her age."

"She looks amazing." Colin winked. "It's no wonder her granddaughter is stunning."

Spencer suppressed a grin, hoping he hadn't noticed the hot flush his words sent through her body.

"So how many boys have asked you to the luau?" Colin asked.

The yacht club held an annual pre–New Year's party—this year it was a Hawaiian luau. When they were younger, Spencer and Melissa used to hide under the elegantly decorated tables and marvel at the artfully carved ice sculptures and fireworks display. "Uh, none," Spencer admitted, looking down.

Colin tilted his head, studying her for a moment. "I find that hard to believe."

Spencer couldn't help but blush. "Why?"

"Because you sure are something else, Spencer Hastings." He playfully swatted at her arm. "And I'm not just talking about your blistering tennis serve!"

"Is 'something else' a good thing?" Spencer asked flirtatiously, her elbow tingling where he'd touched her.

"I'd say so." Then his expression turned serious. "Except for in my family, of course."

"What do you mean?" Spencer asked.

An owl hooted in a nearby tree, and the faint sound of laughter floated over from the club's restaurant. "Well, I'm kind of the black sheep of my family," Colin admitted.

"Me too," Spencer confessed, her heart going out to him. "I feel like I'm living in that *Sesame Street* game 'One of these things is not like the other.' No matter what I do, I'll never be good enough for my parents."

Colin reached forward and squeezed her hand. "Me either. My dad is so hard on me, especially when it comes to tennis. I guess it's why I practice so much."

"But you're such an amazing player," Spencer protested. "What more can he want?"

Colin shook his head. "When I was younger, my dad would make me stay behind on the courts every time I lost a match. I had to do a hundred serves before I was allowed to go home for dinner."

"That's horrible!" Spencer cried.

Suddenly Colin looked embarrassed. "I'm sorry. I can't believe I told you that. I've actually never told *anyone* that, it's just that . . ." He hesitated for a moment. "I just feel so comfortable with you."

Spencer smiled. "I feel really comfortable with you, too."

Actually, Colin was the first guy she'd connected with in a long time. Maybe it could even turn into something serious. She pictured herself boarding a commuter jet every Friday afternoon to visit Colin for a long weekend. And maybe Colin *would* get a wild-card draw in the US Open or another big tennis tournament. She imagined sitting in the stands, big sunglasses on her face, a classy wide-brimmed hat on her head. When the cameras panned to her, the commentators would whisper about how poised and pretty she was. *She looks so intelligent, too,* they would add. *So driven. Like a girl who is really going somewhere. They seem like the perfect couple.*

A pair of Vespas flashed their headlights across the

knoll, casting Colin's face into a spotlight for a second—just long enough for Spencer to see just how dazzlingly blue his eyes were.

Suddenly, Colin's gaze shifted to the left, like he was looking past Spencer and back into the tennis courts. He jumped to his feet, nearly knocking over the remains of her AminoSpa water bottle. She yelped and followed his gaze. The lights on the courts were still on, and a black-haired girl was visible, wearing a little black dress that hugged every curve, shading her eyes. "Hey, Colin!" she said, bounding up the hill toward them.

Spencer gritted her teeth—another groupie? This girl had sleek, catlike eyes, and the most angular, model-thin body Spencer had ever seen.

Colin started toward the girl. Spencer figured he was going to shoo her away, but when he reached her, he greeted her with a long kiss on the lips.

Spencer blinked hard, her stomach dropping to her feet. What the—

The girl pulled away. "I came to tell you I was able to get reservations at Culpeper's tonight. I know the chef from New York, and he's saved us the best table in the house. You need to go get cleaned up!"

Spencer rose and swung her tennis bag over her shoulder, trying to retain as much dignity as possible. "Um, Colin?"

Colin glanced over his shoulder, as if only then remembering Spencer was there. "Spencer, this is Ramona. My girlfriend."

4

SMELLS LIKE TEAM SPIRIT

An hour later, Spencer sat in the kitchen, blinking back tears as the shame and humiliation of her evening washed over her once more. After Colin had introduced Spencer to his girlfriend—his girlfriend!—Ramona had given Spencer a very obvious once-over and said, "Colin said you challenged him to a match. That's so cute!"

Spencer had looked down at her clunky sneakers and childish-looking tennis skirt, suddenly feeling sweaty and young and all wrong.

"That's right," Colin said with an easy smile. "Spencer's a great player. We've just been sitting here chatting, cooling down." He'd spoken in the same upbeat, condescending tone Spencer's father used when talking to the five-year-old twins who lived down the street, as if Spencer had been nothing more than some annoying child begging him for tennis tips.

She dropped her head in her hands. She had been

so sure he'd been flirting with her, so sure that they'd had a true connection. How had she so completely misinterpreted Colin's behavior?

Spencer's mother appeared, perching herself in the seat next to Spencer. She checked the Cartier watch on her wrist and let out a frustrated sigh.

"What time are our reservations again?" Spencer asked. The family had made arrangements to go to Culpeper's, the very same steak house Colin and Ramona were eating at tonight. Spencer could only hope they would be seated far away from each other.

"Eight-thirty," her mother said testily. "We really should get a move on if we don't want to lose our reservation. I'm going to kill your father." She stabbed his number into her cell phone again, but when she hung up a few seconds later, Spencer knew the call had gone to voicemail. "He hasn't picked up all day."

"Maybe he's on the golf course."

"He wasn't playing today. I called the clubhouse." She pulled a wineglass from the cupboard and poured herself a pinot grigio. She had that look on her face that said she was in a mood and should just be left alone.

Spencer beat a hasty retreat to let her mother sulk in peace. She climbed the stairs to the second floor and noticed that Nana's door at the end of the hall was slightly ajar. When Spencer was little, she'd loved snooping in Nana's bedroom—she kept her amazing jewelry collection in a crystal-encrusted box on her bureau. And the navy slip dress Spencer was wearing *could* use a little extra something.

She pushed into the room. The enormous king-sized canopy bed was piled with tons of fussy froufrou pillows. There was a silk-upholstered chaise in the corner, and Nana's vanity, which contained more creams, lotions, powders, shadows, and lipsticks than a Sephora store, stood by the dramatically draped windows. To Spencer's disappointment, the jewelry box, which was usually positioned in the center of the bureau, was gone. She padded into the en suite bathroom to see if Nana had moved it.

Nana's bedroom rivaled a spa's. The bathroom counters were covered in long slabs of marble, a built-in sauna was tucked into the corner, and all the floors were heated. The soaking tub was deep, oval-shaped, and didn't have a grab bar, plastic seat, or any of those other old-person accoutrements to prevent slips or falls—Nana was much too proud and vain for that kind of thing. Nana stocked the fluffiest, plushiest towels money could buy, and she even had her own massage table set up—she got rubdowns every two weeks.

Spencer inspected her appearance in the enormous, gilded-frame mirror. Her blue eyes were wide. Her skin was clear. Her blond hair, which she'd washed during her post-match bubble bath, gleamed, and she looked sophisticated in the sleek Tibi dress she was wearing to dinner. But she didn't look nearly as glamorous as Ramona.

Tears welled in Spencer's eyes. The bedroom door

creaked, and Spencer spun around. Melissa peeked into the bathroom. "What are you doing in here?"

"Nothing," Spencer said quickly, wiping her eyes. "Just looking around."

Melissa leaned on the counter, noticing Spencer's red cheeks and nose. "Are you okay?"

"Uh-huh." Spencer pretended to be fascinated with Nana's perfumes. They were mostly classic scents society ladies wore: Joy, Fracas, Chanel No. 19, and a handmade blend from a parfumier in Paris. But then she noticed Britney Spears's Fantasy at the very end of the line. She couldn't imagine Nana going to a drugstore and actually *buying* it.

"What's with all these toothbrushes?" Melissa asked behind her, gesturing to an open drawer. There were fifteen or so toothbrushes inside, each of them clearly used. Initials were written on the handle in black Sharpie–*JL, AW, PO,* and so on. Spencer didn't see the same initials twice.

"Oh my God," Melissa blurted, pulling out something else. It was a small bottle full of blue pills. The prescription was for Edith Hastings, and the label said VIAGRA.

"Put that back!" Spencer hissed, grabbing the bottle and dropping it back in the drawer, as though Nana might walk in any second and catch them. She slammed the drawer shut quickly and shuddered. "Do you think *Nana* takes that, or do you think it's for Lawrence?"

"Who knows?" One corner of Melissa's mouth rose. "I guess Nana's wilder than we thought."

It was certainly in line with the flirty Nana Hastings Colin had described earlier. Spencer pictured the toothbrushes again. Was it possible they belonged to different guys who'd slept over? *Ew.*

Melissa hoisted herself up on the counter. "So does your bad mood have something to do with that guy I saw you with earlier?"

Spencer's head shot up. "How do you know about that?" She hadn't told Melissa about Colin during their spa day. They actually seemed to be getting along, and ever since Spencer had stolen Wren, boys had been a sore subject for the sisters.

"I left my sweater at the club. When I went back to get it, I saw you playing with the tennis guy we watched earlier," Melissa said. "I hear he's a real hotshot." She picked up a silver-handled hairbrush and ran her fingers over the bristles.

Spencer hung her head in embarrassment. "It's no big deal. I don't really even *know* him. And he has a girlfriend."

"A girlfriend?" Melissa echoed skeptically. "Well, it can't be serious if he asked you out on a date," she pointed out.

"It wasn't a date."

"Oh yeah?" Melissa gave Spencer a little shove on the shoulder. "From what I saw, it was pretty obvious he was flirting with you, Spence. Why would a guy do that if he was fully committed to his girlfriend?"

Because he's a player? Spencer wanted to say. But despite her protests, Melissa had planted a seed of hope in her mind. She thought back to the day's events. "It *was* kind of strange that he didn't tell me about her until she showed up."

"Exactly. He wants you." Melissa cleared her throat.

"Actually, he and the girlfriend are going to Culpeper's tonight," Spencer said.

Melissa's eyes lit up. "Perfect. We'll get to see how they are in action."

Warning bells went off in Spencer's head. "Melissa, why are you being so nice to me?"

Melissa raised an eyebrow. "I'm not. I'm just pointing out a fact. He likes you. You like him. Life is short. You've got to take what you can while you can. You never know when the love of your life will, for example, get hauled off to jail."

Spencer opened her mouth to apologize once more for turning Ian in. She hadn't done it to hurt her sister—she'd done it to get justice for her friend.

"But . . . ," she began.

Melissa waved her hand. "No buts. Just go with me here."

Spencer stared at her sister in disbelief, waiting for her to laugh nastily and tell Spencer it was all a big joke—that Spencer could never get a guy like Colin, and that Melissa still hated her, just like usual. But Melissa just continued to peer at her excitedly. She pushed Spencer's hair behind her ears, ran her fingers over each eyebrow, and then spritzed her with a squirt of Joy perfume.

"Better," she deemed. "Now let's go. We've got a couple to break up."

5

IF *COSMO* SAYS IT,
THEN IT MUST BE TRUE

Culpeper's steak house smelled overwhelmingly like meat, served punch bowl–sized goblets of red wine, and had caricatures of celebrities who'd visited all over the walls. Most of them were famous golfers, singers like Jennifer Lopez and Marc Anthony, and business moguls who were all featured smoking phallic-looking cigars.

Spencer's father had finally turned up from his all-day outing, and the family filed stiffly into a banquette. Her parents had had an under-their-breath argument in the parking lot about where he had been all day, and now they weren't speaking except to tersely agree on the wine. Spencer and Melissa were trying their best to ignore them, canvassing the room for Colin and Ramona.

Suddenly, Spencer grabbed Melissa's arm. *"There they are!"*

Melissa turned to look just as Colin's tall and muscular frame passed through the front door. He had changed into a black button-down, black pinstriped trousers, and a pair of loafers Spencer was pretty sure were Prada. Ramona was with him, still wearing the sexy black sheath dress from earlier. Colin said a few words to the maitre d', but then Ramona interrupted and spoke over him. Colin frowned at her, looking annoyed, and Ramona rolled her eyes at him.

"Hmmm," Melissa murmured. "Seems there's trouble in paradise!"

"Maybe," Spencer whispered, unconvinced as the maitre d' led the couple through the dining room and seated them at a table by the window that blessedly wasn't anywhere near Spencer's family.

Melissa sipped from the glass of red wine the waiter had just poured. "Get up and strut past him right now. You look super hot."

"*Now?*" Spencer felt panicked. It was so public here. Her parents, who were pointedly staring off in two different directions so they wouldn't have to speak to one another, would see.

"Hold your head high. Say hello to Colin, thrust out your boobs, but keep walking. Don't stop and chat. Leave him wanting more," Melissa instructed.

Hold out your boobs? Melissa was the queen of prudes. When a boy had touched her butt during a slow dance in ninth grade, rumor had it she'd slapped him and reported him to the principal. "Where do you get this stuff?" Spencer asked.

"*Cosmo*," Melissa answered.

"Seriously? I thought you only read *Vogue* and *W*."

Melissa shrugged. "It's actually pretty helpful when it comes to guy stuff." She poked Spencer's thigh. "Now go!"

Okaaay. Spencer climbed out of the banquette. She could feel Melissa's eyes on her back, encouraging her on. It actually felt kind of familiar, the way Melissa was helping her. If it wasn't for the fact that they were scheming to break up a couple instead of planning elaborate tea parties and cooking up ways to convince their parents to let them wear their princess crowns to school, Spencer realized it almost felt like old times. When they'd been *real* sisters.

Spencer advanced toward Colin and Ramona, trying to adjust to her shoes. "I think we should take a sailing lesson tomorrow," Colin was urging.

Ramona pouted, her shiny lips folding into a grimace. "I just want to tan and relax."

"You *always* want to tan and relax. If you're not into it, I'm just going to go without you."

"*I'm just going to go without you*," Ramona mimicked, twisting her mouth unattractively.

Spencer took a deep breath and began walking a little faster. When she was a few feet from Colin's table, he looked up and noticed her. She feigned obliviousness, swinging her hips, shaking her butt, and pushing her boobs out as far as they would go. She could feel her hair lift off her neck and float behind her. She felt *fantastic.*

"Hey, Spencer," Colin called out.

She slowed down and faked surprise. "Oh, hey! Nice to see you!"

He breathed in as if to say something else, probably expecting Spencer to stop and chat. But she didn't. She kept walking, holding her head high. After she passed, she couldn't help glancing over her shoulder at him. He was still watching her.

And then her leg hit something hard, and she heard a loud *oof.* She whipped around just in time to see a waitress clamoring to rescue a tray full of steaming plates from tumbling to the floor. But it was too late—the plates slid off the tray one by one, smashing to the ground. At the exact same moment, Spencer's high heels turned, and she felt her legs buckle beneath her. Before she could even catch herself she was on the carpet, her legs tangled under her, her dress riding up her butt, and her elbow landing in something squishy that had just spilled. By the smell of it, it was creamed spinach.

A hush went over the crowd. Everyone turned to stare. The waitress was next to her on the floor, quickly cleaning up a bunch of plates of steak that had fallen off the tray. "Great. You probably just got me fired!" she hissed.

Spencer scrambled to her feet quickly and shot to the bathroom. But as she pushed open the women's room door, she heard faint chuckles and peeked back into the dining area. Colin and Ramona were staring at her with amusement, their hands now entwined on top of the table. *Perfect.* Spencer's fall had probably been the ultimate icebreaker.

Cosmo scheme one: a definite bomb.

6

SAIL AWAY WITH ME

The next morning, after nightmares of laughing crowds and oversized Manolos clawing at her body, Spencer ordered a double espresso to go at the café and met Melissa on the Longboat Key dock under an awning that said FREEWHEELING SAILING LESSONS. Spencer had wanted to stay in bed for the morning—scratch that, for the rest of their vacation—but Melissa had been insistent.

Several small Hobie Cat boats with rainbow-printed sails bobbed in the water. Seagulls circled, squawking loudly, and a bunch of floppy-haired twenty-something guys in Harvard T-shirts passed by in a sleek, gorgeous Beneteau yacht. She couldn't be sure, but she thought she saw one of the guys point at her, causing the whole lot of them to burst into laughter. She scowled and drained her coffee. It was bad enough that she'd discovered a massive purple bruise bloom-ing on her thigh from where she'd hit the tray of food. Now she had to deal with all of Longboat Key laughing at her.

"Colin's already here," Melissa said, slathering SPF 100 on her arms. "There are two other people taking lessons with us today, both of them guys. Colin DeSoto and Merv something. Ramona isn't on the list."

Spencer chewed on her thumbnail, feeling nervous. Not about the sailing lessons—she'd learned how to sail when she was eight and even had a junior license—but she'd never thrown herself so blatantly at a guy before. Besides, what if Colin took one look at her when he arrived and hightailed it away? He now probably remembered her as the girl who'd single-handedly taken out five large platters of T-bone steak instead of the girl who could hold her own against him on the courts.

Melissa squirted another blob of sunscreen onto her palm. "Want me to get your back?"

Spencer turned, feeling surprisingly touched. Melissa hadn't offered to rub sunscreen on her back for years.

Then Melissa drew in a breath and nudged her chin toward an advancing figure at the end of the dock. It was Colin. He was wearing a fitted white T-shirt that showed off every ab muscle and a pair of patterned board shorts. Even his toes, which poked out of a pair of black flip-flops, were cute.

Colin spotted Spencer and stopped. "Spencer?" He grinned in disbelief. "Are you here for the lesson?"

"Yep! Oh, this is my sister, Melissa." She touched Melissa's arm.

"Nice to meet you." Melissa stuck out her hand, and

Colin shook it. He smiled at Melissa and then at Spencer. Spencer's heart soared. If Colin was going to pretend last night had never happened, that was just fine with her.

The second student, a fat, balding guy named Merv, ambled up the dock, and then the instructor, Richard, appeared. "Welcome to sailing 101," Richard told them in an adorable Australian accent. Spencer noticed Melissa checking him out and smiled. Maybe she could have a fling on vacation, too.

Richard went around the circle and learned their names and where everyone was from—Spencer swallowed in surprise when Colin answered, "Connecticut"—that was so close to Rosewood!—then went down a list of boating safety rules. He explained how a Hobie Cat sailboat worked and that they were going to take the boats out in pairs today. "Everyone, find a partner," he said.

Spencer turned to Melissa, but her sister shot her a glare and then touched Merv's arm. "Want to sail together?"

Merv's fleshy lips parted, taking in Melissa's trim figure, pretty face, and scalloped gingham bikini. "*Sure.*"

It was the noblest sacrifice Melissa had ever made for Spencer. Spencer turned to Colin. "I guess that leaves us. Do you mind pairing up?"

"Are you kidding?" Colin grinned. "Something tells me you've sailed before. You have that yacht club look about you."

"Am I that obvious?" she said lightly. "How about you?"

Colin shook his head. "I have never sailed, which is

pretty lame considering how much time I spend down here." He hooked a life jacket around Spencer's neck and tucked his own under his arm. "Safety first." He grinned.

Spencer and Colin climbed into a boat and undid the rope that attached it to the dock. Spencer moved the rudder so that the boat was pointing into the center of the bay, as Richard instructed, and Colin raised the sail. After about twenty minutes of learning how to turn into and against the wind, they were bobbing peacefully on the water. Spencer leaned back and tilted her head to the sun, cursing the freckles she knew would pop up by the end of the day.

"I could get used to this." Colin leaned back in the hull and laced his hands behind his head. Spencer opened her eyes, shading them against the sun. "I tried to get Ramona to take a lesson, but she wasn't into it. She doesn't know what she's missing."

"She's not the active type, huh?" Spencer asked nonchalantly.

"Not exactly," Colin said with a shrug.

Spencer wanted to push Colin for more information, but something told her to sit and wait for Colin to talk on his own.

Colin uncapped a bottle of AminoSpa and sipped. Spencer stared out at the bay. Melissa was across the water with Merv, deep in conversation. Then, she heard a snicker from the shore. She swung around and squinted at the docks, sure she'd just seen someone dart behind a boat. Or was that her imagination?

Finally, Colin sighed and broke the silence. "To be honest, Ramona hasn't been in the mood for *anything* lately. I don't know what her deal is."

Bingo. Spencer gave him a mock-sympathetic look. "Have you guys been together long?"

He shook his head. "Ramona and I are . . . complicated."

Spencer nodded gravely. "I understand complicated," she said, thinking of her and Wren. Spencer turned the rudder so that they wouldn't collide with an oncoming Jet Ski. The boom swiveled toward her, and she ducked. "My last boyfriend and I fought all the time."

Colin leaned over and stared in the water, silent. Spencer couldn't help but notice how closely the water matched his eyes. He looked so sad and torn. Spencer could practically feel him wanting to break up with Ramona for her.

"I can't imagine someone wanting to fight with you, Spencer," he said. "You seem so easy to get along with— and so full of life. I wish Ramona had your sense of adventure."

The sun suddenly felt very hot on the top of Spencer's head. Colin adjusted his seat, casually inching closer to her. There was a tiny bit of sand stuck to his cheek; Spencer reached up and flicked it away. At the same time, he leaned forward, maybe about to kiss her. Spencer shut her eyes and waited.

Suddenly, a whistle blew from the dock.

"Let's bring 'em in!" Richard yelled. "It's getting too windy!"

The romantic mood immediately shattered. Colin sat back on his haunches. Spencer turned toward the rudder, suppressing a groan.

They secured the boat to the slip and climbed onto the dock. Melissa and Merv were pulling in behind them, and Richard was busy helping them out of the water. Spencer faced Colin, wanting to pick up where they'd left off.

"So," he started.

"So." She bit her bottom lip.

A Mercedes convertible pulled into the parking lot and honked. Ramona was at the wheel. Colin glanced at Spencer, a quick look, then sighed. "I should probably get going," he said reluctantly. "Will I see you later, at the luau?"

Spencer forced a smile onto her face. "Yep. See you there!"

She watched him walk down the dock and climb into the car. She might have been imagining it, but she was pretty sure he looked back at Spencer longingly. And from the thumbs-up Melissa was giving her, it seemed her sister had noticed it, too.

7

SHOPPING, WITH A
SPLASH OF AWKWARDNESS

Nana's house was cool and smelled like fresh oranges when Spencer walked through the side door later that morning. "Oh," she said, stopping short in the doorway. Her mother was sitting on a stool at the island, staring at something on TV. Spencer was about to slink out of the room when a headline on the screen caught her eye. *Silver Panthers Terrorize Atlantic City.* There was a shot of two large jungle cats prowling past the various glittering casinos.

"Is this a joke?" Spencer blurted.

Her mother shook her head. "Someone let performing panthers out of their cages in Atlantic City. Apparently one of them almost tore off a woman's arm."

She'd just said more words to Spencer than she had in days, so Spencer dared to sit down on the stool next to her and watch the remainder of the newscast. Animal control teams were working hard to round up the panthers, but the creatures were extremely stealthy.

When the news broke for commercials, Spencer felt her mother's eyes on her. She slid off the stool, prepared to hustle up to her room so her mom didn't have to endure her presence. Then her mother let out a regretful sigh. "I'm sorry about how I've behaved toward you in the past few days, Spencer."

Spencer stopped in her tracks. "It's okay," she said quickly.

"Things have been . . . tense." She touched her forehead. "Your dad and I had a big argument that hasn't exactly gotten resolved. But I shouldn't have taken it out on you."

"Seriously, it's all right." Spencer busied herself with a copy of the *Miami Herald* on the island, too flustered with this sudden change of heart to look her mom in the eye.

Her mother eased off the stool and turned off the television. "I'd like to make it up to you. There's a new boutique called Astrid that just opened up in town. Want to go?"

"I'd *love* to go with you." Spencer's heart began to buoy. They hadn't been shopping together in a long time. They hadn't done *anything* together in a long time.

"Great. Be ready in ten minutes." Her mother swung her purse over her shoulder and shot Spencer a smile. It might have been pinched and tense and still a bit frosty, but at least it wasn't a grimace.

Astrid boutique was a mix of Miami chic and casual beach cool, featuring a lot of caftans, flowing dresses, white denim, and rubber flip-flops that cost over $100.

A Rolling Stones song played over the stereo, and the salesgirls were busily folding merchandise when Spencer and her mom swept through the front door.

Spencer made a beeline to the denim table, and her mother followed her. After sifting through the piles of jeans, her mother cleared her throat. "So you and Melissa seem to be getting along."

"I guess so," Spencer said, surprised that her mother had noticed.

"How is she doing with all the Ian stuff?"

Spencer flinched. "Honestly, I don't know. We haven't really talked about it." She and Melissa had continued to keep their conversations light—mostly they talked about Colin or made fun of the outfits his groupies wore.

"You did the right thing by turning Ian in, you know," she said. "We have no idea what that boy's capable of. And to think we'd invited him into our home with open arms." She shook her head. "I'm considering pressing charges against him myself—for psychological damage. Your father thinks I'm crazy."

"Is that what you've been fighting about?" Spencer asked.

A startled look came over her mother's face. She traced the stitching on the back pocket of a pair of faded blue jeggings. "No," she said quietly. "It was something else."

Straightening up, she pulled a short romper off a nearby rack and held it up to Spencer's frame. "This would look cute on you."

Spencer eyed it suspiciously. "Won't it make me look really young?"

"There's nothing wrong with looking young." She folded the outfit over her arm. "I think you should try it. It's adorable."

"Well, then, you have to try something, too." Spencer pulled a blue-and-white printed maxi dress from a hanger. "Dad would love you in this."

Her mother pursed her lips. "I'm not sure I have the body for that."

Spencer waved her finger in her face. "No negativity! Just try it."

They both found open dressing rooms. Spencer kicked off her shorts and shoes, staring at her bare legs in the mirror. She pulled on the romper. Surprisingly, it didn't make her look as young as she'd anticipated. The high cut caused her legs to look long and tan, and it cinched in neatly at the waist.

Out front, jingle bells on the doorknob tinkled. The salesgirls murmured, and footsteps sounded in the back hall near the dressing rooms. Spencer glanced under the curtain and saw two thin calves ending in slender ankles and silver gladiator sandals. Whoever it was just stood there, not moving.

A tingle traveled up Spencer's spine. She felt like whoever it was could see her through the curtain. She was about to call out, but then the gladiator-sandaled feet pivoted and walked away.

"Spence?" Her mother called from the next dressing room over. "I think you were right about this dress."

"Let me see, let me see!" Spencer cried.

She stepped around the curtain to find her mother standing in the hall. The maxi dress skimmed her narrow hips and brightened her skin. "It's beautiful," Spencer breathed. "You should get it."

Her mother padded barefoot to the three-way mirror in the main showroom. She tilted her hips this way and that, then inspected her backside. "I suppose it *is* nice." She met Spencer's eyes and smiled. "Good choice."

Spencer's heart warmed. When had her mom last complimented her?

Then, Spencer's mother's expression shifted at something in the mirror. A tall, thin, elegant blond woman was flipping rapidly through the racks behind them. A khaki-colored quilted Chanel bag hung from her shoulder, her skin was perfectly tan, there wasn't an ounce of fat on her body, and she had a very recognizable heart-shaped face. Was that . . . ? It *couldn't* be.

The woman looked up and spotted them. Her features registered a note of surprise, and she glanced over her shoulder toward the sidewalk for a millisecond before swinging back to them. "Veronica?" she asked in an all-too-familiar voice.

"Jessica," Spencer's mother croaked.

Spencer resisted the urge to gasp. It was Jessica DiLaurentis. Ali's *mom*.

"My goodness, what a nice surprise!" Jessica DiLaurentis glided over and gave Spencer and Spencer's mom air kisses. "It's so lovely to see you!"

Spencer's mother snapped back into her perfect Main Line hostess mode, all traces of discomfort gone. "It's so nice to see *you!*" she chirped in a clipped, haughty voice she reserved for neighbors, fellow charity board members, and new parents at Rosewood Day she didn't feel were worthy enough to be on school committees. "What are you doing here?"

"We have a house here, remember?" When Mrs. DiLaurentis gave a cool half-smile, it was like seeing Ali's ghost. "We decided to come down here for New Year's. Decompress before Ian's trial." She fingered the giant Gucci sunglasses on top of her head.

"Of course," Spencer's mother said. Her voice betrayed nothing, but when Spencer looked down, she noticed that her mother had one hand tucked behind her back. It was furiously picking at the skin around her thumbnail. "I'm sorry we didn't get to speak more at the arraignment. It was just such a whirlwind."

Mrs. DiLaurentis waved her hand. "We'll have plenty of time to catch up. We've bought a house near Rosewood—in Yarmouth. We wanted to be close by for the trial." Her phone let out a *ping*, and she peeked inside the Chanel bag. "Oh, I'd better run," she said. "It was lovely to see you both. Give my best to Peter and Melissa!"

"Yes, all the best to your family, too!" Spencer's mother beamed.

Ali's mother exited the boutique, still glancing at her phone screen. When Spencer turned back to her own mother, the composed expression had disappeared from her face once more. She ran her hands up and down her hips. The skin on her thumb had been rubbed raw.

"Mom?" Spencer touched her mother's arm. "Are you okay?"

She blinked hard. "Of course. We should go, though. I think the heat is getting to me."

She was about to head for the door when Spencer caught her arm. "Mom. You're still . . ." She trailed off, gesturing to the maxi dress her mother was still wearing. The tags dangled from under her arm.

Her mother looked down and tittered unsteadily. "Goodness. Right."

She walked back to the dressing room as though nothing had been amiss. Spencer stood rooted to the spot for a moment, an uneasy cramp in her stomach. It was natural for Spencer to feel uncomfortable in Mrs. DiLaurentis's presence—she was one of the last people to see Ali alive. But why in the world would her mother fall to pieces in front of their former neighbor?

8

HOW TO GET LEI'D

When Spencer stepped onto the yacht club's parking lot that night for the pre–New Year's party, she could smell the heady scents of grilled pineapple and poi, tiki-torch smoke, and coconut. Since everyone had been asked to show up dressed for the luau theme, Spencer wore a short, floral-printed dress and an orchid flower behind her ear, which kept sending out romantic whiffs of perfume with every toss of her hair. Melissa had on a long printed maxi dress and floral lei around her neck. Spencer's mother had stubbornly refused to wear anything but a white Calvin Klein sheath, though she'd begrudgingly put on a pair of sparkly high-heeled thongs and an oversized floral statement necklace. Her father wore an obnoxious orange and pink Hawaiian shirt under his Armani sport jacket, just like every other man in the room over the age of forty.

As the family walked toward the entrance, occasionally saying hello to other yacht club members they'd met through the years, Spencer's father's fingers flew across his phone's little keyboard. Her mother nudged him. "Weren't you going to leave that in the car?"

"I'm just sending a text," he said distractedly.

"To whom? And since when do you know how to text?"

"I've always known how to text." His phone rang. He answered it with a grunt, then whispered something into it that sounded like *She is?* and then, *Okay, good.*

When he hung up, Spencer's mother was staring at him. "Who was that?"

"Just a work thing," her father murmured hurriedly.

Spencer's mother pursed her lips and fingered her necklace. Melissa leaned over to Spencer. "What's with Dad's sudden air of mystery?" she whispered.

Spencer shrugged. She had no idea, but she didn't like it.

The Hastingses stepped over a threshold and into the luau. Bursts of brightly colored flowers and palm trees covered in twinkling lights transformed the normally stuffy restaurant into a high-class Hawaiian fantasy. A long-haired girl in a coconut-shell bikini top and a grass skirt handed everyone, including Spencer, a piña colada. "Aloha!" she bleated happily, not noticing that Spencer's parents looked like they were ready to throw each other into the roasting pit. "Grab your place cards and find your table! Have a wonderful time!"

Spencer's mother plucked her place card from the long table in the lobby. "We're at table three," she said in a pinched voice, and started across the dining room, the others on her heels. Halfway there, she froze in her tracks. Mrs. DiLaurentis and her husband were sitting at table six, wearing matching puka shell necklaces. Ali's mom looked up and noticed the Hastingses, but instead of waving, she furrowed her brow and looked away.

By the time they sat down at their assigned table, Spencer's mother had already finished her piña colada and had signaled a waiter for another. Her father was still tapping on his phone, a weird expression on his face. Spencer looked around the room, trying to spot Colin. A ten-foot Christmas tree decorated with pineapples and fresh flowers stood in the corner. The band, dressed in Hawaiian gear, crooned onstage. Waiters swirled with appetizers and salads, and a bunch of people were milling around the dance floor and reconnecting. But she didn't see him and Ramona anywhere.

Being in this room again reminded Spencer of the time she'd attended this party in fifth grade. The DiLaurentises had been here too, and Ali had worn a drop-waist dress with fringe at the hem—it had been a twenties theme that year. Ali had hung around with a bunch of prep-school girls from New York City; the five of them had danced wildly to every fast song the band played. Spencer had danced at the edge of the group, thinking that Ali would invite her into the circle, but of course she hadn't.

When Spencer had left the dance floor, feeling like a failure, she'd come upon her dad and Ali's mom talking heatedly in the hallway. She wasn't sure she'd ever seen them interact before. A thorn had twisted uncomfortably in her gut, and she'd cautiously backed away, putting it out of her mind.

Someone cleared his throat above Spencer, ripping her back to the present, and she looked up. "Hey." Colin's eyes flickered between Spencer and Melissa. He was dressed in a Hawaiian shirt, fitted jeans, and black wing-tips. "So you guys made it!"

"Of course we did," Spencer said, her heart starting to gallop. She sat up a little straighter and adjusted her flower. Melissa shot him a cool smile and sipped her drink, turning her attention to the stage and languidly running her fingers through her hair.

"Colin, come *on*." Ramona, who was dressed elegantly in a silver mini-dress and strappy gold heels—no luau outfit for her—tugged Colin's arm. "We need to find our seats."

Colin shot Spencer an apologetic smile as Ramona dragged him away to one of the back tables. Disheartened, Spencer slumped down, sending a mental apology to her yoga instructor for her bad posture. Whatever Colin had been feeling on the sailboat had clearly dissipated.

Melissa touched her arm. "Go ask him to dance."

"What's the point?" Spencer said miserably, throwing her hands up. "He's still with her. I don't have a shot."

Melissa bit into a cherry tomato from the salads that had just been deposited onto the table. "I thought you were thicker-skinned than that, Spence. If you want him, you have to go after him. *Cosmo* says guys love a take-charge girl."

Spencer grunted in response. For the next half hour, she picked glumly at the meal, barely tasting anything. By the time the waiters had cleared their plates and everyone got up to dance, Spencer's parents had changed seats and were sitting on opposite sides of the table, chatting with everyone except each other, Melissa had flitted off to reconnect with a friend she knew from Penn, and Colin and Ramona were slow-dancing nearby. Spencer studied them carefully. They looked happy enough for half a song, but suddenly, Ramona recoiled from Colin, dropped her arms from around his waist, and stood back.

"I just don't understand," she said in a slurring voice. "Why don't you ever invite me to Connecticut?"

Spencer slipped out of her seat and pretended to examine the cheese table, which was conveniently positioned just next to the dance floor and in much better earshot of Colin and Ramona. The manchego looked tempting, but so too did the fight that was brewing.

"Do we have to do this *here*?" Colin hissed, looking uncomfortably around the room. Spencer quickly ducked her head.

Even in the soft light of the party, she could see how Ramona's brow furrowed. "We've been dating for over a year, and I haven't *once* seen your apartment in Darien." Ramona stomped her strappy gold shoe. "And now you're canceling your next trip to see me in New

York. What am I supposed to think? Are you interested in someone else?"

"Jesus, Ramona." Colin threw up his hands in defeat. "I thought we were going to have a nice night together."

He peeled away from Ramona and stormed out of the club, pushing the front doors open so violently they made loud smacks against the walls. Ramona remained on the dance floor with her mouth hanging open, then lowered her shoulders and stomped toward the bar.

Spencer looked around for Melissa, but she was AWOL. Still, she knew an opportunity when she saw one. Melissa had told her to go after what she wanted, and she wanted Colin.

Downing the rest of her father's abandoned glass of wine at the now-empty dinner table, Spencer wove around a bunch of middle-aged women in hula skirts and tanned guys drinking cocktails with umbrellas, and pushed through the double doors into the cool night air.

Cicadas chirped in the trees. Cars honked in the streets. Spencer heard a footstep behind her, then a soft, whispery giggle. She whirled around, but no one was there.

She kept wandering the yacht club grounds until she found Colin standing at the railing on the dock, looking contemplatively at the water. Squaring her shoulders, Spencer moved a little closer and let out a weak cough.

Colin turned. "Oh. Hey."

"Hi, Colin," she said brightly. "Getting some air?"

One shoulder lifted. "I guess so. You?"

"I guess." Spencer walked up to him. They didn't say anything for a few moments. Lights dappled prettily on the surface of the water. The boats bobbed majestically. Then Colin let out a long sigh.

"Are you okay?" Spencer asked innocently.

Colin kicked at the railing. "I think I have some big decisions to make tonight. Sort of like . . . resolutions."

"Well, it's the time of year for it."

"Yeah." Colin nodded glumly.

Spencer poked his side. "Cheer up. It's almost New Year's. It's gorgeous out. And we're at a fake luau. You have to be happy during the holiday season!"

One corner of Colin's mouth rose. "Is that a rule or something?"

"Yep. A rule I just made up." Spencer watched a party boat drift by in the harbor. "And I'm thinking of making some New Year's resolutions, too."

"Spencer setting goals for herself? That doesn't surprise me at all." He grinned conspiratorially, and Spencer felt her shoulders start to sink down as she relaxed into herself. "Care to share what they are?"

"No way," she said earnestly. "Then they wouldn't come true."

Colin paused, opening his mouth like he wanted to say something. The bay lapped against the dock and the air smelled of salt and orchids. A gust of wind blew over the water. For a moment they just stared at one another. Then he reached out and moved a stray lock of hair out of her face, tucking it gently behind her unadorned ear.

Do it, Spencer thought. *Kiss me. Please.*

Suddenly, Colin pulled back his hand and started walking toward the yacht club again. "Where are you going?" Spencer squeaked.

He stopped under a lamp, the golden light making a halo over his head. "There's something I need to do, Spencer," he said quietly. "Something I just figured out."

And just like that, he turned and marched back to the club—no doubt, Spencer thought excitedly, to break up with Ramona. She ran her hands down the length of her face, trying to will her heart to calm down. At that very moment, fireworks exploded in the sky over the water. They flashed against her face, a performance just for her. She was grateful for the noise. Only something that loud could drown out the booming of her heart.

9

SHE NEVER SAW IT COMING

An hour after he left, Spencer realized Colin wasn't coming back to the dock. He was probably consoling Ramona—he was totally the type of guy to do that. Melissa was nowhere to be found, so Spencer made her way back to Nana's house, a secret smile playing on her lips. She couldn't wait for tomorrow, to see how her new relationship would unfold.

The windows at Nana's were dark, and the Mercedes rental was in the driveway. Spencer turned the knob and jumped when Melissa scuttered out of the dark living room and flipped on the entryway chandelier, casting flickers of moving light around the marble floor.

"Hi," Spencer said. She set her clutch on the bottom stair and kicked off her shoes, massaging her heels.

Melissa flashed a bright smile. "Hey! So . . . how'd everything go?"

"Great!" Spencer blurted, settling onto an ornate

antique bench. Melissa dropped down next to her. "Thanks so much for encouraging me to go talk to him!"

Melissa widened her eyes. "Did you guys hook up?"

Spencer shook her head. "But we will soon. He told me he'd made up his mind about something. He's breaking up with her, Melissa, I just know it."

She wrapped her arms tightly around her sister, tears unexpectedly filling her eyes. She squeezed her sister's hands. "Promise me things stay this way."

"Stay *what* way?" Melissa asked.

"Between us. Promise me we . . ." Spencer trailed off to choose her next words carefully. "We don't fight anymore. We help each other. I really miss you."

Suddenly, the doorbell chimed. Spencer felt a thrill of anticipation. Could it be . . . ?

She jumped up, licking her lips and smoothing her hair as she raced to the door. "Play it cool," Melissa reminded her.

She flung open the door and broke into a smile. It was Colin, his chiseled jawline and straight, strong nose casting shadows under his neck from the porch light.

"Hey." His mouth opened up into a slow, smooth smile. Dazzled, Spencer ushered him inside. "Ramona and I are over."

Those words should have made Spencer swoon with joy. Only Colin had breezed right past Spencer and was now standing close to Melissa, a look of rapture on his face.

Spencer stood frozen in place. Why was he telling Melissa all this? She didn't care. *Spencer* cared.

"Really?" Melissa whispered.

"I couldn't stop thinking about you," Colin said in a husky voice, taking Melissa's hand.

Spencer reeled back like she'd been punched. The antique clock on the mantel in the living room chimed twice. What was going on? Was this a joke?

"Can we take a walk? It's a beautiful night," Colin suggested.

"Let me get my purse. Wait here," Melissa breathed. She turned and darted up the stairs. Spencer glanced at Colin, who was staring dreamily after her. She let out a tiny squeak and then took off after her sister, two steps at a time, grateful for all the laps her coaches had made her run.

She burst into Melissa's bedroom, where she was coolly applying some lip gloss, her purse flung over her shoulder.

"What are you doing?" Spencer cried. She didn't even bother keeping her voice down.

Spencer watched a nasty smile spread across Melissa's face in the mirror. "What does it look like, Spence?"

"But . . ." Spencer tried to speak, but no sounds came out. "But you gave me all that advice on how to get him."

Melissa shrugged. "Everyone knows that if you *really* want a guy to notice you, just pretend he doesn't exist."

Spencer's gut churned so violently, she was afraid she might puke up the Hawaiian feast.

"But I thought you and I were *friends*!" Spencer whimpered, tears rushing to her eyes.

"We were *never* friends," Melissa snapped, dropping her gloss onto her dresser, where it rolled around and then off onto the lush carpet. She glared at Spencer. "I *never* forgave you for anything you've done to me. And I never will."

She shot Spencer a cruel smile, then stalked out of the bedroom, down the stairs, and out into the night with Colin, leaving Spencer far behind.

10

NEW YEAR, NEW GIRL

The next morning, Spencer opened her eyes to lovely golden sunshine streaming through the window. Birds chirped in the trees. A bicycle bell jingled on the street. The surf pounded loudly, and there was a soothing smell of freshly brewed coffee and French toast in the air. It was another glorious morning in Longboat Key.

And then she remembered. *Melissa.*

She shot up in bed, the details of the night rushing back to her like black sludge spewing out of a spigot. How Colin had arrived, dashing and gorgeous, to profess his love for Melissa. The twist of her sister's lips as she told Spencer she'd never forgiven her. Spencer had heard them talking on the back patio long into the night, finally turning her sound machine up to level ten to drown out their laughter.

It felt like a punch to the chest. Melissa had never wanted to be friends. She hated Spencer, just like always.

The worst thing about all of it was that Spencer had begun to hope that things really could change between them—no, that they *had* changed.

She pushed her feet into her slippers and padded down the stairs, praying that Melissa wasn't in the kitchen. Thankfully, only her mother was sitting at the table, thumbing through the newspaper.

"Morning, sweetie." Spencer's mother broke the silence. "Did you have fun last night?"

Spencer glanced at her. She was still wearing her robe and pajamas. There was something so vulnerable about seeing her without makeup on. She felt her chin wobble. "Not really," she blurted out before she could stop herself.

"What happened?"

Spencer tried to keep her lips closed, but the need to purge was too great. She spilled the whole story about Colin, explaining that she'd met an amazing boy on vacation, and it looked like he really liked her, but then someone had stolen him away at the last minute. The only detail she left out was that someone was Melissa.

When she got to the end of the story, recounting how she'd seen Colin go off with the other girl, her mother folded her hands on top of the table. "So what are you going to do about it?"

Spencer blinked. "What *can* I do about it?" The decision had been made: Melissa won, yet again. "I lost," she went on. "I should just lick my wounds and move on."

Her mother's brows knitted together. "Since when do

you look at the world that way? Where's the girl who does anything and everything to win?"

Spencer shrugged. "That hasn't gotten me far in the past."

Her mother clucked her tongue. "If you think this boy is right for you, you have to fight for him."

There was a defiant, stern look on her mother's face, and her left hand was curled into a tight fist like she was getting ready to punch someone. "You think so?" Spencer asked. Her voice cracked.

"Absolutely." Her mother's chin-length blond hair bobbed as she nodded. "You need to do everything in your power to throw that other girl out of the picture. You have to fight for what you want."

Something about her tone made Spencer wonder if she was talking from experience. "Does this have anything to do with you and Dad?" she asked in a tiny voice.

Spencer's mother turned away, becoming transfixed with the bird feeder on the patio. After a moment she breathed in, looking like she was going to say something, but then seemed to change her mind and shut her mouth.

"Are you guys having . . . problems?" Spencer tried again.

"It's nothing to worry about, honey." Her mother stood and gave Spencer a tight smile. "Now, do you want a croissant? Maybe I can make you some French toast? Dad picked up that delicious challah bread from Tommy's . . ."

Spencer murmured that she wasn't hungry, then watched as her mother drifted distractedly out of the room. It was hard to know whether her parents were really on the rocks or if this was just backlash from everything that had happened this fall.

She stared at her mother's cup of coffee, which she'd left on the table, and then at a cardigan sweater draped over the back of one of the chairs. It was Melissa's; she'd worn it to Culpeper's steak house the other night. She balled it in her hands, the soft cashmere bending to her will.

Her mother's words swirled through her mind. *You have to fight for what you want.* Maybe there was some truth to that. Before Melissa had come onto the scene, Colin had been into Spencer—she was *sure* of it.

She stood up, feeling the effects of her mom's pep talk zooming through her veins. Forget Melissa's stupid advice—Spencer was going to get Colin back *her* way. Dirty. Ruthlessly. By whatever means necessary.

She sauntered out of the kitchen and up the stairs to her room, suddenly rejuvenated. Little did Melissa know it, but the new year was going to bring forth a new Spencer. And she was playing to win.

11

BATTLE ON THE BEACH

By the time Spencer stepped onto the beach later that morning, the temperature had climbed to almost ninety degrees. Though Nana's house was right on the ocean, it wasn't in the best spot for sunbathing or swimming— that was what the public beach about a quarter mile up the shore was for. If Colin and Melissa were at the beach today, they would be there. When Spencer walked down the wooden steps and scanned the sand, she spied the two of them just to the left of the lifeguard mound, snuggling together on a shared striped blanket. Bingo.

She ducked behind the lifeguard post so they wouldn't see her. Melissa was wearing a polka-dotted bikini and was rubbing sunscreen on Colin's back. She said something in his ear, and the two of them tittered. Spencer wondered if they were talking about her. Maybe Melissa was telling him how she'd fed Spencer all those stupid *Cosmo* rules to win Colin over. Or maybe Melissa was laughing about how she'd stolen Wren back from Spencer, or about how her little sister was too stupid to write her own AP Econ essays.

Well, two could play at that game.

She smoothed out her towel on the hot sand. The beach was crowded, with a ton of people in the water, flying kites, and playing beach volleyball around a net set up near the dunes. A big wave crashed, and suddenly Spencer heard a lilting giggle behind her. She glanced over her shoulder, feeling a dart of worry. That laugh sounded so familiar, like a haunting dream. But it couldn't be A.

Spencer plucked her cell phone from her bag. She knew just the person to remind her that all was fair in love and war. She shot a quick text to Hanna, asking for inspiration. But even after a few minutes, Hanna didn't write back.

Spencer was going to have to do this on her own. Like *everything*, she thought bitterly.

She stood and walked over to Melissa's towel. She cast a long shadow over her sister, but Melissa wouldn't look up from her issue of *Vanity Fair*, not even when Spencer cleared her throat. Finally, Colin shaded his forehead and noticed her.

"Oh. Hey, Spencer." He awkwardly rubbed the top of his head, a sheepish look on his face.

"Hey," Spencer said tersely. She thrust the phone at Melissa. "There's another article about Ian. Your *boyfriend*."

Melissa flipped a page and pushed her sunglasses up her nose, not even flinching.

"The *felon* who's in jail," Spencer added, dangling the phone under Melissa's nose. She'd pulled up a piece about him from the *Philadelphia Inquirer.* "His lawyers just made a statement to the press."

Colin squinted at the phone, then glanced at Melissa in question. Melissa coolly rolled onto her side and took a sip from a can of Diet Coke. After a moment, Colin shrugged and lay down next to her, ignoring Spencer, too.

Spencer lingered over them for another few seconds, phone outstretched, but then started to feel awkward. Melissa had probably briefed Colin that Spencer would be jealous and looking for revenge. *Don't believe a word she says*, she'd probably told him.

Spencer dropped her phone back into her bag, ditched her sunglasses, and marched down to the ocean to cool off. After weaving around a bunch of little kids playing in the surf and a group of guys throwing a waterlogged Nerf ball, she dove headfirst into a wave. The water was cool, refreshing, and salty, and she surfaced and looked back at the shore. Melissa and Colin were now standing in the shallow water, wetting their feet. Melissa stared out at Spencer in the big waves, but when she noticed Spencer looking, she quickly turned her head away.

"Hi." A pudgy boy who looked to be about thirteen years old and who was wearing a soggy T-shirt and a large snorkeling mask stared at Spencer from a few feet away. "You're pretty."

"Thanks." Spencer floated over a wave. Naturally the

only boy who paid attention to her would be a pre-pubescent dork. She could only imagine the laughs she'd get from Aria, Emily, and Hanna when she told them.

The boy lifted something translucent and gelatinous from the water. "Want to pet my jellyfish?"

Spencer yelped and swam a few strokes away.

The boy laughed. "It's fake! See?" He paddled closer, and before Spencer could stop him, he was thrusting the rubbery thing under her nose.

Years ago, a jellyfish that looked just like this had stung Melissa on the leg. She'd screamed and screamed, and their father had told her that the best remedy was to pee on the wound. That just made Melissa scream louder. She'd sulked on the couch for the rest of the day. Spencer had kept her company, making WANTED posters of the evil jellyfish and tacking them up all over Nana's house.

"Uh, do you mind if I borrow this for a sec?" she asked Snorkel Boy, who was still treading water next to her.

His face lit up. "Only if you give me a kiss."

Spencer groaned. But desperate times called for des-perate measures. "Fine," she said, pressing her lips to his cheek. At the last minute, the boy turned his head and touched his lips to hers. Spencer pulled away and wiped her mouth, fighting the urge to gag.

"I'll be back," Spencer grumbled, grabbing the faux jel-lyfish and riding a wave into shore. Melissa and Colin were still standing in the shallow water, inspecting a small tide pool. There was such a big crowd in the water that her sister didn't notice Spencer's approach. Slowly, stealthily, she floated the jellyfish in Melissa's direction and then dove into an oncoming wave.

By the time she surfaced, Melissa was peering at her calf, where the fake creature had attached itself. Then she started to shake her leg vigorously, screaming. "Get it off, get it *off*!" Melissa wailed. The jellyfish remained stuck to her skin, and she screeched louder and louder. Colin's brow furrowed, and for a split second, he looked annoyed.

Spencer waded toward them, ready to pluck the jellyfish from Melissa's leg and tell her that it was just a toy when Colin knelt down, peeled the thing off, and chucked it into the waves. He scooped up Melissa, who was now a blubbering mess, and carried her out of the water and up the dunes. "It's okay," he said. "I'll take care of you. Don't you worry." Melissa lay her head on Colin's shoulder.

Something bobbed at Spencer's feet, and she looked down and saw that the fake jellyfish had found its way back to her. She picked it up by its tentacle and returned it to Snorkel Boy, who was watching her from a few feet away. "I play tricks like that on my sister, too," he said gleefully.

Great, Spencer thought as she slogged out of the water and stomped to her towel. Her get-him-back strategies were on par with a middle-school boy's.

12

SOMETHING BLUE . . .

It was drizzling the following morning when Spencer made her way onto the patio with a cup of coffee, a bowl of Kashi GoLean, and a fresh Florida grapefruit. Her mother was sitting at the table surrounded by a bunch of paints and brushes, a cup of cloudy water, and a terra-cotta ceramic mug Spencer knew she'd bought at the pottery store in town. She had a tradition of painting a piece of pottery every time she visited Longboat Key. She always stashed the finished artwork in Nana's cabinet, but Spencer doubted that Nana actually used them.

"Hey, Spence." Mrs. Hastings painted a blue stripe around the lip of the mug. "Want to paint one of these? I bought a few extra bowls."

"Uh, sure. Just a sec." Spencer's ears suddenly pricked up as she heard her sister moving around upstairs. Melissa had a very anal morning routine: When she was ready for her shower, she carried in a wire caddy from her bedroom full of her face and hair products—she probably thought Spencer might steal a dollop here and there if she left the stuff unattended. Spencer had hatched a new sabotage plan, and she needed to get her hands on Melissa's caddy in a very narrow window of time.

She set down her coffee and cereal and crept back up the stairs. The shower was running in the hall bathroom, but Melissa had stepped back into her bedroom to gather up her clothes as she did every morning. Spencer slipped into the bathroom, spied Melissa's caddy, and grabbed the bottle of Pureology shampoo. Unscrewing the cap, she poured in several heaping drops of blue hair dye she'd found in Nana's cabinet. It wasn't old-lady blue, though, but deep, Manic Panic, Katy Perry blue, the kind Aria had once used to color a thick lock of her own hair as a statement in seventh grade. Who knew why Nana owned such a garish color. Spencer probably didn't *want* to know.

She had just twisted the cap back on the shampoo bottle and edged out of the bathroom when Melissa's bedroom door flung open and Melissa appeared in the hall. She glared at Spencer suspiciously. "What are you doing up here?"

Spencer sniffed. "My room's up here, too."

She was about to turn away when Melissa gave Spencer a saccharine smile. "Look, Spence, I know you're annoyed about Colin. But he and I are much more suited to each other. We're at the same place in life. There's no reason for you to get nasty. That little Ian stunt you pulled yesterday? Totally not cool."

It took everything in Spencer's power not to smother her with one of Nana's monogrammed bed pillows. *Totally not cool?* Did Melissa understand that it was *totally not cool* to steal the guy Spencer was after, too? And didn't she know it was totally not cool to pretend to be on Spencer's side before stabbing her in the back?

Before Spencer could say another word, Melissa stepped into the steamy bathroom and slammed the door shut. Seconds later, the shower curtain rattled closed. Whirling around, Spencer sauntered back downstairs to the patio. Her mother had paused from mug-decorating and was looking at a photo on her iPad. It was a picture of Mrs. DiLaurentis and Ali. They were standing in the Hastingses' backyard at a family barbecue. Spencer's dad was in the corner of the frame, handing Ali's mom a grilled hamburger.

"Why are you looking at *that*?" Spencer asked.

Her mother jumped and minimized the screen. "I, uh, was just scrolling through old photos on our Kodak account. There are so many we need to delete."

"Mom . . ." Spencer fiddled with a spare liner brush on the table. "Is something bothering you about the DiLaurentises?"

Her mother's mouth opened and closed just as a scream pierced the air. A moment later, Melissa burst onto the patio in a terry-cloth robe that said WALDORF-ASTORIA,

NEW YORK CITY on the breast. Her eyes were wild, her skin was still wet, and her dripping hair was a brilliant shade of sapphire. It was even more vibrant and extreme than Spencer could have hoped for.

"Melissa!" Spencer's mother was so surprised she shot to her feet. "What on earth . . . ?"

Melissa pointed at Spencer. "*You* did this. You put something in my shampoo."

Spencer shook her head innocently. "I don't know what you're talking about. You probably just picked up one of Nana's shampoos by mistake."

"You're such a liar." Melissa shook her blue head, her hands quaking with rage. "A pathetic, jealous liar."

"It's a good look for you," Spencer simpered, fiddling with her paintbrush. "And you never know, maybe Colin is into Smurfs."

Melissa let out a piercing groan. Turning to her right, she snatched an unpainted bowl from the table and hurled it at Spencer. Spencer ducked just in time, and the pottery smashed against the brick pavers.

"You bitch!" Spencer screeched. She grabbed the water-filled cup her mother was using to wash her brushes and splashed it in Melissa's face. Green-colored liquid spilled down her cheeks.

Melissa wiped her eyes and gnashed her teeth. She lunged for Spencer, her arms outstretched. "I'm going to kill you," she growled.

"Girls!" Mr. Hastings appeared above them from out

of nowhere, wearing a golf shirt and a pair of plaid shorts. "What the hell is wrong with you two?"

"She put blue hair dye in my shampoo!" Melissa wailed.

"She stole the guy I was interested in!" Spencer shot back.

A look of recognition flashed across Spencer's mother's face. "Wait. *Melissa* stole the guy you liked?"

Melissa scoffed. "I didn't steal him. He chose me."

"That is such a lie!" Spencer yelled and stomped her foot. Her Havaianas made a smack against the floor.

"You two are acting ridiculous," their father boomed. "You're too old to fight like this."

"Your father's right," their mother said, placing her hands on her hips. She strode forward and positioned herself next to her husband. "Melissa, you're twenty-two years old. You should be ashamed of yourself."

Spencer shot a satisfied look at her sister. It had been years since Melissa had been reprimanded.

"Not that you're any better." Spencer's father turned to her, as if reading her mind. "You girls should have learned your lesson about being interested in the same boy. There's no excuse for putting hair dye in your sister's shampoo." Spencer's parents exchanged weary glances with each other, letting out matching sighs.

Melissa reknotted her robe and yanked the patio door open. "I have to call the salon right now and see if I can get this disaster fixed," she said, then flounced away.

Her footsteps could be heard all the way up the stairs. Spencer's father began to sweep up the broken pottery shards with a dustpan.

Her mother turned to her and shook her head. "When I told you to do whatever it took to get that boy, I didn't mean for you to ruin your sister's hair."

"Mom, I—"

But her mother cut her off with a wave of her hand. "Save it."

Then she and Mr. Hastings wandered toward the pool, muttering quietly to each other. Spencer watched as her mother leaned into her father, and her father put an arm around Mrs. Hastings's shoulder. Spencer couldn't help but smile. It was the closest they'd come to embracing in days.

Nothing like two warring children to bring a couple back together.

13

A JUMP INTO THE UNKNOWN

A few hours later, Spencer stood on the dock next to the Finger Lickin' Ice Cream Shop and the jewelry store whose front window featured glittering Rolexes and sleek Cartier bangles. A huge crane extended over the bay, and a big banner that said LONGBOAT KEY BUNGEE JUMP had been stretched between lampposts, surrounded by red, white, and blue bunting.

Just like the pre–New Year's party, the bungee jump was an annual tradition–her family always came and shook their heads at the people crazy enough to plummet over the bay with only a piece of rope saving them from instant death. This year, Spencer was old enough to bungee without getting her parents' permission, and that was exactly what she'd planned to do. It seemed like the kind of thing Colin would be into, and since Melissa would be spending the whole day in the hair salon to de-blue herself, it meant Spencer could finally get some alone time with him. She hoped.

She looked around at the crowds of college kids, twenty-something adrenaline junkies, and men suffering from midlife crises lining up to jump. In fifth grade, the last time her family and Ali's had both visited Longboat Key over the winter holidays, Ali's brother, Jason, had waited eagerly in line, clutching the release form he'd had signed from his parents. Ali and her cabal of friends had stood near him, teasingly asking if he was nervous, if he worried about getting whiplash, or if he'd ever heard the rumor that bungee jumping sometimes made guys' testicles explode. Spencer had snickered at that last jibe, and Ali had spun around and given her a nasty look.

Spencer continued to scan the line. Sure enough, Colin was waiting at the front. She felt a little flutter inside her gut at the sight of him. He was tapping on his phone, his brow furrowed.

Spencer took a deep breath and walked over. "Everything okay?"

Colin looked up. "Oh, hey. Yeah, I was just texting Melissa. She told me she'd meet me here, but I haven't heard from her. Do you know where she is?"

"She told you she was going to meet you *here*?" Spencer made a face. "This isn't her kind of thing at all. She's at the salon, getting her hair done. She'll probably be there all day."

Colin slipped his phone back into his pocket, a strange look crossing his face. "The salon? Seriously? She doesn't strike me as that kind of girl."

"No?" Spencer leaned against one of the wooden posts and watched as a tiny speck of a person plunged from the bungee crane. The crowd applauded. "She's a salon addict. She gets her arms waxed, highlights, a monthly facial, and then there's nails, Reiki treatments, the tanning booth . . . she's super high-maintenance."

"Huh." Colin ran his hand over his chin and looked at Spencer.

A long beat passed. Colin didn't look away until the crane started to groan and the elevator winch slowly pulled the next jumper into the sky. Colin glanced at his phone again. "So was what you said at the beach yesterday true? Does Melissa really have a felon for a boyfriend?"

Spencer opened her mouth, ready to tell the whole story about Ian, but something suddenly made her change her mind. Talking about Ian without Melissa here to defend herself seemed a little crass, even for her. It wasn't like Melissa had known he'd killed Ali, after all. She hadn't even known they'd been together.

"Colin?"

Melissa was sauntering down the dock, her hair now a brilliant shade of honey blond. When she saw Spencer, her eyes flashed, but she swept right past her, wrapped her arms around Colin, and gave him a big kiss. "Sorry I'm late."

Colin picked up a strand of Melissa's new hair and let it fall. "Spencer said you were at the salon."

"Oh, just for a little touch-up," Melissa trilled. She clasped Colin's hand. "I wouldn't miss your big jump!"

"*My* big jump?" Colin's smile was a question mark. "Aren't you jumping, too?"

Melissa blinked hard. Her gaze flicked from the crane to the bungee jumper dangling over the bay. "Um . . ."

"C'mon, you made it just in time." Colin gestured around them, indicating that they were next in line. "You can jump before me. You'll love it—I promise."

One of the bungee workers, a skinny guy with braided hair, looked at the people in line. "Okay, folks. Who's next?"

Melissa's face had gone sheet-white. "Colin, I don't think I can do it," she said in the same damsel-in-distress voice she'd used during the great jellyfish rescue yesterday.

Colin scoffed. "You're being silly. It's really fun—and totally safe. You should live a little."

"Uh, who's going up?" Braided Hair asked impatiently, jingling the chain on his wallet.

Melissa's knees were locked, and she'd sucked in her lips so hard they were white. "Seriously, Colin," she said shakily. "I hate heights."

Colin ran his tongue over his teeth. He stared at Melissa for almost a full refrain of the heavy metal song that was blaring from the speakers. Spencer held her breath, watching Colin's features change as the picture Melissa had painted of herself chipped into something less interesting. It reminded her of the time Spencer's father had been all set to buy a vintage Ferrari from a guy two towns over but had discovered the undercarriage was full of rust and the car actually didn't start.

She pushed around both of them. "*I'll* jump."

"*You?*" Melissa looked shocked.

"Great." Braided Hair stepped aside so that Spencer could climb aboard the little elevator that would carry her to the top of the tower. She tried her best to remain relaxed as he shut her into the compartment and the carriage began to move. Melissa glowered at her. Colin, on the other hand, looked impressed. *Good luck*, he mouthed.

The ride to the top took about a minute. Spencer watched as the people on the dock got smaller and smaller and her view of the bay expanded. When she reached the jumping-off point, an instructor harnessed her up and told her the basics of how to jump—try to remain relaxed, put her arms straight out, and jump into a swan dive so as not to hurt her back. And then it was time to go.

Spencer shuffled toward the edge of the tower, her pulse pounding. The waves lapped peacefully a zillion feet below. The water looked so dark and endless from up here. Suddenly, she was reminded of when she'd dangled over the edge of Falling Man Quarry with Mona Vanderwaal. How black the abyss had been. How certain she'd felt that she was going to plummet to her death. Mona's shrill, desperate screams as she'd fallen, the full *four-Mississippi* counts until she'd hit the bottom.

A faint giggle pierced the silence, and Spencer whipped her head to the right. People on the dock craned up to watch her. A seagull landed on a white and red buoy.

Spencer shook her head. There was no way someone could be laughing at her, all the way up here.

"Are you ready?" the instructor asked, giving the bungee cord another tug to make sure it was secure.

Spencer's mouth felt coated with wool. Her hands began to feel slick, and sweat prickled under her arms. But she couldn't chicken out now.

"Ready," she answered shakily.

The instructors counted down from three. Spencer swallowed hard, thrust her jaw upward, and stepped off the ledge. At first she felt weightless, and then her stomach swooped into her throat. She heard screams around her, only realizing a few milliseconds later that they were her own. The water below her approached faster and faster, her body felt heavier and heavier, until *thwock*—the rope caught and bounced back upward. Soon she came to a stop, and she was dangling over the water. She'd made it. She was alive. She breathed out, listening to the sound of her rocketing heartbeat in her ears.

A cheer rose up from the dock. "Yeah!" Spencer extended her arms. She felt exhilarated and free, like she'd just left all her baggage at the top of the crane. She swung around toward the dock, searching for Colin and Melissa, but she didn't see them anywhere. Suddenly, it didn't really matter.

The crane slowly pulled her back up to the top. The instructor loomed over the edge and unhooked her harness. "That was awesome," Spencer breathed.

"Told you it was amazing!" a voice said behind her.

Spencer peered over the instructor. Colin was standing on the platform, all harnessed up. They were the only two jumpers on the deck. "So I guess Melissa didn't want to jump, huh?" she asked.

Colin twisted his hands at his waist. "Actually, she left." He let out an uncomfortable laugh. "I don't think she really wanted to stick around after what I said to her."

Spencer's heart stopped. "What did you say?"

Colin's blue eyes locked on hers. "That my feelings have changed. That I picked the wrong sister."

The same rush that Spencer had just felt on the bungee jump swelled over her once more. She tried to keep a neutral expression on her face, but she could feel her lips pulling into a smile.

Colin stepped closer and took her hand. Spencer could smell his sandy, sunscreeny scent and tried not to swoon. Just like that, in front of the grubby instructors, hundreds of feet in the air, he leaned forward and pressed his lips to hers. Spencer's eyes fluttered closed. Her heart hammered in her chest. She could feel the instructors shift impatiently behind them, but she didn't care.

The kiss was over too soon, and Colin pulled away. "Want to jump in tandem with me?"

"You can do that?" Spencer looked at the instructor, and he gave a bored nod. She ran her fingers over her harness and shrugged. "Sure. Why not?"

The instructor finished tethering Colin to the bungee,

secured Spencer to the same cord, and the two of them walked to the ledge together. As they counted down, Colin turned to Spencer and touched her cheek. "I don't know what took me so long, Spencer. Can you forgive me?"

Spencer's insides shimmered. Instead of saying anything, she grabbed Colin's hand and squeezed it hard.

And then, together, they jumped into the abyss.

14

TABLE FOR TWO

"Right this way." A Latina waitress who couldn't have been more than five feet tall led Spencer and Colin around a grove of palm trees into a private Mediterranean garden at the back of the Mia Vista, one of Longboat Key's most sought-after dinner spots. Gorgeous purple, blue, and yellow flowers curled around white trellises and a wooden pergola. A beehive-shaped fireplace blazed in the corner, throwing off just the right amount of heat to cut the slight chill in the air, and a jazz band played softly in the corner. They stopped in front of a corner table with a white tablecloth, a glowing white candle, and a glass of champagne at each of their seats— and, of course, a chilled AminoSpa for Colin. In all of Spencer's fantasies, she'd never thought up a first-date spot dreamier than this.

She settled into her chair, smoothing the brand-new dress she'd bought that afternoon over her lap. Colin sat down opposite her, looking extra-tan in his white Lacoste polo. "This is just so perfect," Spencer said.

"We couldn't have picked a better place," Colin said at the exact same time. They both stopped and laughed.

The waitress returned with their drinks and some menus. Colin sipped his AminoSpa on ice, and then burst into laughter. "Remember how much you hated this on our first date?" He reached across the table and took Spencer's hand. She could feel herself blushing. So he *had* counted the tennis game as a date! This whole situation was so surreal. For once, it seemed, she had actually won.

Melissa hadn't been at the house when Spencer had come home from bungee jumping, nor had Spencer seen her in town. Spencer wasn't sure what she would have done if she had run into her. She knew she should feel triumphant for stealing Colin away, but part of her kind of felt . . . crappy. It was a lot like how she felt when she'd kissed Ian in her driveway—as psyched as she'd been to hook up with the hottest senior at Rosewood Day, she couldn't help but feel guilty, even though Melissa was always a royal bitch to her.

But that didn't change the way she felt for Colin, who was staring at her with longing, his eyes soft, the slightest hint of a smile on his face.

"What are you thinking?" she asked.

He half-shrugged, caressing her palm. "Just that you are so gorgeous."

She felt a shiver run down the length of her spine.

"You're not so bad yourself," Spencer said, lowering her lashes.

The waitress reappeared and took their orders. When she was gone, Colin sighed. "It sucks you have to go home soon."

"I know." Spencer pouted. "But maybe I could come back and visit. How long will you be here?" Her mind churned, conjuring up images of snorkeling and sailing and lemonades on the beach after tennis practice.

"I'm going to be here until February. But the thing is, I'm going to be training a lot," Colin said, shifting in his seat. "I want to get into some slams this year, remember?"

"Oh, of course." Spencer sat up straighter. "I would never tear you away from your training. I'd hit balls around with you if you wanted, though you probably want stiffer competition."

"No, that would actually be awesome." Colin used his straw to crush a piece of ice at the bottom of his glass. "Who knows? If things go well, maybe you could come with me to some of my matches." He sat back in his chair and crossed his arms over his chest. "We could go to Australia together. Roland Garros in France. We could hobnob in New York City at the US Open."

"I could sit in the special visitors' box and wave for the ESPN cameras," Spencer said excitedly.

"You'll look amazing in the stands," Colin whispered.

"*You'll* look amazing on the court," Spencer said.

They leaned forward and kissed lightly. Electricity crackled through Spencer's body.

She sat back. "And if, God forbid, you *don't* make it into a slam this year, you'll be coming back to Connecticut, right? I could always drive up to visit you. Rosewood's not that far."

A muscle in Colin's jaw twitched. "Yeah, I don't know about that."

"Why?"

He raised one shoulder. "My apartment's kind of . . ." He trailed off.

"Kind of what?" Embarrassing? Shabby? Or maybe he lived with a creepy uncle or way too many cats.

"It doesn't matter. Let's not worry about that right now." Colin cupped her chin in his hands. "Let's talk about you instead. When did you first realize you had a thing for me?"

"Probably when I discovered we were both organizing junkies," Spencer joked.

Colin wagged his finger at her. "You'd better stay out of my closet. I've got it set up just the way I want it."

Spencer pretended to pout. "But closets are my favorite thing to organize!"

When the entrées arrived, Colin launched into a story about a tennis match that had gone into seven break points that lasted until Spencer speared the last bit of crab onto her fork. She laughed and groaned at all the right places, then tried to tell a story about when a field hockey game had gone into sudden death overtime, but Colin was so enthusiastic that he kept speaking right over her. *He must be nervous*, she thought, smiling at him. It was *so* cute.

The waitress appeared. "Any dessert for the lovebirds?"

Spencer opened her mouth to ask for some coffee and a menu, but Colin jumped in.

"I'm afraid not," he said quickly, checking his phone. He shrugged at Spencer. "You know the drill. Gotta put in a good night's sleep."

Spencer struggled to smile. "Of course. But maybe just a quick—"

"We'll take the check," Colin interrupted.

The waitress glanced at Spencer, mouthed *Sorry*, and left, taking the dessert menus with her. Colin rolled up his napkin, tossed it on the table, and shot Spencer a winning grin. "I'm gonna run to the restroom."

"Okay," Spencer answered, trying to hide her disappointment. She checked her phone—she had one message from Emily, asking when she was getting back to Rosewood—and then examined her manicure, which was still flawless. She crossed and recrossed her legs and then drummed her fingers against the tablecloth.

The waitress dropped their check off, and Spencer left it where it was, crooked in the center of the table, slightly askew toward Colin's still-empty seat.

Colin was taking an awfully long time. *There must have been a line*, Spencer decided. She checked her phone again, and read several blog posts on Go Fug Yourself. She touched up her lip gloss. The waitress returned and reached for the check. Spencer clapped her hand over the leather envelope. "Uh, we haven't paid yet," she said, cheeks flaming.

Fifteen minutes passed. The couple who had been sitting next to them walked out, hand in hand, and a new couple sat down. There was no sign of Colin. Spencer wondered if she'd misunderstood. Had Colin thought they were supposed to meet out front, near the bathrooms? Thinking that must be it, she gestured the waitress over and slipped her her credit card with as much confidence as she could muster. The waitress looked at her sympathetically, but Spencer laughed it off.

The foyer was empty. Spencer hesitated by the men's room door, her stomach beginning to knot. When an older man with silver hair emerged from behind the door, Spencer asked if anyone else was in there. "It's kind of urgent," she explained, her voice high and tight.

The man gave her a weird look. "Didn't see anyone else in there," he finally said.

Spencer bolted for the front door, the uneasy feeling in her now as strong as a heartbeat.

Outside, she took a quick lap around the perimeter of the building. When she reached the parking lot, she stopped short. A man with Colin's same broad shoulders, dark hair, and tight butt was locked in an embrace with a woman in her thirties wearing a killer linen dress. Her sleek blond hair was pulled back in a ponytail and she had her hand on an expensive stroller.

"Say hi to Daddy, Brady!" the woman exclaimed, her voice ringing out over the parking lot.

Spencer gasped audibly. *Daddy?*

The couple turned to face her. Colin's face registered a note of surprise and shock, but he recovered quickly, again grinning that ultra-white smile. "Spencer!" He waved. "Come here for a sec!"

Somehow, Spencer managed to move her feet, one in front of the other, toward Colin. She stared at him, then the blonde, then the child in the stroller. Had she heard correctly? Was he seriously a . . . *father?*

When Spencer was only a few paces away, Colin smiled, his eyes still darting nervously. "Yvette, this is Spencer. She's the girl I told you about, who I've been giving tennis lessons to."

"I'm Yvette DeSoto," the blonde said, her voice warm like honey. She stuck out her left hand. It was weighted down with an enormous diamond sparkler and sapphire-studded wedding band. "I hope my husband hasn't been working you too hard."

The words rang in Spencer's head. She shook Yvette's hand quickly, the champagne in her stomach rising back up her throat. *My husband.* Colin had a wife. But if Yvette was his wife, what did that make Ramona? Or Melissa? Or *her*? Spencer looked down at the baby, who was kicking its little legs and gurgling. And Colin didn't just have a wife. He had a *child*.

For a split second, her gaze returned to Colin's face. She'd assumed he was just out of college, but in the harsh glare of the parking-lot lamp, Colin looked different somehow. Older. The lines around his eyes were deeper, and tiny silver hairs peeked out of the five o'clock stubble on his chin. It was like he was suddenly a completely different person.

After a long moment, Spencer found her voice. "Uh, well, it was really nice to meet you, but I have to . . ." Her voice trailed off, and she turned around and fled, running past Range Rovers and BMWs. When she finally found her way to the empty sidewalk behind the club, breathless and overwhelmed, the faintest giggle echoed through the trees. She was too weary to even look around to see who it was. She deserved to be laughed at for this. She hadn't won Colin at all. She hadn't won anything. Like usual, Spencer Hastings had ended up with nothing.

15

QUIT YOUR CRYING

New Year's Eve morning, Spencer lay on the hammock on the back porch, turning the pages of *Moby-Dick* without really comprehending the sentences. When she got to the word *vile*, she uncapped a blue Bic pen and circled it. Then she circled the words *nasty* and *duplicitous* and *deceitful*. She had been doing this for the past twenty pages, circling every word that reminded her of Colin. It made her feel a tiny bit better.

Spencer had a heartbreak hangover. Her head was pounding and her eyes were so red she'd worn her sunglasses in the kitchen, ignoring the strange looks from her father. She'd cried herself to sleep last night—and then in the shower this morning, and again at breakfast as she burned her wheat bread in the toaster.

She folded the book on her chest and glanced at her phone, which she'd laid on the side table next to the hammock. *No new messages.* Of course there weren't. Of course Colin hadn't texted her. Colin was a player, plain and simple. And he was a cheater. He didn't care about Spencer; he never had.

Still, his lies hurt. Did *anyone* tell the truth, ever? Ali had lied to her, conveniently omitting the part about how she was secretly seeing Ian when she'd chided Spencer for not telling Melissa about her transgressions. Even Spencer's old friends had lied to her—and she had lied to them—keeping huge secrets during their friendship that only Ali knew. And then of course there was Melissa.

"Ahem."

Spencer looked up. Melissa stood there, a cup of coffee in one hand and the newspaper under her other arm. Spencer flinched, ready for another showdown, but her sister's expression was surprisingly neutral.

"Hey," Melissa said in a tired voice.

"Hi," Spencer said timidly.

Melissa sat down on the teak chaise next to the hammock and placed her coffee on the side table next to Spencer's phone. She searched Spencer's face. "You found out Colin has a wife, didn't you?"

Spencer winced. "You *knew*?"

Melissa shook her blond head. "I was at the courts this morning and she was standing on the sidelines, telling all of his groupies who she was. And every break he had, she made him come over so she could straighten his shirt and massage his neck muscles."

"I found out last night—after he ditched me at dinner," Spencer admitted.

"He's a liar in more ways than one." Melissa leaned forward. "You know what else I found out? He's not ranked ninety-second in the world in tennis—he's eight-hundred-something. Certainly not good enough to go to a Grand Slam." She reached for her coffee, took a sip, and shook her head with disgust. "He told me, 'I'll take you to Australia and France with me. You'll be the prettiest girl at the US Open.' And I fell for it."

"He said that to me, too!" Spencer exclaimed.

Melissa clucked her tongue. "He probably said that to a million girls. He has the perfect setup—rich wife hiding in Connecticut, his pick of girls in Longboat Key. It's disgusting. But there's something even worse about him." Melissa covered her mouth with her hand, looking vaguely green. "He's registered in the Masters category at the tournament."

Spencer squinted. "What does that mean?"

"Masters are for players over a certain age. Spencer, he's *thirty-three*."

"*What?*" Spencer shot off the hammock, knocking *Moby-Dick* to the floor. She wriggled violently. "Are you sure?"

"I'm definitely sure." Melissa nodded grimly.

Spencer ran her hands down the length of her face. "I can't believe I kissed him! He's so *old*!"

Melissa thumped a fist on the arm of the chaise. "He

had both of us completely fooled. And now we need to make him pay."

We? Spencer glanced at her sister, about to protest that she was never going to fall for Melissa's sister act again.

"Save your breath." Melissa cut her off before she could even say anything. "What happened between us is water under the bridge, okay? Right now, there are two things we need to do. One: Never tell a *soul* that this happened. As far as I know, you never dated a thirty-three-year-old guy with a wife and kid. And neither did I."

"Agreed." Spencer nodded. Thank God no one from Rosewood had seen what happened.

"And second." Melissa held up a finger. "Before we leave tomorrow night, we need to get revenge."

Spencer leaned against the porch railing. "How?"

"It has to be something good." Melissa cast her head up to the sky. "Maybe something that could ruin his chances of winning the tennis tournament tomorrow. And a fitting payback for all the girls he's played in Longboat Key."

Spencer picked at a piece of splintered wood on the railing, thinking about all of the groupies that had gathered on the sidelines of the tennis courts to watch Colin play. How many had dated him? How many more would once Yvette went home?

She wondered how he kept all his girlfriends straight, imagining his bathroom filled with lots of different used toothbrushes, one for each lover, just like Nana's. Colin had probably been so impressed with Nana and her revolving door of men because he was just as big of a dirty slut. She wondered if he had a secret prescription for Viagra, too.

Suddenly, her head whipped up. "Oh my God, Melissa. I know what we can do."

An excited smile spread across Melissa's face. "What?"

Spencer extended her arm to pull her sister to her feet. "Come on. I'll show you."

16

THE BEST REVENGE

New Year's Day dawned bright and cool. It was the perfect weather for a tennis tournament, and judging by the size and wardrobe of the crowd at the Longboat Key Tennis Club, everyone else thought so, too. Spencer, still wearing her sunglasses, sipped a diet soda and pretended to watch the junior division players while she waited for the signal from Melissa. She was scouring the courts, making sure Colin, his coach, Yvette, and even baby Brady were all accounted for.

"We're on," Melissa murmured into Spencer's ear as she walked quickly past her. Spencer turned on her Toms-clad foot and followed her, ducking her head and feeling grateful that the straw hat she'd borrowed from Nana's closet concealed her identity from the dozen or so Colin groupies who had positioned themselves right near the snack stand.

The walk to the locker rooms was brief and quiet, save for the occasional roar of the crowds in the distance whenever someone scored a point. Suddenly a group of girls in tennis whites passed down the hall. Melissa started laughing.

"*Shhh.*" Spencer clapped down on Melissa's arm. "Do you want us to get caught?"

"This is just so priceless," Melissa whispered, wiping her eyes.

The locker room door creaked open, and a tall guy who couldn't have been much older than eighteen walked into the hall. Melissa peered through the door. "So you're sure Colin's stuff is in there?"

Spencer nodded. When they'd arrived this morning, they'd checked all of the courts being used for the tournaments. A women's match was taking place on the main court right now, but Colin had been practicing on a side court. "His bag isn't with him. It's not with Yvette, either. I don't know where else it could be."

"Okay, then." Melissa pushed Spencer toward the door. "It's now or never."

Taking a deep breath, the girls pulled the men's locker room door open and darted inside. The room was blessedly empty. Spencer scanned the aisles, searching frantically for Colin's lime-green Adidas bag. She thought she saw it and crept down low, ready to pounce, when a loud creak reverberated off the metal lockers. She froze. A pair of footsteps strode away, followed by the sound of the door opening and closing. She let out her breath, waited another few seconds, and then leapt to the bag, which, sure enough, was embroidered with his initials. Her hands shook as she undid the zipper and rooted around the T-shirts, socks, extra rackets, tube of balls, and jar of muscle cream. Finally, she found what she was looking for at the very bottom: a bottle of lemon-lime AminoSpa. *Yes.*

"I got it," she said to Melissa. Melissa pulled out the bottle of Viagra they'd stolen from Nana's drawer and emptied a pill into her palm.

"We should use more than one," Spencer whispered. "More like two. Or three."

Melissa nodded and pulled out two more pills. They used the bottom of the AminoSpa bottle to crush them up until they were a fine powder, then dumped them into the lemony liquid.

"When is Colin going on again?" Melissa murmured.

"An hour, I think," Spencer whispered.

"Perfect."

After the mission was complete, they took seats at the court Colin would be playing on and waited for the show to start.

The women's match finished quickly. The fans filed off the bleachers and a new cheering section shuffled in. Colin's groupies filled the front row. Yvette appeared as well, holding the baby and looking perfectly annoyed. The chair and line judges took their places, and finally, the men's locker room doors opened and two guys walked onto the court.

Melissa grabbed Spencer's hand as Colin proudly paraded toward his chair, green gear bag slung over one arm, bottle of AminoSpa in the other. *Lemon-lime* AminoSpa, to be exact. Spencer had to clap a hand over her mouth to keep from bursting out laughing.

Colin dropped the bag on the court and gazed into the stands, waving dutifully to his wife and shooting his groupies a zillion-watt smile. Then he turned around and took a long swig of AminoSpa, tilting his head back and letting the liquid drip down his throat. Spencer dug her nails into Melissa's palm.

Colin and his opponent batted the ball back and forth for a while until they were ready to play. He won the first few games effortlessly, his serve accurate, his backhand shots impossible to return, his court angles deft and brilliant. The groupies went wild. Spencer wondered if Yvette knew that her husband was a letch, but even if she did Yvette simply held up Brady's arms and clapped them together, smiling proudly at her husband.

Spencer looked at Melissa worriedly. "Why isn't anything happening?"

"Give it time," Melissa murmured.

Four more games passed in much the same way. Colin won the first set easily, and his followers cheered. Spencer's hopes began to drain away. Maybe Viagra didn't work when dissolved. Or maybe Colin had been drinking from a different bottle of AminoSpa.

But suddenly, in the first game of the second set, something began to happen. Colin kept glancing at his crotch, a concerned look on his face. His movements became stiffer, uncomfortable. He missed some easy shots, swiveling around so that his back faced the crowd. When it was his turn to serve and he threw the ball into the air, his shorts pulled in such a way that it was obvious that the crushed Viagra had, well, *worked*.

Melissa elbowed Spencer. A murmur went through the bleachers. A few girls exchanged incredulous smiles. Colin tried for another serve, and this time his shorts hid nothing. A couple people burst out laughing. The line judges' jaws dropped. The chair judge shifted uncomfortably. When Colin double-faulted and covered his crotch with a towel, the judge called out through his bullhorn, "Do you need a minute, Mr. DeSoto?"

"Uh-huh," Colin groaned, walking bowlegged back to his seat.

The laughter intensified. Yvette covered her eyes. Colin stared at his crotch in horror, his face bright red.

"Come on." Melissa looped her purse around her shoulder and stood. "We don't need to see the rest of this, do we?"

"I guess we don't," Spencer agreed. They filed down the bleachers, snaking around the laughing girls and horrified fans. At that very moment, Colin glanced up and looked at both of them.

The sisters burst into laughter. Spencer gave him a three-finger wave. Melissa did, too. Maybe Colin would never know it had been them who'd spiked his drink, but *they* would—and that was all that mattered.

17

STICK WITH ME, SISTER

Spencer and Melissa giggled hysterically the whole four-block walk back to Nana's house. Melissa imitated Colin's stiff-legged waddle. Spencer glanced down at her crotch, pretending she was horrified. "That was the best revenge ever." Melissa gave Spencer a nudge. "I should have known you'd think up something truly evil like that."

Spencer flinched. "It wasn't *that* evil."

"I didn't mean it like that," Melissa said. Then she twisted her mouth. "Okay. Maybe I did. I don't know."

They fell silent. A strong scent of flowers wafted in Spencer's nose, making her queasy. "I'm really sorry about everything," she said quietly as they turned up the driveway.

"I know. I'm sorry, too."

Spencer stopped next to a blooming hydrangea. "We always . . . *do* this. Compete like crazy people. Try to outdo one another. It isn't right."

Melissa shrugged. "It's not like *I* started this."

Spencer stared at her. "Yes, you did. I was the one who liked Colin first. You were the one who wanted to help me, and then . . ."

"*You* were the one who turned in Ian," Melissa reminded her.

Spencer threw up her hands. "That wasn't to hurt you! I swear!"

"Well, it *did* hurt me." Melissa's mouth tightened. She stared in the direction of Nana's house. "And I'm sorry, Spence, but you've hurt me a lot this year. You pushed me down the frickin' stairs, remember?"

"How many times have I said I was sorry about that?"

Melissa sighed and shoved her hands in her pockets. A cool breeze blew up Spencer's shirt, drying the sweat on the back of her neck. She pressed her fingers into her raw eye sockets and sighed. A few minutes ago, they'd been laughing and joking. Everything had been perfect. Now it felt ruined again.

"I just wish I could wave a magic wand and make everything go back to how it used to be," Spencer whimpered.

Melissa glanced at her. "How it used to be *when*?"

"When we were little. When we were friends. When we used to play Castle and spy on Mom and Dad."

Melissa scrunched up her face. "Spence, you were, what? Five years old? Six? Life's a little bit more complicated now. Things have changed."

Tears filled Spencer's eyes. Everything Melissa was saying was completely true. There was no going back. Too much had happened. But did that mean they had to sabotage each other at every turn? Was Melissa saying that their prank on Colin was a one-time thing, not an indication that they could form a stronger bond?

Melissa's face softened, as if she could read all of Spencer's thoughts. "Look, Spence. I don't want to fight with you, either. And maybe, someday, we'll figure out how to make things work between us. But I just don't think there's an easy solution, and I don't think it can happen overnight. I'm sorry."

She gave Spencer a pat on the shoulder, then shrugged and turned for the house. All sorts of feelings swarmed through Spencer at once. Regret. Sadness. Disappointment. But hope, too. Maybe, in time, things *would* improve between her and Melissa. They just had to learn how to work together. When they did, they made a remarkable team. After all, they could bring tennis stars to their knees—literally.

A faint giggle sounded, and Spencer peered off into the bushes. She'd heard that laugh so many times now that it was getting almost commonplace. Her skin prickled all the same, and she felt such an ominous sense of foreboding that her stomach clenched. What if someone *was* watching her? What if this nightmare *wasn't* over?

But that was impossible. Flicking her hair over her shoulder, she turned and headed toward the house, too, putting A and the horror of last semester behind her once and for all.

HAPPY NEW YEAR TO ME!

Now that I've done all my sightseeing, my holiday bliss is complete. And my, my, my have our pretty little liars been busy! Hanna got the boot from boot camp. Emily bribed a cop. Aria got *married*, to an eco-terrorist, no less. And Spencer—well, let's just say she really knows how to get a guy's, er, *blood* pumping.

Poor Spence. What she wants most in the world is a family who doesn't hate her. A sister who will help her get a guy without stabbing her in the back. Parents who will listen to her problems and always be there. Little does she know there's a reason that they treat her like an outsider. Her flawless family isn't nearly as perfect as it seems. The Hastingses have some *huh-yuge* secrets. And who better to tell Spencer than *moi*?

But as exciting as these holiday jaunts have been, my fun is only just beginning. My grand plans will make Mona's peeping-Tom act look more amateurish than Aria's DIY knitted bras. Thanks to me, Hanna's about to fall so far down the food chain she'll never be able to claw her way up. Aria's love life is going to get a whole lot messier. Emily will break her mother's heart into a million pieces. Spencer will destroy her family, once and for all. And soon enough, Ali won't be the only one in Rosewood to die tragically and too young. Sound harsh? Well, what can I say? These bitches ruined my life. And I believe in an eye for an eye. Or in my case, their lives for mine.

So who am I? You'll know soon enough. But until then, I'm the shadow in the window, the whisper in the wind, the nagging feeling that someone is watching, waiting. Spencer and her friends can resolve to be good this new year, but I'll be there to help them stay their sinful selves.

Buckle up, ladies. If I have anything to say about it, this New Year's will be your last.

–A

ACKNOWLEDGMENTS

As I basically see the pretty little liars as extensions of myself and never pass up an opportunity to delve deeper into their lives and secrets, this book was an absolute pleasure to write. I want to thank first and foremost those who made it possible: Josh Bank, for making sense of the idea; Sara Shandler, for her fantastic insight; and Lanie Davis, who went above and beyond the call of editor to make this book shine. Thank you all so much!

Big thanks to Farrin Jacobs, Kari Sutherland, and everyone at HarperCollins for giving this book a shot, as well as Andy McNicol and Jennifer Rudolph Walsh for helping bring it into the world. I've always wanted to write a holiday book, mostly because my holidays have always been so special—thanks to my wonderful family for that! And thanks to my husband, Joel, who stood by me as I wrote this novel, which I amazingly finished before the baby was born. (I'm still not entirely sure how.)

And last but not least, thanks to Kristian, the little nut, for delaying his miraculous arrival until I wrote the very last "The End." We love you so very much!

Don't miss a single scandal!

  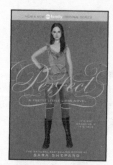 

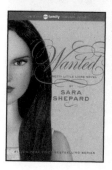 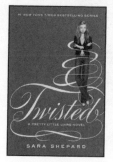 

PRETTY GIRLS DON'T PLAY
BY THE RULES...

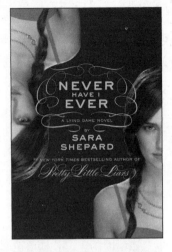
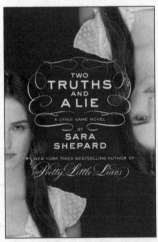
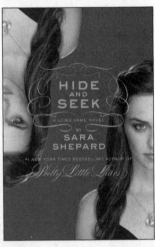

THEY MAKE THEM.

THE HIT ABC FAMILY ORIGINAL SERIES
Pretty Little Liars
Never trust a pretty girl with an ugly secret.
abc family
a new kind of family

  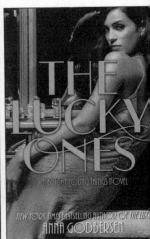